Praise for
A Conspiracy of Alchemists

"Oh my Steampunk God! . . . If you like steam-punk you definitely have to give this jewel a try. It would be a sin not to, really."
　　　　—Butterfly-o-Meter Books

"A wonderful sense of fun on every page . . . Visit [your] nearest bibliographic emporium and seek this rather magnificent tome out."
　　　　—The Eloquent Page

"I truly enjoyed this novel and strongly suggest it to Steampunk fans. I'm convinced *A Conspiracy of Alchemists* will rock your world!"
　　　　—Tynga's Reviews

"Pure fun to read."
　　　　—Karissa's Reading Review

BY LIESEL SCHWARZ

A Conspiracy of Alchemists
A Clockwork Heart
Sky Pirates

Sky Pirates

Sky Pirates

BOOK THREE IN
THE CHRONICLES OF LIGHT AND SHADOW

LIESEL SCHWARZ

DEL REY • NEW YORK

Sky Pirates is a work of fiction. Names, characters, places, and incidents either are the product of the author's imagination or are used fictitiously. Any resemblance to events, locales, or actual persons, living or dead, is entirely coincidental.

A Del Rey Mass Market Original

Copyright © 2014 by Liesel Schwarz

Published in the United States by Del Rey, an imprint of Random House, a division of Random House LLC, a Penguin Random House Company, New York.

DEL REY and the HOUSE colophon are registered trademarks of Random House LLC.

ISBN 978-0-345-54130-7
eBook ISBN 978-0-345-54131-4

Printed in the United States of America

www.delreybooks.com

9 8 7 6 5 4 3 2 1

Del Rey mass market edition: July 2014

Sky Pirates

PROLOGUE

Such is the language of flowers: wormwood whispers of the longing felt for a love that is gone; the willow mourns and the aspen laments.

The seasons have turned one and a half times since I returned from my sojourn with the Traveling folk.

The girl with the auburn hair survived. In the dark days that followed the loss of her warlock, her face had grown angular, where it was once soft. She rarely smiles now and hardness glitters in her eyes, a brittleness that only those who have felt true grief will ever understand.

The great dirty city of London still languishes in the aftermath of those who were lost to *La Dame Blanche*—the Lady in White—and her evil schemes. In the end, over a thousand souls were saved from a terrible fate.

All is quiet in the realms of Shadow and Light. There has been no word from those who wish to see the girl bound in chains. Those who had hoped that she would rise up and bring a golden age have watched with sadness as the Oracle turned her back on the Shadow.

And all the while she searches for him. By day her eyes scan the crowds around her for the slightest glimpse, and by night she trawls the realm of dreams. But sometimes even blind determination is not enough, and day after day her search yields nothing. Dawn after dawn she returns from the Shadow with nothing but sadness.

The Warlock is lost to her now; some say he is lost forever.

And so, in her grief, my mistress takes to the sky. But no

matter how far she travels or how dangerous the work, she cannot outrun the melancholy that haunts her.

The odyssey is not over though. Much as my young mistress wishes it, she cannot turn her back on her destiny. No matter how fast one runs, fate always has a way of keeping pace. And all the while, the wyrd-weavers spin and spin their fine silver strands, weaving all our futures into the crystalline web that binds us all together.

This is a path the girl must walk alone, yet she is not abandoned. I watch and wait, for we remain bound together, she and I.

But there is still hope. When I close my eyes, I hear the soft words of green: lavender speaks of devotion; phlox and olive herald the promise of souls reunited; and lily of the valley whispers of the return of happiness.

For such is the language of flowers. It is the language that only us fairies can hear. And words of green are never lies.

~ The lamentations of La Fée Verte ~

CHAPTER 1

KHARTOUM, 29 OCTOBER 1905

Eleanor tightened her cotton keffiyeh round her face and squinted through the shimmering haze of the afternoon. Before her, the mud-baked flats of the North Sudan spread out as far as the eye could see. They shimmered in the heat, shades of cinnamon, flint and ochre.

Her camel grunted and stepped sideways, instantly disrupting the caravan of beasts as it wound its way along the dusty track.

"Whoa," Elle said. She leaned forward and, using her long riding cane, patted his sand-colored neck to reassure him. In response, he turned his head and tried to bite her foot, leaving a trail of foul greenish snot over the leather of her polished boots.

"Oh you are a beast!" Elle said as she shook her foot and crossed her ankles in the place behind the camel's neck. Even though they had set her stirrups to suit a Western lady, she preferred to ride Bedouin-style as her guides did.

Behind her, one of the guides laughed behind his keffiyeh. "That one, we call him Hamsa. It means "Lion of the Desert."

"Well he's going to be camel stew of the desert if he doesn't behave," Elle retorted.

In reply, Hamsa grunted and farted loudly although he did step into line with the other camels.

The Bedouin guide dropped the fabric from his leathery face and smiled, revealing two rows of white teeth.

"He likes you because you have the fire that burns inside. Not many women can ride the ships of the desert."

Elle smiled back. "Yes, I am quite proficient at piloting ships—only not so much the ones that bite. But say, how much farther do you think we need to travel?" The silence and the vastness of this place made her uneasy. Out here there was nowhere to hide.

"Not too much more. We will be at the place soon. From there you can see for days," her guide replied as he turned his attention back to the invisible path they were following.

They were about half an hour's ride from the fort, which was near Wad Rawah, to the south of the city of Khartoum. And it was here, off the beaten track in the depths of Sudan, that her ship the *Water Lily* was moored, ready to fly a shipment of Nubian artifacts to the British Museum.

When the archaeological expedition that had chartered the *Water Lily* had not returned on schedule, Lieutenant Crosby had ordered a search party of guides to be sent out. It was not unusual for people to run into trouble or lose their way in these parts.

The opportunity to explore this mysterious place had been too strong to resist. So Elle had volunteered to join them. The lieutenant had objected. Elle had argued with him. Vigorously. To this day she had rarely lost an argument—and anyone who had ever tried to disagree with Lady Greychester once she had made up her mind soon learned that resistance was futile. Eventually Crosby had relented, but with much reluctance.

That was before Elle had discovered the quirks of traveling by camel.

"They should have been here by now." Elle peered out

into the distance. Before her the landscape was barren. The sight of it made a lump well up in her throat. Being out here in the vastness of the Sudan was far from a distraction from her inner woe. The emptiness of her surroundings perfectly matched the emptiness she felt in her heart—she felt desolate and alone.

Sensing her inattention, Hamsa lurched forward to bite a lonely tuft of grass, which was poking out from beside a rock. Elle had to grab hold of the saddle to stop herself from being flung over the camel's head and on to the ground.

Elle tried to bring her mount back under control but in her struggle with the camel, her sleeves had ridden up to reveal a series of delicate pink scars that snaked over her hands and up her forearms. She adjusted the fabric of her shirt quickly. Even though the burns had healed up well and were barely noticeable, she did not like to look at the marks. They were a painful reminder of things she preferred not to think about.

Eighteen months had passed since that freezing night in February. The night she had lost her husband and her heart. Despite the desert heat, she shivered at the thought. Had it been that long already?

The Bedouin shaded his eyes and pulled out a brass spyglass and slipped it open. He studied the horizon for a few long moments. Then he let out a shrill whistle. The other guides started chattering and gesturing animatedly.

"What's the matter?" Elle said as she followed the line her guide was pointing out.

In the distance, two fine plumes of dust appeared. Someone was coming.

The Bedouin turned to Elle. "You are lucky he is a racing camel," he said cryptically.

Elle squinted at him. "And why is that?"

The Bedouin shook his head. "Because now we must run."

Elle scanned the dust plume. The familiar glint of sun reflecting off gunmetal caught her eye.

"Bandits!" she breathed.

As if in answer, the distinctive crack of gunfire rose up in the distance.

Hamsa bellowed and soon all the other camels joined in. They could smell trouble and by the looks of it, it was heading directly for them.

"There are too many. We cannot face them with so few guns. We must go back to the fort for reinforcements!" her Bedouin guide said as he gave the signal to retreat.

"Hold up a moment. Shouldn't we stay and lend them assistance?" Elle said.

Her guide shook his head emphatically. "You do not know these bandits. They are of the most bloodthirsty and cruel kind. We have orders to make sure we turn back if there is any sign of trouble. Lieutenant's orders," he added for good measure.

With surprising speed, the small caravan wheeled about and took off in the opposite direction, leaving Elle and Hamsa behind in the settling dust.

Elle did not really need much more persuasion. She had heard terrible stories of violence and cruelty that befell those hapless travelers who chanced upon desert bandits. Her guide's decision to run was not entirely without merit.

"Hold up, wait for me!" she called out, but her companions had no intention of hanging about. That much was clear from the way they were all urging their camels ahead.

Rather clumsily, she led Hamsa round and started following the guides, who were already in the distance. Fortunately her camel needed little persuasion and soon they were kicking up a fair old dust plume of their own. Elle coughed and pulled her goggles over her eyes.

"Hup hup, Hamsa." Elle nudged the camel with her cane and the beast accelerated, his long legs making short work of the distance between her and the rest of the search party. Soon she was bringing up the rear guard of their caravan.

Slowly the minutes ticked by with only the sound of camels moving and the jingles of riding tack as they bounced along, breaking the grim silence. Every time she looked behind her, the dust plume was bigger.

"They are gaining on us," she called out to her guide. He said nothing, but nudged his camel to go faster.

Elle almost let out a sob of relief when the fort came into view. It was one of the few safe outposts within a two-hundred-mile radius of the city of Khartoum.

The fort was a shabby mud-brick building that melded into the landscape so seamlessly that the only way one could spot it was by the scraggly palm trees growing around it.

They rounded a rocky outcrop and entered a wide but shallow wadi that ran downhill from the fort. "Almost there," Elle said.

More shots rang out in the distance. Elle glanced over her shoulder to see what was happening. The dust plumes were much bigger now—a smaller one in front with a bigger one gaining from behind. They were not the only ones under attack, it seemed.

At the sight of the smaller plume, Elle was suddenly seized with an attack of guilt and obligation in equal doses. Instead of providing assistance to people in need as she had volunteered to do, here they were running for their lives. The thought of abandoning someone to the mercy of cruel desert brigands seemed rather poor form, so Elle reined her camel in. Hamsa skidded to a halt with a snort and a puff, his sides heaving from the effort.

Elle lifted her goggles and rested them on top of her head, which helped to keep the loose tendrils of her hair out of her face. She drew out her spyglass. Carefully she turned the little dials until the dust plumes came into focus.

"Dr. Bell," Elle breathed. From her vantage point, she was almost absolutely sure it was the archaeologist she had been chartered to collect. She could just make out the curve of a white pith helmet bobbing up and down in the smaller group.

"Good boy," Elle said as Hamsa stepped about, somewhat unsure as to whether he should stay or run. Camels—unlike horses, Elle had come to realize—tended to do as they pleased. Hamsa snorted and gave her a knowing look, as if he had just read her thoughts. He grunted and extended his lips, revealing a startling clump of gnarled, brown teeth. It was almost as if he was imploring her to turn back to the safety of the fort.

"Yes, you and me both, my smelly friend," she said to the beast. "But we cannot leave the poor doctor out there. It simply will not do."

She stowed her looking glass and unclipped the leather strap that held her Colt 1878 Frontier revolver. The holster was cleverly attached to the side of the leather corset she wore over her shirt ready for a quick draw, if needed.

In a practiced motion, she also reached for the Lee Enfield rifle that was resting in the saddle holster. The rifle was a beautiful thing, brand new and burnished. Lieutenant Crosby had insisted she be issued a weapon before leaving the fort. Which was fine with her as she rarely ventured out without being suitably armed these days; a girl in her position could not be too careful. The company she kept in the course of her business was not always gentle.

She opened the rifle to make sure it was loaded and slid the bolt into place. It made the satisfying sound of well-machined metal upon metal. Satisfied, Elle rested it in her lap. She was ready.

The Bedouin whistled behind her from a slightly safer distance, urging her to follow him.

"Take cover!" she shouted.

There would be no help from her guides in this fight. She was going to have to take this stand on her own until help arrived. Courage be damned.

She lifted the rifle, wrapping the strap around her elbow so the butt sat firmly in the hollow where her upper arm met with her shoulder. She was a passably good shot, but the Enfield was new and she had not had time to set it properly before she left the fort. She would save her pistol for close range, if it came to that.

"Steady on, Hamsa. Good boy," she said in a low voice as she lifted the rifle. The dust cloud was now about five hundred yards away by her estimation, but bullets traveled far in the vastness of the Sudanese plains. However, at this range it was unlikely that she would be able to hit anything with any measure of accuracy. All she could hope for was that her cover fire would be enough to win some time for the doctor. Carefully she exhaled and squeezed the trigger, aiming for the middle of the bigger dust cloud.

The first shot startled her camel for a moment, but he seemed to have been trained to deal with the sound of gunfire. She was rather amazed to see that her aim was true; she could see a camel stumble and a man roll out of the dust on to the ground, where he now lay motionless.

The Bedouin cheered, but Elle pressed her lips together. That was an extraordinarily lucky shot, but there was no pleasure to be found in the shooting of a beast or a man.

Gritting her teeth, she took aim again and fired. Her shot missed, but it did send a few bandits off course.

At that point, the bandits seemed to realize that if Elle could hit them, then they could hit her too. They opened fire with much enthusiasm. Shots started pinging off the ground and rocks around them, much to the dismay of Hamsa who was stepping about in panic.

Elle ducked as a bullet whizzed past her head and she turned to meet her attackers head on. It wasn't much but at this angle she and Hamsa would be a smaller target to aim for. She could see the individual shapes of the bandits clearly now. They would be upon her soon.

"Go. Tell them to open the gates! Get some reinforcements or we'll all be dead in a moment!" she shouted at the cheering Bedouin.

They stopped cheering and swung their camels round.

Elle took aim again. Eight bullets left. Better make them count.

The third and fourth bullets hit a camel. The beast squealed and stumbled. Elle flinched and ducked in order to avoid the volley of shots that was fired in return. One of the shots hit the ground next to Hamsa's foot and he bellowed in surprise.

Elle fired her fifth and sixth rounds, which took the front rider out.

Hamsa let out a low growl and showed the whites of his eyes.

"Easy now. We'll be home in a minute."

Rounds seven, eight and nine she fired in quick succession. This took out one of the bandits on horseback.

The last shot missed, the bullet lost in the rapidly growing spray of dust and hooves.

With shaking hands, Elle stowed the rifle and drew out her Colt. All she could do now was try to send the bandits off course. She fired a rapid volley at them, emptying all the chambers except the last.

The bandits were almost upon her. To her dismay, Elle realized that there was no time to run, because if she did, she would be shot in the back for sure. She stowed her pistol with a grim determination. She would keep the last bullet in the chamber, just in case—for in this world there were some fates that were worse than death.

With the fort firmly in their sights, the bandits seemed to renew their efforts to cut off the archaeologist's route to safety. Elle watched helplessly as the bandits split into two groups in an attempt to outflank the wagon. If they came within firing range of the fort it would be too late for them to catch Dr. Bell.

Elle gritted her teeth. She hated to admit it, but it was time to seek the assistance of the Shadow realm.

She took a deep breath and closed her eyes. It took only a moment to focus on the metaphysical dimension she sought. Just beneath this reality, the space between the two worlds of Light and Shadow lay. The barrier opened up for her almost instantly.

"Come on, boy. Don't falter now," she said to the camel. She nudged Hamsa firmly into the space. Instantly, she disappeared from sight.

Stepping into the space between the two worlds was like being underwater. The barrier between the realms lay before her in a glimmering ribbon of golden light. Touching it was a practice strictly forbidden by the Council of Warlocks. But Elle was the Oracle. She was the force that held the two realms together, and so the barrier was hers to command. And what's more, she did not give a fig about the Council or their draconian laws.

Carefully she pushed her hand into the barrier and felt about until she found one of the globules of power that had accumulated against it. The barrier did not act only as a means of keeping Shadow creatures and humans apart, it also acted as a giant net that caught and retained energy. Elle—and those gifted with the Shadow—used this energy as fuel for their powers. But the net had been growing ever more empty over the years, so harvesting power without authorization was strictly forbidden. Only warlocks with permission from the Council were allowed to access it. Another stupid law, in Elle's considered opinion.

Hamsa squealed at the sight of the barrier. The poor camel was so terrified that he promptly let out a rather large series of droppings. Evidently, in camel terms, being shot at was one thing, but being ridden into a parallel dimension was beyond the pale.

"Easy now," Elle said. She reached out and dug her fingers into the globule of energy. This was a trick she had learned from a rather unpleasant nemesis not so long ago. Her fingers split the membrane and instantly she felt the energy flow into her, filling her up in an exquisite, fizzing sensation.

As soon as the fizzing stopped, she focused her attention on the side of the Light and nudged Hamsa. The camel did not need much encouragement and they stepped back into the realm of Light.

The doctor's party was almost upon the spot where Elle had been. One of the archaeologist's guides let out a shout of surprise when she materialized next to him and veered off just in time to avoid a collision.

"Run! Make for the fort!" Elle shouted.

She dug her heels into the high stirrups and turned Hamsa round to face the bandits who were bearing down on them.

She closed her eyes and reached inside herself for the white-hot ball of energy she had stowed. In one swift move she grasped it and hurled it at her attackers. The ball of light hit the ground just in front of the first riders. It exploded like a bomb, sending camels, horses and men flying.

But the energy of the blast was not entirely spent, and Elle stared in amazement as the aether rose up and collapsed in on itself as it fought for somewhere to go.

"Oops," Elle said as she watched the residual power rise up and turn to wind. Bright blue bolts of lightning crackled and clouds swirled and rose up, turning and whirling with a deafening rumble. Red-brown dust, thicker than the thickest smoke churned in the air, obscuring the blue sky above them.

The explosion, together with the force of the wind, sent the bandits reeling. She saw men and camels stumbling about in confusion.

Elle did not wait about to see what would happen next. She knew she had to retreat or face obliteration. "Go, Hamsa. Go!" she shouted, wheeling her camel about.

Hamsa did not need to be persuaded. He set off at top speed for the safety of the fort. Soon the gates loomed up from the haze of red dust around them.

"Incoming!" Elle yelled at the top of her voice.

She was met by the sound of cover fire as rifle bullets from the stone parapets whizzed over her head. Seconds later she thundered through the gates of the fort.

"To the stables! Take cover!" one of the guards shouted as the heavy doors rumbled shut behind her.

The vast cloud of dust had now all but swallowed the bandits and was spreading, bearing down upon the fort like a huge tidal wave.

Elle urged Hamsa toward the large but rather crowded stable block. People, horses, camels and dogs were all milling about seeking cover from the looming sand. Riders were trying to get their camels to kneel. A horse whinnied and reared up, upsetting a hay trough.

All this confusion was too much for Elle's trusty mount, and the instinct that had allowed his species to survive sandstorms over the millennia took over. Hamsa bellowed loudly before sinking to his knees in a terrified crouch, his head slung low. The momentum of his movements threw Elle from her saddle and she landed with a heavy thump on the ground, just as the stable doors rumbled shut behind her. Outside, the wind howled as the massive cloud of red dust swallowed everything. It was pitch dark; the light from the sun blocked out by the storm.

"Lady Greychester, I presume?"

She heard a match strike. A flame flickered and flared up as it lit a lamp taper, casting a pool of light around her.

Elle looked up to see a formidable-looking woman in her forties. She was dressed from head to toe in a rather austere khaki-colored outfit. The only thing whimsical about her was the pair of round, blue haploscopic spectacles perched upon her nose, presumably to guard against the glare of the sun. Elle noticed with amazement that the glasses must have remained perched there throughout the death-defying chase across the desert.

"Dr. Bell?" Elle wheezed.

The woman smiled and her weather-beaten face cracked into a myriad of lines. She held out her hand to help Elle up. "The very same. How do you do?"

Elle groaned as Dr. Bell pulled her up to her feet.

She gave her jodhpurs a perfunctory pat and winced. Her left shoulder was tender from where she had landed on it, but on the whole she appeared to be in one piece.

"Good heavens, girl, are you quite all right?" asked the doctor.

"I am quite well, thank you. Just made a rather inelegant dismount, it seems." She gave Hamsa a dirty look. The camel ignored her. He was now sitting quietly with his legs folded underneath him—the picture of serenity.

Dr. Bell peered up at the dark sky, which was just visible through the small windows high up in the wall.

"That's quite a sandstorm you've unleashed upon us. Am I correct to presume that you are blessed with the gifts of the Shadow?"

"In a manner of speaking. It's a trick I learned a while ago, but I fear I may have used a tad more force than needed," Elle said, evading the question. Discussing her gifts was not something she liked to do with strangers. Even friendly ones.

"Well, I think that was jolly well done. I thought we were done for out there. The blighters came out of nowhere. I think you may have saved our lives, and for that I thank you."

Elle blushed. "It was nothing."

"Well, shall we go and find ourselves a cup of tea? I don't know about you, but I am absolutely parched," Dr. Bell said.

As if on cue, a young soldier appeared. He stood to attention, spine straight, arms held stiffly by his side. "Lady Greychester. Dr. Bell. The Lieutenant asks that you meet him in his office for debriefing and refreshments at your earliest convenience." He punctuated his sentence by straightening up farther and adding "Ma'am" for good measure.

Elle smiled. "That is the best suggestion I've heard all day." She turned to the archaeologist. "Shall we?"

Dr. Bell nodded, looking rather grateful. "Lead the way, my dear. Lead the way!"

CHAPTER 2

VENICE

A huge moon rose over the city of Venice, transforming the canals to wide ribbons of silver. The velvety evenings had grown chilly and damp with the rising of the *acqua alta*—the relentless winter tides off the Adriatic Sea. Venice, the most beautiful of cities, was now more of an icy morass.

Patrice Chevalier did not mind the cold. He strode along through the narrow alleyways and over the damp-slicked little stone bridges. No, he did not mind it one bit.

The months since his return from London had brought about remarkable changes in his appearance. His new power had wrought his body, melting away the rotund flabbiness that had plagued him all his life until only chunky muscle remained. Gone also was the bristle-broom moustache. The new Patrice was lean and chiseled, and wore his bespoke fur-lined cloak with an air of svelte confidence. To the unacquainted, he was a picture of modern wealth and manliness. Men tipped their hats to him when he walked by, and women smiled at him from behind their open, fluttering fans.

In short, Patrice Chevalier had become the man he had always wanted to be, and he was savoring every moment of it.

His walk through the dark brought him to an old

wooden door just on the other side of the small foot-
bridge. It was an unremarkable, unfashionable address
hidden away in one of the oldest, most run-down parts
of the city. He studied the door for a few moments. This
was the right place, he was sure of it.

Carefully he rested his hand on the cool stone beside
the door. The surface had been worn down to a fine
patina from the many hands that had sought—and been
denied—entry to this place; generations of warlocks had
solicited admission only to be desisted and turned away.

The hex that had been placed on the door also fought
Patrice, for it did not recognize his imprint, but he focused a fraction of his newfound power on it and the
stone soon gave. In the wall above his fingers a faint
symbol of a triangle with an apex eye had been carved
into the stone. It started glowing bright blue as he easily
unwound the protective spell which had been designed
to keep outsiders away. He simply willed it so, and
slowly the door rumbled as it opened.

He wasted no time in climbing the high, narrow stairs
that greeted him and was secretly proud of the fact that
he was hardly out of breath by the time he reached the
top.

On the landing, he was met with the sound of muted
voices. He smiled. He flicked his cloak over his shoulders, straightened the lapels of his jacket and stepped up
to the barrier of power that covered the doorway. He
had found the Meeting of the Council of Warlocks. It
was time to make an entrance.

"Good evening, gentlemen. I'm sorry I'm late. My invitation must have gone missing in the post," Patrice
said with a small smile as he strode inside. Quite casually, he removed his cloak and top hat. No one offered
to take his things so, unperturbed by the slight, he set
them down on a small table by the door.

"Who goes there?" Grand Master Conrad de Montague

half rose from his seat. He sat at the head of an ancient table which stood in the middle of the room framed by large, gracefully curving windows. Also in attendance were eleven other warlocks—the most powerful in the known world.

Patrice noted that the thirteenth seat was still empty—until recently it had belonged to Hugh Marsh, his former associate.

"I am Lord Abercrombie," Patrice said, relishing his newly purchased peerage. "But my friends call me Patrice Chevalier."

"Mr. Chevalier," de Montague said as he fought to regain his composure. "What an unexpected surprise. I see that the last year has treated you well. In more ways than one."

"Grand Master." Patrice inclined his head politely, ignoring de Montague's refusal to acknowledge his new title. "I have indeed found my circumstances to be much improved in recent months."

"While it is always a pleasure to see you, I regret to inform you that this is a private meeting," de Montague said pointedly. "Perhaps you'd like to wait for us downstairs until we finish?"

"Actually, my business cannot wait. You see, I have come to apply for the role of the thirteenth," Patrice said in a smooth voice, gesturing toward the empty seat.

"I'm sorry, but the Council is for warlocks only," de Montague said, giving him a look of disdain.

"I don't believe that to be a problem. As you said, my circumstances are improved in more ways than meet the eye. I think my evading your pathetic door hex is proof enough of my abilities."

"How dare you?" de Montague said, narrowing his eyes.

"Would you have let me in otherwise?" Patrice shrugged.

"I am sorry to disappoint you, sir, but the thirteenth seat can only be filled by unanimous vote. The loss of Lord Greychester came as quite a shock to us. It may be some time before we have a list of candidates we can put to the vote."

"Oh, I don't think a list of candidates is necessary," Patrice said. "I see no reason why I cannot put myself forward for consideration right now. Everyone is assembled, so you may as well vote on the matter."

There was a gasp of surprise from the other warlocks at his brazen approach. A few of them started muttering in protest.

"My good man, that is quite impossible," de Montague spluttered. "It takes more than a cheap touch of the Shadow. In fact, it takes years of training and devotion to become a warlock. You might have come into some money, but I can assure you that you lack the talents needed to ever become one of us."

"I think, Grand Master, that you might find yourself sorely mistaken on more than one of those points," Patrice said, matching de Montague's tone. "You will hear my application now. I must insist upon it."

De Montague snorted and looked disparagingly at Patrice. "Mr. Chevalier, your appeal is quite ridiculous. Request denied. Now please desist with this disruption for you are only embarrassing yourself. Good evening to you." The Grand Master moved to the fireplace where he rang an ornate fringed bell to summon a servant. "Someone will see you out now."

Patrice felt anger rise up inside him, hot and acrid like melted tar. How dare this snobbish weakling treat him as if he were nothing? "I would wait a moment if I were you," Patrice said. Another, more sinister, smile played across his face.

"And why should I do that? You have wasted quite

enough of our time." De Montague's upper lip curled in disgust. "Now please leave, I will not ask you again."

Patrice laughed. He summoned a small amount of the dark energy inside him and channeled it downward, lifting himself off the floor. The light fittings and floorboards in the room began to tremble. Somewhere a small ornament crashed to the floor.

Patrice towered over the Grand Master.

"Prepare to be challenged by one of the most powerful warlocks that has ever lived," he said quietly. "This is no cheap trick of the Shadow. I, my dear de Montague, am the Shadow Master."

De Montague blanched as he stared up at Patrice. "You?" he whispered. "We had heard rumors that a Shadow Master had arisen. It cannot be."

Patrice did not answer. Instead he threw his head back and inhaled as much of de Montague's power as he could in one breath. He felt his lungs fill with the energy of the older warlock, before being absorbed by the ever-growing darkness within him.

De Montague stumbled and fell to his knees. His face had turned gray, and when he looked up at Patrice there was genuine fear in his eyes. "What have you done?" he said as he stared at his hands in horror, which had aged and curled up like claws.

"And how . . . how did you do that?" de Montague whispered. "The power of the warlocks is all but gone. Where did you find this new source of aether?"

"That took hardly any effort at all actually. Do you concede this battle or shall I finish you? I really don't mind either way." Patrice laughed. The low rumble of his voice expelled a vengeful satisfaction from deep within him. He looked up at the other members of the Council. "Gentlemen, a new age for warlocks has come. I have been to the darkest places in the Shadow realm. In death, the path to regaining our former power has been shown to me." The other members of the Council were staring at him in stunned silence. "Are you going to stay loyal to this weak old man while you slowly turn to dust, or will you join me so we may become strong and glorious again?"

"*Potentia Mortis,*" de Montague whispered, using his chair to pull himself to his feet. "You have the darkness of the Underworld within you. It has turned you into an abomination too dangerous to be allowed to live!"

"Well done, Grand Master. I am pleased to see that at least you remember your lessons well," Patrice said.

"The aether inside you is dark, Patrice. Listen to me when I tell you that you do not know with what you meddle." De Montague raised his arms up as if to strike. "You cannot be allowed to wield such power. The dangers are too great. So I must accept your challenge!"

Patrice faced the Grand Master. "Very well, old man, your challenge is met. We shall battle to the death and the winner keeps what he conquers. As are the rules."

"Do not underestimate me. You may be strong, but you are no match for my centuries of experience of the Craft. You do not have all of me," de Montague said with a quaking voice.

"We'll see about that." Patrice raised his arms and struck out at de Montague. There was a flash of light as the two men clashed. They met with deafening force and began to swirl around the room.

De Montague lashed out at Patrice and knocked him back.

Patrice reeled and righted himself. A small trickle of blood ran out of his nose and across his lip. He pulled out a starched white handkerchief from his inside pocket and wiped his face. "Is that the best you can do?" he said. "A burst blood vessel in the nose? Grand Master, honestly." Patrice was annoyed now. Instead of surrendering, the Grand Master had made him ruin his handkerchief. And it was an expensive one too. He reached into the darkness that swirled within him to summon up enough power to strike. He did not like to admit it, but he was still a little unsure of his new gifts. And if he was completely honest with himself, the darkness within him scared him a little. But brute force would be enough to win him this challenge, and win he must, before the other warlocks recovered from their initial shock and came to de Montague's aid. He had come here to exert his dominance; he could not afford to hesitate. No, the time to act was now.

In his mind, he imagined a large ball of swirling black flames, the very same flames that had almost consumed him at the edge of the vortex in Constantinople not so long ago. That day had changed him forever. It was the day he had lost Elle. As he raised his hands to strike out at de Montague, an image of her face flashed through his mind.

A blue bolt of energy flew across the room and struck the old warlock in the chest. De Montague gasped as he absorbed the impact. Patrice launched another blast at him. This time, bright sparks flew everywhere—de Montague was fighting back. The two men were locked in a deathly standoff for a few seconds.

De Montague's face twisted in agony. Sweat turned his forehead shiny as he shook with the effort of holding Patrice at bay. But Patrice held firm, slowly increasing the outflow of power. He watched with satisfaction as the Grand Master's power slowly started to wane. The light emanating from him grew fainter and fainter and then quietly went out. Bright flames appeared around him, catching his clothes, before finally enveloping him.

De Montague gave a cry of anguish and pain. The flames went out as life left him, and his body fell to the floor in a blackened heap.

Patrice watched on as the last remains of the Grand

Master—the supreme guardian of the barrier between the realms of Shadow and Light—turned to dust before his eyes.

The room fell into a shocked silence. No one moved—or even breathed.

Patrice stared at the sad little heap of dust before him with growing delight. He had never used his power with such unrestrained force on another human before, and the results were both frightening and wonderful. He would have to remember how he did that for next time.

The other warlocks continued to stare at him. De Montague had been the oldest and most powerful among them. Their terror and unease radiated from their very core.

"Well, gentlemen, can I have your answer or does anyone else wish to duel?" Patrice said.

"I vote to join," Master Chen, the Chinese warlock, said without hesitation. "I pledge my loyalty to you, Shadow Master." He bowed his head in reverence.

The others all started speaking at the same time and nodding in frightened agreement.

Patrice allowed himself to smile. Slowly and with deliberate enjoyment, he sat down in the chair which de Montague had occupied just minutes before. The seat was still warm.

"Winner keeps what he conquers," he murmured in response to the shocked looks around him.

Master Obanwedya cleared his throat. He was a big man, dressed in the deep red ceremonial robes of the Shaman of Western Africa. "I think I speak for us all when I say we acknowledge you, Grand Master Chevalier, Keeper of the Realms of Light and Shadow." The others all nodded in agreement.

All except one.

"What do you say, Master Lewis?" Patrice said as he met the gaze of the American. Lewis had been a good friend of Hugh Marsh. It was very important to ensure that everyone knew where the American's loyalties lay, for he could be trouble in the future.

"I'd say that you won the battle to the death, and so you are within your rights to claim the title. I never cared for de Montague much, but I will reserve judgment on the rest, if you don't mind. As they say, rather the devil you know than the one you don't," said Lewis.

"Fair enough." Patrice inclined his head. It would take a little time for them to come around, but he did not mind. He could wait. It would not take long for them to support him, not when they understood what his plans for the Council were.

He turned to the parchment, which lay on the table before him. It was an agenda of points that de Montague had intended to discuss at the meeting.

"Gentlemen, shall we continue? Many of you have traveled far for this gathering and I am sure you are all eager to conclude the business." He tore the agenda in half and threw it into the fireplace beside him. The pages burst into flame and reduced to charred black fragments in moments.

"First order of business: I would propose that we finally put an end to the perpetual problem of our current—and rather wayward—Oracle. Indulging her has wasted enough of our time, and I move that she should be brought to order without delay. The time to restore the power of the Council has come," he said.

The other warlocks looked on with varying degrees of hesitation. What Patrice was proposing was both grim and distasteful.

"Motion seconded," said Master Chen, rubbing his hands together.

"Now, allow me to fill you in on the plans I have." Patrice sat forward as he started to outline his vision for the future.

As he spoke, the other warlocks nodded in agreement. A few of them even smiled and, for the first time since he entered the building, Patrice allowed himself to relax. Tonight he had won a crucial victory. If there was one thing that could always be relied upon, it was the greed of men. And right now their desire for power would be the means with which he would retain control.

CHAPTER 3

KHARTOUM

Heat shimmered off the clay-brick houses and dusty streets of the ancient city of Khartoum. Even in late October, the sun was relentless. It turned everything below hot and dusty.

Here the River Nile split the city in two, before winding its way northward to Egypt and the Mediterranean Sea beyond. Elle and Dr. Bell strolled through the central marketplace, which lay just south of the river. They were waiting for the departure time of Elle's ship, the *Water Lily*, to arrive.

Before them the market spread out in a grid of organized chaos. The alleyways and stalls were covered with vast swaths of matting made from woven grass. In fact, wooden planks, grass mats and canvas seemed to cover every possible space between the wooden shanty roofs, in an attempt to shield the place from the blistering sun.

Out of the sun, the air was surprisingly cool, and it was here, beneath the mottled shade, that the merchants of Khartoum sold their wares. Vegetables, spices and finely woven cotton, printed in bright colors, bloomed against the taupe of the clay-brick buildings.

Up ahead, a goatherd whistled fiercely and waved the stick that he used to herd his flock, eliciting sharp words from a nearby stallholder who was worried about the towering pyramid of tomatoes he had erected. Elle noticed that the goatherd had little hooves instead of feet. A faun herding goats, she thought. How quaint.

Dr. Bell flinched at the goatherd's whistle and the sudden movement of the goats around her. "Oh my! I do say that I am still rather jumpy after our narrow escape." The older woman's eyes grew misty. "I honestly don't want to think about what would have happened if it wasn't for your timely intervention, Lady Greychester."

"Oh, please don't say anything more. It was all in a day's work," Elle said with feigned bravado. She didn't want to admit it, but the force of the sandstorm she had created had scared her. It had taken the better part of a day for the wind to die down and the dust to settle enough before they could leave the fort. When the troops finally managed to dig away the sand that blocked the heavy gates, the Bedouin guides had been sent out to search for survivors. They came back with word of thirteen bodies as well as their beasts. All had suffocated in the thick dust.

Elle shuddered at the thought of the carnage she had wrought. The bandits may have been bad people planning to kill Dr. Bell, but such destruction could hardly be justified.

"I must admit that I will be rather grateful to be safely back in the air again," she said. "I do prefer my charters to be a little less confrontational than this one. No offense," she added quickly.

The older woman smiled at Elle. "None taken, my dear. Fighting off robbers is something I've had to contend with as long as I can remember. The moment they see a woman, they immediately assume she's an easy target. You just cannot trust anyone these days." She sighed. "Things were easier when my husband was still alive."

"You were married?" Elle said.

"Oh yes. My husband was also an archaeologist and

we spent many happy years exploring digs in far-flung places." Dr. Bell's kindly expression grew wistful. "My poor Alfred caught a fever in the Congo. We buried him in the jungle. My greatest regret is that I am unable to go there to visit his grave."

"I am so sorry," Elle said. She had to swallow down the awkward lump that had suddenly formed in her throat.

"Never mind. It was many years ago. Although I still miss him every day. He was the love of my life, that man." Dr. Bell patted Elle's arm. "I am happy to say that all the artifacts made it to the fort in one piece, notwithstanding our mad dash across the desert. Human greed is such a terrible thing." She shrugged. "I wish they would understand that my work is not about seeking treasure and riches. It's about studying and preserving history for generations to come."

Elle felt a surge of compassion for Dr. Bell. She suddenly imagined her as a young woman, exploring the world with her husband at her side. The image these thoughts conjured up cut deep, for Dr. Bell's story was not entirely different from her own.

With great effort, Elle disentangled herself from such maudlin reflection. She pointed east, toward the other side of the marketplace where the airfield lay. From where they were standing, Elle and Dr. Bell could see just the tops of the moored airships and dirigibles as they glinted in the hot sun.

"They should have finished loading the cargo by now, I would have thought. Lieutenant Crosby has assured me that the crates would be kept under the supervision of armed guards at all times. Since they were bound for the British Museum, this is a matter involving the Empire so we have their full support. That is lovely, isn't it?" Dr. Bell said.

"Well, then I suggest that we go and make sure they don't drop anything," Elle said.

"Good call." Dr. Bell leaned forward meaningfully. "I have some extraordinarily well-preserved pots which I really would like to see reach their destination in one piece."

"I've never lost a shipment yet. Knock on wood," Elle said. She tapped her knuckles against a wooden beam that held up an awning. This made the canvas shake, which in turn elicited an anxious look from the stall-holder who was watching the dust sift down on the pairs of shoes laid out on the table before them.

Elle held up an apologetic hand.

"Splendid!" said Dr Bell, ignoring the stallholder. "Then I say lead the way, Lady Greychester."

Khartoum had a large strategic military airfield that lay beside the barracks and rifle ranges to the east of the city. The British had built it about fifty years ago in order to accommodate supply ships during the wars that had ravaged this land for more than a few decades. But, with the Empire shrinking, orders had been given for the armed forces to withdraw from the region, so in recent years permission for the use of the airfield by passenger ships and cargo vessels had become more common. The presence of soldiers in uniform was still very much in evidence though. There was no forgetting that this was a place where people died easily, if they weren't careful.

The smell of roasting meat, spices and wood smoke greeted them around the next corner. This part of the market was busier and people thronged around food stalls as they walked through the narrow alleys.

Elle checked her leather holdall, which she wore slung across her body. The leather was worn now and it molded itself around her in the way that leather did when in constant use. Marsh had bought the holdall for her in Florence on their honeymoon—in a time that seemed like more than a lifetime ago now.

Marsh.

Elle stopped in the middle of the pathway and blinked.

She could have sworn she had just seen the shape of a tall man in a carriage cloak and top hat disappear round the corner of one of the stalls.

"What is it?" said Dr. Bell, suddenly concerned.

Elle shook her head. "Did you see him? The tall man in the top hat?"

Dr. Bell frowned and peered into the crowd. "I don't think so," she said. "You don't see many top hats around these parts. Pith helmets, however, are a different matter." She rapped on her own with her knuckles.

Elle scanned the crowds before them. Dr. Bell was right. For the most part, people were dressed in traditional cottons and linens. Here and there the ubiquitous khaki jacket of a soldier broke the pattern. For the most part, everyday life went on in this place as it had done for centuries.

Elle strode along and peered down the alley, but it was empty. "I thought I recognized someone in the crowd," she said. "I'm sorry, it's my mistake. The heat must be getting to me."

"Never mind. I see people I think I recognize all the time. It comes from spending one's life traveling the world." Dr. Bell patted her arm reassuringly.

Elle pressed her lips together and nodded. "Probably just my imagination. Let's get to the airfield, shall we?"

She never stopped looking for him. Not while she was awake, and not during the hours of slumber. But try as she might, and even with all her powers, he remained missing. As she walked, Elle silenced the tiny voice that kept nagging her; that he did not wish to be found; that her search was fruitless because he did not want to come back to her.

* * *

The *Water Lily* was waiting in her landing dock. Elle felt a great surge of affection as she caught sight of her ship. With all the tragedy and changes in recent times, it sometimes seemed as if the little freight dirigible was the only constant presence in her life. Seeing her ship was like coming home.

"Lady Greychester, she's all loaded and ready to go," said the docking agent who greeted them on the landing platform. He handed her the customary bundle of documents she would need to cross international airspace while carrying freight.

"Marvelous. We will be preparing for takeoff right away." Elle smiled at the man. He was one of the many agents she now used. After everything she had been through with her erstwhile docking agent, Patrice Chevalier, it was certainly safer that way. In fact, it was better not to form close relationships with anyone, for that matter.

"Permission to come aboard?" Dr. Bell said smartly.

"Please, after you." Elle gestured to the new hydraulic retractable staircase, which the *Water Lily* sported.

In recent months, Elle had thrown caution to the wind. She had started taking on all the charters no one else wanted. The more dangerous and difficult, the better. And she had done well, in the way that people who had nothing left to lose often did. As time passed, she had gained a reputation for specializing in the transport of rare and exotic freight. And because rare and exotic freight tended to be valuable, most of her charters involved flights where the owner wished to have the freight accompanied. This was a service she gladly provided, and as these small-freight charters were mostly the reserve of the extremely wealthy, Elle had invested in a few luxuries, such as retractable stairs for embarkation. She had even splashed out, in a manner of speaking. Her brass and porcelain water closet, complete with automatic flushing system, had caused more than a few raised eyebrows—although she was sure that her clients were most grateful for this facility on longer flights.

"I have a berth to the port side if you'd care to rest along the way. Let me show you. It's this way," Elle said to Dr. Bell as she led her toward the cabin. "You are of course more than welcome to join me up in the cockpit." She had found that most of her passengers were rather thrilled by the novelty of this. Elle did not mind the intrusion, for the company of the odd passenger or two sometimes made for a welcome diversion from the long lonely hours of flight.

"Wonderful," said Dr. Bell. "Let me stow my things and I will join you for takeoff. If that's in order, of course." She gestured to the battered steamer trunk that had been left outside the little cabin.

"Absolutely." Elle smiled at Dr. Bell. "I'll be busy with the preflight checks. And if you need anything, I'll be just on the other side of these." Elle opened the new set of doors that separated the cockpit from the rest of the ship.

"Would you mind if I checked on the freight before we depart?" Dr. Bell asked.

"By all means," Elle said. "The freight hold is just behind those grates. Be sure to close them once you have finished." She pulled aside the heavy leather curtain that covered the metal gates that demarcated the freight area. These curtains were also a new addition to the interior of the ship.

In the middle of the *Water Lily*'s cargo area was a stack of wooden crates secured by a rope net. Each box was stamped with the address of the British Museum: *Great Russell Street, London, W1*.

"Oh, isn't this a wonderful sight?" the doctor said as

she took in the crates. "The museum is going to be so impressed with these Nubian finds."

"Here is the cargo inventory." Elle handed her the list that was clipped to her docking papers and manifest. "You probably have a far better idea of what you are looking at than I."

Dr. Bell's face opened up in a broad smile. "Don't you mind me, my dear. I will have these double-checked in a jiffy," she muttered, already immersed in the numbers on the crates.

Elle smiled as she made her way to the cockpit. Dr. Bell was a woman after her own heart and she liked her immensely.

Back in the cockpit, Elle ran through her preflight checks without a glitch. Satisfied that all was well, she flipped the switches that activated the spark reactor. The reactor, in turn, heated the water that was stored in large brass tanks. The water turned to steam which was fed into the thruster engines that drove the ship.

The ship's spark reactor glowed and the pressure gauges sang. Elle pushed the levers forward and, with a satisfying rattle and a hum, the *Water Lily*'s engines turned over.

Elle cast an eye over the ship's helium tanks. These filled the balloons from a complex set of pipes that formed the gas system, allowing the ship to rise up and land. All seemed in order, so she flicked the switch on the signal lights to show the docking crew that the *Water Lily* was ready for takeoff.

The ground crew, wrapped in keffiychs to protect against the dust that the airship thrusters kicked up, ran out and started untying the ship's tether ropes.

"Ready for takeoff. Hold on, it can sometimes be bumpy!" Elle called to the back to warn Dr. Bell.

Slowly Elle eased the lever that regulated the gas levels of the overhead balloon and, with the hiss of helium, the chambers filled to capacity. With a gentle creak, the *Water Lily* started to rise up into the air.

Elle eased the thrusters into the forward position and, without so much as a rattle, her ship took to the sky.

"And we're off!" said the doctor as she eased herself into the copilot seat next to Elle with a satisfied groan. "Ah, sitting down in a comfy seat after all those months camping in the desert feels like heaven to these old bones, I can tell you," Dr. Bell said.

"I can well believe you," Elle replied.

Below them, the dusty rooftops and parade grounds of Khartoum grew smaller. As they rose up, the fine curve of the Blue Nile came into view. The water glittered in the sun as it meandered through the city, due north toward the desert. Elle felt an immense sense of satisfaction as she scanned the horizon. The Sudan was a magnificent place that few people had the privilege to ever see. It was moments like these that made flying worthwhile.

"I think that was just about the most trouble-free takeoff I've ever experienced. You might be my lucky mascot, Doctor," Elle said as she wound the lever that retracted the ship's tether ropes.

"Well, let's hope it bodes well for the rest of the flight," Dr. Bell said. "We discovered an exceptional clay chalice that I would love to present to the museum in one piece—after I have written a paper about it, that is."

"Well, the winds are in our favor, so I'll do my best, Doctor," Elle said as she angled the *Water Lily* northward.

"Please, call me Gertrude," the doctor said. "I should like it very much if we could be friends."

"I should like that too," Elle said. "And now, how about a nice cup of tea?"

Gertrude's face brightened. "Now that's a good idea. Shall I get the things ready?"

As they set about filling the teapot with leaves and water, the parched desert sands slipped by below. They were following the River Nile north to Cairo, across the great blue Mediterranean and then onward across Europe to England.

A soft smiled played across Elle's lips as she settled in her seat. She was in her favorite place on earth.

CHAPTER 4

"Now that *is* a nice cup of tea," Dr. Bell said as she took an appreciative sip. It was the next day and they were several pots of brew into their journey. Despite the copious amounts of tea, Gertrude had so far shown no sign of having reached her fill. "It really is the little things one misses when you are out on a dig like that. All I've had for months on end is that terribly strong, syrupy stuff the Bedouin drink. You mustn't misunderstand me. It's perfectly delicious to drink, but it isn't a proper cuppa, now is it?"

"Well, I have plenty of tea, so please have as much as you wish," Elle said.

"Say, where are we now? Is that the Mediterranean?" Dr. Bell peered through the cockpit glass and over the expanse of water before them.

"Certainly is," Elle replied. On the one side, the sun was setting across the vast expanse that was the Sahara Desert. On the other, the shimmering blue of the sea stretched out as far as the eye could see. "If you look at this compass, you will see that we are traveling west, northwest along the coast of North Africa. We will keep going like that for a while until it's time to cut across the sea to Italy. Then we head west to France to get to the Channel and then onwards home."

"How fascinating," Dr. Bell said as she studied Elle's navigational charts. "I've always loved a good atlas and now I feel like I am right inside one." She beamed at

Elle. "Oh, I do see why you love flying so much, my dear. I think I might have chosen the same career had aviation been as advanced when I was young."

"Do have a biscuit," Elle said, offering her the shop-bought blue metal tin that said *McVitie & Price* in smart letters. Her regular home-baked supply had dried up when Mrs. Hinges—or Mrs. Mathilda Chance, as she was now called—had moved back to Oxford with Elle's father, and as far as she could tell, they were both lyrically happy.

But over the last year, Elle had been too grief-stricken for social interaction. The house in Grosvenor Square was now gloomy, its furniture and fittings covered in dusty sheets with only the butler and a maid to keep an eye on the place. Elle had moved out and taken up modest rooms in Knightsbridge, which were close to the airfield in Hyde Park. Her rooms were sparsely furnished, rarely inhabited and not very conducive to receiving guests, meaning that the visits from her father and stepmother had grown more infrequent. The unfortunate downside of her new chosen circumstances, among other things, was a sudden cessation of her supply of homemade biscuits.

Shop-bought, but perfectly acceptable, she thought with a tinge of irritation. She would not allow herself to feel guilty. At least she did not have to face the sympathetic stares and the soft-spoken words of condolence every time she came into contact with anyone she had known. They all meant well, but their kindness did nothing to assuage the bottomless hole of grief, guilt and sadness that sat where her heart had once been. In fact, it made things worse, and the outpouring of sympathy had irritated Elle to the point where she wanted to scream and scratch and weep.

The irritation she felt made her feel even more wretched and guilty, so she decided that it was time to put an end to the funerary procession. No, things were better if everyone left her alone to get on with things. She had gone to great measures to avoid anyone who reminded her of her former life. Even the Baroness Loisa Belododia—her closest friend and confidant—had stopped writing after her letters remained unanswered.

"Don't mind if I do," Dr. Bell interrupted Elle's dark thoughts as she lifted a digestive biscuit out of the tin. "Say, would you be terribly offended if I asked you a personal question?"

"Of course not. But whether I will give you an answer, depends entirely on the question," Elle said.

"That's fair enough." Dr. Bell nodded. "It's just that I was wondering about the man you said you might have seen in the marketplace in Khartoum."

Elle took a deep breath. Gertrude had indeed asked the one question she did not want to answer. Yet, oddly enough, speaking to someone who had suffered a loss similar to her own did not feel so threatening. In fact, the thought of speaking to someone who might understand what she was feeling was almost comforting.

"I thought I might have seen my husband," she said.

"I'm sorry for not mentioning it sooner, but I am terribly sorry for your loss," Dr. Bell said. "I had read about Lord Greychester's unfortunate accident in the papers quite recently. You must remember that the news takes quite some time to reach the Sudan." Dr. Bell shook her head sadly. "Such a terrible business. You have my sincerest condolences, my dear."

"Condolences are not necessary because my husband is not dead. He is merely between worlds at the moment," Elle said. She felt her voice turn sharp as she struggled to keep the annoyance out of her voice. The question as to whether her husband was to be considered alive or dead was a debate she had been forced to endure on countless occasions over the last year and a half and she was heartily sick of it.

The truth was that her husband had been abducted by the villainous Clothilde de Blanc—the Lady in White— who had used him as part of a scheme to take over the world with an army of clockwork soldiers. Elle had fought hard to get him back and she had almost succeeded, but in the end *La Dame Blanche* had had her revenge. In the moments before Elle killed her, she had placed a curse on Marsh compelling him to roam the netherworld as a wraith—always halfway between the worlds of Light and Shadow. The biggest tragedy was that they could never touch, because even the tiniest contact would drain her life force from her. She would drop dead on the spot. So Marsh had retreated into the Shadow, as far away from Elle as he could.

After the accident, distant members of the Greychester family had appeared out of nowhere. Eager to ensure that they received their fair share of any potential inheritances, they had insisted that full rites be held, befitting a man of Marsh's status. Elle had fought them at first, but things became quite ugly when they started threatening to seek legal counsel. In the end, Elle simply did not have the energy to resist the formidable wall of greed and societal convention she had been up against, and so she had let them get on with things. Many a judgmental eyebrow had been raised at the fact that Elle had refused to dress in the customary widow's weeds. At the farce that was the funeral, she had arrived at the graveside in an elegant gray skirt and jacket dressed with black brocade. A military look to face militant relatives, and she had stood, watching stone-faced as they levered the empty coffin into the family mausoleum. Her behavior had caused quite a stir among the society gossipmongers and all manner of rumors had abounded.

"Not dead in the traditional sense of the word, for

sure, but still gone from your life," Dr. Bell continued, quite unperturbed by Elle's sudden broody silence. "I myself am not blessed with any supernatural gifts, but I have spent most of my life studying those who do not dwell in this realm, through the archaeology of the past. And if you don't mind me saying so, even though you take care not to make it obvious, I did notice that you cast no shadow when standing in the sun. And that means you are very much connected with the Shadow realm. The only creature I know of who casts no shadow is the Oracle . . . And that is a most important role indeed."

Elle looked her companion in the eye. Dr. Bell had hit the nail squarely on the head. "Well spotted. But I must ask you to please keep my secret. It is very dangerous for me as there are many who would like to get their hands on the power I hold."

"Of course, my dear, your secret is entirely safe with me," Gertrude said. "And please forgive me for prying. I did not mean to intrude upon your private grief. It has just been such a long time since I've had proper female companionship and so I find myself quite overcome with enthusiasm."

"Please don't worry about it," Elle said. "Besides, I refuse to accept that Hugh is gone. I saw him survive with my own eyes. I just need to find a way to breach the curse so I can bring him back."

"And how is your search going?" asked Dr. Bell. "It is generally believed that mortals who pass over to the other side are not likely to ever return."

Elle closed her eyes for a moment to block out the pain that discussing these matters triggered inside her. Most days it was nothing but a dull ache, but sometimes, in moments like this, she found herself caught off guard and it left her quite breathless. "I am sorry, Gertrude, but this is a very painful subject for me. My search for my husband is a private matter, if you don't mind," she said as kindly as she could.

"Of course, my dear. I was only raising the subject as I wanted to offer you my help." Dr. Bell patted her arm. "Please forgive me."

"Thank you, but I don't think there is anything anyone can do. He is out there somewhere and it is up to me to find a way to bring him back. And I will find a way—even if it's the last thing I do."

"Would you mind if I told you a story?" Gertrude said.

Elle blinked at her. "I suppose."

"Oh, don't be so skeptical. Everyone likes a story. And besides, it will serve to pass the time."

Elle smiled. "Tell away," she said.

Gertrude sat back in her seat, hands folded in her lap as she gazed out over the clouds before them. When she spoke, her voice took on the far-off tone of one remembering a good story.

"They say that east of Siam lies the mythical city of Angkor Wat—it is called the city of a thousand faces and it is hidden within the darkest of jungles. They say that the ancient people of the Khmer once lived there. They drew their wealth from the rich soil and water and became prosperous. Their leader became so powerful that he ruled over a kingdom that stretched from the other side of Siam all the way east to the sea. As is befitting for a ruler of such power, he decreed that the entire city be built as a temple in honor of the gods. And so Angkor Wat rose from the jungle. Rock by giant rock.

"When the city was almost complete, the ruler of the Khmer decreed that a thousand young women should dance a ballet to honor the gods. His officials scoured the land for a thousand of the most beautiful and talented dancers. These women were brought to the city, and they were called the *apsara* maidens. Once there, they were dressed in gold and fine silks. They were given the finest food and satin pillows upon which to rest. They spent their days mastering the most intricate and delicate dance steps ever achieved by the human form.

"Then, when the moon was full and the temple was ready, the thousand maidens stepped out into the night. They danced and danced through the hours of darkness offering themselves to the gods of the Khmer in the most exquisite sacred ballet ever performed. Some say that their dance was so perfect, so beautiful, that it would cause any normal mortal watching to fall into a trance.

"The ruler of the Khmer grew jealous of the maidens, for their dance brought them so close to the divine that the people of the city started worshipping them instead. So, in a fit of jealous rage, he called upon the assistance of the Shadow realm. He wanted to capture the power, the beauty and the purity of the *apsara* maidens for himself. From the Shadow rose a dark sorcerer. A Shadow Master so evil that anything he cast his gaze upon withered to dust. When the moon grew full again, the ruler and his sorcerer disguised themselves in the garden and waited for the maidens. It was not long before they stepped out into the fragrant night air and started their dance.

"As soon as moonlight fell upon the maidens, the sorcerer stepped out and cast his magic. One by one, the *apsara* maidens were swallowed by the giant blocks of stone that constituted Angkor Wat. They all disappeared until only one maiden remained. She was the most beautiful and graceful of them all. Before she disappeared into the stone, she sent up a prayer to the moon goddess for help. But the sorcerer's spell was too far gone to save the maidens from their entombment. All the moon goddess could do was cast her protective light around the last maiden, but not before she too was sent into the stone.

"The moon goddess grew very angry with the ruler of the Khmer and his sorcerer, and in order to shame them into seeing what evil they had done, she worked a spell. In the light of the full moon, the images of the maidens emerged in the walls of the temples and buildings, set in stone so all may see what the Khmer ruler had done. Each carving was unique, an exact likeness of every beautiful apsara who had disappeared. But the most beautiful of them all was the last *apsara* for she had become the queen of the maidens of stone.

"The next day, the Khmer ruler saw the maidens and was so overcome by shame for what he had done that his heart broke and he dropped down dead . . ."

"That's quite a tale," Elle said.

Gertrude smiled. "Some say it is nothing but the truth."

"Oh, I have no doubt," Elle said. She had seen enough strange things in life to know not to dismiss stories of things that referred to the Shadow. They always had the rather inconvenient habit of turning out to be just so.

"I always was of a mind to travel to the Orient. Just think how wonderful it would be to discover an entire lost city." Gertrude looked at Elle.

"Well, I suppose it certainly would bring its share of fame and fortune," Elle replied.

"I would need a competent pilot to fly me there," Gertrude said.

"Would you now?" Elle said.

"Know anyone who might fit the part?" Gertrude's eyes held a strange twinkle that spoke volumes. "I happen to know that such a charter would pay extremely well if the right patrons are secured."

Elle smiled. "Gertrude, if you want to ask me, you should. I am certainly open to persuasion."

"That is excellent news. We should keep in touch once we land in England. I have some work to do overseeing the cataloguing of these Nubian artifacts, but as soon the expedition is finalized and I have started preparing the proposals, I will let you know."

"You know, I think going on an expedition with you might be just the thing I need," Elle said.

"Well, it would be absolutely lovely to have the company of another lady. Especially one who knows how to conduct herself in extraordinary situations."

They sat together in silence for some time after that.

As the companionable silence stretched between them, Elle allowed her thoughts to wander. The warmth of the cabin and the steady drone of the engines lulled her into a state of deep thought. It had been a while since she'd even considered any long-term plans, but somehow the thought of having something to look forward to was rather appealing.

Beside her, Dr. Bell nodded off and started snoring softly.

Suddenly, the *Water Lily* shuddered. Elle shook herself out of her reverie. She caught the movement of a shadow from the corner of her eye.

"Bugger, balls and blast," she said as she scanned the instrument panels.

"What was that?" Dr. Bell sat up and blinked at Elle's peppery use of language.

"Gertrude, are you sure the freight is tied securely down in the back?"

"I suppose so. It's as secure as it's ever going to be."

Another shadow *whoosh*ed past the windscreen and darted off, just out of view. The *Water Lily* shuddered again.

"Say, what is that shuddering sound?"

"Gliders," Elle said. "They are getting into position to fire on us." She adjusted the direction of the thrusters and the *Water Lily* banked to her starboard side, which was just as well, because before them, a giant ship loomed into view.

"Oh my," Dr. Bell breathed as she took in the sight of the 800-foot vessel that floated so ominously before them.

"Oh my, indeed," Elle said between gritted teeth.

The ship floating before them was a leviathan compared to the *Water Lily*. She was a proper warship, fully encased in armor cladding. From balloon chambers to keel, her sleek double-hull bullet shape glittered ominously in the red of the setting sun. Fine spiderwebs of rigging held her together. She was close enough to see that her huge hull was battered and scarred. The ship's broadsides bristled with grappling hooks and cannons. Bits of net and scrim trailed in the air currents and made it look even more eerie and sinister.

Around her, a dozen or so small spark-powered wood and canvas gliders buzzed, ready for action.

"Pirates!" Elle breathed as she watched the ship before her unfurl the skull and crossbones off its prow. "Dr. Bell, I fear our peaceful journey is to be disrupted. We are about to be attacked."

Dr. Bell closed the biscuit tin and placed it in the cubbyhole before her. "Well, I had better put these in a safe place then. Looks like it's going to be a bumpy flight."

"We are small and fast. I am going to try and outrun them," Elle said as she started twisting knobs and pulling levers. As a small commercial freighter, the *Water Lily* carried no cannon. Even if she did, it was unlikely that she would ever be able to take on the likes of the dreadful hulking ship that floated before her. However, what the *Water Lily* lacked in size, she more than made up for in speed and agility; that was her only defense. And right now, Elle was praying as hard as she could that speed would be enough.

She cranked up the spark reactor and angled the ship

in the opposite direction. The *Water Lily* creaked and the engines hummed.

"Let's give them a run for their money, shall we?" she said to Dr. Bell, and with a surge of power they took flight.

The pirates had expected the *Water Lily* to adopt evasive maneuvers, it seemed. Elle watched through her rearview periscope with a growing sense of trepidation as a swarm of gliders slipped into formation behind them. And just then, as if the universe was truly conspiring against them, a stiff headwind fueled by the heat of the desert rose up and met them head-on.

The *Water Lily* groaned as she hit the hot updrafts. Elle shook her head in frustration as she pushed the engines harder.

The pirates had been clever. They had waited until she was on course and facing the headwinds before they chose to strike. The little out-fliers suffered far less from wind drag than the dirigibles did, and soon they were almost upon her.

One flew past almost touching the windglass. The scruffy pilot, dressed in goggles and a dirty aviator cap, waggled his wings as if to taunt her, while he made another loop in front of the cockpit. It did not take much to work out their plans, judging by the large reel of rope and grappling hook attached to the side of the glider.

Elle pushed the thrusters till they were fully open and jammed the autopilot controls into place.

"Watch that gauge," she said to Dr. Bell. "If the line dips below the red, call me."

Dr. Bell nodded. "Will do." The older woman was looking a little wide-eyed and pale.

Elle strode over to her storage cubby and unlocked it. She pulled out her shotgun and a box full of cartridges. The shotgun was inlaid with silver and emblazoned with the Greychester family crest, but that was not something she wanted to be reminded of right now. It was one of the few items she had taken with her when she had left Greychester House.

"Gertrude, do you know how to use a shotgun?"

"Do I ever! I am a crack shot. Been grouse hunting since I was a mere slip of a girl," the older woman said with a touch of pride.

"Well, then take this and shoot anyone who comes through that hatch," Elle said, pointing up above them. "We won't be able to defeat them, but let's hope we can fend them off long enough for me to fly us out of here."

Dr. Bell took the shotgun and started to load it. "Do you think you could perhaps perform your sandstorm trick?"

Elle shook her head. "No, it's too dangerous. If I summoned that amount of updraft out here we will only end up blasting ourselves out of the sky in the process," Elle said. "I do have another idea, though."

"Then get to it, girl!" Gertrude said. "I for one would prefer to go down fighting and not end up being pirate quarry, if you don't mind."

"Right then, I'll be back in a jiffy." Elle closed her eyes and focused on the barrier. Here, high up in the sky, the barrier was less prone to wear and tear by Shadow creatures so it was thicker than it was closer to the ground. She took a deep breath and slipped into the space between the worlds. As soon as the golden light enclosed her, she started looking about for the globules of energy, but to her dismay, she saw none. Before her, the barrier stretched out, all glorious and pristine. She felt her heart sink, since without the snags caused by wear and tear, there was nowhere for any excess energy to accumulate. Elle looked about in a state of indecision. If she followed the barrier down to look for globules of energy, she might lose her place in relation to the realm of Light. If she went the wrong way, she could end up stepping back into thin air, miles away from the *Water Lily*. Dr. Bell would be left to fend for herself unaided and Elle would most likely end up falling to a gruesome death.

No, she had to turn back. As she turned, she looked up and saw one small globule high up above her. Using all her strength, she jumped. As she drifted through the aether, she reached out and grabbed hold of it. It split and she absorbed it almost instantly. It wasn't much, but it would have to do. She took a deep breath and slipped back to the Light.

"They've been dropping hooks on us," Dr. Bell said as soon as she reappeared.

"How long have I been gone?"

"A good ten minutes or so. I was getting a tad worried." Dr. Bell was indeed looking rather anxious.

"Right, well, time to see if we can fend them off." She grabbed hold of the controls to turn the ship round. She pulled the steering lever, but nothing happened.

There was another large thump above them and the ominous clinking sound of grappling hooks dragging against the fuselage. She tried to turn again, but the thrusters would not budge.

She consulted her periscopes with growing dismay. "The bastards have snagged my thrusters and they are busy tying them down!" she exclaimed. Long cable lines were being reeled back to the pirate ship by the gliders.

The engines of the *Water Lily* suddenly started whining loudly as the thrusters reached their limit. The ship lurched forward but the tether ropes that held them rang taut.

Elle felt her herself go cold with fear. The *Water Lily* was stationary, hooked like a fish by the large ship behind them.

She reduced the power to the thrusters, and the hull creaked as the ropes picked up the slack.

The next move for her would be to kill her engines and dump helium in the hope that the sudden dip would dislodge the grappling hooks, but as they drew closer, she could see vicious bilge hooks being lowered from the hull of the pirate ship. They were waiting for her to duck so they could ensnare her.

"Gertrude, I need your help," Elle said, thinking quickly.

"Tell me what to do."

Elle strode over to the flight console. "I want you to sit in this seat and hold this." She pointed at the steering controls. "When you hear the ropes release, I want you to push forward on the thrusters as hard as you can. Do you think you can do that?"

"Leave it to me," Dr. Bell said.

"Let's give these blighters a run for their money then, shall we?" Elle said. She grabbed the large rigging machete she kept in one of the cubbyholes. It was a broad steel blade, about a foot long—an essential tool for severing snagged rigging. With the blade in hand, Elle climbed the maintenance ladder that led to one of the upper hatches.

"We have got to sever those ropes before we are reeled in, come what may."

She flung the hatch open and gasped as she felt the freezing air hit. The wind whipped the loose strands of hair that had escaped from her aviator cap into her face, and the icy air made her eyes stream. She pulled her goggles over her eyes and blinked.

Four thick ropes now tethered the *Water Lily* to the pirate ship. Her engines were fighting bravely, but Elle could see the ropes tightening and straining as the pirate ship slowly reeled them in.

She closed her eyes to steady herself against the wind and dizzying height. All she needed to do was sever these four ropes. That would give them enough time to get away before the pirates managed to rally their gliders in order to launch another attack.

Carefully she reached inside herself for the globule of power. She drew a little of the energy forth and aimed at the space before her where the ropes spanned. She breathed in and out, in an attempt to steady herself. There would be one chance only to succeed at this.

She raised her arms and flung the white ball of light at the ropes.

There was a flash of light. The air crackled with bright blue flashes of energy, before they went out with a fizzle and a pop.

"No!" Elle gasped. The wind and the thin air up here made combustion difficult, and the amount of power she had managed to grab from the barrier was simply too little. Without something to direct the energy, such as the barrel of a cannon, the blast had simply dissipated in the wind before it had had any effect.

Aether would not help her out here. She was on her own and this was going to have to be done the hard way. Bracing herself against the cold, she hoisted herself up out of the hatch and onto the roof.

She grabbed hold of one of the rigging ropes which held the hull of the *Water Lily* to her balloon. The icy wind took her breath away, and far below the earth stretched out a mass of desert and sea. She gritted her teeth, for this was no time to be cowardly. Step by tiny step she edged her way along the edge of the fuselage toward the tethers. Her movements were slow, hampered by wind and cold, but eventually she made it. With a small sob of relief, she sank to her knees next to the rope. Her hands shaking, she pulled out the blade and started hacking at the rope.

Elle gave a cry of triumph as she watched the strands of the rope wind and untwist of their own accord as the rigging blade hacked into it. The rope twanged and whizzed as the tension was severed, but the end of the rope closest to her shot up and hit her squarely on the chin.

The blow nearly knocked her out and she fell back hard. She grabbed hold of the rigging just in time to stop herself from flying over the edge. But in her scrabble, she let go of the machete. She watched helplessly as it skidded to the edge of the fuselage and then, slowly, slipped over and disappeared into the nothingness below.

"Eleanor! Come back inside. It's no use and you're going to get yourself killed!" Dr. Bell called from the hatch where she had appeared.

Elle stared at the taut tether ropes in despair. Without the rigging machete, there was nothing she could do. She would have to find another way. Carefully she edged her way to the hatch but the fuselage was slippery from condensation and she felt her foothold falter.

"Here, take my hand!" Dr. Bell said as she grabbed hold of Elle and they both dropped down into the ship.

Inside the *Water Lily* the engines were still screaming. Steam was hissing from a blown pressure valve.

"Sorry. I tried," Elle managed to gasp as she caught her breath. "I was able to get one rope but it recoiled and hit me in the face. I lost the blade." Her jaw and neck were throbbing as if she had been punched in the face, and it felt like one of her molars had become loose. She reached out to steady herself from the wave of dizziness which had overcome her. She would have a nasty bruise on her face—if she lived long enough.

In answer to her thoughts, the ship creaked and listed slightly to one side as the remaining tether ropes tightened and strained.

Elle strode over to the controls and eased off on the thrusters. The engines slowed down to a slightly lower revolution per minute. The *Water Lily* lurched again as the tether ropes picked up the slack.

"Perhaps we should see if we can negotiate with them. The artifacts for our lives," Dr. Bell suggested.

Elle shook her head. "They'll take the artifacts no matter what we do. They are just a bonus. The real prize is the *Water Lily*. These men want the ship and there's no telling what they'll do with us once they have it. Pirates are animals. They are the roughest and lowest of men. It might be a fate worse than death," she said in a low voice. This was her worst nightmare. Suddenly all the arguments she had had with Marsh about her safety when flying came sharply into focus. Elle did not want to admit it, but she was utterly terrified.

"It's time to abandon ship," she said with a grave expression.

"What do you mean?" Gertrude looked at her in surprise. "Surely you are not suggesting we jump overboard."

"Not exactly, but you are going to have to trust me," Elle said.

The older woman nodded. "Do it," she said.

Slipping into the barrier up here was going to be exceedingly dangerous, but it was their only option now. Elle was simply going to have to try and hope for the best. She closed her eyes and reached out for the barrier. Then she stopped and frowned.

"What is it?" Gertrude whispered.

"There is nothing here," Elle said. She closed her eyes again and concentrated harder. Before her, in the place where the barrier usually opened up for her, there was nothing but air. She focused more of her attention on opening the space, but it was in vain.

"Elle, what are you doing?" Gertrude said again, this time with more urgency.

"It's gone," Elle said.

"What is gone?"

"The barrier. Our means of escape. It was here a few

moments ago, but now I can't seem to open it." She stared at Gertrude in disbelief. "Gertrude, you saw me disappear."

"Maybe they've done something to stop you from escaping," Gertrude said.

"Or perhaps my powers have failed me," Elle said, feeling a sudden urge to panic. "I had them just a few moments ago. Why are they not working?"

Gertrude laid a hand on Elle's shoulder. "This is the problem with aether. It's so very unpredictable."

"Gertrude, we are trapped. I'm so sorry. I thought I could whisk us out of this mess. What are we going to do?"

Gertrude looked in Elle's eyes. "If we are truly trapped, then I say we stand and fight. I'll not go down without protest. That's for sure." Dr. Bell's face grew stern.

The *Water Lily* groaned again as the ropes tightened more.

Elle looked about in frustration. There had to be a way . . . "I am going to try something," she said over her shoulder.

She took hold of the controls and pushed them in the other direction. The engines slowed down dramatically and almost stalled midair. Immediately the ropes slackened. Elle pushed the purge valve to dump helium. With the reduced gas levels, the *Water Lily* started sinking rapidly.

"Yes!" Elle said as she watched one of the grappling hooks slip loose and fly past the windglass. Now all she had to do was to create enough clearance to miss the bilge hooks attached to the hull of the pirate ship above them. With a little luck they could slip past at a lower altitude. Once clear, the other hooks would slip free. It would be a fast plummet to the ground before she'd be able to refill the balloon, but she was sure the larger vessel would not be able to turn around fast enough to catch them.

With grim resolve, she grabbed hold of the thruster controls in order to swivel them about. The sky went dark as the large hull of the pirate ship blocked out the sun. The *Water Lily* dipped in a desperate bid for freedom.

Suddenly there was a loud clanging noise. The ship shuddered and listed sharply to the port side. The sudden jolt caused a universal pressure release, and with a hiss of steam the engines went out.

Elle grabbed her periscope and swung it round. The pirate ship was directly above them. Above her, the *Water Lily*'s balloon billowed limply below it. Her rigging cables creaked as the hull swung in the bottom drag caused by the hull of the bigger ship.

The *Water Lily* was securely caught in the row of grappling hooks attached to the bottom of the hull of the pirate ship. And judging by the flapping of the balloon canvas, she appeared to have bled out all of her gas.

"That's not terribly good, is it?" Dr. Bell said.

"No, it's not," Elle replied. Her duck-and-cover maneuver had been too little, too late, and they were now stuck, with no means of escape. Elle felt a wave of panicky fear rise up into her throat. They were in very big trouble indeed.

CHAPTER 5

The sharp rattle of her communications console startled Elle out of her fear-induced stupor.

Elle grabbed the speaking tube. "What?" she said rather rudely.

"This is the captain of the pirate ship *Inanna*. You are completely immobilized. Any further resistance will only result in your death."

"How dare you attack my ship, you vile bastard? Have you no honor? I will never surrender to you!" she shouted.

The captain just laughed at her fury. "Prepare to be boarded. Any resistance will be met with violence. You have been warned." The console lights went out as the communication was terminated.

There was a series of loud thumps overhead as the pirates dropped down onto the roof of the *Water Lily*.

"I'm so sorry," Elle said to Dr. Bell.

Dr. Bell just closed the shotgun and aimed for the hatch. "Oh, I think we could still give them a run for their money. I for one am not prepared to give up my artifacts so easily. Not after all I've been through to find them."

"Right on." Elle pulled her revolver out and cocked it. "We fight until we cannot fight any longer, but please be careful, Gertrude."

Dr. Bell just gave her a reassuring smile. "Never you

mind about me. I can take care of myself. You should rather pay attention to staying alive yourself, hmm?"

"Right. United we stand, divided we fall." She gripped her pistol. "Bring it on, you rotters."

Slowly the hatch above them creaked open. A pair of heavy rubber-soled, steel-tipped boots appeared at the top of the ladder. Attached to the boots was a pair of legs, clad in brown canvas trousers, soon followed by a broad leather belt and the bottom of a shirt and waist-coat.

Then there was the eardrum-ripping boom that only a shotgun could make, as Dr. Bell dispatched the pirate before he could even draw his weapon. The cabin filled with gun smoke as he dropped to the floor with a dull thump, his face covered by the leather aviator mask.

Then the fight broke out in earnest as the rest of the pirates boarded the *Water Lily*.

Elle took out the next two men who came through the hatch. They too dropped to the floor on top of their departed compatriot.

Then the shooting started in earnest as more pirates than Elle and Gertrude could take aim at dropped through the hatch. Chaos ensued as the pirates boarded the *Water Lily*.

Elle ducked behind the flight console as bullets pinged all around her, at that moment feeling deeply grateful for the solid-oak paneling of the *Water Lily*. The noise and smell of gunfire left her deaf and almost blind but she had to keep fighting. With fingers that were slippery with fear sweat, she reloaded the Colt and took aim.

The pirates who stole through the hatch looked a rag-gedy lot, and judging by the way they moved, they were quite used to fighting in close quarters. They easily avoided her shots, which grew more urgent and less ac-curate as the cabin filled with invaders.

"Gertrude, take cover!" she yelled, but it was too late.

She watched in horror as one of the pirates raised his pistol to take proper aim at her shotgun-wielding friend.

Elle saw the man's face draw into a satisfied grin as he pulled the trigger. "Gertrude! No!" Elle shouted as the shot hit the older woman squarely in the stomach. Elle raised her Colt and shot the pirate in the face. His head exploded like a melon, with bright red gore splattering against the wood paneling behind him.

Dr. Bell gasped and let go of the shotgun as she slumped against the woodwork.

"Stop!" Elle shouted. "Please stop shooting. We surrender!" She stepped out from behind her hiding place and held out her revolver to signal surrender.

One of the pirates grabbed Elle by the collar. He pressed the muzzle of his pistol against her temple.

"Enough with the shooting, little girl," he sneered through tobacco-yellowed teeth. "Drop the gun."

Elle felt the cold of true terror as her Colt was wrenched from her grip.

Someone grabbed her arms and dragged her hands up over her head. She flinched as they tied her wrists together. The rough rope bit into the delicate scarred skin of her wrists. The pirate pushed her to the floor and she landed heavily on her knees next to where Dr. Bell lay.

"Gertrude," Elle gasped.

The older woman lay back with her hand on her belly. She looked pale. Deep red blood seeped through her fingers and onto the wood of the deck. "Oh dear, I seem to have gotten myself in a spot of bother," she muttered.

"Hold on," Elle whispered as she dragged herself onto her knees. "We need to keep pressure on the wound. She pressed down with her bound hands, but dark red blood kept seeping through her fingers. "They must have a doctor on board who can help. Pirates always have medics on their crew." She did her best to stop her voice from trembling.

"Oh, I don't think we'll have time for that, my dear," said Dr. Bell. "I think the bullet has gone right through me, quite possibly severing my spine. You see, I can't feel or move my legs at the minute."

"There has got to be something we can do," Elle said. "I am not letting you die. Not like this."

"Stay alive," Dr. Bell whispered. "Do what you must, but stay alive," she added before she closed her eyes.

"No, please,"' Elle said. She felt a sudden, unbidden tear trickle down her cheek.

The pirates had evidently found what they were looking for: Loud whoops of excitement along with the violent crunch of crowbars on wooden crates rose up from the freight hold.

The big pirate with the beard and the yellow teeth came striding into the cockpit with his huge fist clamped round a jeweled goblet. "Nubian gold," he sneered. "The Cap'n is going to be pleased."

"Take whatever you want. Just please could you get my companion to a doctor? She needs help," Elle pleaded.

The pirate laughed. "Then she shouldn't 'ave been shooting at us in the first place. The Cap'n did warn you there'd be trouble if you did that."

"Please," Elle said again. "She's going to die if you don't help us."

The pirate strode over to them and cast an eye over Dr. Bell. He scratched his beard and sucked air through his teeth as he regarded the wound. "That bullet's gone straight into the gut," he said after a few moments. "There ain't a doctor alive that can cure a shot like that. She'll be a goner in a few hours, for sure. But I've orders to take you alive so you'd best wait here quietly until the Captain calls for you."

"If you've orders to take us alive, then you should get us to your sick bay. If she goes, I do too," Elle said.

The pirate ignored her. Instead, he strode over to the cockpit. "My, but it's hot in here. Must be from the shooting. He shrugged off the black canvas coat he was wearing and flung himself into the pilot seat. Then he put his great hobnail boots up onto the flight console and stretched out. "Ah, that's a nice chair. I think I might take it for myself." Then he grabbed the communications tube and barked a few orders into it.

"Pity you ripped the balloon on this one. She's a pretty little freighter. But I reckon she'd fetch a nice price, ripped canvas or not." His face broke open in a dirty grin. "A bit like her little pilot. What d'ya say?" He guffawed at his joke.

Elle just glared at him with cold anger. There was much she wanted to say to this vile man, but she had to stay calm for Gertrude's sake.

She watched with naked hatred as the pirates carried the crates up through the hatch and into the hull of the *Inanna*.

Elle's back ached from sitting in such an awkward position and her hands were numb, but she held on to Dr. Bell, willing her own life force into her and hoping for a miracle. From time to time, she felt the strange trickle of energy slip between them. It was, after all, the function of an Oracle to channel the energies of the worlds, but she had no knowledge of the healing skills of the Shadow Realm. Gertrude was growing quieter and paler by the minute, and Elle could see that what she was doing was not enough. There was so little aether up here that there was not much more she could do.

The pirate with the yellow teeth eventually strode up to them. "That one still alive?" he inquired.

"Please. You must help her," Elle murmured. "Look, I'm a good pilot. I can navigate. Let me work in return for her treatment."

The pirate laughed heartily at her offer, but he did

stand back and survey them for a moment. Elle could almost see the cogs and gears turning inside his meaty head. "That's a mighty fine offer, but who says we don't already have a good navvy on board?"

"I'll do anything . . . anything you want if you just get her to a doctor," Elle said.

The pirate scratched the back of his greasy neck. "Well, as I said before, I have strict orders to bring you aboard alive."

"And what if we resist?"

"Well, then I have orders to shoot you. Not kill you, mind. Just maim you a little. Seems our Captain wants a word with you." He shrugged. "You should count yourself lucky that we only have orders to put the two of you into a life-raft balloon and set adrift out there if you refuse." He wiped his huge hand on his none-too-clean shirt, leaving a brownish streak of what may have been blood or engine grease across it. "Millions of square miles of nothing but sand and sun," he said sniffing.

"If I come without protest, will you ask your doctor to help my friend?"

The pirate shrugged. "Can't promise anything, but if we bring her on board, Doc said he'd look."

Elle closed her eyes and took a deep breath. "Very well then, I accept," she said. She could play at being a willing prisoner if it meant there was a chance of getting Dr. Bell some help. They could find a way to escape later.

The pirate grinned through his thick beard and the skin around his eyes crinkled with pleasure. "Well then, Osbert Heller's the name. First mate and bosun of the *Inanna*.

"Eleanor Chance," Elle said.

"Well, welcome aboard the *Inanna*, Eleanor Chance," he said in a tone that was anything but welcoming.

He turned and whistled. "Elias! Finn! Get a stretcher

and take the old lady to the infirmary. See if Doc can do something for her. Cap'n wants to see the other one. Chop-chop."

With that, Heller gripped Elle with his enormous hands and dragged her to her feet. She barely had an opportunity to ensure that Dr. Bell's head did not hit the floor before she was hoisted along and shoved up the ladder that led out of the hatch. Outside, boarding scaffolding had been lashed to the fuselage leading up to an open cargo hatch in the hull.

Elle also noted, with some dismay, that more large iron hooks and tether ropes were holding the *Water Lily* in place now. There would be no escaping from here without a fight. And it was a fight she was not so sure she would win on her own.

"Up the ladder then," Heller said as he shoved her toward it. "And no funny tricks or your friend won't see the doctor."

Elle gritted her teeth and started climbing the ladder. This was not an easy task, considering the fact that her hands were bound. She slipped once or twice on the rungs. Each time she stumbled, Heller gripped her painfully and hoisted her up before him. "Come on, girlie. I thought you were a pilot," he growled. "Steady on now."

When Elle's head reached the top of the ladder, she was unceremoniously seized by the collar and dragged inside.

The first thing that hit her was a blast of warm air, slick and damp with the smell of metal and engine grease. She stumbled along the narrow gangway that led from the cargo hatch. She was on board the *Inanna*.

Inside, the ship was enormous, with walkways and doors stretching off to all sides. Everything was painted in the same drab shade of anticorrosive paint that prevented the ship from rusting. This was indeed a warship, she thought as she looked around. It was solid, impenetrable and a million times different from the pretty wood paneling and hand-painted windowpanes of the *Water Lily*.

Elle felt a strange sense of claustrophobia envelop her. All her senses felt dull—as if she had her head inside a metal bucket. Iron, she thought. This ship is made of iron.

Even with her navigational skills, Elle was soon lost as she was manhandled down yet another narrow corridor by Heller. He kept one of his large hands clamped securely around her elbow, forcing her to walk in front of him, their footfalls clunking along the metal walkway.

As they walked, Elle stared sideways at Heller's hip. Peeking out from underneath the leather waistcoat was her Colt, tucked away into his belt. It sat there, its pearl butt jiggling just out of reach.

She resolved that retrieving it would be the first thing she did. A bullet between this hideous man's eyes would quite possibly be the second. She was secretly relieved that no one had bothered to check her for other weapons. Her stiletto sat tucked securely in a front pocket of her corset. It would take more than a cursory search to find it. She would sort out her escape later. For now, saving Gertrude was all that mattered.

They came to a closed door and stopped. Heller reached over to turn the round metal wheel that operated the opening mechanism. As he moved, Elle caught the distinct smell of engine grease, unwashed body and stale tobacco. Elle closed her eyes and tried to block out the awfulness of him brushing past her.

The door swung open with a clang.

"Permission to enter the ready room with the prisoner, Captain," Heller said.

"Permission granted, Mr. Heller," a man said from inside.

Without further ceremony, Heller shoved Elle through the door. She stumbled but he was still holding on to her so she ended up being half dragged until he dropped her into a heap on the floor.

"Miss Chance. Or is it Lady Greychester? It's nice to see you again," the Captain said.

Elle looked up and felt all the blood drain from her face. "You!" was all she managed to stammer. Before her was none other than Captain Logan Dashwood.

He gave her a lazy smile. "The one and only," he said.

Suddenly furious, Elle found her feet and yanked her elbow out of Heller's grasp. "How dare you steal the *Water Lily*!" she shouted at him. "Dr. Bell is likely to die because of you!"

Dashwood sat back in his chair. "My dear Mrs. Marsh, if I recall correctly, you stole the *Iron Phoenix* off me in Amsterdam. You had no compunction about leaving me stranded with my crew at that point. We could have died too, you know."

"There was no shooting. No one got hurt!" she said. "I won that fair and square."

"Oh no you didn't. You never let on that you were gifted by the Shadow. Took me for all I had, if I recall rightly."

"You were the one who was cheating." Elle lurched at him, the intention to kill upon her, but Heller had grabbed hold of her and dragged her back.

"Easy now. That's no way to address a captain, now is it?" he said.

"Let go of me, you hairy gorilla." Elle spat.

Dashwood sat back in his seat, enjoying the spectacle. "It's all right, Heller. Let her be."

Heller set Elle back onto her feet. She straightened her coat and glared at him.

He shrugged and ambled up to the doorway where he

leaned against the door, crossed his arms, and regarded Elle with hard eyes, slightly narrowed.

At well over six foot and with a chest as broad as an oak, this was not a man she wished to tangle with, she realized.

"Not only did you steal my beautiful ship, you then crashed her into the ground near Battersea," Dashwood said, drawing her attention back to him.

"I was not flying her and you know it," Elle said.

Dashwood was right though. He and Ducky Richardson—one of her oldest friends—had come to lend their assistance at the Battersea spark monastery in London during her attempt to rescue Marsh from the lair of the Lady in White. The rigging of the *Iron Phoenix* had become entangled with another ship, with disastrous consequences. Both had crashed into the ground, causing untold damage.

"Does Ducky even know you're a—a pirate?" Elle said.

"Oh yes. In fact he's been on a few raids with me," Dashwood said smoothly. "I think he quite enjoys the excitement of it all."

"And what about Dr. Bell? What did she ever do to you to deserve this?"

Dashwood's face colored for a second. "Look, I am sorry about your friend. My men had orders to take you alive and unhurt. You shouldn't have opened fire on us. Accidents happen."

"And you think that justifies your actions?" Elle said, horrified at his glib attempt at shifting the blame.

He sat forward, his eyes suddenly intensely blue. "You gave the lady a shotgun instead of surrendering like you should have. *You* are the one with blood on your hands, Mrs. Marsh. Not me."

Elle stared at him in disbelief. There was no point in

arguing with him. "Can I see her, please?" she said, changing tactics.

Dashwood nodded. "Heller, take her to the infirmary. My surgeon is doing all he can, but she's in a bad way. You may go and say goodbye." He stepped closer to Elle and regarded her with a look of concern. "Perhaps you should ask the doc to look you over too. That is quite a bruise you have on your chin." He ran his finger gently over the place where the rope had caught her earlier.

Elle flinched and turned away. "I am perfectly well, thank you very much. I do not need your sympathy, especially since none of this would have happened had it not been for you. Mark my words, this is not over Captain Dashwood."

Dashwood started laughing. "Oh, you are quite right. You and I have many things to discuss in the coming days."

The infirmary was painted a sickly shade of light green. Patches of rust bloomed up and down the metalwork. In one of the bunks, tucked away behind a canvas curtain on the far end of the infirmary, Elle found Dr. Bell.

"Gertrude," she whispered. "Just stay still, I am working on a way to get us out of here."

Elle glanced around. The doctor was a solid-looking man with slightly bowed legs. He was almost completely bald, save for one long wisp of hair, which appeared to be held in place by the rubber headband that also held a surgical light over his eye. He was busy bandaging the arm of one of the crewmen. His white frock was splattered and stained with red. It had taken almost all of Dashwood's crew to capture them, yet Elle took no satisfaction from the fact that the infirmary seemed to be full of wounded men. So much bloodshed over nothing.

Gertrude's lips were very pale. A bright red stain bloomed through the bandages wrapped around her stomach. "Eleanor, we have only known one another for a few days, but I feel like we have been friends for a long time." Dr. Bell coughed and winced with pain.

"Save your strength," Elle said.

Dr. Bell smiled at her. "It's all right my dear. I just wish someone had told me that dying was so painful. Doctor gave me some laudanum and I am quite giddy with it, but it still hurts."

"Gertrude, please don't say things like that. You are going to survive this." Elle held the older woman's hand in hers.

Dr. Bell gripped her fingers. "Before we run out of time, there is something very important I need to tell you."

"I'm listening." Elle leaned forward to catch the words.

"You must listen to what I have to say. Remember the legend of Angkor." Dr. Bell drew a deep breath and winced.

"The hidden city?" Elle said.

"The *apsara*." Dr. Bell struggled to sit up a little and gripped Elle's lapel even tighter. "I know she would deem you worthy. The *apsara* will be able to tell you how you will find your husband. I am absolutely sure of it. Promise me you will go and seek her counsel. Offer her something that is sacred to you and ask her."

Elle started shaking with fear and distress. "I promise. Gertrude, please rest now. You must not get so excited. All this will start the bleeding again," Elle murmured.

Dr. Bell let go of Elle and lay back, her eyes closed. "The bleeding has not stopped since I was shot. It has been seeping into my insides all this time. The only reason it has slowed is because there is no blood left to lose . . . and there is no getting better from that. I know I am not long for this world."

Elle felt hot tears well up in her eyes. "No. You will

survive this. You will be all right," she said, more to convince herself than anyone else, but she knew deep down that what Gertrude was saying was true. There was no recovery from a gut shot like hers.

"Promise me you will seek the answer . . . and even if you don't find the answer . . . don't live your life alone like I did . . ." Dr. Bell's voice trailed off as she drifted out of consciousness. She did not speak again.

Elle sat with her for what seemed like a very long time. She sat and listened to the labored breathing of her friend, mingled with the gentle humming of the ship's engines. She sat perfectly still until the only sound she could hear was the engines.

Elle closed her eyes in despair. Gertrude Bell was dead.

CHAPTER 6

Elle sat alone in the dark next to Gertrude's shrouded body for a long time. Around her the ship's sickbay grew quiet as the injured pirates cleared off one by one; those who couldn't walk were either shrouded like Gertrude or fed laudanum to rest. Amidst the general hubbub, a strange numbness settled upon her.

I bring death and destruction upon anyone who is too close to me. Marsh, Gertrude . . . all of it is my fault. Perhaps I should just give in to de Montague's requests and hand myself over to the Council of Warlocks. They may as well do their worst. At least then I would be of some use to the world.

Her only answer was the gentle creaking of the ship.

"Oh, voices of the Oracle, where are you when I need you?" she said softly.

There was no answer. She did not expect one either, for she had banished her guardians in a fit of anger not so long ago. Since then, there had been no word from them. She had tried a host of chants or rituals to bring them back but none of them had worked. It was as if the voices had disappeared into thin air—never to be heard from again.

She sighed. *When will I ever learn to control my temper?* she thought as a great wave of despondency swept over her.

A soft tap on the metal door interrupted her thoughts. Heller lumbered into the small infirmary. At the sight of the shroud, he pulled off his cap and scrunched it up in his giant hand. "Captain wants to see you," he said, sounding somewhat awkward.

"Well that's convenient, since I would like to see him too. In fact I have more than one bone to pick with him. Let's go." She pushed past Heller and stomped a few paces down the narrow corridor before stopping. She turned to Heller. "Well, are you going to show me the way or am I to wander around on this godforsaken ship by myself until I find him?"

Heller's eyes grew wide with surprise. He put his cap back on. "It's this way," he said as he led her away.

Dashwood was waiting for her on the bridge. He sat sprawled out in his leather captain's chair, one leg slung over the arm. He wore knee-high leather boots like she did, she noticed.

"Mrs. Marsh. How fares your companion?" he said.

"She passed away a little while ago." Elle swallowed the lump that had formed in her throat. "And I hold you responsible for her death."

Dashwood straightened up. "I am truly sorry about your friend." He held up his hand as if to ward off her fury. "This was supposed to be a quick, clean heist. The plan was never for anyone to get hurt or killed on board. You have my word on that."

"I want my ship back," she said, ignoring his apology. "Now!" She crossed her arms and glared at him.

Dashwood's expression lit up with a glimmer of surprise at her fury. "I'm sorry but I can't do that. Finders, keepers and all that. It's the code. She's mine now."

"What are you going to do with the *Water Lily*?" Elle demanded.

"Well, I was going to sell her as an airworthy vessel, but seeing as you managed to shred her balloons to fine ribbons, I would have to repair her in order to do that."

"Good. I hope it is so expensive that you have to spend every penny you have," she spat.

Dashwood grinned at her. "Well, yes. A complete balloon replacement is going to be very expensive, and to be honest, I don't really fancy laying out cash when I don't have to, so now I am forced to consider my options."

Elle did not like the sound of that. "And what might these options be, Captain?" she demanded.

Dashwood looked slightly uncomfortable as he met Elle's gaze. "I have given orders for the crew to strip her down and take all we can use. We can sell the spare parts and the fittings as salvage. The rest will be jettisoned when we're done."

"You can't do that!" This news was almost too much for Elle to bear. She lunged forward to grab Dashwood by the throat, but he was quicker than her. In one swift move he grabbed her wrist and swung her round so her arm was twisted and pushed up against her back. "Mind the face," he said next to her ear.

Elle struggled against him and managed to stomp on his foot with her boot. She felt Dashwood flinch slightly when her heel connected with his toes, but to his credit, he maintained his hold on her.

"I don't want to hurt you, Mrs. Marsh, but I will if I have to. Now stop fighting with me," he said as he fought to contain her struggles. "I swear I will tie you up if you don't stop right now," he said.

Elle could feel the rapid beat of his heart against her cheek. Up close, his chest felt solid and warm against her, his face so close to hers that she could feel the stubble on his chin against the sensitive skin of her neck. His touch sent a strange surge of excitement through her, which was entirely inappropriate, given the circumstances. This left her feeling utterly bewildered. She did not want to be tied up, but she also definitely did not want to give him the satisfaction of obeying his commands, so after a few more attempts at freeing herself from his grip and a well-placed elbow shoved into to his ribs, she stopped struggling.

"Heller, fetch me some rope," Dashwood said. He was slightly out of breath from wrestling with her, and his carefully combed-back blond fringe had become dislodged.

"Right away, Captain." Heller disappeared out the door and reappeared a few moments later with a skein of tough-looking rigging cord.

"Wait! You said you wouldn't tie me up if I stopped struggling," Elle said.

Dashwood rolled his eyes. "I was planning to go easy on you, on account of the fact that you are a lady and all, but I will not allow you to attack me in front of my crew. So my apologies for the rough handling, Mrs. Marsh, but yet again you have made extreme measures necessary." And with that he thrust her away from him and over to Heller who wrapped his enormous hands round her wrists as if they were nothing but lily stems.

"Tie her securely and put her in the brig while we work on the ship," Dashwood said as he smoothed back his hair. "I'll decide what to do with her once I've dealt with the loot. Perhaps we can get a ransom or something. Her late husband was worth a few dollars and I'm sure her family could muster up some money to have her back safely." He shook his head. "Although, she is such a harpy, I bet they'd probably pay money for us to keep her here."

"Aye, aye, Captain," Heller said. He was still smiling at the captain's joke, when, without much ceremony, he started looping the rope around Elle's shoulders, drawing it so tight that she gasped.

"No! Let me go! This is not fair! You promised!" Elle kicked and struggled as Heller dragged her out of the cabin and down the stairs, but her protests made little difference; fighting Heller was like wrestling with a mountain. A large, hairy, bad-tempered mountain. She did manage to land a solid blow on his thigh as he carried her down the narrow ladder, but that was about it. Heller just grunted a little but continued with the task undeterred.

"Better do the legs too, sir," Heller called up to the Captain as he dropped her onto the landing. "She's got some mighty sharp edges to her, this lady."

"Gag her too, if you must. Her mouth is the sharpest thing she has," Dashwood said from the top of the stairs.

"Wait!" Elle stopped struggling.

The men looked at her. "If you are going to strip down the ship, at least allow me to take my personal possessions off first." She looked up at Dashwood. "Please. I promise I'll go quietly if you let me get my things."

Dashwood sighed. "I can see you are going to be far more trouble than you're worth, Mrs. Marsh, but as a courtesy—one captain to another—I will allow it. But only because you have given me your word that you will behave. I hope you will keep it."

"You have my word," she said.

"Very well then, you have fifteen minutes to collect your things. But if I hear that Mr. Heller here has had one ounce of trouble out of you, you will live to regret it. Mark my words."

"Thank you," Elle breathed.

"Heller, take Atticus with you. Keep both eyes peeled; she's a crafty one. If she tries anything, shoot her in the knee."

Elle blanched. "Wait, you can't do that."

"My dear Mrs. Marsh, I am the captain of this airship and my word is law. Up here, I can damn well do as I please."

"But—" she said in a voice that came out slightly smaller than she had intended.

Dashwood shook his head in disbelief. "No more arguing! I told you once before that you would land yourself into some trouble if you went gallivanting around in airships. You are lucky that it's me and not some other captain or you would be dead right now. It's a harsh world up here; only the fittest survive. So yes, I can order my men to shoot you in the knee or anywhere else, if it pleases me. I will too. If it pleases me. And you will thank me for my mercy, for there are far worse fates which could befall the likes of you."

He looked at his first mate. "Heller?"

"Right away, sir," Heller said. He gave the rope a tug and dragged Elle to her feet. "Come along then, let's get your things." With that, he set off with a lumbering gait and Elle had to stumble-run to keep up with him.

Back on the *Water Lily,* Elle stared at the inside of the cabin with dismay. She had managed to convince Heller to untie her, but he was not happy about it and he stood by the hatch ladder scowling the rope looped in his hands.

The signs of plunder were already evident. Someone had made a sweep of all her cubbyholes and the contents were strewn all over the floor. The halfjack of brandy that she kept in case of emergencies lay empty on the floor among her papers.

"Hurry up now. No dawdling," Heller said. He folded his massive, hairy arms across his chest.

Her other guard was the one they called Atticus Crow. He was a weedy-looking fellow with dark eyes that darted here and there as he took in the interior of the ship. Crow was also dressed in a black canvas sou'wester which was so old that it had patches of what looked like gray mildew on it. Under the coat, he wore a pair of brown overalls with brass buttons and a pair of hobnail boots. On his head, he wore a black pilot's cap and goggles, the straps tied loosely under his chin. Crow was a good name for him, Elle thought, for the large black coat made him look just like a hunched-up bird.

She found her holdall, which she had stowed in the secret compartment under her seat. She noted with much relief that the raiders had missed the hatch and her things were all still there. She went over to her navigation table. Her compass had fallen round the back of it, and with the distraction of the loot in the hold, somehow the plunderers had missed it too. It had belonged to her father once and she carried it everywhere she went. With it were a few sky charts, that she rolled up and stowed in her holdall. From under her small sleeping bunk, she pulled out the canvas rucksack that held her other things. Inside it, underneath the underwear, was a box of bullets—ammunition for her Colt. She shifted it carefully so the box would not rattle.

She slung the rucksack over her shoulders and hooked her holdall so the strap sat across her chest. She then looked around the cabin for anything else that she might need. Her eye caught Dr. Bell's travel trunk, which was still sitting in the passageway. Someone had had a go at breaking the lock, but it was still intact.

She pushed the key into the battered lock and slipped it open. The trunk contained a number of books and papers along with the late doctor's toilette and an assortment of clothes.

She closed it and locked it again.

"I'm ready," she called out to her guards. "But one of you is going to have to help me with this." She bent down and lifted one side of the trunk.

Atticus grunted, took hold of the other end and then lifted it out of the hatch. "What's in here? It feels like it's filled with rocks," he said.

Elle did not answer. Instead she just shoved harder at her edge of the trunk.

At the top of the ladder, Elle stopped and looked across her ship one last time. That uncomfortable lump in her throat was threatening to turn into a full-blown sob as she took in the fine wood paneling and the hand-painted water lilies inlaid in the windowpanes. Then it was time to go.

"The brig is this way, missus. Captain's orders," Heller said as he helped her on board the *Inanna*.

"What about my things?" she said.

"They are to be left in the hold until the captain decides what he wants to do with you. Now come along; you promised you wouldn't be any trouble," he said.

Elle let out a slow breath and allowed herself to be led to the brig, which was somewhere deep in the airless belly of the ship.

She heard the door slam and the lock crunch as the key turned in it. Defeated and exhausted, Elle sank down on to the cold metal deck and rested her face in her hands. What a terrible, awful mess this was.

CHAPTER 7

Elle spent three nights in the cold and damp brig before Dashwood finally took pity on her. During this time, she tried over and over again to open the barrier so she may slip away into the Shadow realm, and to freedom and beyond, but it was all to no avail.

Try as she might, the barrier would not manifest. It was as if something was preventing her from finding it. Up here, high in the sky, surrounded by the iron bars of the brig, the pull of the Shadow realm felt weak and distant, and each time she sought to enter the barrier, she would black out and wake to find she had collapsed on the floor. She kept trying until her temples pounded and blood trickled from her nose.

On the fourth day, she was transferred to one of the crew cabins. Heller came to collect her himself. "By the way, the captain says not to try any funny Shadow business. This ship's been warded against tricks. She's got iron in her bones, so you can forget about escaping that way, girlie," he said as he shoved her through the door.

Elle turned and looked at him. "An iron-boned ship?" So her suspicions had been correct.

Heller nodded. "Aye, we took her off a Trader. Even the ship's grappling hooks are hexed. If you look at them closely you can see the magic inscribed on the metal. Captain says the slavers used the hooks to stop their prey from escaping in midair." He shrugged. "Not sure how that all works, but I can tell you we found some pretty funny creatures lurking in the hull when we took her." He pointed to the hatch. "See, over here is one of the markings."

Below his stubby finger, Elle could make out the faint markings of some ward or talisman engraved into the metal.

Elle felt her mouth go dry. Because part of her existed in both the Realms of Shadow and of Light, she was not usually so heavily affected by iron, as those who dwelled exclusively in the Shadow would be. But even she had felt the power of whatever made up this ship. The hexes were most likely the reason the aether would not work when they were first caught. She had been too distracted by the danger at the time to think about it, but if the *Inanna* had been an old battleship that had been converted to a slaver specializing in the trade of Shadow creatures, then it all made sense. The thought made her feel sick.

"Never you mind," Heller said, reading her thoughts. "We cleaned her up good and solid when we took her. Had her refitted for the crew as you can see. The captain even let the Shadow creatures we found chained up in here go free. They were worth quite a bit of gold, but he let them go just the same."

Elle shook her head. The world was so full of evil it was almost too much to comprehend.

"Anyways, I'm under orders that you are to be confined to quarters and so it shall be," he said as he closed the door. Elle heard the wheel that operated the lock in the door spin, followed by the crunch of metal on metal. The door was resolutely locked and she was completely on her own.

Days passed in silence. The only company Elle had was the low hum of the ship's engines.

The tiny cabin was fitted with two narrow bunks,

bolted one above the other. In one corner was a small water closet and basin with a little shaving mirror embedded in the metal. Along the other side of the cabin were storage lockers. She still hated the place, but at least the berth was more or less clean and dry and, more important, she did not have to share it with anyone.

She even had an extra blanket and a small porthole. These were items of luxury for ordinary crewmen aboard a ship like this, and she found herself feeling strangely grateful for being afforded them.

She spent hours staring out of the grubby little porthole, thinking. Outside was nothing but endless sky and clouds. They were flying at high altitude; a feat only the very big airships could achieve, and so apart from the fact that they were traveling in a westerly direction, it was impossible to tell where they were or where they were going.

She was let out of her quarters once to attend Gertrude's funeral. There among the other pirates, she stood dry-eyed, staring bleakly at the row of bodies wrapped in canvas. In all, six people had died in the siege of the *Water Lily.*

Well, Gertrude, we gave them a run for their money, she thought silently as she watched the crewmen dispatch the bodies through a cargo hatch. They were far out over open water and the weighted canvas would sink down into the vast expanse of sea below.

To his credit, Dashwood said a few heartfelt words about the waste of human life and how everyone should take this as a lesson in humility, but Elle was too distraught to listen. She just stared out of one of the portholes at the white clouds that drifted below them.

Locked back inside her cabin after the funeral, Elle had crumpled to the ground. Alone, she had wept over the loss of her friend and her ship and the monstrous unfairness of it all.

She had stared at her stiletto for a long time, wondering briefly whether it might not be better to simply put an end to her misery, but Elle was not the sort to take the coward's way out. No, she would hide the blade and bide her time, for at some stage these pirates would slip up. She just needed to be ready for them.

From what she could see, the *Inanna* was of the rigid design models, which meant that the gas balloons and hulls of the ship were all housed inside giant metal rings that formed her distinctive double-hull shape. The rings in turn were covered with specially reinforced canvas and metal plating. Even if the web of rigging that held the two together was severed, the upper and lower parts could still float independently. She was armor plated, armed and designed for long-haul flight, so with her spark reactors filled, she could remain airborne for months before she needed to touch down on land. That was not good news, Elle realized. They could well be on the other side of the world before her chance of escape came.

Getting home was going to be much harder than she had initially thought.

Some days, when she listened carefully, she could hear the sound of hammering and the buzz of spark-powered saws cutting through metal from below. It was the sound of the crew working on stripping down the *Water Lily*. Every clang and buzz was a blow to her heart. But every night before she went to bed, she resolutely scratched a line into the metal of her bunk.

She had lost her ship. She felt the grief of it as if the *Water Lily* had been a person. And in a way the loss was just as great. For it had been the *Water Lily* and the escape that her work brought that provided Elle with sanctuary from her grief in the dark months that followed the loss of her husband. All was lost now, she thought bitterly. She had only two goals left in life now.

One was to escape from this ship, and the other was to honor her promise to Gertrude. If there was even the slightest hope that it would bring him back, she would find the lost city of Angkor Wat. She had vowed that she would restore Marsh to the realm of Light and she would not stop until she managed it. Even if it was the last thing she did in this life.

But amid all of her ardent resolve, she found that she could not quell the nasty thought that perhaps Marsh did not wish to be found.

On and on it niggled while she lay in her bunk in the quiet, dark hours. Perhaps Marsh chose the realm of Shadow as a convenient means to be rid of their marriage. Perhaps he did not really love her as he said he did. Perhaps she made him so unhappy that dwelling in darkness in the form of a half-alive wraith was a preferable alternative. These thoughts made Elle very sad and she tried to push them down deep inside of her with a force that only someone as stubborn as she could muster.

She did not have to wait long for her prospects to change, though. On the fourth day alone in the cabin, there was a thump and a rattle at the door.

Atticus Crow appeared. "Captain says you can have these now," he said, dumping her rucksack and her holdall onto the bunk. Then he turned and shoved Gertrude's trunk into the narrow space on the floor. "I don't know where you're going to put all that stuff, though." He sniffed. "Which is why ladies don't belong on ships, I says."

Elle was too thrilled to see her things to care about his nasty comment. The thought of wearing fresh underwear filled her with such joy that she honestly did not care what Atticus Crow or any of the other crewmen thought.

And so her solitary confinement continued.

* * *

In the late afternoon of the eleventh scratch, Atticus Crow appeared at the door again.

"Dinner," he said awkwardly as he put a tray down on the small table which was welded to the hull.

"Thank you," Elle said in a low voice. She was busy leafing through one of the journals she had found in Gertrude's trunk. They were the chronicles of a lifetime's work. It wasn't the full set—the earlier ones were presumably at home—but she had been captivated by Gertrude's easy style of writing and her wonderful illustrations. Gertrude, it turned out, had been blessed with the most amazing ability to draw, and her work was littered with fine drawings and diagrams.

She found the journal that was marked *Siam*. It was a slim volume in a soft leather cover. This was the volume that told her how to find Angkor Wat. She had studied it over and over, trying to memorize every detail.

Atticus stared at her for a few seconds as if he wanted to say something.

Elle looked up from the page she was reading, but said nothing.

He turned bright red and pulled something wrapped in a dirty piece of cloth out of his coat pocket. "I saved this for you. I saw you looking at it when we went to get your things, so I thought you might want to keep it," he said as he held the ragged bundle out to her.

Elle opened it and bit her lip. It was a small pane of glass with a fine water lily inlaid on it.

"I thought you might want it to remember her by," Atticus said. "We are jettisoning the scrap tomorrow."

Elle looked away, unable to say anything.

"It will get better." Atticus cleared his throat again. "I was press-ganged when I was just a lad myself. They locked me up at first too, so I would forget about running away. I think I must have spent my first year crying.

I was only little and the other fellas used to tease me something terrible. That was years and quite a few ships ago, but I still remember."

Elle stared at him, surprised by his sincerity.

"Anyway," Atticus continued. "The captain's not so bad. He's better than most. You'll see—you just have to give him a chance."

"Thank you." She was oddly touched by this strange rough man's kindness.

"Don't mention it," he said. "I'll let you get back to your readin' now," he said, casting an eye over the journals that were spread out on the bunk.

"Say, is that a map?" His little eyes lit up at the sight of the fine illustration on the page.

"Er, not exactly," Elle said. She moved to her bunk and started closing journals and shuffling papers. "They are scientific notes on archaeological digs."

"So it's like looking for buried treasure?" Atticus appeared even more interested.

"In a manner of speaking, but this is more like looking for history. So no gold or treasure," Elle said, doing her best to keep her voice even.

He nodded slowly. "Hmm, sounds like hunting for treasure to me. There was plenty of gold in them crates we took."

"Well, thank you for the glass pane," Elle said, trying to divert his attention from the papers. "It was very kind of you to save it for me."

Atticus nodded. "Always makes me sad when they strip a ship," he said. "Makes me feel like someone's died." He turned to leave the cabin, casting a final long look at the papers she was holding in her arms.

The moment the door was locked, Elle flung the journals and notes onto the bed and regarded them. She shook her head in frustration at her stupidity. Allowing someone like Crow to see those notes was just about the most foolish thing she could have done.

She picked up the fork that was on her dinner tray. It wasn't the ideal tool for the job, but it would do. She dragged the mattress off the bed and, using the tines of the fork, she unpicked the stitching on the side until she had a space that was big enough. Carefully she slipped the journal into the stuffing. She tucked the innards back and folded the canvas cover over as best she could. She lifted the mattress back onto the frame and pushed the open side against the hull. She would sew up the hole as soon as she managed to find a needle, but hopefully the hiding place would do for now.

Carefully she made up the bed again. With a little luck, if they decided to search her, Dashwood and his crew might overlook it in favor of the trunk.

After stowing the rest of the journals back in the trunk, she sighed and flopped down on the narrow bunk. The metal frame and the thin mattress groaned in sympathy under her.

How could she have been so careless?

The only way she could convince them to let her go was to make them believe that she was of no value at all. That was already difficult, given that Dashwood believed she might be worth something because of her title and connection. If rumor got out that she was in possession of treasure maps, there was no way these men would let her go. She closed her eyes in frustration. Her means of escape had just slipped away a little further.

CHAPTER 8

Patrice Chevalier was not amused. The source of his discontent lay on the starched linen tablecloth next to his cooling cup of café au lait. It was a telegram.

He shook his head and stared out of the finely arched windows of his Paris apartment. Up here, he had a most excellent view of the Avenue des Champs-Élysées.

Outside his windows, the citizens of Paris were going about their business. Fine ladies wove in and out of the elegant shops, with servants and automatons to carry parcels in tow. Steam cars rattled over the cobbles, their rivets and metal glistening in the thin, wintery sunshine of a morning in early November. The people below were like sheep, he decided. They were prone to traveling in herds, and utterly oblivious to the impending disaster that was threatening to befall the world.

The Oracle was missing.

Patrice sighed in frustration and picked up his cup. This was not the way he wanted to start his career as Grand Master of the Council. Damn and blast that woman.

Somewhere deep inside the building, an expensive-sounding doorbell rang. In fact, everything about Patrice Chevalier's new apartment was the height of sophistication. Situated in the most desirable of neighborhoods, the imposing baroque building spoke of a grandeur and affluence, and his view of the city had caused more than one lady caller to suffer from the vapors the moment they entered.

There was a soft knock on the finely painted gilt-edged door.

"Entrez," Patrice said.

At his command, Mr. Chunk, his right-hand man, appeared. Mr. Chunk was a man who had lived his entire life under an unfortunate name. Contrary to his nomenclature, he was lithe and athletic in the scrappy, stubbly kind of way that was typical of street fighters and pugilists. He was short and compact with sinewy muscles that played under the fabric of his shirt, no matter how he tried to hide them. Mr. Chunk also had the gift of mental agility, which many underestimated. This was why Patrice liked him so much. No one ever expected much of Mr. Chunk and he surprised them.

Mr. Chunk gave a short, awkward bow. "I'm sorry to disturb you, sir, but you have a visitor. Are you available to see him?"

"A visitor?" Patrice frowned. He had arrived in Paris only the evening before and had tried to be as discreet as possible. It concerned him slightly that anyone should know his whereabouts. He would have to take care to be more guarded in the future.

"Who would be calling on me this early? It's not even ten o' clock yet."

"A Mr. Crowley, sir," Mr. Chunk said.

"Aleister Crowley the occultist?"

"I think so, sir. His card didn't say." Mr. Chunk held the visiting card out to Patrice.

Patrice scanned the card. It was white, cut from expensive-looking card. The one side simply said, *A. Crowley, Esq.* The other side contained a series of magical symbols printed in a vertical row. The symbols fizzed slightly when he touched the paper. *I have important information for you . . .* they whispered.

Patrice dropped the card on to the tablecloth and waved a dismissive hand. That was an impressive trick. He would have to remember to ask Crowley how he did that. "Very well, send him in. Let's see what he has to say."

A few moments later Patrice rose as Mr. Chunk ushered their guest in.

Aleister Crowley was the kind of man everyone noticed. He was burly, with a bristly, jowly face that was perfectly ordinary in its ugliness, but for a gaze that hinted at a fierce intelligence. He moved with a silence and grace that belied the coarseness of his features, and his presence filled Patrice's drawing room entirely.

"Please sit. Would you care for a coffee? Have you eaten? I am sure I could ring for something to be sent up for you."

Crowley cleared his throat. "No, thank you," he said softly as he sat down.

Patrice took a seat opposite him and folded his hands in his lap. "And to what do I owe this unexpected pleasure?"

Crowley gave him a smile that sent shivers up and down Patrice's spine. "Well, I am in Paris only temporarily. I am busy with preparations for an expedition to British India. There is a particular mountain that is just begging for me to mount." He gave Patrice a dirty smile. "But then I heard rumors that you were due to arrive and so I simply had to come and make your acquaintance."

"Well isn't that kind of you," Patrice said, returning the creepy smile with one of his very own. "I am at your service, monsieur."

"So a Shadow Master has taken control of the Council of Warlocks," Crowley said.

Patrice did not answer.

Crowley looked greatly amused. "Oh, Conrad de Montague and I go back many years. He blackballed me for membership to some of the London clubs when I was at Oxford. He was most indiscreet about . . . certain things," Crowley said. "This in turn barred me from becoming part of the set to which one must belong in order to negotiate membership of the Council. My career as a warlock was forever ruined. It was all frightfully boring."

"I am sorry to hear that," Patrice said.

Crowley waved a dismissive hand. "Oh I have managed well enough on my own. You are, I take it, familiar with my work?" He paused and waited for Patrice to nod. "So I am sure you now understand the reason why I have hated de Montague for so many years. And my joy at hearing of his demise." Crowley folded his hands in his lap, mimicking Patrice's gesture. "Mr. Chevalier, you did me a most excellent favor when you killed him and I thank you for it."

Patrice nodded slowly. "I suppose I did," he said.

"Come now, Mr. Chevalier, there is no need to be so modest. Achieving what you have is a most outstanding feat and I regard you with the greatest of admiration."

"Thank you, sir," Patrice said. To his surprise, he found himself starting to warm to his guest.

"And, as you have done me the great favor of vanquishing my nemesis, I am here to offer you my services in return."

"And what would you possibly be able to do for me?" Patrice said.

Crowley gave a condescending look. "Well, while you might be vibrant and powerful, your background has left you largely unschooled in the grim realities of occult politics, my good man. By virtue of our education and breeding, most of us are seasoned warriors by the time we reach the top. But you are positively virginal, if you don't mind me saying so." He sat forward and arched a sparse eyebrow. "And take it from someone who knows. You need to be a seasoned warrior in order to survive the constant dogfight that is the Council."

Patrice felt himself grow angry. How dare this—this bullfrog of a man presume to condescend to him in this way?

"I would hazard that some new contender will challenge you for leadership before this year is out," Crowley said, quickly interrupting Patrice's thoughts.

"Is that so?" Patrice said.

Crowley regarded Patrice with his eerie gaze. "If you don't watch out, it is you who will crumble to dust."

"You are entitled to your opinion," Patrice said.

"What you need is a mentor. I could be that mentor, if you'll let me."

"That is a most generous offer. But if what you are saying is correct, why not challenge me and take my place? What possible benefit could you gain by helping me?"

Crowley smiled. "It is true, I have always coveted de Montague's place on the Council, I will not lie to you about that. But you, Mr. Chevalier, by assuming leadership, have changed the playing field forever. You have been touched by that which dwells in the deepest, darkest recesses of the Shadow realm and you have lived to tell the tale. I have spent years studying those dark recesses and I can only guess at what must be going on inside you. I mean, just look at you. You are a work of art, such beauty and grace and intelligence. Looking at you now—it's, it's . . . like watching a panther from the jungle," Crowley drawled. "It sets my pulse racing."

Patrice felt himself blush. "I suppose I am rather unique," he said, looking away.

"Exactly so!" Crowley exclaimed. "And we cannot let

a rare and beautiful creature like yourself be swallowed up by the filth of the system. It would be a complete travesty, so hence my offer to help you."

Patrice narrowed his eyes. "Admiration is all fine and well, but what's in it for you?"

Crowley's smiled broadened. "Well firstly, I get to spend time with you, you delicious beast. And, as I understand matters, you still need to fill that thirteenth place at the table. If you like what I can do for you, I would be honored if you could consider me for the place. As a token of your appreciation, of course." His eyes grew dreamy. "Just think of all the wonderful things we could do together, you and I."

Patrice nodded slowly. He wasn't entirely comfortable with the advances Crowley was making. They left him feeling flattered and slightly aroused at the same time, which was rather disturbing. He shifted uncomfortably in his chair.

Crowley did have a point, though. Patrice knew he needed help. He had almost been sucked into the swirling vortex the alchemists had created in their plan to use darkness to take over the Council not two years before. And he had barely escaped from it with his life. He had spent months limping along half in reality and half not, until his run-in with the Lady in White. She too had nearly finished him, but in the end he emerged transformed: a self-made warlock.

He was the first of his kind, not born of the ancient bloodlines. It was all thoroughly nouveau and exciting, but also deeply dangerous.

"And how would you help me if I were to agree?" Patrice said.

"I gather you have heard the rumors?" Crowley said.

"Depends on the rumor," Patrice said.

Crowley laughed. "Oh, you do like to tease, don't you? The one about a certain, rather important young lady who went missing very recently on her way back from the Sudan."

"*Ouais,*" Patrice said without thinking. Immediately he regretted the informal answer as he allowed his careful, cultured French to slip in his moment of excitement. "*Mon Dieu,* how on earth do you know about this?"

Crowley nodded, seemingly oblivious to Patrice's slip. "The London papers are full of reports of the lady pilot and her ship that disappeared on the way back from North Africa. A terrible tragedy they are calling it. Her poor father is said to be distraught.

"And *I* know who the Oracle is, so it really was not difficult to put two and two together. Such an inconvenience when an Oracle goes so young. It throws everything into disarray until a new one takes over, don't you think?"

"She is not dead," Patrice said.

"Are you sure?"

"Yes, of course I am sure. I am the Shadow Master. I can sense shifts in the divide. I would know if there were a gap in the Shadow and Light continuum and there is not. She is still alive and holding the layers of the realm together. The question is just where."

"That's even worse, in a way," Crowley mused. "Knowing she is out there, but not being able to reach her. What exquisite torture."

Patrice sighed. Crowley had hit the nail squarely on the head. This was precisely the thing he had been brooding over before the man had arrived.

The Council had people searching on both sides of the divide for Eleanor, but so far their search had turned up nothing. Perhaps it was time to seek assistance. Being Grand Master was certainly proving to be far trickier than he had envisioned. Maybe having someone who could provide him with advice on how to navigate this quagmire might not be such a bad idea, after all.

"So what are you proposing to do about the matter?" Crowley said, interrupting his thoughts.

"We are searching, but she seems to have disappeared into thin air."

"And so soon after your appointment to office." Crowley shook his head and tutted. "I am sure this would have set tongues wagging. How are things in Venice these days? The floodwaters this season are worse than ever. Venice is sinking, I have heard it told."

Patrice swiveled round and glared at Crowley, for he had gone one step too far. "I am sorry if I appear to be rude, but who exactly do you think you are, bursting into my apartment at such an early hour and then accusing me of incompetence? I should ask you to leave, sir."

Crowley lifted a placatory hand. "Now, now, Mr. Chevalier, there is no need for Gallic histrionics. As I have told you only a few moments ago, I am here because you and I share the same goal. We must find this Oracle. She must be taken in hand. We cannot allow the world to drift along with the barrier unguarded. Or else pretty soon we will have every Shadow creature in the realm clambering for a foothold here in the Light. Each one will be seeking to establish its own little base of power. And when that happens, we will be stuck in a world where warlords battle one another for whatever foothold they might gain." Crowley paused for breath. "And you never know who or what might be slipping through or what their plans are. I mean, just look at that awful business in Battersea last year. I would not relinquish my position so easily, would you?"

"Certainly not," Patrice said, recalling images of *La Dame Blanche,* which involved armies of indestructible clockwork soldiers. And she was small fry compared to some of the Shadow creatures out there.

"Well, what do you propose we do?" Patrice said.

Crowley folded his hands over his fine brocade

waistcoat and thought for a moment. "They say there is a man here in Paris. He is born of the unholy union of a human and a creature of the Shadow. This has given him a few . . . what shall we call them . . . unusual quirks. One of these quirks is that he can summon demons up from the darkest recesses of the Shadow to do his bidding. They call him the Summoner."

"The Summoner?"

"Yes. He is a most useful fellow to know. All you need to do is give him something that used to belong to the person you seek and he does the rest. And before you know it, you have whomever you are looking for."

"And where shall I find someone like that?"

"Well, he is a regular attendee at my masses. He holds a rather important position in our rituals—for obvious reasons. I have been asked to say mass this evening as I am here in Paris for only a short time. If you'd care to join us, I am sure he'd be happy to assist."

Patrice pondered the matter for a moment. "And you are sure this Summoner would be able to find her."

Crowley inclined his head. "If he cannot find her, my dear fellow, then no one can."

"Very well then, Mr. Crowley. I shall see your man this evening."

"Ah, how marvelous." Crowley beamed. "And please, call me Alec. All my friends do." He held out a small black card with an address inscribed on it in red. "Mass is said at midnight, but you are welcome to join us for supper at the café from about ten o' clock onward. Oh, the congregation will be so delighted to meet you. The dark forces will flow with such potency with a Shadow Master there."

"Till this evening, Mr. Crowley," Patrice said politely.

Crowley rose from his seat. "I look forward to it," he said with a little wink, as Patrice escorted him to the door.

"Oh and one thing, Mr. Chevalier, do try to keep it discreet. We don't want our little alliance to bear too much scrutiny too soon," Crowley said with one more of his strange smiles that made Patrice feel stirrings in places where he really wasn't supposed to.

Then Crowley was gone.

Patrice stared at the card in his hand and shook his head in disbelief. What a strange morning this had turned out to be.

CHAPTER 9

The journey to Montmartre seemed to take forever. From the backseat of his new Rolls-Royce 20hp, Patrice watched the streetlamps pass in the misty gloom as Mr. Chunk negotiated the uneven cobbles. He had purchased the car for the princely sum of £650. The fact that one could buy a large house for the same money gave Patrice much pleasure. Which was just as well, for he was in short supply of pleasure at the moment.

He shivered in his coat. The night was cold and damp, and he was in no mood for pretend-occultist nonsense.

The prospect of sitting through one of Mr. Crowley's masses was not filling him with any measure of delight, but as much as he hated to admit it, he needed help. So far, negotiating the politics of the Council had proven to be tricky. The other warlocks were still too stunned to take action, but it would only be a matter of time before they started plotting against him. He needed someone like Crowley to help him negotiate the pitfalls. And if it meant trawling the underbelly of Paris, then needs must.

"Are we there yet?" he asked Mr. Chunk, rather irritated.

"Not long now, sir," Mr. Chunk said as he turned the car into a dark side street. "Boulevard de Clichy is just up ahead."

The motor slowed as they pulled up outside a building with an elaborate doorway that resembled the head of some demonic creature surrounded by molten lava rock.

The doorway was the monster's huge jaws, splayed wide between large fangs. They were outside the Café de l'Enfer. Hell.

"I suppose this must be the place," Patrice said dryly.

"It's the very address as it says on the card, sir," Mr. Chunk replied as he opened the door for his master, seemingly oblivious to Patrice's sarcasm.

"So it is," Patrice said. He narrowly missed drenching his fine handmade leather boots in a puddle as he alighted from the car.

"Welcome to the gates of hell, monsieur," the doorman said. He was dressed in a ridiculous red satin devil suit, complete with horns and pointy tail.

"I am a guest of Mr. Crowley's," he said as he handed over the little card.

The doorman nodded and stepped aside. Behind him was a smaller wooden door, hidden in the shadows. He knocked on the wood six times in rapid little bursts.

Patrice rolled his eyes. This was beyond the realm of ridiculous.

There was a shuffling sound before a small peephole opened in the door.

The doorman muttered a few words.

The peephole closed and he heard the slide of the latch and the door opened with a shudder.

"Enter and be damned," the doorman said with a flourish as he ushered Patrice inside. Patrice just shook his head as he brushed past the man. *Crazy Bohemians,* he thought.

Inside was a little vestibule, lined with swathe upon swathe of purple velvet. Black candles flickered inside lanterns against the wall, and it took him a few moments for his eyes to adjust to the gloom.

"Good evening. We have been expecting you, monsieur." Before him stood a woman dressed in a hooded cloak that covered her from head to toe. She had been waiting for him in the shadows.

She lifted a lantern from the wall and took a few steps along what seemed like a tunnel. *"Entrez, s'il vous plait,"* she said in soft tones.

Patrice hesitated.

"This way please." She beckoned for him to follow.

Patrice followed her down the tunnel and down a set of stone steps.

"What is this place?" he asked his silent companion.

"Here there once stood an old nunnery, long buried under the city," she replied. "We are all gathered in what used to be a chapel. You are late, monsieur. You were missed at the feast," she said in a matter-of-fact tone.

"I was unexpectedly detained," Patrice said. It was the closest thing to an apology he would offer to a lowly servant.

They stepped through the narrow doorway and down another flight of smooth stone steps that led into the chapel.

"Please make yourself at home. May I take your coat?" she said.

Patrice blinked and coughed. The inside of the chapel was also lit with row upon row of candles, which made the space hot and airless. The rising smell of damp, unwashed bodies and acrid incense nearly knocked the breath out of him.

Through the haze, he could make out the shape of other attendees. They sat on narrow wooden benches, heads bowed, whispering to one another.

"Mon Dieu, what is that stink?" Patrice said to the woman. He pulled out his handkerchief and held it over his mouth and nose.

"The incense is henbane and mirkwood mixed with other herbs and substances. The fragrance pleases the Lord of Darkness and we seek to please him. You will get used to it before long," she said as she held out her hand to take his coat.

Patrice blinked the tears that the fumes had caused from the corners of his eyes.

"No, here is fine for me. I shall hang on to my things, if you don't mind." It would be wise to be in a position to make a rapid exit from this place—before death by suffocation set in.

The woman dropped her hand. "Suit yourself," she said in a tone that was exceedingly rude for a servant. "We will begin in a few minutes," she said over her shoulder as she disappeared down the aisle.

Patrice sat down on one of the narrow benches at the back and squinted into the gloom. At the front of the chapel an altar had been erected. It was covered with a cloth of black velvet, and a series of daggers, chalices, chains and other silver paraphernalia was laid out upon the fabric. The wooden pulpit was also painted black, and a cloth adorned with a red pentagram surrounding the head of a goat was draped over the front.

More thick, black candles dripped wax from the various chandeliers suspended from the rough roof. There was no mistaking what this place was. It was a sanctum dedicated to Baphomet: the Demon-ruler of the Underworld.

Patrice could not help but smile at Crowley's brazenness. He had hidden his cult in plain sight: below a hell-themed cabaret club in the heart of Bohemian Paris.

He took a deep breath and instantly regretted it, because the stale air made him cough. The source of the intense smell came from a silver brazier that was situated next to the pulpit. It was oozing the foul sweet-smelling smoke in little tendrils.

The room swam before his eyes. The smoke made his head spin and he wondered whether the brazier contained something more than just mirkwood incense. He suspected it did, for he was no stranger to the effects of opium and hashish.

In the front rows, the whispering of the other attendees grew more frantic and then, quite abruptly, died down to a hush.

The silence was broken by the sound of cymbals crashing, followed by the low hum of a chant. Patrice clutched his coat to his lap and shifted in his seat. The Black Mass had begun.

Two altar boys dressed in black robes entered from an unlit entrance at the front of the chapel. Each one carried a chafing dish held high.

Patrice blinked through the gloom at the tableaux that was forming. In fact, it took him a moment to realize that the altar boys were no children. They were in fact grown men, dwarf-size in stature. They chanted as they stepped along in a slow procession. Before the altar, they lit the chafing dishes with tapers. More pungent incense filled the chapel. The ladies seated in the front rows swooned and started loosening their laces in a most unseemly manner.

In the midst of all this undressing, the high priest stepped out before them. He was dressed in red satin robes embroidered with elaborate symbols. On his head he wore an animal skull with two large horns protruding from the forehead. In the center of the skull, a black pentagram was carved.

As the high priest reached the pulpit, he made eye contact with Patrice. It was Crowley.

"Arise, brother. Please join us. Don't be shy, we are all here in the service of the Shadow," Crowley beckoned for Patrice to approach.

Patrice sighed and rose. He stepped forward, leaving his coat on the seat behind him.

The imps picked up sets of cymbals from the altar and started bashing them together, causing quite a racket.

Amid the noise, Crowley started muttering all manner of profanities and blasphemies. He spoke them with such fluency that they blended together into something almost beautiful in its obscenity. The soliloquy was punctuated by the imps beside the pulpit who echoed the worst of the words in places.

The ladies in the front row were by now in a rather advanced state of undress. They cooed and sighed, quite content in their euphoria. A few of them were even sat back against their seats, with their eyes rolled back, breasts exposed, offered up to Baphomet, their master.

"We call forward the Summoner!" Crowley said, breaking off his soliloquy.

Another robed figure stepped forward and, for the first time, Patrice felt a shudder of apprehension. The man in the robe said nothing, but Patrice could feel the thrum of true Shadow power that emanated from somewhere deep within the folds of his hooded cloak.

"Is there someone here who would call upon the Darkness for assistance?" Crowley gave Patrice a meaningful look.

"Ahem. I do," Patrice said. His voice cracked and he had to clear his throat, which was sticky and dry from the smoke.

"Have you brought us a relic?"

Patrice felt inside his breast pocket and pulled out a scrap of dark blue fabric that had been torn from the ceremonial robes Elle had worn that night in Constantinople when everything had changed. He had found the scrap of fabric in the rubble afterward and had carried it with him all this time as a bizarre keepsake. Of all the women who came and went through his life, Elle was the one constant. He could not be rid of her, no matter how he tried. And the strange thing was that he did not want to be rid of her either. Her presence was in his blood, a hunger that would not abate.

Crowley made an elaborate gesture indicating that Patrice should hand over the scrap of fabric to the Summoner.

Carefully, Patrice laid the scrap on the outstretched palm of the cloaked man before him.

"You seek the woman to whom this belongs?" the Summoner said.

"I do," Patrice said.

The Summoner held the fabric to his face and inhaled deeply. Then he threw his head back and howled. It was an unnatural sound that grated the soul, pitched somewhere between nails scraping on chalkboard and a scream. Patrice felt his blood curdle, but somehow he managed to hang on to his composure.

The Summoner broke off his howl and for a moment there was nothing but complete silence in the chapel. The air became even hazier and then the ground trembled, making the items on the altar quiver and jingle.

From the floor a dark shadow rose up. At first, it was just an indiscernible black mist, but it grew and took shape until it resembled a rather dangerous-looking black dog.

"Arise whelp of Cerberus. Son of the Guardian of the Underworld!"

The outline of the dog seemed to be fighting with itself as it moved and morphed, folding over itself as it materialized before them. It sprouted two heads, each splitting in half to reveal two massive sets of jaws lined with terrible teeth.

The hound stared at the Summoner with no small measure of expectation in its eyes.

I have been summoned . . .

The voice of the creature rasped and wheezed inside Patrice's mind.

The Summoner smiled and threw the scrap of fabric into the air.

The dog lifted its two heads and caught the fabric in one of its mouths. With a sharp snap of its jaws, it swallowed the strip of cloth.

"Find the woman who last wore that and bring her to me," the Summoner commanded.

"Um, and she must be hurt as little as possible," Patrice interjected.

There was a collective gasp from those assembled, and Patrice suddenly wondered if he had spoken out of turn.

The hound rose slowly and padded across the chapel to where Patrice stood frozen to the spot. It lifted its heads; endless seconds ticked by as it sniffed at Patrice, pressing its noses into his clothing.

Patrice did not move. He did not even dare to breathe. The hound was filled with a strange swirling power that felt very much like the darkness which swirled within his own body. The presence of another creature confined in the space of the chapel that drew its power from the same source as him made him want to claw and scratch at his skin, but he held himself in check, because those teeth looked incredibly sharp and the creature they belonged to looked as if it would not hesitate to use them.

The hound turned away from Patrice and inclined its heads slightly at the Summoner.

So it shall be done, it whispered. Then it promptly disappeared out of the chapel doors in a trail of swirling blackness.

The chapel went silent for a few moments. The only sound that could be heard was the rapid breathing of some of the ladies.

"Brothers and sisters, the Dark Lord Baphomet has blessed us with the presence of one of his most favored demons! We should give thanks to him," Crowley exclaimed. He started his soliloquy again and pretty soon the mass was back in progress.

The woman who had admitted Patrice inside stepped

up to the altar. She was no servant, but a priestess of some sort, he saw now. She threw her cloak back to reveal that she was completely naked. The flickering candlelight played off the contours of her oiled skin, highlighting the curves in an exceedingly erotic way.

The other women in the chapel took this to be a signal, and they threw off the last remnants of their own clothes, much to the delight of the male attendees.

Patrice took a step back in order to avoid being hit in the face by a flying stocking.

The woman in the cloak dragged the velvet cloth with the silverware off the altar and flung herself onto it, where she spread her legs in a theatrical manner. The imps threw back their cloaks to reveal their own nakedness and within moments, the three of them were writhing together on top of the altar.

In response, the members of the congregation fell upon one another with great enthusiasm. Within moments, the Black Mass had descended into an unattractive and undignified orgy.

Patrice had to sidestep the mottled, pasty limbs of a couple who were flailing and rutting on the floor by his legs.

He curled his lip in disgust. The smell of sweaty bodies and coupling, mingled with the cloying incense, was suddenly too much for him to bear. He liked to think of himself as avant-garde, open-minded in every sense, but while what was happening before him was certainly risqué, it was also utterly devoid of any sophistication or style. And lack of style was the one thing he could not abide.

He fought his way through the writhing limbs to retrieve his coat, and he was out of the chapel before anyone could stop him.

In the vestibule, he paused and took a few deep breaths. The smell of wet cobbles and Paris at night, just detectable from the crack under the door, was like a balm to his poor, tortured olfactory organs. With an immense sense of relief, he pulled on his coat and stepped though the door into the street.

Mr. Chunk was waiting for him inside the motor. When he saw his master he stepped out and held the passenger door open for him. From the blue glow of the reactor, Patrice noticed with relief that his man had kept the boilers hot and ready to go.

"Bless you, Mr. Chunk," he said, as the man held the door for him.

"Everything all right, sir?" Chunk said as he got into the driver's seat.

"Mr. Chunk, I think I might need a drink after all that. I think I saw a wineshop on the main road, just before we turned into this alley."

"Right on, sir," Mr. Chunk said as he regarded his master in the novel little rearview mirror the motor sported. He engaged the gears and the Rolls-Royce pulled off with a satisfying roar, leaving the smut and banality of the Café de l'Enfer behind.

The wineshop was little more than the front room of a house. It was sparsely furnished with benches and tables rattling on the naked floorboards, but it was clean, and a fire glowed in the fireplace. Above all, it was mercifully quiet.

The shop owner wiped his hands on his black apron and poured Patrice a generous shot of cheap cognac. "You look like you need it, monsieur. You are as white as a ghost," he said.

Patrice took a deep gulp of the cognac, allowing the alcohol to cleanse and disinfect the back of his throat where the horrid bitter perfume taste of incense still clung.

He looked down at his hands, which were shaking

faintly. That dog creature had scared the living daylights out of him. It had stared at him with such intelligence, such knowing in those few moments, that Patrice had almost felt its thoughts. He had no doubt about the message the creature wanted to convey: They served the same master. The dark power that flowed through Patrice flowed through the dog too and that bothered him slightly.

He wasn't sure, but he sensed that the dog knew who or what it was hunting too. He had sensed its glee at the thought of tracking her . . .

Someone coughed gently beside him, catapulting him back to the present.

He looked up. An old man in a frayed green coat was sitting next to him.

"*Bonjour*, monsieur," the old man said.

Patrice glanced up at the clock. It was indeed morning—very early in the morning.

He gave the man his most dismissive nod, turning away to ignore him, but the old man would have none of it.

He stuck out his hand. "The name is Jack. I have other names too, but you may call me that for now."

Patrice frowned at him and did not extend his own hand to meet the greeting.

"No?" Jack looked at him with amusement. "Oh, we can shake hands later. For now we don't know one another that well. But we will soon. Oh yes we will."

"If you'll excuse me, I would prefer to drink alone," Patrice said with as much icy politeness as he could muster. He balled his hand into a fist. The next step would be violence; he had just about had his fill of irritating people for one evening.

Jack smiled. "Fair enough, I will leave you to your drink soon. But first we must speak about what you have just done."

Patrice looked at the man. "What do you mean?" he said.

The old man chuckled. "Ah yes, don't think I don't know about that nunnery that hides just around the corner. Some dark things go on in there, I hear it told."

In the half-light of the low-burning candles, Jack's face looked strange, slightly otherworldly. Patrice summoned a little of his power and reached out to him. He touched the man's aura and recoiled as if he had been burned.

Jack held up his hand. "It's very rude to touch someone's aura without permission, now isn't it?"

"Perhaps," Patrice said. "What do you want from me, old man? Be quick about it before I send you back to the other side."

"Why did you summon one of the dogs of Hades, warlock? Do you know what evil you have just unleashed upon this world?"

Patrice blanched. "How did you know about that?"

"I know lots of things," Jack said. "Now, why did you summon the son of Cerberus?"

"I'm looking for someone," Patrice muttered. He was growing rather annoyed with this line of questioning.

Jack gasped. "You sent it after *her*, didn't you? Do you even know what a creature like that would do if he found our Oracle?"

Patrice swiveled around at the word. "Keep quiet!" he hissed. "You don't know who else might be listening."

"I am listening too." A tall man in a tatty carriage cloak stepped out of the shadows and stood behind Jack. His voice was little more than a whisper.

Patrice felt the blood drain from his face. "You!" he muttered. "You're alive?"

"Oh, I'm not sure you could call him that," Jack said. "Let's say my friend over here is between worlds at the moment. A wraith, for lack of a better word. You know all about being trapped between two worlds, Mr. Chevalier. Don't you?"

Patrice was still staring at the wraith. Its face had grown pale and gaunt, and its dark hair hung in tatty strands into eyes that were dark and haunted. The wraith seemed to flicker slightly—as a lamp that was about to run out of spark would. There was no mistaking the features, though. It was Hugh Marsh, Viscount Greychester, or at least a shadow of the man he used to be. And he did not look happy at all.

"Now, back to the subject. I really must protest the use of the hound," Jack continued, quite unperturbed by the shock on Patrice's face. "The lady in question owes me a few favors and I really don't want to see her ripped to shreds and devoured before I have a chance to call upon them, you see."

"What?" Patrice turned his attention back to Jack.

"I said that I don't want to see our young lady torn into a thousand doggie treats. For a Grand Master you really are very slow, sir," Jack muttered.

Patrice shook his head. "The hound has instructions to find her and to bring her to us unhurt."

Jack tutted. "So easily fooled? Did you specify *how* she was to be brought to you?"

"I—I assumed unhurt meant alive and well," Patrice stammered. A cold fear suddenly gripped his insides.

Jack pursed his lips. "Oh, I do hope for your sake that is so. Unhurt can mean different things to different demons. And my friend over here will be most upset if she is damaged in any way."

Marsh let out a soft hiss in reply.

"I know what I am doing. How dare you suggest otherwise?" Patrice said, indignant at the suggestion that he was not in control.

"Oh, there is no need to be like that." Jack leaned forward and tapped Patrice's lapel with his forefinger. "I do hope you have procured a dog leash. The strongest one you can find," Jack said.

Marsh leaned forward and Patrice felt a chill run over him. "I am watching you, Patrice. If one hair on her head is harmed, I will tear you to pieces with my own hands." His whisper was barely audible, but it was enough to strike a chilling fear.

Patrice grew angry. "Enough!" he said. "You are no match for me. Look at you. You are nothing but a half-wasted shadow."

"Try me," Marsh said. A deep anger simmered in his dark eyes.

Just then, the shop owner cleared his throat. "Gentlemen. It is very late and I wish to close now," he said pointedly.

Patrice downed the rest of his drink and rose. As he stood, Jack gripped his arm. "Remember to keep an eye on that dog. Do not let it turn on you."

"Excuse me." Patrice freed himself from Jack's grip and strode past them and out into the street. Enough was enough. He wanted to go home and slip in between his fine, crisp bedsheets and sleep until the sun burned away all the distasteful images that were swirling around in his mind.

"Home. As fast as you can manage, Mr. Chunk," he ordered. It was time to call an end to this night.

CHAPTER 10

It did not take long for Atticus Crow to spread the word that Elle might be hiding treasure maps in her cabin.

The next evening, Heller's lumbering frame filled the doorway to her cabin.

"Cap'n said to ask you if you'd like to join him for dinner. The invitation is not optional. Just so you know."

"Tell the captain I'd be delighted to join him," Elle said with a tight smile.

"Well, come along then. Grub's up." Heller stood aside and indicated for her to follow.

Elle pressed her lips together as she squeezed past him into the narrow passageway. Somewhere from deep inside the ship, she could smell meat in gravy cooking. Wasn't it strange how the smell of stew could penetrate almost anything, she mused. Her stomach grumbled in agreement.

"Been holding out on us then, have you?" Heller said as they walked along.

"Whatever are you talking about, Mr. Heller?" Elle said, looking up at him.

"Oh come now. You didn't think we would not find out, did ya?" he said.

Elle just shrugged. It was good to know that news did not take long to travel on this ship, she thought. She might be able to use that to her advantage someday. Someday soon if she could help it.

* * *

Captain Dashwood's quarters were a revelation. Situated at the bow of the *Inanna,* his cabin had a bank of windows that lined the port side, which allowed him an uninterrupted view of the night sky.

The captain was sitting in an overstuffed, purple Queen Anne chair, which was set at an angle to a Georgian writing table. To the other side of him was a large teak desk that was covered in all manner of charts and papers.

"You sent for me?" Elle said, nudging the fine wool of the Turkish carpet with her boot. To the one side of the captain's desk was a doorway that led to a room with a dining table and chairs covered in the same purple velvet as the one he was sitting in. To the other side, a set of polished wooden doors closed off an area which was presumably his sleeping quarters. Crystal chandeliers hung from the ceiling, and dainty spark lamps with fringed shades decorated the carved half-moon occasional tables against the wall.

Dashwood's quarters looked more like the boudoir of a French madam than a pirate's lair.

Dashwood looked up from the papers he was studying. "Ah, yes. Mrs. Marsh, do sit down." He motioned toward a chaise longue that stood to the side of his desk, then he glanced at Heller. "Thank you, Mr. Heller, you may leave us now."

Elle perched on the side of the chaise, but kept her back straight as a ramrod. She focused on the oil painting that hung on the wall behind Dashwood's head. It was of an ocean-faring ship—a schooner, if she wasn't mistaken. The painting was from the days before the discovery of spark. Spark was the bright blue amalgam produced by the thaumaturgic melding of static electricity and aether. Centuries before it was discovered that spark had the ability to heat water quickly, great ships had sailed the oceans on missions of trade and war. The discovery of spark had brought the world into the Light. It had given man the ability to fly and had heralded a golden age entirely driven by steam. The freedom of taking to the sky and flying wherever one wanted had also opened up endless possibilities for making a living, and as ships grew bigger and faster, even despite the fact that piracy was a crime punishable by death, the number of pirates and the slightly more legal freebooters who made a living from procuring and hauling freight had grown steadily.

She stared at the schooner against the wall. It was plowing through the waves of the ocean with spray on all sides. Empires had risen and fallen since those days. And as the realm of Light grew, so the Shadow realm retreated. She wondered what would happen once there was no aether left to make spark. No one seemed to be concerned about this. Instead, great industries forged ahead, sucking every bit of energy they could from the world, sparing no thought for the future.

"I trust your accommodation is adequate and all your needs have been met," Dashwood said politely, dragging her thoughts back to the present.

Elle blinked. She had been locked up on her own for so long now that she was starting to lose the ability to speak. The manner in which her mind was drifting was rather worrying.

"My berth is quite adequate, sir," Elle said. "I have not been harmed . . . so far," she added quickly.

Dashwood's handsome features darkened. "We are not monsters here, Mrs. Marsh. I far prefer to think of us as businessmen."

"Business must be booming," Elle said, looking around the opulent cabin.

"It is indeed. I have added a few personal touches since I took this old tub off its previous captain. I kinda like it," he said. "What do you think?"

"Look, Captain, I'm sorry if I'm being impolite but let's dispense with the small talk, shall we? I would like to know what exactly what is the point of this meeting?"

Dashwood stared at her with a glimmer of amusement in his clear blue eyes. "Well, for starters, I thought you might enjoy a bit of company. You must be getting rather lonely sitting all by yourself in your cabin for all this time. I thought that perhaps I might tempt you into a game of cards after dinner." His voice held a slight edge to it.

"Thank you, Captain, but I would decline your invitation," she said.

Dashwood's eyebrows rose in surprise. "What's wrong, Mrs. Marsh? Afraid I might beat you this time? That's not very sporting of you, now is it?"

Elle shook her head. "Not at all. It's just that you've already taken everything I had left in this world. And I have a strict policy of not gambling beyond my means." She smiled sweetly.

Dashwood rose and stepped out from behind his desk. "And you didn't take everything I had from me? Twice?"

Elle frowned. "Twice?"

"Oh yes, our acquaintance goes back further than Amsterdam. The *Iron Phoenix* was not the first ship of mine you have managed to destroy."

"What on earth are you talking about?" she said, genuinely puzzled.

Dashwood let out a bitter chuckle. "Oh, I was hired to salvage a strange new flying device in Italy a few years ago. It was supposed to be a simple sky-grab. I was to be paid a lot of money for the job too. It would have set me up for life. But then I ran into you and the warlock. And between the two of you, you managed to blow up my ship before I had the chance to net your flying contraption. I escaped with nothing but the clothes on my back." His face grew stern at the memory.

Elle blanched. "You? You were the one who attacked the gyrocopter? Do you realize that you could have killed us all with your stupidity? What were you thinking, filling the tanks of a battleship with hydrogen?"

Dashwood looked away. "Mistakes were made. As I said, it was supposed to be a simple snatch and grab. We never intended to fire the cannon."

"I don't believe this." She shook her head in amazement.

Dashwood folded his arms. "Oh yes. Once we were on the ground, I swore then that vengeance would one day be mine. I have spent more than two years tracking you. I even went legitimate for a while. Then Richardson joined my crew. He was a trove of information, which was most helpful."

"And you have been following me all this time so you might extract some petty revenge for something that was nothing more than your own foolishness? What's wrong with you?"

"I did what I had to do. You have no right to judge me," he said.

"Judge you?" Elle shook her head again.

"It was hard going for a while. I had to scrounge to keep my crew together. There were things I did back then that even I am not proud of. But then you strolled into the mess room in Amsterdam like you were about to attend a country picnic. I could not believe my luck. Your ship would finally be mine, but things didn't work out the way I had planned, now did they?"

She had beaten Dashwood in a game of poker that day. The stakes had been high as they bet their respective airships in the last hand. In the end, Elle had shown Dashwood up to be the cheater that he was by using her own powers to stop him from seeing her cards. She walked away with Dashwood's ship, the *Iron Phoenix*.

"But that would mean we are even," Elle said. "You've had your way with the *Water Lily* and you've taken the museum's artifacts. So why keep me locked up? You have what you wanted, so why not just let me go?"

"Well, the plan was to seize your ship and make you buy her back for a rather tidy ransom. You know, teach you a lesson, and make a bit of cash—no harm done. But then you had to be all noble and take a stand. Instead of surrendering like any other sensible person, you had to fight back and cause bloodshed. And now we're stuck with one another and I can't ransom you or let you go because I have no guarantee that you won't go and tell the authorities where I am the moment we touch the ground." Dashwood scratched the thin layer of stubble that covered his finely sculpted jaw. "And I would rather prefer not to be hanged or banned from certain patches of airspace. It's bad for business." He sighed and looked at her. "Things never seem to work out the way I plan them when you are involved, so I am not taking any chances this time."

"And what is your plan now?" she said, feeling a little faint.

There was a soft knock at the door and one of the crew entered. He had pulled on a white serving jacket over his grubby overalls and was pushing a serving trolley with silver cloches on it.

"Thank you. Just leave it there," Dashwood said. He strode across the cabin and pulled out two crystal glasses from the drinks cubby. The drinks cabinet was an elaborate piece of carpentry shaped like a globe set into the wood paneling. It operated with an intricate series of gears that whirled the shelves round so one could easily find the bottle one was looking for. From where she was sitting it looked like it came complete with a built-in ice production compartment. Fresh ice on a ship. What luxury.

Dashwood dropped a handful of ice cubes into two glasses and poured a generous measure of whiskey into each. He set one of the drinks down in front of Elle.

"Drink, Mrs. Marsh?" he said as he took a seat in the chair opposite her. "This is a really nice single malt. I have grown quite fond of it in recent months."

Elle wrapped her hands round the glass, testing the weight in her hands. The glass was heavy-bottomed, made of good, solid crystal. It would make a nice dent in the side of his head. "I hate whiskey," she said, setting the glass down in front of her.

"Well, cheers to that," Dashwood said and took a swig from his own glass.

"So, you were saying?" Elle prompted, in an attempt to bring the conversation back to the point.

"Ah yes, back to business," he said after crunching an ice cube between his teeth.

Elle shuddered. Did he not even know how to drink from a glass? He had really nice teeth though. They were all white and even . . . not something one saw often in a pirate.

"I thought you and I would discuss your new position on my crew over dinner," he said, dragging her attention back to the present. Elle blinked and frowned. Clearly being locked up was driving her a little dotty.

"You are a woman of many talents, Mrs. Marsh," he said. "And I could certainly use some of them. And even though you seem to do everything in your power to belie the fact, you are still the Viscountess Greychester. And the heiress to a considerable fortune, from both your husband and your uncle, I believe."

"Not that it's any of your business, but none of that money is mine. There are . . . disputes over the estate.

And no one knows what to do about death duties because my husband is not dead," she said.

"Semantics," Dashwood replied, taking another sip of his whiskey. "Whether it be your money or not, I am very sure arrangements could be made to invest in certain business ventures, should I choose to demand it."

"You wouldn't dare!" Elle said.

Dashwood smiled at her. "Wouldn't I?"

She did not respond. Instead, she lifted the glass and took a swig of whiskey. The burn of alcohol mixed with peat filled her mouth and throat, warming her all the way to her stomach. Dashwood was right, she thought with irritation. She normally didn't care for whiskey, but it *was* a very nice single malt.

"That is extortion," she said in a low voice. "And you had better know that my husband's money is tied up in probate. His solicitors would never agree to anything like that. Even if I told them to do it, the ultimate decision still lies with them. So the money and the title—it's just an illusion. In real terms, all I had was my ship and you have already taken that."

"Oh, there is no need to be look so distraught, Mrs. Marsh. Your fortunes are safe for the moment." He set down his empty glass. The ice inside tinkled as if it agreed. "You see, I believe in keeping a close eye on my enemies and you have proven beyond a doubt that you are far too dangerous to set free, if you don't mind me saying so. So my preference at the moment is to keep you right here, where I can keep an eye on you."

"And what if I refuse?" she said.

Dashwood shook his head. "If you refuse, then I will lock you back in your cabin until you agree. And you will agree with me. Everybody does, eventually."

"So you really are going to press-gang me into being a pirate?"

Dashwood sighed. "Those are old-fashioned and ugly

monikers. We prefer to call it 'private contracting' these days. And you are not being press-ganged. Let's call it a negotiation."

"And if I agree?"

He gave her a most charming smile and gestured to the table. "Well, then we shall discuss those treasure maps you have been hiding in your trunk over the most excellent dinner Cook has prepared for us."

Elle sat back against the chaise and let out a long breath. She was utterly trapped.

"I will regard the maps as a joining fee to our organization. I will offer to make you a special member of this crew, which means you get a cut of the loot as opposed to just wages. We can negotiate the size of your cut as soon as you are ready."

"But they are not treasure maps. They are the journals of a woman whom I have grown to admire and regard with deep affection. When I get home I intend to have them published so the whole world can know what an exceptional scientist and person Gertrude Bell was."

"You will do no such thing," he said.

Elle set her glass down and stood up from the chaise longue. "It is not your place to order me around. You are not my captain. Now if you will excuse me, I think I will go back to my cabin. Please be advised that I am going on a hunger strike. Once I am dead, you will have no cards to play. As I see it, you need me alive, Captain. It is all I have left to bargain with."

Dashwood rose and moved up to her. "You will do no such thing!" Suddenly he was so close that she could feel his breath on her cheek. "I don't know how many times I need to apologize for the death of your archaeologist friend, but here it is again. I am sorry. Her death was an accident. And we haven't even begun to discuss the good men *I* lost because of your actions. Tell me, do you mourn their passing?"

Elle took a step back and felt the edge of the chaise longue against the back of her knees. The low-lying sensation of feeling trapped suddenly rose to the point where it was threatening to overwhelm her and she had to fight to suppress the sudden surge of panic. "Please," she whispered. She pressed her palms against his chest in order to push him away. "Please, just let me go."

Her gentle touch seemed to have the desired effect. Dashwood remembered himself and took a step back. He coughed uncomfortably. "As I see it, your Dr. Bell spent years exploring the secrets of ancient civilizations. These ancients usually have treasure—ergo, the journals contain treasure maps," he said.

Just then, there was a knock on the door.

"Enter!" Dashwood said, sounding strangely irritated at the interruption.

Elle turned to see who it was and gasped with shock. It was Heller, and under his arm he held the bundle of journals she had stowed in Gertrude's chest not too long before.

"Ah, Mr. Heller. I see you have found what we have been looking for. Please put those down on my desk."

Elle turned to Dashwood with blazing eyes. "How dare you search my things!" she said. "I am a lady. Have you no decency?"

"Ah, so you *are* a lady when it suits you." Dashwood's eyes lit up with amusement. "You should remember that as long as you refuse to cooperate, you are my prisoner. And as my prisoner, I may do with you as I please. The fact that I'm being civilized about the whole matter is entirely my choice, but things could be a lot worse for you if you continue to antagonize me."

Elle's panic turned to anger. "I demand that you let me off this ship right this instant. You have no right to keep me against my will! People will come looking for me. Important people. I will be missed, and when I am found, you will hang for this, *Captain*. You mark my words."

Dashwood tutted and shook his head. "I am sure they will search for you, but even if they find the jettisoned wreck of the *Water Lily*, which is highly unlikely, they will assume the worst. You will simply become the tragic story of a lady pilot who went missing under mysterious circumstances and was never found."

"So what now? Must I become a thief? A murderer like you?" she said.

"I told you, we are businessmen. Privateers if you will. It is an honorable profession which goes back to the time of the Elizabethans, you know."

"Call it what you will," she said. "Taking stuff that does not belong to you is still wrong."

Dashwood gave her a cynical smile. "Don't be such a hypocrite, Mrs. Marsh. What would you call taking those artifacts you and your precious Dr. Bell were carrying away from the Sudanese? Is your respectable British Museum not doing exactly the same thing in the name of research?"

"But at least we don't murder and pillage," Elle said.

"Don't you?" Dashwood arched a sarcastic eyebrow. "Don't tell me you've never killed anyone. That's not what they say in the papers when they write of your heroics. I recall you being rather trigger-happy when we boarded the *Water Lily*. Five of my men died because of you. Five." He held up his hand, palm out, his fingers all extended.

Elle looked away in shame. Dashwood was right. She had led the Battle of Battersea against the clockwork army that *La Dame Blanche* had created. And in her search for clues she had killed a man. She had shot him dead in a park at point-blank range. There had been others since; she could not deny the fact.

"And besides, what else is there for you now?" Dashwood continued. "You have no husband. Your ship is gone. From the gossip in the airfield mess halls, I hear that you've gone all reclusive and dotty. No friends, no social gatherings. Just the poor, brave, grief-stricken Viscountess Greychester soldiering on, taking strange charter booking after strange charter booking. And all this to forget the tragic loss of your husband, yet you remain frozen in time, same as the day he left you," Dashwood said. "If this were a Dickens novel, you would be Miss Haversham in an airship."

The truth of his words hit Elle like a barrage of heavy artillery. She turned away to hide her face, but he gripped her shoulder and swiveled her round so she faced him. "Your choices are quite simple. You will either join my crew and take your rightful place among us with courage and loyalty, or you will remain my prisoner until I decide what to do with you. I might not be able to ransom you off to family, but there may still be some profit in you yet. I just need to find the right buyer."

Elle felt herself grow cold. The last thing she wanted was for Dashwood to start turning his mind to selling her to someone. As the Oracle, there were more than a few nefarious parties who would pay handsomely to have her delivered to them. That would be a very bad fate to suffer indeed. She was just lucky that Dashwood did not seem to know that she was the Oracle. And she intended to keep it that way.

"I need a little time to think," she said softly.

He let go of her shoulder and smiled. "Certainly. I take it that I will be dining alone, then?"

She looked up at him. "I'm sorry, I—I just need some time to order my thoughts."

Dashwood made a sweeping motion with his arm. "Think it over as much as you want. Just remember that you have nowhere to run." Then his eyes hardened. "You have until tomorrow."

Back in her cabin, Elle lay in her bunk and stared into the darkness for a long time. She heard the signal whistle for the shift change. Rubber boots squeaked and thumped on the metal stairs as crewmen manned their stations and went about the daily business of eating and sleeping. Life aboard a pirate ship was, for the most part, surprisingly mundane.

Around her, the ship creaked, pitched and rolled as it plowed through the air currents.

She lay awake until late night turned into early morning and a gentle silence fell over the ship. This was her favorite time of day—those magical few hours before the light broke, when it felt like the whole world was asleep except for her.

The greatest irony of her current situation was that being a crew member aboard a big airship like this one was the one thing she'd dreamed of doing for as long as she could remember. Granted, she had hoped that it would be one of the large commercial airships that plowed through the skies and not a pirate rig, but the principle was the same. To be part of the breed of men and women who sailed the skies was all she had ever wanted. Until Hugh Marsh came along. He had stumbled into her world and everything had changed. And she had been happy with that change. But as soon as everything had settled in, the whole thing had shattered into a million tiny, irreparable fragments.

She gave a small, cynical laugh. Perhaps life was granting her this, her most ardent wish, as a vicious joke.

Dashwood's words had struck a nerve. That nerve had been connected to sensitive thoughts she had buried deep within herself. She had been so preoccupied with her grief that she had managed to entirely avoid thinking about who and what she really was.

Dashwood was of course entirely right. She was a

killer. She had killed more people than Dashwood could ever know.

She counted them off in her mind, trying to recall their faces as she always did. She needed to remember their faces. There were the two men she had shot in cold blood in Battersea Park. Then there were the dozens of alchemists and nightwalkers who died in Constantinople. Patrice. She did not want to think about Patrice right now. Then there was *La Dame Blanche*, whom she had beheaded, although she was not entirely sure that the witch could be counted as a person, given that she was more monster than human.

But worst of all, she had killed Marsh.

The thought sent another spasm of grief through her. Not a day went by when she did not blame herself for leaving him, and the terrible things she had said to him. Had she not left her husband in a huff that day, he would never have met with Commissioner Willoughby. He would never have gone in search of the Duke of Malmesbury's son, and had he not gone in search of the missing man, he would never have ended up in the clutches of the evil Lady in White.

Elle could not deny that slicing *La Dame Blanche*'s head off had given her some measure of pleasure, but once the heat of the quest for revenge had cooled, the fact remained that she was nothing more than a bitter woman with blood on her hands. So much blood.

The saddest part of it all was that the violence and the bloodshed seemed so utterly pointless when viewed against the one true tragedy of her life. In the end, Marsh had chosen to leave her. He could have stayed. They could have fought to find a way to break the curse, but he had taken the decision to leave her and stepped through the barrier into the world of Shadow. It was such a small thing, that step, but it had shattered her heart completely.

As much as she hated to admit it, Dashwood was right. She had become a recluse. She had avoided everything and everyone who had reminded her of that awful time. She had been extremely efficient at pushing everyone away until they were all gone. She even pushed away Gertrude, whom she had known for only a short time and who wanted nothing more than to be her friend. With the *Water Lily* gone, what else was there left for her in this world, she wondered?

The answer was only emptiness.

She sat up and rubbed her face. Despite the fact that she had been cooped up in this little cabin for days, she was unbearably tired. It was the kind of weariness that no amount of sleep could cure.

Perhaps it was time to move on. Perhaps joining this crew was her chance to try something new. Perhaps a change in environment might help her find her way back to the world. Not permanently, mind you. These pirates were far too rough and unpleasant for any long-term commitment. But they would do for a little while—at least until she was ready to move on.

Yes, that's what she'd do. She would pretend to be a pirate. She would bide her time until they trusted her. She would use that time to plan her next steps. Of course, she would have to find a way to get word to her father and Mathilda. It was not fair to leave them believing she was dead. No, she would send a message as soon as Dashwood let his guard down, to let them know she was alive.

If she played her part carefully enough, Dashwood and his crew might even let their guard down completely. And if they did, she would escape. And once she was free, she could find a way to search for the lost city.

Elle smiled to herself. Yes, with a little luck, her plan might just work. All she had to do was bide her time. All that was needed was one unguarded moment in a port.

Somewhere for her to slip away. On shore, away from this iron-boned ship, it would simply be a matter of opening up the barrier between the two worlds and slipping away. They wouldn't even know she was gone.

Dashwood was wrong. She did have a choice.

She stood and stretched. Outside, the blanket of clouds below was turning soft shades of lavender-gray, not unlike the feathers on a pigeon's breast. The sun would rise soon. It was a strange thing, the sun at this altitude, she thought. Strange because the sun always shone up here, no matter how hard it rained on the ground.

Elle rubbed her arms to warm herself from the chilly air that seeped in through the seams and rivets of the ship.

She nodded to herself slowly. She would give Dashwood her answer today. Yes, it was time to start living again.

CHAPTER 11

It was Heller who came when she banged on the door of her cabin and called to be let out.

This morning he was dressed in a magnificent leather waistcoat. The expanse of leather would probably have been big enough to be a coat on any lesser man, but on Heller it just about covered his barrel chest and belly. The waistcoat was adorned with all manner of shiny things sewn onto the leather in a pattern. There were coins, some of them gold; silver pins; and in one or two places, Elle could have sworn she spotted jewels—a ruby earring winked at her from the breast pocket, a diamond cravat pin sparkled in one of the buttonholes. *This twinkling garment of shiny things must be Heller's pride and joy,* she noted. An outward expression of his success as a pirate.

Heller gave her a quizzical look, his sharp black eyes missing nothing.

"I'd like to see the captain, please," she said.

"As you wish. But I must warn you, he's not a morning person."

"I don't care. I must see him without delay."

Heller shrugged and stood aside to let her walk in front of him along the narrow walkway.

Elle did not stand on ceremony. She knew the way now and she started marching off toward the captain's chambers, as Heller stumbled to keep up with her. She had things to say and she wanted to say them before she lost her nerve.

The captain's quarters were deserted when she arrived. A whiskey glass sat on the desk where it waited patiently to be cleared away. Without pausing for breath, she pushed through the set of louvered doors that led to his private berth.

Dashwood was in his singlet and trousers. Behind him was an unmade bunk, the pillow still holding the indentation from where he had slept.

He looked up from the washbasin, where he was busy brushing his teeth, with a look of mild surprise.

The sight of him in such a private setting made her reel, and she almost ran back the way she came, but he spoke before she could.

"Mrs. Marsh! Good morning," he said, placing his toothbrush on the washstand.

Her eyes were drawn to the little black amulet that hung around his neck, suspended from a strip of worn leather. It was infused with the power of the Shadow, and while she wasn't entirely sure how it worked, she knew it allowed him to sense people's thoughts. It was a handy trinket to own, for it made him an infallible poker player. Fortunately, she had noticed what he was up to when they had met in Amsterdam, so she had been shielding herself from him ever since. The amulet must have been rendered useless by the iron in the ship, she thought, for she had not sensed it before now.

"And to what do I owe this early and rather unexpected visit?" he said.

She stood before him and placed her hands on her hips. "You asked for my answer today and so I shall give it to you."

He folded his arms over his chest. "And what might that be?" he said.

"It is yes. My answer is yes."

"Well that is indeed good news." He stuck out his hand and she took it. He had a firm grip and he held her smaller hand in his with confidence. "I welcome you to the crew of the *Inanna*."

"Thank you," she said with more enthusiasm than she felt. "Where do I sign?"

Dashwood gave her one of his lazy smiles. "Here, a man or a woman's word is their bond. You signed when you shook on it."

"So, where do I start?" Elle said, her mind moving to matters at hand.

Dashwood picked up a towel and wiped the small bit of tooth powder that had accumulated in the corner of his mouth. "You can start by taking out the slops," he said, gesturing at the washbasin.

"Slops?" She stared at him in surprise.

"Penance for barging in on your captain unannounced," he said. "Next time, it's lashes."

Elle looked at him in surprise. "Lashes?"

"Oh yes, Mrs. Marsh. I think you might find that I run a tight ship round here. And I have no compunction about dragging you over my lap and punishing you. Would you like to test me?" His expression was that of a man who was not joking, and Elle felt a shiver of apprehension run up her spine. Discipline was essential to the successful management of an airship and right now was not the time to test the mettle of her new captain. So instead, she held her tongue and edged past him to retrieve the washbowl. He watched her, the amusement on his face barely hidden. She gritted her teeth as she took up the washbasin with her head held high. He might treat her like a skivvy, and she might even have deserved it, for being so insolent, but she would not give him the satisfaction of seeing her falter in her resolve. She would be obedient and she would earn his trust, if it was the last thing she did.

"Very good," Dashwood said. "And once you're done with that, you can do the rest as well," he said, gesturing to the bed and beyond to his open quarters. "Don't forget the chamber pot."

"Aye, Captain," she said.

"You will find that there is no maid service on board, Mrs. Marsh. We all pitch in when it comes to cleaning."

"Yes, Captain." She nodded.

"And once you're done here, please report to Mr. Heller so he can issue you some work overalls. This is a crew of men who know a thing or two about the world. We don't have time for delicate sensibilities."

" 'Delicate sensibilities'?" she said.

He gave her a sideways look. "As becoming as that corset and those jodhpurs might look on you, Mrs. Marsh, I can't afford to have you distracting my men with your womanly wiles. You are to wear overalls that cover you at all times while you are on duty."

"O—Overalls?" she stammered.

"Is that clear?"

Elle was about to protest, but thought better of it when she saw his expression.

"I might be able to control my own urges, but I cannot vouch for the rest of my crew. As I said, we run a tight ship, but I cannot watch everyone every minute of the day.

"Y—You have urges?"

It was his turn to blink and Elle watched with surprise as a wave of red briefly washed over his cheeks and the backs of his ears.

"It's for your own safety. And that's an order."

Elle nodded. As a woman in her line of work, she was used to men leering and making the odd comment. One or two even made a pass at her in the early days of her career, but she fended them off without too much trouble. But Dashwood's words, here in this intimate setting, cut through all her defenses, leaving her feeling most unsettled. Perhaps he was right. Being locked up alone for days had made her lower her guard. She would have to be more careful in the future.

And besides, work was likely to be messy and there would be no way to replace any of her clothes that became worn out or damaged. She would need her good clothes for the day she walked away from this ship. "Aye, Captain," she said softly and bowed her head— the model of demure obedience.

This seemed to placate Dashwood. He nodded with approval. "Have some breakfast and once you are done, report to the bridge."

"Aye, Captain," Elle repeated.

Dashwood smiled. "I think, Mrs. Marsh, that you will do just fine here."

"Please call me Elle," she said as she left the cabin.

The *Inanna* had started out with a crew of fourteen plus the captain. Now they were a skeleton crew of ten, if she included herself. Half of the crew worked the night shift, the other the day. They operated on shifts that rotated, because a ship the size of the *Inanna* needed round-the-clock tending.

Most of the crew was between shifts when she entered the mess a little later that morning. She was, as ordered, dressed in her new crew overalls. They were a little too big for her and so she had rolled up the sleeves and trouser legs. She had cinched the fabric around her waist with the leather corset she normally wore over her shirts. She had also tied a brightly colored handkerchief around her head to keep her curls from falling into her face. The resulting look was far more appealing than Captain Dashwood had intended, and Elle felt rather pleased with herself when she met the crew.

Atticus Crow grinned at her from where he was busy spooning scrambled egg into his mouth. "Ay-up, lads! Meet our newest crew member! Int she lovely?" He waved with his fork at her.

The others turned to stare.

Heller cleared his throat from where he had been pouring himself a cup of coffee.

"That's all right, Crow. Let me do the introductions," he said.

Heller was first mate, bosun and quartermaster all rolled into one. This meant he was in charge of anything valuable, and if anything were to happen to the captain, he would take over. The men listened to him when he spoke, she noticed.

"Now listen up," Heller said. He paused for effect, which was a bit superfluous, given that everyone was already listening. "This lady here is going to be our new navvy pilot following the recent loss of young Wes Jones."

A few of the men swore and one spat on the floor.

Elle felt her smile fade. Perhaps joining a crew after killing a whole load of them was not the smartest move.

"Oi! I'll have none of that!" Heller raised his voice. "Wes Jones was a good pilot, but he knew the risks when he volunteered to be part of the boarding party, same as everyone. We live as we die, without regrets."

"No regrets," a few crew members mumbled.

Heller cleared his throat. "Miss Elle over here is a pilot of renowned skill. She has the hours and you all know she was the captain of the *Water Lily* before she fell."

There were a few more mumbled comments. Heller waited for a few moments till silence fell again.

"As I said, she will be our new navvy. We've made do without a navvy so far, because we've been laying low while we dealt with the last haul. But the fact remains that this ship can't fly if she don't know where she's going, and we can't know where we're going without a navvy. Agreed?"

No one said anything. Somewhere in the background one of the men burped loudly. Heller gave them a sharp look. "Captain's orders. We are all to give her the respect a lady of her standing deserves. Right-o?"

There was a bit more grumbling in the background, but no one objected any further.

"What would you like us to call you?" Heller said.

"My name is Eleanor. Elle for short," she said.

"That's not a very interesting name!" one of the guys in the back called out.

"My surname is Chance. Or it used to be," she said.

"Ah, better!" Heller exclaimed. "Round here we tend to have names for everyone. I think we should just call you Chance for short, eh?" He grinned at her. "What do you say?"

"Fine by me. Chance it is," she said with more confidence than she felt.

"Let's hear it for our new navvy then!" Heller said.

There were a few reluctant cheers before everyone went back to their respective dinners or breakfasts, depending on which shift they were on.

"Let me introduce you," Heller said as he took Elle by the elbow.

There was a fellow named Mick, who was apparently on the lam after escaping from a sentence he had been serving in Australia. From his grimy clothes and the myriad of gadgets he carried around strapped to his overalls it was easy to tell that he was the ship's mechanic. Elle made a note to befriend him; she was a woman in the market for a few new gadgets.

Then there was the ship surgeon, Dr. Mackenzie, who was Scottish, and a cook everyone called Fat Paul.

"You would do well to keep on the good side of Fat Paul," Heller said out the side of his mouth. "No one knows his real name, but some say that he was a cook in the kitchens of the Tsar himself. Some say he escaped execution after a whole banquet-load of guests fell ill one day. We found him in a tavern in Kiev."

Elle stared at Heller.

He laughed. "Anyway, he's a genius with a meat cleaver. And so as to ensure you don't starve, you should be nice to him." He looked her over. "You are only the size of a penny and you could do with a good feed, by the looks of you."

Elle nodded and smiled at Paul, who nodded back, wiped his hands on his big grease-stained canvas apron and went back to spooning large helpings of bacon onto plates.

Atticus Crow was one of the three pilots the *Inanna* needed in order to remain airborne. He operated the controls to the giant spark engines that ran the thrusters which drove them forward. It was his job to control the velocity of the ship. They called him the thruster pilot.

The other pilot was a thin, humorless man named Mr. John Kipper. He wore his shirts immaculately starched, with the collars buttoned up as high as they could go. He operated the complex sets of tanks, valves and recyclers that filled and emptied the cavernous helium gas chambers which kept the ship afloat. He was called the altitude pilot and it was his job to ensure that the ship ascended and descended safely.

The remaining two crewmen were brothers, Elias and Finn, who were both freebooters. They were called all-rounders because they could do almost anything on board. They had left the American South to find adventure. Normally the ship would carry four freebooters, but given that two had recently departed this world, only Elias and Finn remained, and they seemed the most unhappy about Elle's appearance.

The third pilot needed to fly the ship was the navigator pilot. The person stood at the helm and made sure that the ship stayed on course. To Elle's surprise, once they left the mess, Heller guided her to the steering panel on the bridge and started explaining the intricacies of the ship's navigational system to her.

"Captain says that you are supposed to be good with maps. At least that's what he's been told." Heller gestured to the panel. "Best we point her in the right direction."

"Right then," Elle said, scanning the charts before her. From a cursory glance it looked as if they were somewhere above the Atlantic Ocean.

"Say, where did you say we were going?" she asked Heller.

"I didn't." He grinned at her, and in that moment she realized that he was joking. "Never you mind, Chance," he said, ruffling her hair. "You'll get used to us yet. We're not a bad lot when all is said and done."

Despite her apprehensiveness, she found herself smiling at Heller.

"San Francisco," Heller said, pointing at the chart. "Got a delivery or two to make."

"Right, so due west then," Elle said, more to herself than to anyone else.

"Due west," echoed Mr. Crow as he pushed forward levers and adjusted the flow into the thrusters.

Slowly the ship creaked as she made a wide arc through the air, righting her course as she went along.

Elle scanned the maps spread open on the large table before her. The maps were held in place with little brass clips, and there were metal markers with magnets which one could use for positioning. Carefully Elle checked their coordinates and placed the marker to show the *In-anna*'s position in relation to the earth.

They were heading for the other side of America, she thought with a sinking heart. Their destination could not be farther from home if she had picked it. But orders were orders and these would have to do for now.

CHAPTER 12

SAN FRANCISCO

The thin winter sun was fighting its way through the relentless mist and drizzle when the *Inanna* set down in the city of San Francisco. She bumped against the docking trellises and came to rest with a shudder.

Elle looked up from her navigation table. Her mouth was set in a determined line of concentration, for she had never berthed a ship this large before.

"Nicely done, Chance!" Atticus slapped her on the back and gave her a little shake of appreciation.

"You're not too shabby yourself, Mr. Crow. Although you *did* have a docking bay big enough to park two airships. What was that maneuver?"

The other crew started laughing and, to her surprise, Elle laughed too. Despite her misgivings, she was finding that it was quite fun being part of a crew. She had been on her own since she left the flight academy because none of the commercial ships would hire a woman. But here among these men she found no such prejudice and she had to admit that she missed the camaraderie she had known in flight school.

She was still the only woman on board, but somehow she did not feel as lonely.

It was also rather nice for someone else to worry about the welfare of the ship for a change. She stole a glance at Dashwood. This morning he was dressed in his green velvet coat with brass buttons down the front. His boots had been polished to a bright sheen.

"Ready to disembark, Captain," Heller said, following her gaze and eyeing Dashwood's outfit. "I see you've brought the old captain's coat out. Am I to tell Fat Paul that you will be dining out this evening? With a lady friend, perhaps?" Heller, it seemed, was the only one who could get away with teasing the captain.

"Mr. Heller, let's see if we can off-load some of that cargo we brought with us from Edinburgh," Dashwood said with a small smile, avoiding the question. He turned to look out of the window but as he did so, Elle could have sworn she had seen a slight blush form on the planes of his cheeks.

"Right on, sir." Heller turned from them and started shouting orders.

Elle kept her eyes on the charts before her. If Dashwood was due to go drinking and womanizing, this could be a golden opportunity. Granted, she was a world away from home, but as long as she could escape, she would be able to find her way back.

"A word please, Mrs. Marsh," Dashwood said, interrupting her thoughts.

"Sir?" Elle turned to him.

He took her by the wrist and before she could say anything, he had strapped a slim metal cuff around it. It clicked shut with the decisive sound of something that had been tempered by the Shadow.

"What are you doing?" Elle withdrew her arm and started tugging on the cuff. It was making her skin tingle with a sensation that could have been only from the Shadow.

One side of Dashwood's face lifted in a regretful smile. "This binds you to me. We can't have you running off the moment I turn my back, now can we?" He stepped closer to her. "And I, for one, am planning to be rather . . . distracted later today." The suggestiveness in his gaze left no doubt as to exactly what activities he was planning.

"How dare you? I am not some dog that needs to be kept on a leash." She tried to drag the cuff over her hand but it remained resolutely stuck. "I demand that you remove this thing at once," she said.

"Once we are back on board safely, I promise I will remove it. But while we are ashore, you are bound to me." He held up his arm. Around it was a similar cuff. "The two are linked, so no matter where you go, I will be able to follow you. I will always be able to find you, no matter where you run."

"So I am to be your prisoner then?" she huffed. "I do have rights, you know!"

Dashwood smiled at her. "You keep forgetting that I am your captain and my word is law. I may do as I please, and right now it pleases me not to have you escape the moment my back is turned." He studied her face for a few moments. "You weren't thinking of escaping, by any chance. Were you, Mrs. Marsh?"

Elle closed her eyes in frustration. She was starting to develop a serious dislike for mysterious bracelets that could not be removed once worn. And this one had just neatly put an end to her plan.

"No, Captain. I wasn't," she said in a low voice.

"Fantastic. Then the cuff need not cause you any bother. And I promise you, it's only until we are back in the air. All right?"

She did not answer.

He offered his arm in a gesture that was absurdly gentlemanly, given the circumstances. "Shall we?"

Elle ignored his gesture and stood aside so he could pass. "Lead on, Captain," she said with a stiff smile. Despite her protestations, she was itching to be on land. They had been airborne for the better part of a month now and she was starting to crave the oxygen-rich air that one breathed closer to the ground. It was not an unusual phenomenon. Sky sailors called it "the craving."

On the ground, San Francisco looked even prettier than it did from above. Elle watched in fascination as the city's trolley service ran up and down the hills, disappearing into the fog.

This morning the city was shrouded in a fine mist that turned the buildings sweaty with damp and the streets muddy and black from grime.

Elle shivered in her leather coat as they walked away from the bustling air docks. At least Dashwood had allowed her to wear her own clothes this morning, she thought resentfully.

San Francisco was a busy place and not the backwater gold rush village she had pictured. Everywhere she looked, crates of freight were being unloaded at a breakneck pace. Wagons with giant loads of lumber rumbled by, leaving dark slashes in the mud.

Elle studied a group of women waiting patiently under a corrugated iron awning. Each had a cloth bundle or a battered carpetbag with their belongings. They stared forlornly at the dismal drizzle, faces drawn in apprehension.

"Bit of a shortage of women in this place. So they fly them in from abroad," Dashwood said next to her. "Those lovely brides are most likely destined for the ranches and gold fields farther inland. Probably waiting for the trolley to take them to the station."

"Brides?" Elle frowned at the thought.

"Surely you must have seen the advertisements in the newspapers?" Dashwood said.

Elle nodded. "I have. It's just that I never thought

women actually answered them . . ." she trailed off, lost in thought.

"Life's hard if you don't have any money, Mrs. Marsh. Those women are looking for a better life. Some say this is the land of opportunity. Not everyone manages to land themselves a husband that is richer than a Roman emperor," he said with a hint of disdain in his voice.

"I'll thank you to keep your comments to yourself, if you don't mind, Captain. The subject of my marriage is not something I wish to discuss with you," she said in icy tones. She was still very angry about the cuff around her wrist and she was not about to take his little dig at her circumstances.

Dashwood held up his hands. "Just trying to open your eyes," he said.

"My eyes are extremely open, thank you very much." She turned to him. "So what exactly have we come here to do?"

Dashwood smiled again. "Whiskey, my dear Mrs. Marsh." He gestured for her to follow him. "Come on, we have an appointment."

They started walking down one of the long, broad avenues. It was strange how American cities were laid out in perfect grids. Although poverty and squalor were still in evidence, there were no dark alleys or crooked lanes in the brave cities of the New World. She spared a sideways glance at a huddle of street children in a doorway who stared at them with hungry eyes.

"Captain, wait!" Elle said as she stopped beside the children. She felt in the pockets of her coat, but she had no money. She started shrugging off her coat in order to give it to them.

"Wait," Dashwood said. He pulled a handful of coins out of his pocket and handed them to the children. Dirty little hands scrabbled for the money.

"Can't have my navvy dying of exposure without a coat," he said.

Elle sized him up. "That was really nice of you," she said.

He shrugged. "Now I don't want a word out of you once we get to our meeting. I only brought you along so you could watch and learn. In silence. Do you understand?"

"I'll do my best," Elle said as they started walking up a steep slope.

The venue for Dashwood's appointment turned out to be a saloon called Crazy Jerry's. It was a tin-roofed place not too far from China Town. The barkeep smiled as he recognized Dashwood.

"Ah, Captain Dashwood. Nice to see ya," he drawled as he wiped his hands on his apron to shake Dashwood's in greeting.

"Jerry!" He greeted the barkeep with a warm handshake and a wide grin, but Elle was not convinced that they were old friends.

"Who's she?" Jerry said, nodding at Elle.

"New navigator pilot. I'm busy showing her the ropes," Dashwood said.

"That's a bit of a risk," Jerry said, rubbing his chin. He started laughing. "You're even crazier than I thought. And you honestly let her drive your ship?"

"She does all right. As good as any," Dashwood answered.

Elle stood slightly behind him, but said nothing. Being spoken about as if she was not there was one thing, but having her skills criticized was quite another. She was sorely tempted to give this man a piece of her mind, but Dashwood gave her a warning look before she could say anything, so she remained where she was, silently annoyed.

"The boys will be along with the wagon in a few minutes, but I brought this for you to taste." Dashwood reached into the deep inner pocket of his coat and produced a bottle of amber liquid stoppered with a cork. "Top-of-the-line merchandise all the way from Scotland, as promised." He placed the bottle on the counter with a flourish.

The barkeep eyed the bottle with no small measure of skepticism. "I hope for your sake that's the case. Them fellers been a bit thirsty round these parts. Good whiskey has been in short supply. We've had to make do with my cousin's moonshine on some nights," the barkeep said as he stepped round the back of the bar. He pulled out three greasy-looking shot glasses and set them out on the counter. He pulled the cork and poured out three measures.

"Drink up," he said.

Elle eyed the cloudy whiskey in the glass with little enthusiasm. The whiskey smelled strange, something earthy and sweet that she could not quite put her finger on.

"Oh, none for me," she said. "I'm on duty and it is only ten o'clock in the morning. I tend to limit my whiskey drinking until afternoon."

"You first," Dashwood said, aiming a devastatingly charming smile at the barkeep.

The barkeep laughed. "Oh no, my friend, you go first." He gestured at the drink.

Dashwood gave a nervous laugh.

Just then, Heller and Atticus Crow burst through the swing doors of the saloon with a wheelbarrow filled with whiskey bottles.

"Free drinks for everyone!" Heller said in a loud voice.

Heller's arrival had the desired effect. Even at this early hour there were punters inside the saloon. The promise of a free drink seemed to galvanize them into

action. More materialized from corners Elle had not ob-
served that the saloon possessed, and the barkeep was
suddenly overwhelmed with requests for glasses. Some
of the drinkers didn't even wait, and pulled out stoppers
with their teeth, swigging from the bottle.

"Gesture of goodwill! For the special people of San
Francisco," Dashwood said with a flourish. He was
grinning from ear to ear now. "So, shall we agree on a
price?"

Elle watched the captain with growing suspicion. Was
it her imagination or did he look slightly nervous? Elle
studied the way he held his shoulders and the way he
watched the punters dig into the hooch.

"Anything the matter, Captain?" she asked sweetly.

"Not at all," he drawled. "We have a schedule to
keep, is all."

He turned to Jerry, who was doing his best to fend off
the tide of customers who were suddenly inside his es-
tablishment. "Fifty cents a bottle. Six bottles a case. I
have a hundred cases; what do you say we call it an even
three hundred?" he said.

Before Jerry could answer, a punter to the side of the
bar suddenly spat his whiskey out onto the floor and
swore loudly. "Dawg-naggit. It's rotgut!" he shouted.

Before him, the gray-blue mist of a specter hovered. It
was drifting up and down as it keened sorrowfully.

Elle turned to Dashwood. "Oh, you have got to be
joking."

"Afraid not," he said with a shrug.

The specter's keen had intensified as it searched for the
human remains it was supposed to be tethered to, but
these were probably back in Edinburgh and in the process of being dissected by a student of medicine at the
university.

Rotgut whiskey, Elle thought with a shudder. As if it
wasn't bad enough that the whiskey in the shipment had

once been used for preserving corpses in aid of medical research, rot gut also carried the inherent risk of being haunted. Much in the same way that absinthe fairies spirited into liquor, ghosts appeared when the corpses they had been tethered to were soaked in alcohol. This wasn't a problem until the body was removed from the keg and disposed of. The realization that its earthly tether was no more was usually more than most specters could handle, and judging from the shrillness of the keening filling her ears, Elle estimated that things were about to get very ugly in Crazy Jerry's saloon.

Elle took a step away from the counter and looked about. Suddenly, the whole saloon was filled with specters, hovering in midair as they emerged from the bottles that held them.

One of the saloon girls screamed, which in turn set a few of the ghosts howling and set off the other specters. Within seconds the entire saloon was filled with the angry spirits of the departed, demanding vengeance for the terrible wrong that had been done to them.

"Dashwoo-ood! If we survive this, I am going to kill you myself!" Jerry shouted.

"Ah, I think there may have been a bit of a misunderstanding on that front," Dashwood said. "They assured me that all the spectral energy had been removed when they strained the whiskey. I promise."

The air filled with ear-piercing shrieks as one by one the specters transformed into poltergeists. Glass started breaking and mirrors split due to the force with which they changed. One of the punters pulled out his shotgun and started firing at the ghosts. This was a completely pointless course of action and only caused other on-edge punters to start firing back. Elle ducked behind the counter as an empty bottle flew past her head and smashed against the wall behind her. Within seconds, a full-blown gunfight complete with howling poltergeists had erupted.

"Aw crap," Dashwood said under his breath as he crawled beside Elle. "I thought they'd take a bit longer to show up, but I guess they didn't take too well to the flight." He ducked as a chair flew past, narrowly missing his head.

A few of the ghosts turned on the punters and soon bodies were flying about the room as more shots rang out.

"Heller! Take the men and get to the ship!" Dashwood shouted. "Each man for himself until we get there!"

"Aye, Captain," Heller called from behind a piano on the other side of the room, where he was busy laying down cover fire with a sawn-off shotgun.

Another bullet whizzed past Elle's head, closely followed by a keening poltergeist, this time so close that she felt the air move against her cheek. Enough was enough.

The only way out was blocked by specters and half-drunk trigger-happy brawlers. She sighed. There was only one way out of this mess and that was via the Shadow. This was most inconvenient, given that she was still tethered to the captain. He would have to come with her if they stood any chance of survival.

"Take a deep breath and don't let go of me!" Elle shouted, as an upturned table smashed into the wall behind them, sending long splinters of wood flying everywhere.

Before he could react, she grabbed a handful of Dashwood's green velvet coat and closed her eyes. Quickly she reached out to the barrier between Shadow and Light. She had not touched the barrier since Khartoum, weeks ago. She could feel it the moment she closed her eyes, humming with energy at the edge of her consciousness.

She reached into the meta-space and dragged herself and Dashwood into the void. The aetheric turmoil the specters were creating made the transition between worlds feel like crossing the English Channel in a force-ten gale, but she held on to the captain and forged ahead. They hit the golden murk headfirst. The barrier wobbled and engulfed them with a big slurping sound.

Dashwood looked like a man drowning. His eyes were wide as saucers, and she had to grip his collar and his biceps hard to hold on to him as he struggled against the aether. She gave him a little shake to make him look at her.

He stared at her in horror, his mouth agape.

Keep still, she said into his mind. *You are quite safe as long as you hold on to me.*

He nodded, looking more than a little distressed. Even here, the sound of shotgun fire could still be heard as well as the ghostly shrieks of the poltergeists.

Slowly Elle counted the moments, holding on as long as she dared. Dashwood looked like he was about to expire from lack of breath. She could tell him that it was perfectly safe to breathe in here, but his bright red face and the bulging veins on the side of his neck gave her a small measure of satisfaction. Good, let him think he is drowning for a little while longer. It would serve him right for everything he'd done to her.

When she reached ten, she moved them gently back toward the point where they had entered the barrier. She could see the small rent glimmering in the distance. When they reached it, she shoved Dashwood out, and without ceremony they spilled back onto the sawdust and plank floor of Crazy Jerry's bar. Or at least what was left of it.

Dashwood wheezed and coughed violently where he lay, gasping for breath.

Elle stood up. She dusted herself off as she glanced about. The bar was deserted. The floor was covered in smashed glass and what looked suspiciously like spilled and spattered blood.

"What in the name of all that is holy was that?" Dashwood said from the floor. He wheezed and resumed his coughing fit.

"That, I believe, was me saving your life, Captain," Elle said. "And you're welcome." She held her hand out to help him up, but he refused and stood up by himself.

"Where is everyone? What time is it?" he said.

Outside, it looked like it had grown dark.

"I have no idea." Elle shrugged. "Time and space work differently inside the barrier."

Dashwood stopped patting himself down, looking for injuries, and eyed her sharply. "Are you trying to tell me that that was *the* barrier? The magical one that's supposed to keep out all the Shadow creatures?"

"The very same," Elle said quietly.

"And how in the blazes did you manage to do that?"

Elle gave him what she hoped was a mysterious smile. "Now that would be telling, would it not?"

"Tell me!" he shouted.

Elle shook her head. "A lady does not give up all her secrets, nor should she."

Dashwood ran his hand through his blond fringe and turned away from her in exasperation. Then his surroundings seemed to register with him. He shook his head at the lamentable state of the saloon as it came into focus. "Things don't look like they went very well in here after we left," he said.

"Shh!" Elle grabbed his arm. "Look," she said in a low voice as she pointed at the roof. Up among the rafters a cluster of poltergeists hung, swaying silently like sleeping bats. A few of them were groaning and moving, obviously disturbed by the noise Elle and Dashwood had made.

Dashwood nodded. "Better not wake them further," he mouthed.

Slowly they started creeping across the floor to the doors. Every step made the plank floor creak. Every creak made the poltergeists stir a little. Elle did not dare breathe until they reached the door and were well into the street.

"Well, the deal's gone south, so I suppose we had better get back to the ship. I, for one, don't want to take my chances on running into Jerry right now," Dashwood said beside her.

"I think you might be right," Elle said. "Say, where did you say you got that whiskey?"

"Oh, I have a friend in Edinburgh. At the medical college," Dashwood shrugged. "He gave me an excellent price on that shipment. Even guaranteed that it would be problem free. Said it had been triple strained."

Elle shuddered as she thought about soupy human bits suspended in whiskey, but decided to bury the thought firmly and deeply inside her mind. "Well, neither one of us knows how to rid a place of ghosts, so I suppose your work here is done, Captain," Elle said. There really wasn't much more she could say in those circumstances.

"Come along then, Mrs. Marsh," Dashwood said.

Elle said nothing, but followed him nonetheless. There was nothing more she could do.

It was raining in Paris. The cold drizzle sifted down over the gray rooftops and spires of the city with a relentlessness that spoke of the harsh inevitability of winter.

Somewhere deep in the shadows of an alleyway, something stirred. A great black hound lifted his two heads off his paws, where they had been resting, and sniffed the air.

The hound did not mind the rain, for he was not affected by cold or wet or even hunger. Those were the concerns of creatures with warm blood in their veins. He was a creature of pure darkness—the offspring of the unholy coupling of creatures of the Shadow.

Slowly he blinked and stared into the distance with his yellow eyes. Something—a shift in the aether—had stirred him to wakefulness, from where he had been waiting in the shadows.

He did not mind it. He was patient; he had all the time in the world.

Around him, the shadows had grown thicker and the alleyway more ominous. The lesser Shadow creatures of Paris had long since retreated from the area with an air of reverence. Those who dwelled in the Light could not see him, but avoided the place, for his presence was known to make a person's hair stand on end without them ever knowing why. He was the undefined creepiness that bore no name.

The scent of the woman he was tracking lay imprinted in his memory. She smelled of freesias and engine oil. And of Shadow. He knew it very well, for he had been playing the smell over and over in his mind while he waited.

He lifted his noses up to sniff the damp air. There it was again. The scent carried faintly across the aether along the barrier—a ribbon of scent as distinctive as sunlight.

Slowly the hound rose from his place of rest. His terrible shaggy form grew large and detached itself from the shadows that had concealed it. Somewhere off in the distance, a dog howled. More joined in until the cold night filled with the hunting cry of the pack.

The hound threw back his heads and howled in

answer. It was a terrible bloodcurdling sound that could silence all others of his kind, for he was the pack leader. The alpha. Then he let out a low growl of satisfaction. This is how it always started: He just had to wait for his prey to make the first mistake. That first tiny, seemingly insignificant error that invariably led to the end. He had the trail now. She was far away, this quarry, but he could run tirelessly for a very long time. The hound started running through the alleyways of Paris. He moved like a shadow, just out of sight, but every now and then an unsuspecting passerby would stop and look about, unsure as to why they felt the need to do so. Then they would shiver as the cold evil whispered by, and they would walk on a little faster than they had before. As he ran, the hound allowed his tongues to loll out the corners of his two mouths. Yes, he had the trail. The hunt had begun.

CHAPTER 13

The *Inanna* left San Francisco and made her way to the open air without much delay that very evening.

"No need to hang about looking for more trouble, now is there?" Heller said to Elle with a wink as they piloted the ship into the safety of international airspace.

"Oh, I agree. I think we have caused more than enough trouble for one day," Elle said as she watched the city slide by below. "What about the captain?"

Dashwood had stomped off to his quarters the moment they were on board without so much as a thank-you when they parted.

"Oh, I'd wager he's in a bit of a sulk about his shipment. It's ruined his night good and proper," Heller said. "Me and the boys had to leave it behind on the wagon when the trouble kicked off. I suspect his nose will be out of joint about the money. Thought he had a sure thing going there, our captain did." Heller shook his head. "Suppose me and the lads will have to wait till next time before we get our wages."

"But surely he should be here, commanding?" Elle glanced over at the empty chair.

"Nah, we got it in hand. Captain gave strict orders that he was not to be disturbed unless the ship was on fire."

Elle sank into her own pilot's chair. Here, safely on board the *Inanna*, she suddenly felt very tired. She stared at her wrist where Dashwood had removed the cuff.

She hated the Shadow realm. Every time she allowed the energy of the Shadow to flow through her, something went catastrophically wrong. People died. And every time she channeled this power, a small bit of her own life force disappeared along with it. She had been warned to be careful about channeling energy, but until now she had paid these warnings little heed. The fact that she was starting to feel the effects of the barrier every time she made the crossing worried her. She did not know much about her kind, but she did know that it was this very sapping of life force by the Shadow that was the reason why most Oracles died young. Many did not make it past the age she was now.

She rubbed her eyes and studied her instruments. They were lit up in pale blue against the night sky in the windglass. Too many people had died because of her. Too much destruction had been sown. It was time for her to take responsibility for her actions. No more running and hiding in the Shadow when things became tricky. No, it was time for her to face things on her own without the help of magic.

Her dark thoughts made her feel even wearier. It was warm on the bridge and the gentle hum of the ship's engines was always comforting. Despite her best efforts to stay alert, Elle felt her eyelids droop lower and lower as she drifted off . . .

. . . the world shifted and changed around her. Dark trees sprang up, their branches clawing up at the sky.

No, Elle thought as she fought against the forces that pulled her along, but something had grabbed hold of her and it was dragging her deeper into the Shadow realm. She scrabbled and grabbed at passing branches and roots, but they turned to nothing under her fingertips. Faster and faster she moved until everything around her turned to a dark blur, and then, quite abruptly, there was silence.

"Where am I? Who's there?" she said, more than a little annoyed.

"Easy now, little Oracle, you are among friends," Old Jack said.

She heard the sound of magpies squawking as Jack's dark forest took shape around her.

"Jack! I should have known," she said.

An old man appeared by her side. Carefully he opened his cloak and set a burning lantern on the ground between them. "A good evening to you, my Queen. It is lovely to see you, as always," he said with a reverent bow. "Please forgive the rather undignified journey here, but the iron bones of your new ship form an almost impenetrable barrier."

"Yes, they do," she said. "How did you get past the hexes and the iron?"

Jack smiled. "Oh, I have my ways. Don't ever doubt that old Jack will get something done when he puts his mind to it. But you are not fully away from there. I have only managed to pull part of your spirit here. The rest of you is still napping when you should be keeping watch."

"What gives you the right to drag me out of my time and space like that?" Elle said.

"Desperate times call for desperate measures," Jack said.

"I'm sorry, but your problems are not very high on my list of matters to solve at the moment, Jack. As you might have gathered, I have a few pressing problems of my own to contend with at the moment."

Jack gave her a knowing smile. "Now, is that a way to speak to an old friend and someone you owe a great debt to?"

Elle closed her mouth. Jack was right. She did owe

him a number of favors, that were sealed within a sacred pact. She had been dreading seeing him again.

"Very well, Jack. What do you want?" she said.

Jack sat down on a tree root and groaned. "Ah, my back. I am not as sprightly as I used to be." He motioned to the place beside him. "Do sit down, my dear."

"I'd rather stand, if it's all the same to you."

"Suit yourself," he said. "I must say, I had such a lovely holiday in the Light realm. Thank you for asking." He stretched, lifting his bony arms over his head. "A little time away from it all really did me a world of good. It's very hard work running an enchanted forest, you know. Always keeping an eye on everything. And the administration! You wouldn't think it, but you will not believe the amount of paperwork that needs to be done," he said as he made himself comfortable on the log.

"As I said, what do you want, Jack? The *Inanna* could be crashing into the side of a mountain at any moment, for all we know. I have neither the time nor the inclination to become involved in the games of fairies."

"I have eyes on your post. My magpies will warn us if there is danger in the realm of Light."

"That does not bring me much comfort," she said. "If I recall, your magpies can be rather unpredictable and mean. They would be the last ones I'd trust with navigating a large ship."

Jack rested his chin on his hands. "We have much to discuss, you and I, but I will get straight to the point if you wish."

"Please do," she said.

"Well, I called you here mostly to warn you about touching the barrier. And entering the Shadow realm." His expression grew sharp. "Don't do it. Under any circumstances."

"It's a little late for that, don't you think?" she said, gesturing at the forest around them.

"We are safe here for the moment, because I have made it so. And also, no one dares enter my realm here among the trees without my say-so. For now." Jack grew serious. "Please, my dear, if you value your life, stay away from here. Do not go into the barrier like you did today. It is too dangerous. I implore you."

"How do you know about that?" Elle said.

"I have been keeping my eye on you. I can feel it when you enter this world. And so can others."

"Others?" Elle was suddenly worried.

"I don't want to alarm you, but since your recent and rather tragic loss . . ." Jack paused and cleared his throat. ". . . there are those who plan to take you. So many grand plans for the Oracle. You know what I am talking about, don't you?"

Elle's mouth suddenly went dry, for she knew exactly what Jack was talking about. So the Council of Warlocks had stepped into action. And they were supposed to be the good guys.

Jack leaned in and looked at her intently. "You must find yourself a protector, Oracle. *He* is the only one who can keep you safe from them."

Elle felt her heart constrict. "Jack, I have tried. I have done nothing other than search for him these past months, but he will not be found."

"He will be found, my dear, but he knows also that as matters stand, the two of you absolutely cannot be together."

"What do you mean?" she said.

Jack pointed at her with a gnarled finger. "You are a vessel. You are filled with the energy that holds the universe together. He is a complete void. A wraith. A shadow of his former self." Jack made a pouring motion from one hand to the next. "Things always go from full to empty and from empty to full, and so it will be with the two of you. Just one touch from him would drain you until you are nothing more than a husk. Death would be instant." Jack looked her in the eyes. "And that is why he chose to walk away from you. He made the sacrifice so you might live."

Elle felt a tight knot of grief rise in her chest. "What am I to do, Jack? I feel so lost and alone."

"Find a new protector."

"How am I supposed to do that when—"

"I know he wants you to be happy. He told me so himself. Go and live a full life. You have his blessing."

"His blessing?"

Jack nodded. "Yes, he has set you free, little one. Move on. Find a protector who dwells in the realm of Light and stay away from the Shadow. That is all that can be done about the matter."

"You have seen him?" Elle felt her vision blur and she fought to bring her breathing under control.

"I have." Jack stopped talking and looked up into the darkness, nostrils flared. His head was cocked to one side as if he were listening for something.

Elle felt a cold shiver creep over her.

Jack's gaze snapped back to her. "It is coming. We do not have time to talk further. You must go now, before he catches your scent." Jack gripped her hand firmly "Go safely, little Oracle. Stay in your iron-bound ship where he cannot smell you out. That is all I can say." Then he disappeared as swiftly as he had appeared.

"Jack?" she whispered, but she was met only by silence.

Somewhere in the distance, she caught the sound of forest twigs crunching underfoot. Elle swiveled round. "Who's there?"

She strained to see through the darkness, which was

all around her. Somewhere in the distance, she saw a faint movement.

Then, in the flicker of one of the thin moonbeams that shone through the trees, her eyes caught the outline of a tall man in a ragged carriage cloak. He turned to her, and for a moment she caught the sight of his pale face in the moonlight.

"Hugh!" she called out. "Wait. Please!"

But the moonbeam flickered and disappeared behind a tree, and he was gone with it.

"Go home, little Oracle. Go home and stay away from the Shadow," the trees whispered around her. "It is coming for you. You must run!"

The darkness suddenly felt claustrophobic. She looked this way and that, unsure as to what she needed to do, but all around her was darkness.

A cold mist curled around the trees and swirled along the ground. Elle peered at the blank grayness that surrounded her.

"Hugh, is that you?" she whispered, but she was met with nothing but ominous silence.

Another twig snapped, a leaf rustled and the cold shiver she felt earlier intensified, making the hair at the back of her neck stand on end.

Something was out there.

For a moment she spotted the soundless shape of something moving though the mist. Something big and shaggy that walked on four legs.

From just beyond the mist, she heard a low growl. The sound made every cell in her body react. It was the sound a predator made when it knows its prey is helpless and the hunt will end successfully and soon.

Elle looked around for something to defend herself with. At her feet was a fallen branch. It was too thick to lift but one of the smaller branches had snapped half off. The bark of the branch was wet and the spongy bark turned her hands black, but she managed to wrench the stick free.

Balancing the stick in her grip, knees slightly bent, she found her balance. She lifted the branch up, ready to strike. It wasn't much, but it would have to do.

"Come on, then!" she spoke into the mist. "Let's have you."

Something moved, and from the swirl, a giant two-headed hound emerged. It was blacker than the blackest darkness, save for the two sets of enormous yellow eyes that glowed from the blackness and the long, bone-yellowed fangs protruding from its two terrible jaws. It was a creature straight from the deepest recesses of the Shadow. And it had come for her.

"Who are you?" Elle said.

The creature just licked its lips with a red tongue and stared at her.

"What do you want from me? I command you to speak," she said with more confidence than she felt.

I have come for you, the creature said into her mind.

"Why?"

I have been sent for you.

Elle felt her hackles rise. "Who sent you?"

I am thrall to the Summoner. He has been asked to do this by the Shadow Master. The hound shifted its heads slightly and Elle could just make out the glint of a black metal collar around its neck.

"I am sorry, but I am not coming with you," she said. "This Shadow Master of yours has no right to command me."

There is no choice in the matter. It is my fate to hunt you until my task is done.

"There is always a choice."

The hound shook its heads. It sank down onto its haunches, hackles raised, ready to pounce.

Elle raised her stick up, ready to defend herself just as

the hound leaped at her. She turned and flung herself sideways, just managing to avoid its snapping jaws. She brought the stick down as hard as she could. The wood cracked against one of its skulls with a satisfying thwack.

The beast landed on the ground behind her with a heavy thump. It shook its two heads as it turned around in order to launch another attack.

Elle did not hesitate. She dropped the stick and flung herself in the opposite direction. She ran faster than she ever thought she could, her feet skidding in the wet leaves and mud. Branches dragged at her legs and bulging tree roots threatened to trip her, but she kept going.

The hound let out a strangled yowl of frustration and set off after her. She could hear the rustling thumps its paws made as it bounded through the underbrush.

It was much faster than she was and she could hear the rasp of its breath as it gained ground behind her.

She steeled herself and swerved off to the right, hoping that the hound would be slowed down by the sudden change in direction, but in her heart she knew it would be only a matter of seconds before its jaws sank into her.

Elle rounded a tree, but an errant branch hit her squarely in the chest. She gasped in pain but grabbed hold of the branch in order to keep her footing, for the ground was slippery with damp leaves.

At that moment, the hound leaped out of the underbrush.

Elle dragged the branch back and let go, just as the hound launched itself into another leap. The branch recoiled and hit the hound squarely in both of its faces. It let out a yelp of surprise before crashing to the ground, momentarily stunned.

Elle did not wait about to see what might happen next. She closed her eyes and slipped into the barrier. It took her a few precious seconds as she frantically sought the portal she had been dragged through. Her heart was pounding in her chest and her breath came in quick little gasps. There was no time to cover her tracks. Any second now the beast would step into the barrier and if it saw which way she went, her escape would be doomed, as it would follow her into the Light, for sure.

With a small sob of relief, Elle slipped through the breach just as a pair of jaws appeared behind her in the golden light of the barrier. She spilled back into her sleeping body where it sat at the navigation station. Quickly she spoke the words she had been taught in order to seal up the rent. She counted the moments this took in fast, exasperated breaths.

Far in the distance, she could hear the fading sound of frustrated howls as the hound searched for her. She could feel it sniffing, probing the barrier for evidence of her escape until the last of the gap closed.

The spell along with the iron that bound the ship meant that she would not be able to access the Shadow realm again from this point in the realm of Light, which was no bad thing—not with that monster waiting for her.

Here, high up in the air, surrounded by iron, there were fewer places to access the barrier. They were constantly moving and so, with a little luck, the creature would struggle to keep up with her.

When the portal was sealed, Elle collapsed onto the floor and gasped for air. She was not used to running so fast and the weeks of being confined in a small cabin had left her feeling weak and unfit.

She rubbed her eyes. That escape had been far too close for comfort. She pulled herself into her pilot's chair and looked about to see, with no small measure of relief, that she was alone. At best, Dashwood would punish her for falling asleep at her post—whether such sleep was her fault or not. At worst, he would throw her in the brig for deserting.

"I brought coffee," Atticus Crow said from behind her.

Elle nearly leaped out of her chair in fright as she swiveled round to look at him.

He regarded her with amusement. "I know how long and boring these night shifts can be, and as I found myself unable to sleep, I thought I'd come and have a look at the stars." He set the mug down next to her.

"Th—Thank you, Mr. Crow. I'm sorry, you startled me."

He smiled at her. "This old ship can be quite spooky at night. More than one crew member has reported seeing something strange during the quiet shifts. Happens on all ex-slavers."

"I suppose you are right," Elle said, taking a sip from her mug. The coffee was strong and sweet. Exactly what she needed. "Thank you for the coffee," she said.

Crow just nodded and sat down in the empty seat next to her. "Think nothing of it. Next time, it's your turn," he said with a lopsided smile.

"It's a deal," she said.

Crow frowned. "Say, you look like you've been in the wars." He pointed at her. "Does the captain know you got all bashed up at Jerry's?"

Elle looked down at herself. The skin on her chest, just visible from the V in her shirt, was bright red and covered in fine scratches from where the branch had struck her. And if the stinging sensations in her cheek and neck were anything to go by, she had scratches there too. It seemed like injuries sustained in the other Realm carried across even when body and spirit were separated. "Oh, it's nothing," she said as she wiped at her cheek.

"Might want to ask Doc to have a look. A little cut

like that can get quite nasty if it becomes infected. I think I saw him in the infirmary on my way back from the mess. I could watch the bridge, if you want."

"Would you mind?" Elle said. Of all the crew, Atticus Crow had been the nicest to her and she felt a sudden surge of affection for him.

"You run along now. I'll hold the fort," he said.

"Thank you," she said. "I'll only be a moment."

Elle did not go to the infirmary. Instead she ran to her cabin, where she dabbed Vaseline camphor ice onto the scratches from a tin she kept in her holdall. She sucked in a breath as the ointment stung her skin. She was furious with Jack. How dare he drag her into such danger? And had Marsh been there all along? Why had he not shown himself? Was he really that determined to have nothing to do with her ever again?

These thoughts were simply too overwhelming. She had to get back to the bridge before Atticus or any of the others started to suspect something was up. She didn't want to think about the fact that perhaps her husband really did not want to see her ever again.

"One thing at a time," she said, finding it hard to breathe. She put away the ointment, did up her shirt and headed out the door, her skin still stinging from the camphor. For now, she would heed the advice of old Jack. The Shadow realm was off limits for the foreseeable future. She would stow away her thoughts about Marsh for later. Later when she was alone, she would allow herself to think on the matter.

CHAPTER 14

The next morning, as soon as her shift ended, Elle strode into Dashwood's quarters. Her back ached and her eyes were red from the long night at the helm, but she had spent the quiet hours of her shift deep in thought. Being chased by a two-headed monster from the underworld tended to give a girl cause to stop and consider. And consider she had. In fact, she was a woman on a mission this morning.

She had decided to heed Jack's advice. She needed her protector back even if it meant that they could not be together as man and wife.

Now all she had to do was get the captain on board, in a manner of speaking.

"Mrs. Marsh. To what do I owe the pleasure of this morning's visit?" Dashwood half rose from behind his desk and regarded her warily. Clearly the whiskey debacle and their little trip to the netherworld were not quite behind them yet.

"Treasure," she said, getting straight to the point. She was tired and in no mood for witty banter.

Dashwood's eyebrows rose. "I seem to recall the last time we spoke you were quite adamant that you knew nothing about any treasure."

"That was then, this is now." She dropped the last remaining volume of Dr. Bell's journals down on to Dashwood's desk.

"And what have we here?" he said.

Elle flicked open the pages to the place where she had found Gertrude's reference to the *apsara*.

"The mystical city of Angkor Wat. It's in the middle of impenetrable jungle. If it is there at all."

Dashwood peered at the page. "I'm listening."

"Dr. Bell wrote that she found this reference in an ancient Khmer scroll." She tapped the finely drawn illustration with her index finger. "See, it's a pictogram that describes the route to the city. It is said to be covered in gold, and floating on a lake."

"Sounds promising." Dashwood stared at the row of pictures. "What does that one mean?" He pointed at one of the pictures, which looked very much like a giant multiheaded snake.

"I don't know, but I'm sure we'll find out when we get there."

Dashwood sat back in his seat and watched Elle. "Why come to me with this now?"

Elle crossed her arms and met his gaze. "Following recent events, I have come to change my mind."

"Really? And which events would those be?"

Elle sighed. "Well, San Francisco gave me cause to believe that I could trust you in a fight," she said.

Dashwood sat back in his chair. "Funny, San Francisco gave me exactly the opposite impression of you."

"I saved your life and you know it," she said.

"Only to nearly drown me in that place," he said.

"Oh come on, Captain. You were in no danger of drowning. One can breathe in the barrier as easily as one can breathe here in your cabin. It was just your own fear that prevented you from doing so."

Dashwood blanched. "And you did not think it necessary to tell me this at the time?"

Elle shrugged. She didn't really have an answer for that.

"And while we're on the subject, what exactly was that stunt? What kind of a Shadow creature are you?"

"I am as human as you are, Captain," Elle said.

"I don't believe you," Dashwood said.

"Well, I am. You can choose to believe me or not."

"You, my dear Mrs. Marsh"—Dashwood pointed at her—"are hiding something, and I need to know what it is."

"I'm sorry, but I can't say," she mumbled and stared at her boots.

"Oh, so now you're suddenly all coy." Dashwood sat forward in his chair. "That means I have stumbled on the truth. So I would caution you to think very carefully about your next answer, for it may determine whether I let you stay here or whether I put you out to the sky through one of the hatches."

Elle stared at him in horror. "You wouldn't make me walk the plank, would you? That would be . . . it would be ungentlemanly."

Dashwood tutted and shook his head. "As I have told you before, I am no gentleman. But I *am* a businessman. And you, madam, are bad for my business. So either you tell me what this is all about or I will have no option but to get rid of you." He crossed his arms over his chest.

Elle stared at him. Despite her best efforts, she could not help the first glimmer of moisture that welled up in her eyes. Her gamble had failed. If she kept silent, Dashwood would set her off the ship and she'd be dead, either dropped from midair or left at a port where, being away from the protection of the ship, that demon dog would get her; if she told him the truth, he would sell her to the warlocks, and she would be dead anyway.

Dashwood's expression softened. "Look, if I'm going to agree to go searching for treasure in snake-infested jungles, I need to know who—or what—I am taking along with me. Is that so unreasonable?"

"I suppose not." Elle took a deep breath. "I—I possess the ability to slip into the gap sometimes. It's a trick. An illusion, if you will," she said.

Dashwood shook his head. "It all adds up now. Married to a warlock. The fact that you cast no shadow. The poker game. The whole business in London where my ship crashed."

"As I said, there was nothing to be afraid of. You were perfectly safe."

Dashwood sighed. "I hate all that Shadow realm stuff. Nothing but trouble ever comes out of messing with the Shadow. Apart from a few trinkets which I buy from a trusted source, I tend to steer clear of such things."

"And a wise philosophy to live by, that is."

"That still does not answer my question."

"The gift I have . . . It—It is something I have no control over. It's a family quirk that goes back generations. But it's perfectly harmless—nothing you should concern yourself with . . . sir," she added for good measure.

Dashwood stared at her for a few long moments without saying anything. Then he sighed and ran his hand over his jaw. "Fine. Whatever. As I see it, you are a passably good pilot and against all odds, my crew have grown to like you. Decent pilots are hard to find so, Shadow gift or not, you may still be worth more as part of my crew than not."

"Do you mean it?" she said, almost too relieved to believe his answer.

He waved a dismissive hand. "As long as you give me your word that it's just a small trick and not a serious source of power."

"Yes, sir," Elle said, mentally crossing her fingers behind her back.

"And please don't tell anyone else. My crew are a superstitious lot and them knowing that we have someone of the Shadow on board will cause all kinds of problems. Then it'll be out the door with you. Do I make myself clear?"

"Crystal clear, sir," she said.

"Very well. You are dismissed."

"So we are going to find the treasure?" she said hopefully.

Dashwood narrowed his eyes. "Give me one reason why I should I risk my ship and my crew on an endeavor that may or may not yield a profit?"

"Those factors never seemed to bother you before."

Dashwood gave her a look. "Touché," he said.

Elle took a step closer. "Captain, I need to find the city. You are in the market for making some cash. I would have thought that those two things would be enough for us to make a bargain."

Dashwood's eyes narrowed. "I am a pirate. I love gold and money as much as the next man, but I have already lost more than one ship because of your schemes, so you will forgive me if I'm a little wary."

Elle lifted her chin. "And I have lost a ship to yours. I think that makes us even, Captain."

Dashwood suppressed a smile. "Oh, I don't think we have even begun to get even, Mrs. Marsh. I had to abandon my first ship in midair. Do you even know how hard it is to keep a crew motivated when it's your fault that the very thing that unites them has gone up in flames?" He had grown a little red around the ears as he spoke.

"As I've said before, I am very sorry that happened."

"As sorry as I am about your friend?" he said.

Elle sighed. He could make a good argument when he wanted to, this captain. "Very well, I will let it go if you will."

"Agreed," he said.

"So, on to the business of Angkor. By my estimation, we could make our way to Bangkok and then onward—"

Dashwood held up his hand. "For the love of all that is good and beautiful in this world, will you just stop talking, woman? I should have put you in a life balloon and sent you on your way the moment I had taken your ship."

"Then why didn't you?" she said.

"Because, jettisoning a woman on her own across the desert with a wounded companion is so . . . so dishonorable that even I cannot justify the act," he said. "You, madam, are nothing but trouble. You sow chaos wherever you go." He threw his hands up in the air in exasperation.

"Are you in or are you out, Captain?" Elle crossed her arms and lifted her chin to meet his gaze. "Because I am going to find the lost city of Angkor Wat whether it be with or without you."

"Actually, I'm not," Dashwood said. "We've been through the journals and you were right, there is no treasure in any of them. So apart from a few squiggles on the page you just showed me, I have no proof that the city exists. I have even less evidence to show that even if we find it—and that's a big *if*—that there will be treasure." He pressed his lips together. "And I *know* you are not seeking this place because you are looking for gold, which probably means there isn't any and if you want to go there, then there is probably a whole lot of trouble waiting there. I will not let you use me or this ship for your own private agenda. So no, count me out, thank you very much."

"You said you would!"

"I never said any such thing," Dashwood said.

"That is a very foolish decision, Captain. I know you will regret it," she said, desperately trying to bring him round.

Dashwood shook his head. "No, mark my words: If you want this, then it can only be bad for me. This is probably the first sensible decision I have made since I became captain of this vessel. I have a hold full of Egyptian artifacts which need a buyer, as well as the mess in San Francisco to sort out. That's more than enough trouble for the moment."

"Ah yes, I believe you are somewhat out of pocket after that last little incident," she said. "Tell me, when was the last time you paid the crew?"

Dashwood turned red. "I would be lying if I said that I wasn't in need of some cash. I might consider going after treasure, maybe in a month or perhaps three, once I'm ready, but I am not turning this ship around to blunder across a jungle at the mere say-so of a known troublemaker. I have learned my lessons when it comes to you, Mrs. Marsh. My decision is final."

"I think you will find, Captain, that I am a very determined woman once my mind is made up. I must find the city and I will not rest until it is done."

This is what she had resolved in the silent hours of her shift. She needed to find Marsh and confront him. She needed to know where she stood.

"Not on my ship you don't." Dashwood rubbed his temples "Now if you'll kindly excuse me, I have work to do and you've given me an almighty headache." He shooed her away. "For the second time, you are dismissed."

Elle turned back from the door to say something, but met with Dashwood's most forbidding and captain-like stare.

"Or would you like to spend a few more nights in the brig for disobeying an order?" he said.

She did not reply. He was still her captain and orders were orders. And she really did not want to spend another night in the freezing cold brig. She was too tired for that.

"As you say, Captain," she said, relenting.

The captain's sudden about-face was very frustrating. But there had to be a way, she thought, as she made her way to the mess. She would get some sleep and try again later. Perhaps she would find a way to send word to her father or the solicitors that managed the Greychester estate. Once they knew she was safe, and on an expedition, she might be able to convince them to put up the money to hire Dashwood and the *Inanna*.

Although she seriously doubted Dashwood would agree to such an arrangement, no matter how much money she offered. Plus, she was almost entirely sure that neither her father nor the partners of Messrs. Jinx, Hubble and Trust would consider such funding a wise investment. She groaned inwardly. Why was life always so complicated? No, there had to be a way to do this without incurring the wrath of probate lawyers—all she needed to do was find it.

CHAPTER 15

LONDON

Patrice stared across the snow-covered lawns that spread out before the house on his estate. Winter looked to be harsh this year and the snow lay thick on the ground. But even in the freezing cold, Mr. Capability Brown's gardens looked breathtaking.

He turned from the window and stretched his hands out in front of the huge fire blazing in the fireplace. His days of being cold and hungry were definitely over, but somehow, no matter how much money he had, he was still unhappy. The missing Oracle formed the center of this discontent.

It had been a full three weeks since his trip to Paris, but there had been no further word about the Lady Greychester.

Patrice rang the bell and Mr. Chunk appeared. "You rang, sir?"

"Ah yes, Mr. Chunk. Please fetch the Summoner from downstairs. I would like a word with him."

Mr. Chunk inclined his head and retreated. A few minutes later, there was a shuffling, scraping sound outside the door before the Summoner was deposited on the rug before Patrice.

The man trembled and blinked at the bright light of the room. He had been held in the dark cellar ever since

Patrice had grabbed him off the street and dragged him back to England with him.

"Monsieur. I see you are still alive," Patrice said.

The man fell to the floor and started sobbing. "Please. Please allow me to go home. I have done nothing to deserve this," he begged.

"Now, now. That's quite enough of that," Patrice said. "You know my terms, sir. You may go as soon as that creature you summoned brings me the girl. Now tell me quickly how things fare with your pet. You are filthy and it's leaving a mark on my rug."

"Please, the hound has no news. He caught her scent a couple of days ago . . . f—followed her into the Shadow realm, but she escaped. D—Disappeared through a rent in the barrier. He has been hunting and hunting for her, but there is no sign," the Summoner whimpered through cracked and broken lips.

Patrice reached back and slapped the Summoner in the face. "Good grief, man. You are supposed to be a powerful occultist with the command of beasts from the darkest parts of the Shadow realm. Stop sniveling and get ahold of yourself."

The Summoner just wheezed in distress in the place he had fallen.

Patrice slapped him again. "How can she vanish with no trace? I thought your hound is supposed to be unstoppable. Is he or is he not the pup of Cerberus himself?

"He is, he is," the Summoner said. "But it's as if she has simply vanished into thin air. He will find her. She cannot hide forever. We just h—have to be patient."

Patrice balled his fist in frustration and slammed it down on his desk. "In the name of all that is Dark! I am sick of waiting and of hearing empty promises!"

The Summoner flinched and started keening softly.

"Please let me go home. I have a wife and a child. I am an insurance clerk, for goodness' sake!" he whined.

"Mr. Chunk!" Patrice bellowed. "Take him back to the cellar. And send to the village for a bricklayer."

"Right away, sir," Mr. Chunk said.

"Monsieur, you had better hope that your hound starts sniffing properly. You have one day, and if I do not have a clear idea as to where the girl is by then, I shall instruct the bricklayer to close off the small cellar. You will rot there until the place becomes your tomb."

"No! Please. I will do better . . . Please!" the Summoner started babbling hysterically as Mr. Chunk dragged him off.

Patrice sat staring at the sifting snow for a long time as he thought things over. Thin air, he mused. It was just like Eleanor to confound everyone with the simplest of tricks. Patrice smiled suddenly as the realization hit him. Of course! How could he have been so stupid?

He stood and walked over to his drinks cabinet where he poured himself a glass of the finest cognac. He smiled slowly as he took a deep drink from his snifter. He knew where to find Eleanor Chance. It was time to take matters in hand.

Finishing his drink, he set the glass down and headed upstairs to select the clothes he wished to pack. He needed to go to London without delay.

The Dirty Mermaid was not an easy pub to find. Hidden along the dank alleyways of the Isle of Dogs, far out on the other side of London, the only sign that it was, in fact, a tavern was a crude image of a mermaid in a rather lewd pose carved into a plank above the door. This was the place where pirates, bounty hunters and other men of general ill repute drank. Patrice loved it immediately.

"I'd like to say a few words," Patrice said to the landlord as he stepped into the center of the tavern.

"We don't talk to strangers round these parts, sir. 'Specially not ones in fancy coats. Best be on your way before there's trouble," the landlord grunted and turned his back on Patrice.

Patrice held his temper in check. It would be so easy to transform the greasy man into wallpaper paste but, tempting as it was, it would not serve his purpose right now. A little restraint was needed sometimes.

Instead, he lifted a purse from his coat pocket and dropped it on to the table with a soft, expensive-sounding clunk. The noise drew a few stares.

Patrice picked up the purse and tipped its contents out on the table. The coins tinkled and clattered onto the wood where they lay shining in the candlelight. Everyone inside the Mermaid stopped what they were doing and stared at the gold.

"I am looking for a woman. Her name is Eleanor Chance. She also goes by the name Marsh or Greychester. She has red hair, and if you stare at her closely enough, you will see that she casts no shadow," Patrice said in a loud voice.

Silence descended upon the tavern. He had their attention now. Patrice gestured at the little heap of gold coins on the table. "This here is but a small sample of the riches I have set aside for the man who brings her to me. If you make a few inquiries, you will find that I am Lord Abercrombie. I am a man of considerable means and this girl is very important to me." He paused for a few moments in order to create the right effect. Then he gestured with a sweep of his arm. "I hereby pledge to pay one hundred thousand pounds sterling to whomever brings me the girl. Delivered to my door, alive and kicking, right here in London."

Everyone stared at Patrice and, somewhere in the background, he could have sworn he heard a pin drop.

Patrice pulled a card out of his breast pocket and held

it aloft. "Here is the address. I will entrust its safe-keeping to this fine fellow," he said as he held the card out to the somewhat nonplussed landlord.

"And now, ladies and gentlemen, I bid you a good evening." He spread his cape and vanished in a puff of smoke. It was a simple, if not garish, trick that was usually within the repertoire of cheap illusionists. He would not normally stoop to such frippery, but it was a rather unwashed audience and it definitely had the desired effect. There was a moment's pause before pandemonium broke out as everyone rushed to grab up the coins.

Patrice chuckled to himself as he watched the chaos from the shadows across the alleyway.

That should do it, he thought to himself as he turned and strolled down the alley to where Mr. Chunk was waiting with the motor. If anyone could ferret out Eleanor Chance, it would be this riffraff.

As always, it was the sound of money that spoke the loudest.

CHAPTER 16

"Evening, Chancey," Heller said as Elle sat down next to him in the mess. Dinner for him and breakfast for her this evening was sausages and beans served with hunks of fresh bread. On the two shifts one would be either waking up or going to bed, so Fat Paul tried to make dinner and breakfast as similar as possible.

"Hello, Heller," Elle mumbled. She had not slept well. Her sleep had been filled with dark dreams of being chased by awful baying creatures.

Dashwood had put Finn on the day shift and he had ordered her to split her night shift between the bridge and the engine room. It was, she believed, a fitting punishment for her insolence the last time they had met in his quarters a few days ago. He had also given orders that some of Finn's duties be transferred to her, so she found herself clambering inside mucky engine parts and scrubbing out spark conduits. Adjusting to hard physical labor was proving to be a bit of a challenge. She ached all over and her body did not want to be awake when it was so dark outside.

They were somewhere across the south Atlantic Ocean. The captain had directed them to head south after San Francisco and across Panama into the Atlantic. She had been navigating east across night ocean for days now, which was extremely dull work at the best of times.

"Caught some right rough turbulence this afternoon."

Heller chuckled. He bit into a large chunk of bread and chewed with gusto.

"It was a bit bumpy, wasn't it?" Elle stared at her beans.

"Oh nah. It's about what's to be expected in these air currents this time of year. Have you sailed the straits before?"

"I haven't," Elle admitted. "Most trade routes tend to avoid the area." And for obvious reasons. Treacherous air currents and sudden storms plagued this part of the world and played havoc on navigational instruments. Pirate ships prowled the cloudbanks, waiting for easy quarry. Much like the *Inanna* was doing at this very moment.

She looked up at Heller, who was busy spearing his sausages with his fork. Funny how he had frightened her when they first met, she thought. Now he was almost a friend. But then again, she was a pirate now, in every sense of the word. She dug her fork into her beans and took a bite. Yes, she was a pirate trapped on a ship where the captain's word was law. And in this case it was a captain who hated the sight of her.

"Why the long face, little one?" Heller said. "It won't do to see a pretty face like that so sad." Heller stared at her with concern.

She sighed. "Oh, Heller, I feel so alone here. I feel like I have no one to talk to."

Heller wiped his black beard with the back of his hand. "I suppose it must be hard for you, being the only woman and all. I know it's not the same, but you can talk to me. I like listening to others. It's what makes me a good first mate."

"Oh, I don't know," she said.

"Go on, try me." Heller sat forward with concern.

"Can I trust you?"

He frowned. "Of course."

"Well, you know Dr. Bell left me all her notebooks?"

Heller nodded. "Me and the captain have been through 'em. The captain was mighty upset when they turned out to be a load of old cobblers with no maps or treasure in them."

"That's just the thing, Heller. The captain missed one of the notebooks. One I held back."

"You didn't!" His expression grew alive with interest.

"I did too. I held back the one journal with a map in it until I could be sure that the captain could be trusted." Elle pulled the journal out of the leg pocket of her overalls. She opened it and smoothed out the page. "See this here?" She pointed at the pictogram. "This is a map to the Khmer city of Angkor. The greatest temple city that has ever been built."

Heller's eyes grew wide. "And temples have gold . . ." he murmured.

"Well, I can't promise that, but I can say that this will lead us to the greatest temple ever built. Built by one of the richest people who have ever lived. The map speaks of the fact that the temples were lined with gold, but it is all for nothing." Elle rubbed her eyes. They felt scratchy and tired.

"Why so?" Heller said.

"Well, when I showed the maps to the captain, with a plan to find the place, he said no."

"He did?" Heller frowned. "That doesn't sound like our captain. He's normally first in line for treasure. Unless there's a good reason . . ."

"There's no reason other than the fact that he doesn't trust me," Elle said quickly.

"That seems mighty foolish," Heller said.

"I know." Elle skewered a bit of sausage and bit into it. "So here I am, on a ship that's ready and able to go, but I can't because my captain doesn't like or trust me enough to give it a go." She put down her fork. "I wish you hadn't destroyed my *Water Lily*. I would have been off this tub and in search of the city by now."

Heller stared at the map with such concentration that Elle could almost hear the cogs and gears moving inside his head.

"Tell you what," he said after a good few minutes. "Let me talk to the captain. He'll listen to me."

Elle eyed Heller. "Would he? Or would he be angry and accuse me of talking to the crew behind his back?"

Heller thought for a moment. "Hmm, that's a good point. But I tell you what, let me have a word with some of the lads and then we'll see what we can do about changing his mind," he said.

"Thank you, Heller." Elle laid her hand on his arm.

Heller grinned. "See, I told you I was good."

Elle pushed aside her breakfast, which had started to congeal on her plate. "Well, I had better head up to the bridge. This old bird is not going to navigate herself."

"You do that," Heller said with a far-off look in his eyes.

Elle's shift dragged by without event as the *Inanna* plowed on through the clouds. No one said a word, or gave even the slightest indication that Heller had spoken to them, and she went about the business of scrubbing out vents and conduits. Just before dawn, dog-tired and covered in grime, Elle stumbled to her bunk, where she fell into a deep, dreamless sleep.

The next evening, however, when she came down for breakfast, it was a whole different story.

Elle felt all eyes on her when she entered the mess hall. Fat Paul gave her an extra chop on her plate. The boys from engineering even made a space at the table for her to sit. Heller was nowhere to be seen. Every so often one of her crewmates would nudge the other and nod.

Elle picked up her fork and contemplated the lamb

chops and mashed potatoes on her plate. Good, solid stodge to keep everyone going. The one thing Captain Dashwood did not appear to scrimp on was catering, but then again, a fed crew was a happy crew, so it made sense.

A kerfuffle at the entrance of the mess broke her reverie and she looked up to see that Dashwood had stormed in. The captain didn't usually enter the mess, and there was a great deal of shuffling and the rumble of chairs scraping as crewmen rose to acknowledge him.

Dashwood ignored them as he strode into the mess. "Eleanor Chance!" he roared. He was quite red in the face actually.

Elle stayed where she was. This was going to be trouble and she would do well to show no fear. "Here, Captain," she said in a voice as steady as she could muster.

"Who in the seven hells do you think you are, lady?" he bellowed.

She set her fork down. "Captain?"

"I said, exactly what do you think you're doing?"

"I'm sorry but I have no idea what you are talking about."

"I am talking about this!" He threw the journal onto the table before her.

"The city of Angkor. What of it?"

A hush fell across the mess. Everyone was staring at them.

"I'm sorry, Captain, I'm afraid I still have no idea what you are on about," Elle said.

"I will not have you inciting mutiny on my ship!" he shouted. "Or do you really want me to hang you by that little neck of yours?"

"Mutiny?" Elle said, rising from her seat. "Who said anything about mutiny?"

A few crewmen coughed uncomfortably behind her.

"Come now, Captain. That's taking it a bit too far

now. Me and the fellas were only engaging in idle gossip," Heller said behind them. He had followed Dashwood into the mess. He gave Elle a reassuring look. "We all like tales of booty and riches. Even you do," he said in soothing tones.

Dashwood's face was like stone. "Anyone who even thinks about supporting these crazy notions will be made to take to the wing. Do I make myself clear?"

There was a soft gasp from more than a few crewmen. Taking to the wing or walking the plank was a rather nasty punishment which was usually meted out for the worst of crimes. It entailed being thrown out of the back of the cargo hold with a rope round one's waist. If the fall did not rip a man in two, the extreme cold would cause certain death.

Elle put her hands on her hips. "Excuse me, Captain, but don't you think that you are overreacting just a tiny bit?"

"Overreacting?" Dashwood roared as he turned on her. "I take you in. Give you a place here. Feed you, clothe you, put up with your irritating demands and . . . and the first thing you do as soon as my guard is lowered is try to steal my crew. I say mutiny certainly warrants my reaction, madam."

"Steal your crew? Have you completely lost your mind?" Elle said.

Dashwood glared at her. "That's it. Another week in the brig. And don't try me, because the next step is lashes. Lady or not."

Elle paled. "But I've done nothing wrong—"

"Um, Captain, me and the boys would like to say a word," Heller interrupted.

"What?" Dashwood swung round to face him.

"Well, seeing as this is not the navy, and we are all freebooters here, me and the boys feel that we should put the matter to a vote. They say the lost city is paved with gold. I, for one, would at least like to prove that such a rumor was wrong . . ."

There were murmurs of agreement among the crew.

"I don't believe this." Dashwood threw his hands up in dismay.

"Angkor Wat does exist and were it not for you scrapping my ship, I would be on my way to it right now," Elle said. "In fact, I intend to procure a ship as soon as I am able to do so." She turned to the crew. "You all know that I was the captain of the *Water Lily.* I am a very resourceful woman, so do not doubt that I will find the money to fund such an expedition myself. The only thing stopping me is the fact that Captain Dashwood is keeping me prisoner on this ship when every prisoner here is free. So any man who wants to join me in finding the city would be welcome on board."

There were a few cheers, which were abruptly cut off by Dashwood's murderous glare.

"Begging your pardon, Captain," Heller spoke again. "It has been a while since we've seen any proper money. What with the haul in North Africa not being worth much and all that went wrong in San Francisco . . . the boys are eager for a bit of action, is all."

"Who else feels this way?" Dashwood said.

A few more men grunted their agreement.

"Is this the crew I have? A bunch of milk-livered sons of whores who are ready to run the moment someone whispers the word *gold*?"

Dashwood looked apoplectic, his hands balled into fists by his side. She would have to step in and do something soon, or else there would be bloodshed.

"Why don't you just let me go, Captain?" she said. "You know I don't belong here. You said so yourself. Set me down somewhere. And perhaps also anyone who wants to find Angkor Wat. We would be on our way, never to bother you again. That way you will be rid of all the troublemakers." She took a deep breath. "I will see if I can find us a charter. It won't be an easy journey but I promise to be fair to anyone who follows me. Let us agree to part ways with no hard feelings, shall we?"

"Who else wants to go off and die on this crazy half-cocked idea? Any man who does, step to the other side of the room now," Dashwood said. He was still seething, but Elle noticed with no small measure of relief that at least he was listening to her.

"I do. The lass is lucky. Everyone has seen it," Heller said. He stepped to the other side of the mess. "Sorry, Captain," he mumbled.

Elle held her breath. One by one, every single crewman stepped across the line to her side.

Dashwood looked like he was about to explode. "So this really is a mutiny then," he growled. "I never thought I'd live to see it on a ship of mine."

"It doesn't have to be. All you need to do is give the order," Elle said softly.

She watched the captain wrestle with his thoughts and in that moment she almost felt sorry for him. There really was nowhere for him to go in order to salvage his pride. His crew had overruled him.

"Seems I have no choice in the matter," he said. "But mark my words. This will go terribly and horribly wrong. This woman is not lucky—she is cursed."

"Thank you, Captain," Elle said, before he could say any more. She felt a deep surge of relief wash over her.

"Hold on a moment. We are not done negotiating. I have one condition: If I am going to risk this ship on your crazy half-baked plan, then any haul of treasure is ours," he said.

Elle shook her head. "Sorry, Captain, fifty-fifty. I provide the map and you promote me to chief navigational pilot. And day shifts only. Fair is fair."

Dashwood regarded her for a long time. "Eighty for me—twenty for you and I let you live."

Elle laughed. "You have got to be joking. I could have you put into the brig and dropped off at the very next port. Can't I, boys?"

A few of the crewmen guffawed.

Dashwood narrowed his eyes and Elle knew she had won.

"Sixty-forty. The *Inanna* takes the bigger share and not a penny more," he said between gritted teeth.

"And I am promoted," Elle said. "No more scrubbing out thruster chambers."

Dashwood cursed. "Done." He stuck out his hand and shook hers. He gripped her hand so hard that she could feel her knuckles pop and she had to clench her teeth so as not to flinch.

"Long live Captain Dashwood!" Heller started cheering, and soon all the men joined in.

"Why do I still have the distinct feeling that you are not telling me everything?" he said as he withdrew his hand.

Elle gave him a sweet smile. "I think you'll find, Captain, that sometimes ignorance really is bliss. You keep your eye on the Khmer gold and I will keep an eye on the rest."

Dashwood shook his head in resignation. "I just can't win with you, can I?"

"It's not about winning, sir," Elle said.

Dashwood shook his head. "All right then, all hands back to your stations. Chance, report to the bridge. We set course due northeast immediately. Engineers, I am going to need some steam. Who wants to stop off in Socotra to refuel?"

There was a unanimous cheer from everyone.

"Aye, Captain." Elle touched her eyebrow in a small salute.

Elle wasn't so sure about stopping off in Socotra. It was the infamous pirate city. The stuff of legend. For hundreds of years, pirates had prowled the oceans, plundering as they went, but with the dawn of the Age of Steam and airships, they had taken to the skies. Robbing airships was even more profitable than robbing seafaring vessels. In addition, a pirate could go anywhere he wanted to in the sky. There were more places to hide, and in response a number of pirate cities had sprung up across the world. They were free places where spoils could be traded and they offered all manner of diversions and entertainments for crewmen with a bit of gold in their pockets.

In retaliation to this mass migration of pirates to airships, the sovereign nations of the world sent naval airships out to hunt pirates and bring them down to earth, where they were tried and in most cases executed. The act of piracy was punishable by death. Great armadas of battle cruisers patrolled the freight routes, armed to the teeth and always on the lookout for a fight.

As air traffic increased, so the freedom pirates once had diminished. One by one these great pleasure cities had been found and invaded. Most of them were either burned to the ground or taken as outposts.

But not Socotra. Some said that the city was hidden somewhere deep in the storm clouds that brewed across the ocean. Others said that only those with pirate blood could enter through its gates, but Elle was sure that these were all just tall tales.

The fact remained that its location was a closely guarded secret and so it had remained hidden from all but those who were allowed to enter for hundreds of years. It was the last truly free outpost where freebooters could meet and trade without fear of persecution.

Elle smiled at Atticus Crow as he passed her on the gangway. He grinned at her, his eyes twinkling with excitement. Perhaps she was being overly cautious. She'd never been to Socotra. Perhaps the place was not as bad as people said. Besides, what harm could come of a little shore leave if she kept to herself? Perhaps a few nights in a pirate cove might be just what the doctor ordered. It might even be fun, who knows?

Around her the rest of the crew jumped to attention to the captain's orders.

As she left the mess, Heller winked at her. "That was nicely played, lass. Nicely played indeed," he whispered.

"Thanks, Heller." She gave him her widest smile.

Out in the corridor, Elle let out her breath slowly and smiled in triumph. She was going to find the city of Angkor and, hopefully with it, some answers.

CHAPTER 17

TIGER CITY, SOCOTRA

A week after the *Inanna* had altered course to the east, the island of Socotra came into view. It was not the kind of place one would find on any ordinary map. In fact, many had died over the years so that the location of the city could remain a secret. The island was located off the east coast of Africa and south of the Yemen, in the heart of the Arabian Sea. The secret city of the sky pirates was a place only the most intrepid and skilled pilots could find—and then only if one knew someone who could tell them how to navigate the treacherous air currents and storm banks that shrouded it.

Half the year, the high sea cliffs were blasted by blistering hot dust from the desert winds that came from the north and west. These winds lay down layer upon layer of gritty air pockets—air turbulence violent enough to split a ship in half. The other half of the year, the monsoons from the east turned the skies into a boiling storm, just waiting to swallow any unsuspecting ship whole. It was, however, the richest and most coveted pirate cove in all the skies, so traders and freebooters frequently came here, regardless of the danger.

Elle watched with fascination as the *Inanna* docked against one of the rickety plank-and-rope landing docks set high against the cliff tops that surrounded Tiger City.

Below them, the sheer rock face dropped down into the stormy sea.

Elle and the rest of the crew—all, with the exception of Heller, had been granted shore leave—followed Dashwood along the stone walkway leading up to the enormous wooden gates of the stronghold. Behind the walls, stone buildings rose up, almost perfect in their rectangular symmetry. The side of each building featured rows of perfectly square windows, neatly painted with white frames.

"This is all rather neat and clean for a pirate city," Elle mused. "I must admit that I was expecting much more squalor and depravity."

"You just wait till you see what's inside," Fat Paul said. "You'll find depravity by the spade there." He was leafing through the lists he had made; the *Inanna* was sorely in need of supplies.

As a peace offering, Dashwood had even granted everyone a day's shore leave and the crew was anxious to make up for lost drinking time. Everyone except Heller had gone ashore. He was charged with guarding the ship while they were docked. It seemed that Captain Dashwood had not quite forgiven his first mate for his part in the coup.

There was an air of anticipation when Dashwood reached the gate. "Now remember, we want to keep our heads down. And no talk about you-know-what. The last thing we want is everyone and his dog beating us to the chase, now do we?"

There was a murmur of agreement from everyone.

"Don't you worry, Captain. You can count on us," Atticus Crow said.

"That's what I am worried about," Dashwood muttered. He turned to Elle. "Would you care to do the honors, Mrs. Marsh?" Dashwood motioned to a thick rope that was attached to a large gong strung high above their heads.

"Why, thank you." Elle smiled at him. Ringing the gong was a privilege reserved for ship captains only. Was Dashwood trying to make peace with her? He had even let her come ashore without a cuff on her arm this time. This was a good sign, she hoped.

"Two rings, the first separated by a count to seven from the second," he said. It was the code needed to gain entrance to this place.

Elle pulled the rope, counted to seven and rang again. The gong reverberated with each pull and then returned to silence.

A muscular man in a leather jerkin opened the pedestrian door. He had a long moustache which was segmented by little silver cuffs and hung all the way past his chin. On his head he wore a round metal cap. He looked them up and down for a few moments.

"The captain and crew of the free ship *Inanna* seek admittance," Dashwood said.

The man grunted, scratched his wide belly where it protruded from the leather tunic he wore and held out his hand.

Dashwood placed a purse full of coins on his outstretched palm.

The doorman weighed the money in his palm for a moment and then stepped aside with a nod to allow them in through the gates.

There was a brief cheer as the crew passed through the doors, the men elated that they were free to do as they pleased within the walls of the pirate city.

"To the left, to be searched," the man with the moustache growled.

Elle stepped into the queue of people waiting to be searched by the guards. Tiger City was a place where anything went. Women, drink and gambling were all available in abundance. There was, however, one rule, and that was that no one was allowed to enter the city armed. To be found in possession of a weapon in Tiger City was an act punishable by immediate death. Dashwood had made them all empty their pockets of weaponry before they came ashore.

"Not hiding anything inside that corset now, are you, pretty lady?" the guard asked her as she stepped up to the wooden box they used as a search platform.

Elle gave the pirate her most winning smile. "Of course not."

"Off you go then." The guard gave her a quick slap on the bottom to encourage her in, as she stepped off the box. Elle's eyes widened at this ill treatment, but the guard had already moved on to the next man. Instead, she took a deep breath and pressed her lips together. As much as she wanted to take the guard to task, it would only attract attention. And the last thing she wanted was for someone to find the slim blade she had tucked inside the secret compartment in her corset. There was one other rule in Tiger City. That was the rule that everything started and ended at the gate. She was taking a huge chance bringing a blade in here, but after her little talk with Jack she could not afford to take any chances.

"Easy now, Mrs. Marsh," Dashwood said in a low voice next to her ear as if he were reading her thoughts. "He was not very gallant, I agree, but this is not the place to pick a fight." He gripped her elbow as if to reiterate the point.

She glared at Dashwood. He just gave a low chuckle as he walked alongside her. One by one, Elle's compatriots fell to the call, peeling off into the numerous brightly painted taverns and houses of ill repute that lined the streets.

Pretty soon, only Elle, Dashwood and Fat Paul were left.

"Let's get the supplies out of the way first, shall we?" Dashwood said as they headed up to the supply caves that were carved into the rock face behind the city.

The city sat high up into the cliff face, its foundation carved from the very rock that made the mountain. The thick walls that encased the city were flanked on each side by huge, wooden landing platforms and sky docks lashed to the outcrops with ropes as thick as a man's forearm. On these docks, Sky schooners, clippers and an impressive array of other nonregulation aircraft of all shapes and sizes drifted gently in the sea air. Elle felt a pang of sadness when she spotted a smallish wooden freighter among the hulls. The ship could have been the *Water Lily*'s twin.

Below the city, a long stone staircase spilled down to the bottom of the dry valley that stretched before it. Tiger City was proud of its reputation as a place that had never been invaded from the ground. Any army mad enough to brave the arid valley and climb the stone stairs would be too exhausted to fight by the time they reached the top, so no one bothered.

"It's quite beautiful," Elle said as she admired the whitewashed walls and green clay-tiled roofs of the place, as Dashwood paid the pirate merchant for a consignment of barrels of beer. The emblem of the brewers had been singed off the side of the barrels with a branding iron. It would be anyone's guess what make or type of ale it was.

"Yes, it is rather. Place was abandoned for years till the sky ships found it."

"A haven for those who prowl the skies," she murmured.

"It's a strange place this," Dashwood said. "I've never been across the island, but some men say that it is full of brightly colored lizards as venomous as snakes. Plants that grow upside down." He leaned in closer as he spoke. "Some even say that dragons live here."

Elle stared at him. "Seriously?"

Dashwood started laughing. "No, but you seem very eager to believe old tales."

Elle shrugged, feeling suddenly embarrassed. "Who knows," she said, looking off into the distance. "There is more in this world than you and I could ever know." She would not have believed that two-headed dog-monsters existed either, but they did. But that was not something she could share with her captain.

"Now if you'll excuse me," Dashwood said as he stowed his purse. "I think there is a card game with my name on it round here." He patted the amulet around his neck. "As long as you stay away, I should be fine."

"Just don't gamble away the ship again, Captain," Elle called after him.

He spread his arms in a theatrical gesture. "What do you take me for? It is you, my dear Mrs. Marsh, who should take care not to get into any trouble."

"Me?" She mimicked his gesture. "Never."

Dashwood stepped closer and looked down at her. "I mean it. Please don't get involved in any Shadow business while we are here, all right? I really don't want to have to come and drag you out of a mess when I'm half drunk and holding a winning hand. Do I make myself clear?"

Elle swallowed. Dashwood's proximity made her feel rather uncomfortable. "I promise, I will be as quiet as a mouse. No one will even know I am here," she said.

"That's my girl." Dashwood's voice was suddenly softer, less harsh.

Elle cleared her throat and stepped back. "Why, Captain, if you carry on in this manner, I will seriously start to think that you care about me," she said.

Dashwood tipped his fedora and gave her a smile. "Just guarding my investment, Mrs. Marsh. See you later." With that, he turned and headed off down one of the side streets.

For the first time in what seemed like an age, Elle found herself completely at liberty to do as she pleased. The sudden sense of freedom felt wonderful.

She thought with a pang about her father and Mathilda. News of her disappearance must have reached them by now. Were they looking for her? Surely they must be anxious for news of her. Sadly, the price for secrecy was the fact that Tiger City had no post offices or telegraph lines, so apart from leaving a letter behind the counter with one of the taverns in the hope that someone might pick it up and post it on the way, there was no way she could send a message to anyone at home that she was alive. The risk that someone might read the letter and she might be discovered was too great. It was not a chance she could take right now. Not with that thing tracking her. And besides, Angkor Wat was in her sights now. She would have to wait until they reached another port.

So instead, she wandered around the ramshackle market that filled the narrow lanes and spread out into the open spaces. Here one could buy almost anything imaginable. She stopped and admired a selection of silver cutlery with their insignias filed off. To Elle the tableware looked suspiciously like it had been looted off a passenger ship.

The next stall held skeins of velvet in every color and she was sorely tempted to buy some, were it not for the inconvenience of transporting it back home.

In the next lane she bought a cup of frozen gelato, almost as delicious as the type one could buy in Venice.

The next stall sold all manner of leather goods, and she found a rather fetching jerkin to wear over her corset. Since her promotion, she had packed away her overalls and had reverted to her jodhpurs and leather coat, but she still sometimes caught some of the crew staring at the leather corset she wore over her shirt. The jerkin would also be handy when it got really cold. She had found herself shivering while walking the gangways late at night.

It was strange, but here in Tiger City no one seemed to give her outlandish choice in clothing a second glance. In fact, she even spotted one or two lady pirates wandering about, dressed like men. Elle did not approach them or acknowledge them, but somehow, knowing that she was not completely alone was just about the nicest thing she had encountered in quite some time.

Eventually she got bored with the market and decided to find somewhere to sit. The warm afternoon sun was setting and an icy wind nipped at her as it whispered through the buildings. She shivered and ducked into a little tavern.

Inside, it smelled like roasting meat and apricots and cinnamon. "What will it be, miss?" the tavern keeper asked.

"Could I have a small brandy?" she asked. "Something to warm me from the inside. And say, do you sell food?"

"Indeed we do, miss. What can I get you?" the tavern keeper said. "We have some excellent roast goat."

"Then I shall try it," Elle said.

"A small brandy?" a man at the counter beside her said with mock outrage. "What kind of a pirate are you?" he guffawed. "Give the girl a proper drink, will you?"

The tavern keeper grinned and tipped more of the drink into the glass in front of Elle.

"Salty Ben's the name," the man said. He was a short, grizzly-looking fellow in a tricolor hat so ancient that it was impossible to guess what its original color had been. He stuck out his hand in order to introduce himself.

"Eleanor." Elle shook his hand.

He narrowed his eyes as he studied her face. "You have pretty hair," he said, casting a glance at her head.

"Thank you." Elle took a sip of her brandy and turned away slightly in an attempt to end the conversation, but Salty Ben seemed intent on maintaining the discussion.

He studied her more closely. "Say, you seem different from the other women here."

"That's because I am a pilot," she said.

Ben looked her over again. "No, it's more than that. Something not quite right about you." He narrowed his eyes and stared at her intently.

"I'm sure you must be mistaken," Elle said quickly.

Just then, the tavern keeper slid a plate full of roast meat and flatbreads before her.

"Thank you," she said as she handed him a coin.

"Hmm, looks good," Salty Ben said, peering into her plate.

"If you'll excuse me." Elle gave him a little smile. She picked up her plate and drink and slid off her high chair. She spotted a free seat at the very end of a low rectangular table. No one seemed to object to her sitting there so Elle set down her plate and sat down.

Opposite her, an old-timer was telling a story of drunken ribaldry involving the very first air balloons flown over the Crimea.

She half listened as she ate her dinner, which was, as the tavern keeper has promised, quite delicious. As she ate, her thoughts turned to the navigational charts she had left on her table back on the bridge. In order to reach Angkor the *Inanna* was going to have to cross some rather treacherous airspace and it would be up to her to make sure that they did not go off course.

Elle was so engrossed in her own thoughts she did not notice that the old-timer had changed stories. Or that everyone in the tavern was listening intently.

". . . I'm telling you, this happened just the other week . . . I was there—I saw it with my own two eyes. The man just walked into the Mermaid and dropped a bag of gold on the table. Coins spilling out on to the floor and everywhere," the man opposite her was saying.

"Get out of here," a second one said.

"Nope. Said he was some fancy lord or summat."

"And then?"

"Ah, this is the best bit. After he threw coins at everyone, he announced that he would pay a hundred thousand English pounds to the man who brought him the girl. Insisted that she had to be alive and kicking."

The men around the storyteller howled with delight.

"A hundred thousand pounds! Who in their right mind gives away a hundred thousand pounds?"

"Crazy rich men!" the first crowed. "But I swear on my life as I sit here, that's what he said."

"So who is this girl then?"

"I don't know the name. Said she had red hair. Said something about a shadow, but I was too busy getting me share of the coins." The man who had spoken wiped his lips, which had become shiny with spittle. "And the best bit is—after he made the grand announcement, he disappeared. Poof! Went up in a cloud of smoke like a circus magician."

"Ah, he was a conman and he was just having a lark," one of the men said. "I bet you there's no money to be had."

The old-timer shook his head. "No, he was completely serious, I tell you. I saw the gold for myself. Tell you what, though. I'd love to see the look on that mad French geezer's face if someone did show up with a girl at his house. What would he do then?"

There was another round of raucous laughter followed by numerous lewd comments about Frenchmen.

"Well, go and find yourself a redhead and claim your prize!" someone shouted. "I'm sure there's more than one or two for hire round here."

Elle sat frozen at the spot. Her dinner had turned to sawdust in her mouth. She wanted to ask more, but she was too afraid to attract any attention to herself. Suddenly, Old Jack's warning about finding someone in the realm of Light to protect her made sense.

Slowly she put down her fork with a growing sense of apprehension. If there was anyone in this world who had the money for a ransom that high, it would be Patrice Chevalier.

She downed the last of her brandy and set aside her plate. Careful not to attract any attention to herself, she gathered her things and rose.

"Hey, where you going?" Salty Ben said as he popped up next to her.

"Have to go now. Sorry I can't stay to chat," she said as she slipped past him and headed for the door.

"Wait! Come back!" he said, but she was out the door before he could stop her.

Once outside, she stepped into the first alley she could find. Hidden by the chilly shadows cast by the side of the building, she rested her back against the wall. She forced herself to take deep breaths, willing the manic hammering of her heart inside her chest to slow.

So Patrice had set a bounty for her capture. She would have to be very careful.

But first she needed reinforcements. Just in case.

Carefully, she traced her steps back through the market until she found the spot where Dashwood had left her.

At the end of the alleyway she saw the lights of one of the gambling houses. She ran down the passageway and slipped in through the doors. Inside, the place was lit with little spark lamps. People were sitting round velvet-covered tables, hunched over their cards. To the side was a baccarat table and by the sounds of things, a lively game of dice was under way. This was as good a place as any to start her search, she surmised.

A few men looked up when Elle entered but soon went back to what they were doing.

This was definitely Dashwood's kind of place, but a glance around the room told her that he was not here.

She slipped out the door on the other side of the room. The door, as it turned out, led into a hallway with a set of stairs. She heard a soft giggle and looked up. Above her, two half-dressed girls were leaning against the balustrade, chatting.

Yes, this was definitely her captain's kind of place. Of course the card house would be attached to a brothel. Of course it would.

The hall and landing were draped in swathes of red velvet. Beside her was a yucca palm tree in a brass bucket.

She felt the back of her neck prickle with apprehension. Carefully she opened the door to the card house a little, just as she saw the shaggy tricolor of Salty Ben enter.

He scanned the card room, the expression on his face turning to a scowl. He was definitely following her. Of that she was sure.

Escape through the card house was now impossible. The only way was up. Hopefully she'd find an open window or something to climb out of. As quietly as she could, Elle made her way up the stairs, trying not to let the fall of her boots echo too much on the stone slabs of the steps.

Behind her, she heard voices. It was Salty Ben arguing with someone downstairs. A woman joined them, loudly protesting the fact that only paying customers were allowed.

At the top of the stairs Elle ducked behind the balustrade and listened. When they saw her, the two half-dressed girls stopped talking. They gave her a wary look. Elle lifted her finger to her lips, imploring them to say nothing.

To her relief, the bond of universal sisterhood prevailed. The girls nodded, linked arms and disappeared into one of the rooms. Elle heard the distinct sound of a lock turning in the door. Well, the bond of universal sisterhood prevailed up to a point, she thought.

Below her, the voices were raised now. The door slammed and she heard Salty Ben stride toward the stairs, with the woman chattering loudly behind him. She needed to find a better hiding place and quickly too.

Behind her, more velvet draped the walls of the landing and the corridor too. In the distance she could hear a woman moan accompanied by the sounds of beds creaking. That could only be one thing. Slipping into one of these rooms was out of the question. Walking in on someone in that situation was likely to cause more noise than it was worth.

The voices were now at the foot of the staircase.

No, the hallway would have to do. As quietly as she could, Elle ducked behind the nearest swathe of velvet. She dropped the fabric behind her and, as she turned, she let out a small squeak of surprise as she collided headfirst into a solid wall of chest muscle. Her hiding place was already occupied, it seemed. And when she looked up, she found herself staring into the startled face of none other than Captain Dashwood.

They stood, chest to chest in the half-light for a few moments while they both recovered from the shock.

"Why, Mrs. Marsh," Dashwood drawled. "We appear to be lurking in the same dark corners this evening."

"Shh!" She put her finger to her lips. "I think someone is following me."

"Are they now?" Dashwood arched an inquiring eyebrow at her. "Well that's rather inconvenient, isn't it?"

Elle moved until her back touched the wall so as to put as much distance between her and the captain as possible, but the space available had its limitations.

"Captain, are you drunk?" she whispered.

"I might be." He swayed as he spoke.

"What are you doing here?"

"Oh, well, things went really well at the card tables, but not so well with the ladies." Dashwood closed his eyes a little. "I fear I may have upset a few of them. So now I'm laying low till the coast is clear." He swayed a little again, and as they moved she felt his arms go round her. He was surprisingly strong and solid, even when a little squiffy, she realized.

"Well, this is rather nice," he said, leaning into her.

"No it's not. Keep quiet before they find us."

"Perhaps I should step out of here and see who dares to harass a member of my crew," he said. "What do you think? Shall I show them a thing or two?" She felt his hand go to the place on his belt where he normally carried his pistol. He dropped his hand to his side when he realized that the holster was empty and started laughing. It was a deep sound that reverberated through her.

"Be quiet. This is not funny," she hissed.

She reached up and started unlacing the top of her corset. There, just inside the laces, was the secret pocket that held the small stiletto she always carried. Not even the bottom-slapping guard had dared to look down her front, she thought.

"Why, Mrs. Marsh," Dashwood said in a low voice, which was still far too loud. "You naughty, naughty girl."

"Please, Captain, be still," she whispered.

"Now, that is impressive," he said as his gaze drifted to her exposed cleavage while she pulled the blade out.

"Not even I am brave enough to bring a blade in here. Also, very impressive hiding place," he said, nodding at her cleavage.

"Captain! Be quiet." She gave him a little shake. "You need to sober up before we are both caught. This is not a game. I am in serious trouble here," she whispered.

"Yes, ma'am," he said. She could feel his amusement radiating from him.

The sound of boot steps on the tiles silenced them both. Elle put her hand over the captain's face before he could make another sound. "Be. Quiet," she mouthed at him. To her immense relief he remained still, his arms still securely around her.

The footsteps were much closer now. She could hear the creak of leather and the jingle of buckles as her pursuer moved along. He too was trying to walk as quietly as possible.

Elle gripped her stiletto, holding it at the ready.

A dark break in the strip of light that glowed at the bottom of the velvet appeared. Moments ticked by with exaggerated slowness as they waited in silence.

Then, Salty Ben dragged the fabric away. He grinned at her. "Ha! Got you n—" he started to say, but he never managed to finish his sentence. Instead, his eyes grew wide in shock as Elle drove the stiletto into his chest.

Salty Ben gasped as the blade sank into his heart, and then he fell to the ground, dead as a doornail.

"Oh dear," Dashwood said, looking down at the dead man, leaking blood on the carpet at their feet. "That is not good."

Elle stared at the body, horrified at what she had just done.

"Mrs. Marsh, I would strongly recommend we leave this place," Dashwood slurred next to her. "On account of the fact that I really don't want to be hanged tonight."

"Right," Elle said as she untangled herself from his embrace. "This way," she said, as they both took flight down the stairs, out the side door and into the alleyway.

Behind them, a woman screamed and people started shouting.

"Run!" Dashwood said next to her. The cold fright of murder and the sprint down the stairs had almost sobered him up. He grabbed Elle's hand, dragging her along as they ran.

Behind them, a bell started tolling. Men were running through the streets, raising the alarm. There was only one rule in Tiger City and now they were about to die for breaking it.

"They're closing the gates!" Elle said as they rounded a corner and caught sight of the entrance to the city.

"We'll make it!" Dashwood said. They both started running faster until they were sprinting flat out. Once through those gates, they were in no-man's-land and no one could touch them. Everything started and ended at the gates.

The mustached guard in his leather jerkin appeared before the gates, blocking their escape with his large, hairy body. He braced his legs, ready to meet them.

"Elle, when I say so, you go for the gap between his legs. You get out of here and back to the ship, do you hear me?" Dashwood said.

"Right," she said, even though she had no intention of leaving him behind. He was her captain, after all.

A few feet before the guard, Dashwood yelled, "Now!"

Elle threw her weight to the ground and skidded on the gravel straight through the guard's bandy legs. As she slipped through, she lifted her fist and slammed it into the man's crotch.

Her move caught the guard completely by surprise. His eyes bulged and he doubled over in pain just in time to meet Dashwood's right hook. The second blow finished him off and he toppled over like a fallen tree.

Elle and Dashwood slid through the gap in the gate just before it closed behind them. They kept running, because behind them a mob of angry pirates was gathering on the parapets of the city walls. Some of the men started hurling rocks down. These smashed to the ground, and Elle had to dodge them a few times before they were out of striking range. After what seemed like an eternity of running, the welcoming ladder of the *Inanna* came into view. Elle and Dashwood scampered up it and into the ship without hesitation.

"Evenin', Captain." Heller was waiting by the doors for them. "Everything all right?" He gave them both an inquiring look as he took in their disheveled states.

"All crew present and accounted for. You two were the last on board." Heller chuckled. "Seems like no one was having any luck tonight. There has been much grumbling about empty pockets round here. But it looks like we can close her up."

"Oh, thank the gods," Dashwood gasped. "I was dreading the thought of having to leave crew behind." He was leaning forward, with his hands on his knees, gasping and panting for breath.

"I'm sorry, sir, you were going to leave crew behind?" Heller looked even more puzzled.

"They're after us. I had to stab him. He was after me," Elle gasped as she stumbled into the hold and collapsed onto her knees utterly spent and winded.

"What? You stabbed someone?" Heller's caterpillar eyebrows knitted together in consternation. "In Tiger City?"

"There's no time to explain. Just get Atticus to take off!" Dashwood said.

Heller gave the captain a puzzled look.

". . . Before that mob behind us have time to open the gates and come after us."

"Aye, Captain." Heller pulled at the wheel that operated the doors, and once they were closed, he sealed the hatch firmly.

"That should keep 'em out while we fire the old girl up, Captain," he said. "Now you catch your breath while I sort out the orders. Shall I meet you on the bridge as soon as you're ready?"

"Yes, carry on at will, Mr. Heller. Just get us out of here," Dashwood said.

It was not unusual for ships to take off and berth in Tiger City at unsocial times of day and night. Pirates did, after all, keep unconventional hours. But the departure of the *Inanna* was an incident that was remembered in Tiger City for many years afterward.

Many sets of eyes watched the giant ship lift off and sail to the freedom of the night sky.

"She's heading due east," said one pirate as he stared at her receding lights.

"Aye, heading for the Orient. I heard someone say some of the crew were talking of treasure hidden in a lost city. In the jungles of Siam, of all places. Said the whole place was built of gold."

A few pirates said "Arr" in agreement.

"There's a redhead girl on board. The one old Geoffrey told us about. I reckon Ben sussed her and she killed him in cold blood when he went to claim his prize," another said.

There were more mutters about the unfairness of the fight.

"I think that story about the hundred thousand pounds is true. I reckon that's why she stabbed him," yet another said.

"Now that's a sweet haul, if ever I've seen one," a fifth pirate added. "Just imagine. A hold full of Siamese gold and a trunk full of pounds waiting for you when you get home. The man who gets all that will be richer than the king of England himself."

There were more nods of agreement.

"There's a lot of jungle between here and China. More than you'll ever imagine. I'd say that's a perfect place for a bird as big as the *Inanna* to disappear," a pirate named Colin said.

"A lot of jungle indeed," old Geoffrey muttered. Someone had helped him up the stairs.

"A fine haul indeed," someone repeated.

"The kind of treasure one could only imagine," someone else said.

"Come, let's get a head start before the others," another said.

They began to walk away, nodding in agreement. "Hang on, we saw her first. We should have first dibs," Colin said.

"No, we saw her first!"

"No, we did!"

"I say it's every pirate for himself. Finders, keepers," old Geoffrey declared.

By this time, more pirates had started slinking down the steps from the parapets. Not to be outdone by another, this very quickly became a scramble to get to the ground.

And so that night, Tiger City saw almost every ship in its port take to the sky almost simultaneously. All of them in pursuit of riches. And their target, the *Inanna* and the valuable cargo she held.

CHAPTER 18

"Eastward ho!" Elle called across the bridge.

"What's the weather doing, Mrs. Marsh?" Captain Dashwood asked. He was sitting in the captain's chair, every bit the master of the ship this morning.

"Fair as is, Captain, but for a few banks of cloud east, northeast. The monsoons are more or less over, so she should be fine."

"Very well, full steam ahead, Mr. Crow. Daylight's a-burning!"

The *Inanna* creaked and she surged through the sky. Atticus pulled the signal lever so that the position on the round dial read, *Full steam ahead.* Far below in the engine room was an identical signal linked up to the one in the bridge. When Atticus adjusted the signal on the bridge, the one in the engine room responded accordingly, telling the engineers how much power was needed for the thrusters. It was a most effective and fast method of communicating across the 800-foot expanse of the ship.

Below the hulls of the *Inanna*, acre upon acre of impenetrable jungle stretched as far as the eye could see. They had been traveling at a steady speed for the better part of two weeks with no major incidents. Behind them lay the subcontinent of India, and the Bay of Bengal nestled beside the Kingdom of Siam. Before them the seemingly limitless jungles of French Indochina stretched out in an emerald carpet of trees.

Elle felt a shiver of excitement. After their escape from Tiger City, the journey had been so uneventful that she had felt the first stirrings of boredom. All those miles were behind them now and somewhere in the jungle below was the city of Angkor. Their destination, if Dr. Bell's notes were accurate, was almost in sight.

She glanced over at the captain. Neither of them had spoken about their encounter behind the curtain and the escape from Socotra, but since that night things had been almost cordial between them. She had even joined him for dinner along with Heller and Mr. Crow on a few occasions and they ended up laughing and talking until late.

The crew were in high spirits, and she had heard laughter coming from the mess when she came to her shift this morning. Yes, the spirit of adventure and the whisper of riches were definitely in the air. Elle allowed herself a little smile of triumph. It had not been easy to get here, but for once in her life, things were going well.

She frowned as she scanned the horizon. The puffy white cloud bank that had been resting in the distance was rapidly growing darker. In fact, the clouds were moving rapidly across the sky toward them like nothing she had ever seen before.

"Um, Captain, I think we should keep an eye on those clouds," Elle said.

Dashwood rose from his seat and came to stand next to her at the observation window.

"Have you ever seen anything like it?" Elle said as she watched flashes of lightning play in the growing mass. "We are out of the monsoon season, so this sort of storm should not be happening."

Dashwood pulled out his brass telescope and studied

the sky. Elle watched the good-natured smile fade from his expression.

"Storm riders," he said, snapping his telescope shut.

The crew on the bridge all grew silent at the words.

"Mr. Crow, do you think you could coax a bit more speed out of the old girl?"

"Certainly can, sir," Mr. Crow said. He too had paled in the last few moments.

"Set a course westward—back the way we came. Bring her round as fast as you can."

"Aye, Captain." Mr. Crow shifted the brass signal, pushing it right into the red.

Atticus and John Kipper exchanged a worried look.

"I need bearings! Now!" Dashwood snapped.

"Um, aye, Captain." Elle scanned the compass and the charts. "Forty degrees," she said. "Do you mind me asking—who are we running from?"

"You have got to be kidding me." Dashwood shook his head. "I don't have time for this."

The *Inanna* creaked and groaned under the pressure as Mr. Crow brought the massive thruster engines about. Slowly, she started changing course, cleaving a wide arc through the sky.

"Mr. Heller, I want every hand on deck. Now," Dashwood said.

"Aye, Captain." Mr. Heller started winding the crank handle that sounded the alarm. The braying of the microphones echoed through the ship, causing everyone to jump to attention.

"What?" Elle said. "What did I say?" Elle asked over the noise of the alarm echoing through the decks below.

"Aeternae," Mr. Crow said.

"I thought they were just made-up stories," she said.

"Trust me, Mrs. Marsh. They are as real as you or me," Dashwood said. "And judging from the size of the storm clouds they are brewing, they have one seriously powerful electromancer on board."

"So what do we do—just run?"

"As fast as we can. The Aeternae mainly hunt over open ground. They brew up a huge storm to confuse and incapacitate their quarry. Then, once the ship is helpless, they board it and strip down everything they can—and that includes metal, flesh, and bone."

"There ain't nothing more horrible than a ship that's been picked clean by riders," Mr. Crow said. His eyes were trained on the gauges and instrument panel before him, his shoulders tense.

"And how is running going to help?" Elle said.

"They avoid cities because cities usually have other electromancers. Other electromancers can access their storm clouds and neutralize them. Ergo, if we make it to the airspace over Bangkok, they might just abandon the hunt."

"But Bangkok is more than a day away, Captain," Elle said, looking up from her charts.

"Well then, we are simply going to have to run as fast as we can, for a whole day if need be, now won't we?" the captain said. "Now find me the shortest route!"

Elle just stared at him as fear boiled in her stomach. She still woke in the night thinking that she was on board the *Water Lily* with Gertrude, the sound of gunfire deafening her ears. And she also had ample experience with the dangers of those who utilized the powers of the electromancers. Being raided again, this time by creatures with Shadow power, was just about the most terrifying thing she could imagine.

"Bearings!" Dashwood barked.

Elle jumped and turned to her charts.

"Mr. Crow?"

"Full steam ahead, sir. We are going to give them a run for their money, for sure."

"Take her up as high as you can, Mr. Kipper. I want as much clearance as we can get in case we need to dive," the captain said.

"Aye, Captain," Mr. Kipper said. Even he was looking slightly perturbed.

The next hour passed in tense silence. The only sound on the bridge was the creaking of fuselage and the desperate hum of the *Inanna*'s engines, which had been pushed to their limit.

Elle scanned the horizon with her optics. Her viewfinder locked on a shadow in the distance and she froze. She turned the little wheels of her spyglass until the image came into view. An airship painted black as night was heading toward them, her dark balloon curving gracefully above the carved hull.

"Captain! Off the starboard side. Looks like a Chinese junk," she said.

Dashwood peered into the direction she indicated. "Why are they not running from the Aeternae?" he muttered.

"They look like they are gaining on us," she said.

Dashwood frowned.

"Captain!" Finn burst on to the bridge "Captain!" he gasped.

"Ships aft. They are in our slipstream, sir. A clipper and two schooners. One of them has just raised their colors. Pirates, sir," he gasped.

"What?" Dashwood said. "Mrs. Marsh. With me, please." He snapped as he strode out of the bridge and along the gangway to the poop deck that held an observation platform. By the time they reached the deck, two more ships had appeared in view.

"What is going on?" Dashwood murmured.

"I have no idea, sir," Elias said, looking up from his spyglass. "They just appeared from nowhere. Seems like they've been tracking us since Socotra."

Dashwood swore. "If we survive this, I am going to kill with my bare hands the man who blabbed about our destination!"

A tense silence filled the deck. No one even dared to breathe.

"Elias, you are in charge of the poop deck. I want someone on the communications tubes at all times. Updates every five minutes. Every five minutes, do you hear me?"

"Aye, sir!"

"Finn, man the cannons. Call Fat Paul and the Doc up here to help you. Tell Mick to keep her engines running no matter what. We are going to need every pair of hands we can find to fight off these bastards. Hopefully the riders will go for one of these other ships, if we manage to hit one hard enough to slow them down."

No one spoke.

"Do I make myself clear?"

"Aye, Cap'n."

Their answer was punctuated by the dull thunder of cannon fire. The *Inanna* shuddered as a blast of spark bloomed in the air beside them.

"Battle stations!" Dashwood shouted.

"Officers to the bridge!"

Elle ran after him as he strode along the gangway, his coattails flapping behind him.

When they reached the bridge, Heller grabbed Elle by her elbow. "Here," he said as he thrust her Colt into her hand. "Found some ammo for it too." He pushed the paper box into her other hand. "Save yourself, if it comes to that, lass. Don't let them take you."

"Thank you, Heller," Elle said. She gripped his large hand.

"Bearings!" Dashwood shouted behind them. "Mr. Heller, you have orders to fire at will. Now move it!"

"Aye, Captain," Elle said as she stowed her pistol and resumed her post.

The Aeternae were now much closer. She could glimpse the outline of their dreadnought through the clouds.

More cannon fire exploded around them. The ship recoiled as the *Inanna* returned fire.

"Mr. Crow, I need more power," Dashwood said. "On Mrs. Marsh's bearings. Mr. Kipper, take her down as fast as you can."

They all turned and looked at the captain. "But, sir, that would place us in a headlong collision course with the pirates . . ."

"Do it! Now!" he barked.

The *Inanna* groaned as her hull absorbed the pressure exerted upon her as Mr. Crow and Mr. Kipper adjusted course. Elle kept her eyes trained on her instruments while the storm rider cloud grew bigger and bigger before them. Behind them, the flotilla of airships trailed in the *Inanna*'s wake.

"When I give the order, I want you to dive. Full steam. Nose to the ground. Do I make myself clear?" Dashwood said.

"Aye, Captain," they all answered.

The captain was planning a risky maneuver which intended to flick the ships behind them into the Aeternae's storm cloud, using the *Inanna*'s thruster updraft when she dived.

There were no guarantees that the other ships would follow. There was also no guarantee that they would be able to level off before they plunged into the ground either, but right now the maneuver was their only option. Elle bit her lip before she could say anything. Now was not the time to question the captain's authority. This was do-or-die time.

She checked her Colt at her side. She had loaded it in

the few spare moments she had between Dashwood's commands. She hoped Heller had taken good care of her Colt and stored it safely. If there was any dirt in it, it could misfire or jam. There was no time to worry about it though. They had far bigger problems to face.

The *Inanna* bucked forward and rocked as she took more fire from behind. There was a slight shudder as something impacted on the side of the hull just below them.

"What was that?" Elle said.

"Keep your eyes on the navigation, Mrs. Marsh. Let me worry about the thumps and knocks, all right?" Dashwood said.

"Yes, listen to your captain," a strange voice said from behind them, followed by a snigger.

Elle turned round to see two men armed with shotguns at the entrance to the bridge. One was wearing a battered tricolor hat. She could have sworn it was the same hat worn by Salty Ben in Socotra.

"I know you. You were at my table in the tavern," she said before she could stop herself.

He lifted his hat with a flourish. "Colin at your service, ma'am. And this is Ed. We have come to collect the bounty."

"Bounty? What bounty?" Dashwood said. He had drawn his pistol, which caused both Colin and Ed to take aim at him.

Colin started laughing. "He don't even know about the gold mine he's sitting on top of, do he?"

"What?" Dashwood barked.

"We've come for the woman, Captain. The redhead— the one who don't cast no shadow. There's a hundred thousand pounds sterling in it for us, if we deliver her in London."

"A hundred thousand pounds," Ed said before he started giggling.

"That's right. Now hand her over before it's too late. You have a battle to finish."

Dashwood glared at Elle. "What is he talking about?"

Elle shrugged. "Um, that's why the man I killed in Socotra was following me. There's a bounty on my head, apparently—"

"Enough chatting. Give us the girl," Colin said. He shucked his shotgun like a man who meant business.

"I don't think so," Dashwood said. He lifted his pistol and shot Colin squarely in the chest. Colin's eyes widened in surprise for an instant, before the life went out of them. His legs buckled and he sank to the ground with a thud.

At the same time, Ed shrieked and started firing his shotgun repeatedly. Everyone ducked as the buckshot sprayed across the close confines of the bridge. The windglass turned opaque in a spiderweb of cracks.

On impact, Mr. Kipper groaned and slumped forward onto his controls, his insides spilling in a slick of blood and gore across the flight instruments.

With Kipper no longer at the helm, the *Inanna* screeched and started plummeting to the ground. Everywhere, lights started flashing and alarms started ringing. The change in pressure made the cracked windglass shatter. Tiny fragments of glass sprayed everywhere and an icy wind rushed into the cabin, scattering charts and instruments.

Elle felt herself being flung across the deck, but her fall was broken by something warm and solid. Dashwood. His arm flopped over her, the muscles limp and motionless. Elle looked at his face. His eyes were closed and blood streaked over his cheek from where he had hit his head. He was alive, but out cold. Which was just as well, given the fact that at that moment they were plummeting to the earth below—and certain death.

I must try to save the ship, Elle thought. *The crew. Hellhounds be damned, there is only one way I know. I can do this if I try.*

Elle closed her eyes and focused her attention on where the barrier should be. Perhaps it was the presence of the Storm Riders, but the *Inanna*'s hexes seemed to have weakened and when she gave it all she had, Elle could just about make out the faintest glimmer of the barrier. It was a long shot, but right now it was the only option left.

The warlocks are never, ever going to forgive me for this, she thought as she summoned up every bit of energy she had within her. She grabbed hold of the barrier and tore at it with all her might. She felt an awful ripping sensation as a large rent opened up between the worlds. She willed the *Inanna* toward the opening with all the strength she could muster.

The ship creaked and bucked, and she nudged it forward. She felt her muscles strain, and something wet trickled from her nose, but still she held on with everything she had. Then the fuselage slammed into the barrier with a deafening crash and the impact caused the barrier to split open further, but the hole was still not big enough for an 800-foot battleship. With the sickening crunch of distressed metal and the hiss of balloon gas, the *Inanna* lodged herself in the rip, marooned half inside and half outside the dividing space of the realms of Shadow and Light. Half the ship had disappeared into the barrier, and was now invisible to those looking at it from the Light side. The other half remained suspended in midair. Elle had effectively flown the ship into a wall and now the *Inanna* was stuck there with no way of passing through.

Around her, Elle heard pipes bursting and gauges popping. Steam and engine fluid started to spray everywhere. Blue spark crackled over the surfaces, igniting patches of flammable liquid.

"Abandon ship! To the life-raft balloons. Use the outriders if you must! Save yourselves!" Heller shouted and began to help Atticus clamber out of the broken doors that led away from the bridge.

Lights flickered, and somewhere in the distance the low boom of a ship's horn sounded. Above her, someone was giggling hysterically. It was an awful gurgling sound. Elle looked up to find Ed the pirate hanging just above them. A jagged piece of metal torn loose from the hull was protruding from his stomach, skewering him to the spot, wound bathed in a slick, red gore which dripped down onto the floor next to them.

"Aeternae. They sound their hunting horns before they board a ship," he said. "They are coming for you," he rasped. Then he started laughing again weakly, before his eyes closed as the last bit of life drained out of him. His body went limp.

Elle looked down at Dashwood. He was still unconscious.

Damn you, Captain. I can't leave you here for those things, she thought. She had no way of telling where they were in relation to the two worlds, or even how high up in the air, for that matter. For all she knew, the hound was waiting for her on the other side, jaws wide and ready to tear her apart.

Off in the distance, she heard the sound of boots clambering over metal, followed by the brief, terrified screams of crewmen, before they were silenced. She heard cannon fire, but it seemed to be directed away from them. The captain's plan must have worked, she thought. The Aeternae had turned on the other pirates, and from the sound of it they were exchanging some pretty heavy-duty cannon fire.

If she was going to survive this, now would be the

time to move. She grabbed hold of the captain and lifted him up so his arm draped over her shoulder. She allowed gravity to take over, letting him roll over her so she could drag him, draped over her back.

"Let's see if they have any gliders left on this thing," she said to his unconscious form as she sidestepped the dead pirate Colin.

Dashwood was heavy but moving downhill helped, and she managed to pull him through the broken doors and along the sloping gangway. Around her the air rang out with the screams of the Aeternae and gunfire.

The *Inanna* was constructed out of a honeycomb of air ducts that made her light and strong. It was the secret to her staying in the air. Elle opened an air duct through one of the service doors and slipped inside.

The duct seemed to be clear and quiet. "Come along then, Captain," Elle said, sucking in a breath as she heaved. He let out a loud groan so she stopped and rested against the hull for a moment. The metal beneath her felt strangely warm to the touch, which was rather worrying.

"Captain," Elle whispered. She patted his cheek. "Captain Dashwood, wake up."

He groaned once more and opened his eyes slightly before shutting them again. "What happened?" he mumbled. "Why aren't we moving?"

"Captain," she whispered and patted his cheek again, this time a little harder. "You can't sleep here. Come on, you have to walk." Elle dragged him up. "Both legs, there you go."

Dashwood stumbled but managed to stay upright. He groaned again.

"Be quiet. They'll hear us. This way," she said as they shuffled down the duct. Dashwood, for once, allowed himself to be led along until they reached the row of launch conduits that held the ship's gliders. To her dismay, they were all empty. The rest of the crew must have taken them, she realized with both relief and despair.

"What are we going to do?" she muttered to herself, stumbling into the hold.

"Balloon," Dashwood mumbled.

Elle spotted a wicker safety basket still in its launch bracket. This was, she realized, the very same life raft that Dashwood had intended to use to jettison her and Gertrude in the desert.

"Come on, Captain," she said and hauled him into the basket.

"No . . . must stay on the ship . . ." he mumbled.

She ignored him and started unclipping the balloon, hooking it up to the valve that fed off one of the helium chambers that held the *Inanna* aloft. She heard the gas flow into the balloon with a soft hiss.

The sound of gunfire was now very close, although she wasn't sure why they were firing. Presumably more pirates had boarded the ship and were facing the storm riders.

However that might be, she did not have time to wait for the balloon to fill completely. The ride down would be bumpy, but it would have to do. Elle hopped into the basket alongside Dashwood and pulled the release catch. The escape chute shuddered and slid forward, tipping the basket out of the ship, the balloon inflating behind them as they moved.

"Stop . . . must stay on the ship . . . I'm the captain . . ." Dashwood put up his arm in an ineffective attempt to climb out of the basket. His movements made the wicker wobble dangerously to the side.

"Stay still or you'll kill us both," Elle said curtly.

She heard a clang of metal overhead, but there was no time to wonder about it. With a final shudder, the escape balloon slid loose and they were in the air. The half-filled balloon above them wobbled and dipped as it took the weight of the basket.

Elle held on to the basket to stop them from tipping out; they were drifting downward and sideways at a speed that—though not quite lethal—was fast enough to be alarming.

Suddenly the basket shuddered as something hauled itself over the edge. Elle let out a scream as one of the Aeternae fell into the basket next to her.

It was hideous. Dressed only in a coarse tunic and trousers fashioned from animal skins, its long black hair tied in greasy braids hung over its shoulders and down its back. From its forehead were numerous saw-like bone protrusions that resembled blades. Elle stared into its yellow catlike pupils in horror.

The creature hissed at her, baring its sharp teeth while at the same time drawing a long, vicious-looking blade from a scabbard on its leg. This then was one of the legendary man-beasts who had attacked and killed Alexander the Great's men all those years ago.

She had just enough time to unclip and draw her Colt before the storm rider sprang on her. She pulled the trigger right as the blade came down, the shot ringing loudly in her ears and making her wince. The Aeternae gasped and slumped forward, pegging the knife into the basket beside her head. Elle gasped in shock and quickly wriggled her way out from underneath the creature, wanting to get away from it as fast as was possible. It smelled of decay and when she looked closely at it, she saw that its hair was crawling with lice.

Shuddering, Elle freed herself from the corpse and moved to look over the edge of the basket. Their descent had increased. With a third body on board the basket was too heavy and they would surely die if they hit the ground at this speed.

Biting back her supreme disgust, Elle grabbed hold of

the storm rider's dead body and hoisted it up onto the edge of the basket. It was time to lose some ballast. She took a deep breath and heaved it over the side. The body tumbled downward into the sea of green below.

The reduction in weight slowed their descent a little, but it was not enough to keep them airborne. Elle looked up and spotted the tear in the balloon above her. She closed her eyes and reached out for the barrier, but there was nothing. Crashing the *Inanna* into the divide must have done something to it, because there was no energy or golden light to be found as she cast around desperately for anything that might stop their fall. She let out a wail of despair as she watched the treetops of the jungle growing bigger.

"Captain, I just wanted to say I'm sorry about everything. And thank you. Not for stealing my ship, but for making me part of a crew again," she said.

Then she closed her eyes and braced herself.

This is how I am going to die. Here, alone in the middle of nowhere. And I am never going to see Hugh again, she thought, as the basket clipped the first treetop and bounced off it.

They were plowing into the canopy. The impact of the basket hitting the dense foliage knocked Elle's head back against the side of the basket. The basket tilted in a whirr of greenery and sky. The last thing she remembered was grabbing hold of the edge of the basket as they skidded down. Elle was lurched forward. She felt her vision blur and then everything around her went dark.

The end, it seemed, was now.

CHAPTER 19

The hound had been walking for many days now, prowling the long, golden corridor that formed the barrier between Shadow and Light. On and on he walked, ever searching for a way out. Every now and then, he would catch a whiff of her scent. It would hang in the air for a few moments and before he could catch it, it would dissipate, leaving him growling and pacing up and down in a state of perpetual fury.

He shook his heads and let out a long growl of frustration. His quarry was starting to make him very angry. He never let his prey put up that much of a fight. He was supposed to be the hunter and it was against the natural order of things for him to be trapped here while she skipped around the skies, free and unhurt. The hunt-lust that was building up inside him threatened to drive all reason from his brain, and he was tempted to give in to the red haze that would send him into a frenzy and spell death to anyone—or anything—unlucky enough to encounter him. But he resisted. He had a task to fulfill and he would not stop until it was done.

The hound stopped and sniffed the air. He could feel a strange pressure building up around him. He sank down on his haunches, ears flat, nostrils flared. Something was about to happen. He could feel a sudden shift in time and space. It resonated deep inside his bones.

The air around him started humming and his ears

filled with the most awful high-pitched noise. It was the sound of the very fabric of the universe ripping.

The hound ducked as a massive shockwave surged through the barrier.

He felt himself catapulted through the air. Everything around him was blindingly bright, and then suddenly he was in the realm of Light, falling, tumbling down to the ground as the air rushed by. The ground grew closer, and then he found himself crashing through treetops. Painful branches slapped at his faces and ribs. Then branches made way for the huge leaves of the upper undergrowth. Over and over he tumbled, bouncing off the foliage, his legs tangling through vines, before the greenery gave way to a steep slope. He hit the ground, the angle of the slope inflicting only one glancing blow. Over and over he rolled until he landed with an almighty splash into a river.

The hound started paddling as fast as he could, but white water boiled up around him and his paws scrabbled against slimy rocks without any hope of purchase. Round and round he spun as the current dragged him along. He gasped and swallowed water and then, without any warning, the riverbed gave way below him as he tumbled over the precipice of a waterfall. He slowly arched through the air, suspended in the spray for a few seconds, before crashing into a deep pool below. He kicked and paddled as hard as he could, fighting for the precious air he needed to survive in this realm, until finally the river, having grown bored with him, spat him out.

Bedraggled and weak, the hound dragged himself up onto the riverbank where he collapsed onto the damp ground. He retched the water from his lungs until both of his throats felt raw. Exhausted, he rested his heads on his paws, closed his eyes and lay there for a long time, panting for breath. He was battered and bruised. Every inch of him ached and his lungs felt as if they had been stripped raw inside, but at least he was alive.

Slowly the shadows of the undergrowth unfurled and spread across the ground toward him. He inhaled the power of the trees and the plants around him and slowly his broken bones mended and his torn muscles healed. The dog lifted his heads off his paws and peered into the undergrowth.

Around him, the jungle grew silent as small creatures watched fearfully from their hiding places. Sunlight dappled the jungle floor in front of his paws.

A huge spider crept past and wiggled its mandibles at him before retreating into the bark of a fallen log.

He was alive. Yes, he was alive and he could still hunt.

He took a deep breath and drew the humid air through his nostrils. There it was—the faint smell of freesias and engine oil—drifting to him on the almost still breeze. Every nerve stood on end and he felt himself quiver with excitement.

She was here. He could feel her presence deep within him.

Slowly the hound rose. He shook himself off, urging the last of the river out of his thick, black fur. Then, noses to the ground, he started moving through the undergrowth.

The hunt was on again, and this time his prey would know no escape.

Patrice sat up in bed and clutched at the breast of his silk pajamas. The source of his sudden—and rather inelegant—awakening was a fierce, white-hot pain that tore through his chest.

Gasping in agony, he rolled over and turned on the spark lamp next to his bed. Light filled the room and he fell back against the down pillows. He lay there, staring up at the silk canopy of his bed, eyes wide, and waited for the moment that would surely be his last. But it did not come, and as he lay there, the pain slowly ebbed until he could manage to sit up and ring the bell pull.

Something was very wrong. He had not felt like this since his descent into darkness.

"You rang, sir?" A bleary-eyed Mr. Chunk stumbled into his room, still buttoning up his jacket.

"Mr. Chunk, a terrible malady has come over me this night." Patrice ran his palm over his chest, where the scars that *La Dame Blanche* had left still lay. "I feared that this night would be my last."

Mr. Chunk's eyebrows knitted together with worry. "Shall I fetch the doctor?" he asked.

"No-no." Patrice shook his head. "This is not something that can be cured with ordinary medicine."

"Sir?" Mr. Chunk looked confounded.

"Help me downstairs." Patrice struggled out of bed and, leaning heavily on Mr. Chunk, he stumbled downstairs to the library.

"Please, light the fire. I am so very cold," Patrice mumbled.

Patrice stumbled over to the panel that would open the secret entrance to behind the bookcase and pushed the lever. With a gentle rumble, his private sanctum opened up. He had recently had this secret chamber redecorated. What was once old and cobweb-lined was now exquisite, filled with all manner of secret texts and artifacts that had once belonged to the man from whom he had inherited all his wealth. In the middle of the sanctum was a circle, inlaid in fine mosaic.

The symbols in the mosaic glowed as he stumbled into the middle and sank to his knees. Carefully Patrice stretched his arms out and closed his eyes, willing himself into the golden light that separated the two realms.

Nothing happened. He tried again, this time willing himself into the space where he knew the barrier should lie, but around him was no light. The barrier hung around him in dark, ragged tatters.

What has happened? he wondered as he watched a cluster of wood sprites slip across into the realm of Light, each carrying a rabbit skin with which to disguise themselves once they reached the other side.

One of them stopped for a second and looked at him. "Quick! Get in there before they close it again," he said, before scampering off after his friends.

Someone has damaged the barrier, Patrice realized with growing dismay.

And if there was no barrier, there was no need for warlocks.

He watched a pair of nains clatter over the divide. Evil little dwarves; part of the satyr family, with hooves instead of feet. Their high-pitched giggles disappeared into the night.

This needed to be fixed and quickly, by the looks of things. And as Grand Master of the brotherhood sworn to be the guardians of the barrier, it looked like it was a task that would fall to him.

Patrice lifted his arms and reached into the depths of his power. Slowly he started chanting the dark words that brought forth the aether. The ground started to tremble. Artifacts and chandeliers rattled, and suddenly a burst of energy surged up. It strummed and throbbed as it gushed along the remnants of the old barrier, filling in the gaps and repairing the rips. Patrice let his sight extend across the length of the barrier. He could almost feel every snag and flaw, as the energy he was exuding glided into place. But then he felt the barrier hit something large and very solid. A giant battleship, crammed into the space between the two realms.

He let the resistance give and a new wave of power surged up and spliced the ship in half. The ship exploded in midair and remnants of fuselage scattered into both worlds.

His strength gave out and his legs buckled underneath him as he sank to the floor. He felt his palms press against the cool mosaic beneath him and he fought to steady himself. For a few long moments, all he could hear were his deep breaths, filling his lungs with much-needed air. Then laughter started to bubble up inside him. He threw his head back in triumph as he felt the energy of the barrier surge within.

"Oh, Eleanor, you are priceless," he said, once his laughing fit had abated. It did not take much mental agility to figure out that she had tried to move something too large for her abilities through the divide. "An airship, of all things? What were you thinking, you stupid, stupid girl?"

The impact of the dirigible must have shortcut the system that held the barrier in place, and with it the whole thing had collapsed. Luckily it was only a temporary collapse, thanks to him. Patrice sat back and smiled. It was a most fortuitous turn of events. And what an opportunity it was—for now it was the Shadow Master's power that maintained the barrier between Shadow and Light.

He now held the ultimate control.

"Excuse me, sir, are you all right in there?" Mr. Chunk knocked discreetly on the paneling.

"Fine, Mr. Chunk," Patrice said, his mind still reeling with the implications of what he had just achieved. He struggled up from the floor, straightened his pajamas and stepped out of his sanctum.

"Mr. Chunk, prepare my toilette, please."

"Sir? But it's three o'clock in the morning," Mr. Chunk said as he stood and left the half-made fire he was busy laying.

"It might be three o'clock in the morning here, Mr.

Chunk, but it's midday somewhere else in the world and I have much I need to do."

"As you wish, sir," Mr. Chunk said and stepped back to attend to his duties.

Patrice sat down in one of the leather wingbacks by the cold fireplace. With a flick of his wrist, bluish flames sprang from the ashes, filling the room with warmth. He smiled to himself with a deep sense of satisfaction. Oh, what an opportunity this was indeed.

CHAPTER 20

Slowly Elle opened her eyes. The world drifted in and out of focus for a few seconds as her vision adjusted to the light. She saw an ant perched on a large green leaf, just inches from her nose. It was extraordinarily large compared to the ants she knew in England and it had reddish brown bands round its belly.

The ant rose up onto its hind legs and wiggled its antennae at Elle, tasting the air.

She frowned at it. What was this little creature trying to tell her? She was sure there was something she needed to remember, but somehow it all seemed too much of an effort. All she wanted was to close her eyes and drift back into the blissful darkness of sleep, but the ground beneath her was damp and cold, and the knobbly roots of trees were digging into her ribs.

No, she had to wake up. With great effort, she opened her eyes again. There were three ants on the leaf now. They all wiggled their antennae at her and she watched in fascination as a fourth joined them—then a fifth.

The ants turned to one another and then back to her. It was rather comical as it looked exactly as if they were having a conversation.

Were they discussing the fact that a giant pink lump of flesh had just fallen from the sky? She could almost sense their excitement at her arrival.

Fallen from the sky . . .

The thought made Elle sit up abruptly as realization

came flooding back. The world tilted and spun for a moment before it righted itself again. Then the pain set in. Every muscle and bone in her body ached. She looked down at herself. She was covered in mud, but her arms and legs seemed to be in working order. There didn't seem to be any bleeding anywhere, and she was definitely alive.

She groaned and rubbed the large lump on the side of her head. Something must have knocked her out on the way down.

Down where? Was she on the Light side or in the Shadow? It was hard to tell. She looked down at herself again. She was covered in leaves and bits of vine and other strange fragments of jungle debris, some of which looked suspiciously like cobwebs. Her limbs felt normal and not strange, like they did when she was in the Shadow.

This was the realm of Light, she was sure of it.

Above and around her there were only trees and plants. They stretched so high above her that she could not see the sky. Everything seemed to be alive and mobile in the steamy heat.

She checked her holster, but it was empty. Her gun. She needed it. With frantic movements, she started rooting through the undergrowth in search of it.

"I'd watch where I put my hands if I were you. Those are fire ants. If they touch you, you will know all about it," Dashwood said from behind her.

She swiveled round to see him sitting on a log. "Captain! You're alive."

"Just about." He touched the side of his head where the blood had dried into a dark crust. "What on earth happened?"

"Pirates broke into the bridge and started firing. The glass shattered and I think you were hit by all the stuff that flew about the cabin when the air rushed in. Then the Aeternae came on board. Heller gave the order to abandon ship and we crashed in the escape balloon."

She did not want to start explaining the finer intricacies of exactly *why* they had been under attack in the first place, and she hoped Dashwood would be too concussed to ask.

Dashwood ran his hand through his blond fringe. "The rest of the crew?"

"Mr. Kipper was shot." She shook her head.

Dashwood looked away. "Kipper was a good man. A bit maudlin, but a brilliant pilot."

"I think Heller got most of the crew out, sir. They took off in the gliders. With a little luck they should have made it to Bangkok."

"And . . . the *Inanna*?"

Elle shook her head again. "The Aeternae were on board. Along with other pirates. There was a lot of shooting and fighting when we launched in the escape balloon." Elle bit her lip. Now was not the time to tell the captain about the fact that she crashed his ship into the barrier. Every instinct was telling her to keep quiet about the Shadow realm for now. She would tell him later, if there was a later. Because at this moment they had far more pressing matters with which to concern themselves.

"You should have let me go down with her," he said softly. "A captain should go down with his ship."

"I did what I had to do. I wasn't going to let anyone die unless I couldn't help it."

Dashwood leaned back and looked up at the tree canopy above them. He let out a low whistle as he scanned their surroundings.

"What?" Elle said as she followed his gaze. The trees were unbelievably tall and around them there was nothing but thick, lush jungle.

"I don't think we could have chosen a worse place to crash if we tried," he said.

"I don't think it's that bad." She rose and started pacing about. "At least we are alive and mostly unhurt, which is quite something, given the circumstances."

Dashwood let out a little laugh. "I suppose. I think *how* to stay alive is going to be the hard part. By my reckoning, the nearest civilization is about a day's flight from here."

"I'm sure if we walk a little we'll find a way out of here. Let me see if I can find my bearings," she said and started pacing toward one of the large trees.

Dashwood grabbed her elbow to stop her from walking. "You've never been in the jungle before, have you?"

"No, but I'm sure it's just the same as everywhere else," Elle said. "North is still north, isn't it?"

Dashwood shook his head slowly, his expression serious. "We have no idea where we are and no idea in which direction we need to go. We also have no idea how long we were knocked unconscious after the crash." He pulled his watch out of his pocket and studied the cracked glass. "And my watch is busted, so without the sun, there is no way of telling the time."

"Fair enough," Elle said. He was being annoyingly sensible. "So what do we do now?"

"Well, if we're lucky, we will have been out cold for a short time only, which means it is early afternoon now. I'd suggest we try and sort out some shelter for tonight."

He kicked aside a rotten log. It broke apart to reveal a myriad of crawling insects. "This place is full of critters. They are all hungry and we are the food. We are going to have to find somewhere safe to sleep where we won't be eaten alive."

Elle shuddered as she watched a very large, flat spider with long skinny legs skitter across the leaves. She really hated spiders and this place looked to be crawling with them. "You know what, for once, I think I agree with you entirely," she said.

"We need to look for water. Try to make a fire. And if we make it through the night, we can do what we can about getting out of here."

"Very well then," Elle said. She studied the thick undergrowth. To her right, the jungle appeared slightly different. It was hard to tell for sure, but it looked as if the leaves of the plants had been crushed and some of the vines had been torn, like something large had passed through there. She pointed in the direction of the broken foliage. "We need to look in that direction."

She set off before Dashwood could stop her again.

"Wait!" he said, and then she heard him stumble after her.

She pushed aside the vines and undergrowth as she followed the trail for about a hundred paces.

"What are you doing?" Dashwood said, coming up behind her.

"Look," she said, pointing upward.

Before them, about six feet off the ground, was their escape balloon. Or at least what was left of it. The canvas hung flaccid from a mass of tangled rigging cord and the basket was on its side, but intact.

Elle took a running leap up to the tree and grabbed the edge of the basket. She hung there for a few seconds before the whole tangled contraption collapsed onto the jungle floor. She had to duck to get out of its way as the canvas settled on the ground.

"Well, that's handy," Dashwood said, walking up to the basket.

"Would this be of any use?" Elle dragged the storm rider's knife out from where it had become lodged in the wicker. Up close the bone-handled blade looked bigger than it had when it was in the Aeternae's hand. The blade was long and broad and deathly sharp.

"Where on earth did that come from?" Dashwood said, examining it.

"One of those storm riders jumped into the basket with us on the way down."

Dashwood stared at her, his surprise evident on his face.

"I shot him and managed to tip him out of the basket before he killed us both." She shrugged. "Which reminds me—do look around to see if you can find my gun." She pointed at her empty holster. "I think I dropped it while I was hauling the dead guy out of the basket."

Dashwood shook his head in amazement. "I think you have just doubled our chances of survival with this." He held up the blade and examined its edge. "I vote we make camp here for tonight."

"Agreed." Elle slapped her neck where a large mosquito had settled. "And perhaps a fire to keep these biting insects at bay."

"Ants and mosquitoes are the least of your worries," he said. "This is tiger country and we need to do something to stop ourselves from becoming a tasty snack." He lifted his coat to reveal his six-shooter safely tucked in its holster. "I am not so sure we'll be able to stop a tiger with this, but at least we'll be able to scare it away."

"I'm not so sure we should be shooting at tigers at all, Captain," Elle said. "We are in their home, not the other way round."

Dashwood gave her a strange look.

"What?" she said.

"You know, you truly have a unique way of looking at the world. Has anyone ever told you that?"

She smiled. "A few."

At that moment, the jungle responded with the most theatrical of gestures. Without any warning, fat, cool raindrops started to splatter on the leaves and ground.

Harder and harder it rained until the deluge poured off their heads and shoulders, drenching everything in seconds.

Dashwood threw his head back and opened his mouth, sticking out his tongue to catch some drops in his mouth. "At least we have water," he said after a few seconds of doing this. "Now let's try and clear a bit of space so we can make shelter. See if you can salvage some of those cords. We can cut the canvas of the balloon to make a tarpaulin and some hammocks. Stay here. I think I saw some bamboo a few paces that way," he said and strode off through the undergrowth, with the storm rider blade at the ready.

Elle wiped the rain off her face and trudged over to the basket. Suddenly alone, the shock that had been nibbling at the edges of her nerves finally set in. She felt her whole body go numb and she started shaking as the enormity of the situation hit her. They were lost and stranded in the middle of an impenetrable jungle. One misstep and they would die.

She stood like that, staring at the basket, for a good few minutes, as the rain continued to splatter down onto her head.

Then she balled her hands into fists. *No, I am not going to die here. I am going to live. And I am going to find the city of Angkor so I can save Marsh. That is what I will do.*

Her flight school training then took over and she reached forward and started to untangle the lines, winding them into neat bundles as she went. The rope was wet and made her fingers ache but she kept going, taking great pains to ensure that each skein of rope was perfectly wound. Somehow, maintaining standards out here seemed incredibly important.

"Here, let me help you," Dashwood said from behind her. He dropped a bundle of bamboo logs that he had brought back. "We can use a few of those thick ones to carry water in. Let's use the basket as a base," he said as he flipped it over to form a sturdy platform.

"And how about we spread the balloon over those branches to act as a roof?" Elle added. "We can cut it into smaller bits once it stops raining." Suddenly her mind started whirring with ideas as to what they could do, and a strange sense of exhilaration filled her.

They started pulling the canvas across the branches, tying the edges down with the cords, and soon the two of them were huddled under the makeshift shelter.

Dashwood built a little fire on top of the metal plate which formed the base of the basket. He piled up slivers of bamboo and a little bit of dry tree bark he had found. Carefully, he opened up a bullet and with the tip of the knife poured the gunpowder into the tinder.

"I thought we were saving those for shooting tigers," she said.

Dashwood just smiled at her. "Do you want to be warm or do you want to go hunting?" he said.

"Warm. Definitely warm," Elle said.

"Now all we need is one little spark," he said softly, so as not to disturb the delicate kindling.

Elle sighed. She did not want to reveal more about herself to him, but this was a serious emergency. They needed fire.

"Here, let me," she said. She closed her eyes and reached for a bit of aether she had stored. Gently she touched the gunpowder, focusing her energy at it. A tiny spark crackled off her fingertip, and the gunpowder flared and lit the tinder.

Dashwood's eyes grew wide. "How did you do that?"

Elle did not answer. She just smiled at him as she slowly fed the slivers of bamboo to the flames until they took.

Dashwood patted his throat and looked down.

"What is it?" she said.

"I seem to have lost my amulet in the fall," he said. "Pity. It was most handy."

"We'll be all right without it," Elle said.

"Do you know what? I think I am inclined to agree with you on that," he said.

And so they sat, huddled in their smoky shelter as the world grew dark around them.

"Well, it's not exactly the Ritz, but at least we are sort of dry," she said.

"It's going to be cold tonight," he said.

Elle nodded. It wasn't even properly dark yet and she was already feeling the chill of being wet creep into her bones.

"I'll take the first watch, if you want to get some sleep," he offered.

"Not that I'd be able to do much if anything attacked us," Elle said. She listened to the many sounds of the jungle coming alive in the darkness.

Dashwood laughed. "And this coming from the woman who fought off an Aeternae warrior with her bare hands. You know those guys are supposed to be invincible?"

"Desperate times call for desperate measures, Captain."

He was silent for a while. "Why did you save me, Mrs. Marsh? I mean, you could have left me for dead and gone with Mr. Heller."

"I couldn't," Elle said. "Besides, I owed you one for Socotra."

"But if you had, you would most likely be enjoying a cocktail in one of the bars in Bangkok right now."

"And instead, I am sharing a rather precarious perch on a basket in the middle of the jungle with who knows how many creepy crawlies. Present company included."

"Exactly my point," he said. "Even if you are some strange voodoo witch that can cross into different worlds and shoot sparks from her fingers."

Elle looked away, suddenly self-conscious. "You were right about me," she said.

"And how is that?" He was watching her closely, she could tell.

"I am trouble. Every person who comes into contact with me ends up either hurt or dead. Or they end up suffering some terrible disaster. It's like I'm cursed."

"I'm not going to argue with you about that," Dashwood said. "That's three ships you've cost me now, is it?"

Elle didn't answer immediately. Instead, she fed a few more bamboo slivers into the fire. "When I saw you on the floor, covered in blood, I just couldn't let yet another person get hurt. I had to do something. So here we are."

"I see," Dashwood said. "Well, I am grateful. I know I should be noble about going down with my ship, but I am quite glad I didn't die today."

"Well then, you are very welcome, Captain."

"And just so you know, I am going to reserve being angry with you for not telling me about the bounty for later. There will be much yelling at you when we get out of here."

"I look forward to it," Elle said dryly.

They were both silent for a long time as they listened to the rain drip-dripping onto their canvas.

"So what now?" he said.

"I think I want to carry on searching," Elle said. "Walk till I find help and then see if I can continue my search for the city."

"You have got to be joking," Dashwood said.

Elle shook her head. "No, I am completely serious. I have to find Angkor Wat. There is nothing else for it."

Dashwood thought about this for a few moments. "I think you are completely off your rocker, Mrs. Marsh."

"That may be the case, Captain. But a vow is a vow and continue on this path I must."

"I can't guarantee that I'll go with you. I, for one, am all for cutting my losses and going home."

"Well, then, I suggest we review this alliance when the time comes. Agreed?"

She felt Dashwood laughing at her in the dark. "One day at a time, Mrs. Marsh," he said. "One day at a time."

Somewhere deep in the jungle, a shadow stirred.

The great two-headed hound shook the rain out of his shaggy coat and sniffed the air. There she was. Freesias and engine oil.

He too had felt the shift in the barrier earlier. First there was nothing; he had watched the smaller Shadow creatures skitter across the void in abandon. Then the space had filled with a strange, dark energy which he found familiar. Whatever had caused the barrier to be temporarily down had been restored and that was all he needed to know.

The hound did not spend much time contemplating the how or the why of it, for these matters were beyond the limits of his understanding. He did, however, recognize that a certain darkness was now infused in the barrier. It was the same darkness that flowed through him.

All he knew was that this was a good thing; where his trail had been muffled and confused before, the scent now carried to him across the aether, clear and bright as a ringing bell. He could almost taste it on his tongues.

She was not far. He could smell the green of the bruised jungle that surrounded her.

The hound opened both his massive jaws and panted

with anticipation. His red tongues lolled out from between scimitar-sharp teeth in a grimace that was the closest thing to a smile his kind could muster.

Yes, she was close.

Here in this place, the hunt would be the best yet.

CHAPTER 21

Elle sat hunched under their makeshift tarpaulin cut from the canvas of the balloon.

It had been raining for a whole day and night without any sign of respite. In the end, they had decided to start walking and had trekked through thick jungle until they both felt that they could walk no more. Every bone in Elle's body ached and she was so numb from the cold that she did not even feel the ruts of the bamboo frame underneath her.

Below them in the crook of the tree a pathetic little fire smoldered. The damp smoke made her head ache and her eyes water, but at least it kept away the relentless barrage of mosquitoes and other biting insects that feasted on them at every possible opportunity.

Dashwood sat next to her, his legs drawn up before him. He was studying the edge of the blade in the dwindling light.

"Strange how such a simple instrument turned out to be the one thing that is keeping us alive," he said.

Elle was too miserable to answer. She stared at her forearm. On her skin, just over the place where the scars crisscrossed, was something black and squidgy. She nudged it with her finger, but it remained resolutely stuck to her skin.

"Leeches," Dashwood said.

Elle shuddered, but she was almost too tired to care. "If you have one on your arm, then you're guaranteed to have them in other places too," he said. "Better check. Would you like me to help?"

She grunted at his joke, which was almost funny in this context. "Now that's a comforting thought," she said. "Tell me, Captain," she said, changing the subject, "how do you know all this stuff? You seem to be an unending source of knowledge of the jungle."

Dashwood did not answer. Instead, he reached down and stuck a bamboo sliver into the fire. He waited for it to catch and then lifted the glowing tip up and leaned over to her. "Hold still," he said, as he stuck the bamboo into the leech. The creature squirmed as it sizzled, leaving a bubble of bloody spittle that Dashwood lifted off her arm. With an expert flick of the wrist, he cast it onto the ground below them.

"That is so disgusting," Elle said.

"You're welcome," Dashwood replied. "And I know this stuff because I used to be in the military. I really am a captain, you know."

He was quiet for a few moments.

"My family made their money on the gold fields in California. I was born in San Francisco and I joined the army as soon as I was old enough." His face grew grim. "I saw too much at too young an age, but the army was my life. I was drafted into a unit of Rangers that the government used for special missions. They sent us to Cuba. No one knew we were there. The Cubans were fighting the Spanish for independence. Investments were at stake. Tobacco, rubber, sugar." He stared off into the distance, remembering. "And so we were sent there by the government in Washington to see if we could sway the conflict. The war of ninety-eight only lasted a couple of months, but we were there long before war was formally declared. I spent months crawling though the mud and jungle. I saw what the Cuban rebels and the Spanish did to one another there while the world looked the other way, so I deserted."

He flicked a damp leaf off his arm.

"I ran away in the night. Stowed away on a merchant ship. Talked my way into joining her crew. And that was how I became the freebooter you see before you today."

Elle stared at him.

He looked away. "Not much of a story, but now you know. I can't even go home to see my mother, because if I do, I will be caught and placed before the firing squad for being a coward and a traitor."

"You may be many things, Captain, but you are no coward," Elle said.

He did not answer, and they both stared into the dark in silence for a while.

"What about you?" he said.

"Not much to tell," Elle said. "My father is a scientist. Specializes in spark thaumaturgy. He is the younger brother, so we never had any money because my uncle Geoffrey inherited it all along with the title and the peerage. My mother died when I was young, so I don't remember her. I grew up, failed spectacularly at being a debutante and snaring a husband, so I decided that the only sensible thing to do was to become a pilot, so I did and here I am, as you see me today."

"I'd say you did all right in the husband department. You must be a fairly comfortably off widow, yes?"

"I am not a widow," Elle said. "My husband is still very much alive."

"And you're sure about that?" Dashwood said.

"You were there." Elle said. "That night strange things happened."

"Indeed they did. Hence my question."

"I believe so. I honestly do," she said.

Dashwood sighed. "Look, this might not be my place to say, but speaking as a man, I don't think I would leave you if I were in that situation. I would find a way to stay."

Elle gazed into the flames for a long while. Could Marsh have stayed with her if he had really wanted? Perhaps she really was a widow, after all. Everyone in the world seemed to think that. Everyone except her. Perhaps it was time to face the fact that she might not find Angkor Wat—or Marsh, for that matter. In fact, she would be lucky if she survived this whole ordeal at all.

Oh, voices of the Oracle. Do you know how much I need your counsel? What should I do?

As usual there was no answer from them. Elle hugged her knees a little tighter.

Dashwood gave a little laugh, breaking the silence. "Do you know it took me weeks to get away from the Misses Pankhursts? They took me home, trussed me up before the fire, fed me more tea and suffrage literature than any man could possibly absorb. And then they would not let me leave!"

"Really?" Elle said. "They seemed like such capable women. What on earth would have made them want to hang on to you like that?"

Dashwood was silent.

Elle gave him a sharp look, and then her eyes grew large with the realization. "You didn't!" she said.

"Miss Pankhurst is a fine woman with a modern outlook on life. She had no objections at the time." Dashwood shrugged. "The objections came when it became apparent that no marriage proposal would be forthcoming."

"Captain, you are incorrigible," Elle said. "If I had a parasol, I would be clipping you about the head and face with it right now."

Dashwood laughed. "In the end I had to escape through a window when they were all asleep."

"Poor Christabel. I really hope her heart did not break too much because of you," Elle said.

"I hope so too," Dashwood said, surprising her.

"Say, I thought the jungle was supposed to be this hot, steamy place," Elle said, changing the subject. Discussions about the captain's liaisons were making her uncomfortable. She nudged the edge of the tarp with the thin bamboo cane she was using to poke the fire. "I'm British and I am certainly up for a bit of rain, but this is worse than Wales."

"It's called the rain forest for a reason, you know," he said.

"I suppose," she said. "But no one said it could be so cold at times."

"We should keep moving," he said. "Find something to eat."

Elle groaned at the thought of food. "Oh, what I would give for a lovely plate of roast chicken right now." She closed her eyes as her mouth filled with saliva. "Followed by strawberry tarts. My stepmother makes the best roast dinners ever."

Dashwood groaned next to her. It was a sensual sound that emanated from somewhere deep within him. "Steak and eggs. And chocolate fudge cake," he said.

"Hmm, that would do too," Elle said, lost in dreams of food.

"I had hoped that perhaps some of the crew would find us. Or that we would stumble on the *Inanna*. It's strange that there is no sign of any wreckage anywhere. We must have drifted further than I thought . . ." His voice trailed off.

"I know," Elle said.

"There's something very wrong about all this." Dashwood looked at her. "Why on earth would all those ships go after us? And the storm riders on top of it all. I mean, those guys tend to be so careful about selecting their prey that one hardly ever sees them." He shook his head. "What on earth could have made them venture out this far?"

Elle held her breath. She did not want to discuss this with Dashwood because it meant revealing things she did not want to tell.

"Surely the rumored treasure of Angkor Wat can't be all that. I had never even heard of the place before you told me. And pirates are looking for gold all the time, so it's not like our little expedition was that out of the ordinary. Why did they all go to the trouble to follow us from Socotra? Surely not out of vengeance for the death of one man."

Elle closed her eyes. "I don't know either," she lied.

"Perhaps it has something to do with the fact that you are the widow of an extremely wealthy and powerful nobleman with connections to the Shadow world," he said. "Maybe your family put together the reward for your safe return. Although I'm sure I would have heard about it if that were the case."

She looked at him sharply.

"I read." He shrugged.

"There are some people out there who would pay a lot of money to get their hands on me." It was as much as she dared to say.

Dashwood thought about this for a little while. "There is more to this. I can feel it in my bones."

Above them, thunder rumbled. "We need to find people. We need to find food and shelter," Elle said. "Who knows how long we'll last out here—"

Dashwood put up his hand to signal for her to keep quiet. On the tree trunk next to him, a giant black spider had appeared. It was hairy and bigger than the size of a hand. The creature sat perfectly still, its thick, articulated legs poised gracefully, mesmerized by the fire they had made.

Ever so slowly, Dashwood lifted the blade he was holding and skewered the creature against the tree. The spider carried on wiggling even though it was clearly dead.

"Arghh! That is the biggest spider I have ever seen!" Elle shuddered.

"It's also the tastiest spider you will ever eat," he said.

She shook her head. "No. I'm sorry. But no."

Dashwood shrugged. "I have seen these in the markets in Siam. The local people fry this type of tarantula and eat them as a delicacy. Apparently they are quite delicious." He picked up a thin piece of bamboo from their stash and carefully set about affixing the spider to the stick.

Elle stared at him in horror.

"What?"

"You're telling me you're going to eat that spider?" she said.

Dashwood shrugged. "Of course I am. It's food and I am very hungry. And if you're very nice to me, I might even share it with you." He lifted the stick in order to examine his dinner, which had now mercifully stopped wiggling. "Don't tell me you are going to turn all girly and squeamish on me, Mrs. Marsh. I knew it was only a matter of time before your highfalutin sensibilities took over."

"I am not highfalutin," she said.

"Oh yes you are. And the sad bit is that you don't even know it half the time."

Elle bit her lip. She was not about to be upstaged by this man. Not here. She stared at the spider with a mixture of revulsion and fascination. For some unbelievably strange reason her treacherous stomach rumbled in response. The thought made her entire body break out in goose bumps, but somehow the notion of eating a spider didn't seem all that ludicrous. Perhaps if it was cooked properly . . .

Elle shook her head. It had been two days since they'd eaten a real meal, and if she wanted to live to see the city of Angkor, she had to do whatever was necessary to survive this.

She had to.

The matter decided, Elle hopped off their platform and wiped her hands on her trousers. "Well then, Captain, I will see if I can find us a bit more of that dry wood. You should look around to see if there are more spiders about. Perhaps that one has a friend."

Dashwood started laughing. "Brave words, but will you put your money where your mouth is when it comes to the crunch?" He waved the spider at her.

Elle crossed her arms and lifted her chin defiantly. "If spiders were good enough for Miss Muffet, then they are good enough for me," she said, taking the blade from him. "Fire her up, Captain, I'll see what I can do about finding more wood."

It had stopped raining. Elle was chopping down whatever she could find that was dry enough to burn in the underbrush. They were going to need a big fire, she decided. Fortunately, the jungle was quite dense where they were and there were quite a few patches of dry bamboo, so it was easy work. When she returned a few minutes later, Dashwood had indeed found another spider and he was slowly turning their dinner on a little spit he had set up over the flames.

"I caught you a tarantula all of your very own," Dashwood said.

"Oh, how wonderful," Elle said with growing trepidation as she sat down next to him.

"You know what, Mrs. Marsh?"

"What?" She stared in fascination as the little hairs on

the legs and bodies of the spiders caught alight and glowed red for a few seconds before turning to ash.

"When I first met you in Amsterdam, I thought you were a stuck-up wife of a rich man, playing at flying airships because you were bored and had more money then brains. But actually, you're all right." He handed her the tarantula.

"Thank you, I think." Elle took the stick gingerly and stared at the charred spider on the end of it. She turned it this way and that, somewhat unsure of where to start.

Dashwood watched her with a growing expression of amusement on his face.

"Well, bottoms up," she said. "This probably tastes better hot than cold." She shut her eyes tightly and took a large bite of the cooling mass of legs and body. She did this deliberately as she wanted to fit as much of it into her mouth as she could. She knew she might not be brave enough to do it twice.

Roast tarantula tasted exactly how one would imagine a spider would taste. Burnt crispy with a hint of ash on the outside and all gooey on the inside. Elle swallowed, feeling every nerve in her body shudder in revulsion, but she persevered. The spider was food, she told herself. And she needed food to survive. And besides, she was not going to allow Dashwood to show her up.

She swallowed the chewed mass and opened her eyes. Strangely enough, it really did not taste that bad once you made a point of forgetting that it was a giant, hairy spider.

Dashwood was staring at her in shock, his own spider still untouched and cooling on the stick in his hand.

"Is something the matter, Captain?" she said sweetly. For effect, she took a second bite, finishing off as much of her dinner as she could in one big gulp.

Dashwood had turned a little green around the gills as he stared at his spider. "I was only kidding. You know,

doing it to see if you'd scream. I didn't think you'd actually *eat* the spider," he said.

"Oh no you don't, Captain. You've killed and cooked
it, so you had better eat it. Those poor creatures did not
die just so you could tease me." She put her stick aside,
immensely grateful that the spider had not been bigger.
"Come along now, chop-chop. Waste not, want not."

She watched Dashwood, a smile hovering on her lips,
as he took a bite. He looked as if he was about to expire
with revulsion as he chewed and swallowed and gagged.

Elle sat back on the platform with a growing sense of
satisfaction. What a story this would be to tell one day.
If they survived long enough to tell it.

The next morning, bright, dappled sunshine broke
through the chilly mists that lurked on the forest floor.

Elle woke with her head on Dashwood's shoulder. In
search of heat and comfort, they must have gravitated
toward one another during the night.

"Good morning," Dashwood said next to her.

"Good morning." Elle rubbed her face. She looked
about her. "Well, that was rather silly. Both of us falling
asleep like that. Who knows what could have crept onto
us in the night," she said, looking about.

"You looked like you needed the sleep, and I didn't
have the heart to wake you," he said.

"How very gallant of you," she said.

Dashwood slipped out from under their tarpaulin and
stretched. He straightened his crumpled shirt as much as
he could and strolled off into the bush to attend to na-
ture's necessities.

Elle sighed and pulled out her compass. It was most
fortunate that she always carried it in her pocket for
good luck, as she would have lost it in the crash if she
had stowed it. She stared at the needle as it wound round
and found north. Knowing the general direction was re-

assuring, but without a fixed point of reference she needed to take a bearing, they were still as good as lost. She looked around.

"So, where to next?" Dashwood said as he stepped out of the underbrush.

"Well, we have been walking in an easterly direction, sort of. That's the best I can do," Elle said. She looked up at the tree that formed the basis of their makeshift sleeping arrangement. The trunk was split into a number of thick boughs that had been most useful for lashing their tarpaulin to. In the morning light the boughs also looked infinitely climbable.

"I think I'll go up there and see if I can find a landmark," she said. "At least we know there are no tarantulas left in the tree."

"I'll give you a hand up," Dashwood said. He knitted his fingers together in order to form a stirrup for her. Elle clambered up the tree. Higher and higher she went until the branches started bowing.

"Can you see anything?" Dashwood called out.

Elle scanned the sky through the boughs of the tree. "Looks like there is a mountain to the southeast," she said.

"Yeah?" Dashwood was looking up at her.

"Let me just take a bearing." She pulled her compass out and started lining it up with the sun. It was a tricky task as she needed the compass to lie straight, which meant she had to lock her legs in order to let go with her hands. Carefully she wedged her boot into the notch between two thick branches.

She was so engrossed in her compass that she did not notice the green snake she had disturbed with her boot. Silently, it slithered up the branch next to her.

"Got it!" Elle called down as she placed her compass in her pocket. She put her hand out to steady herself and it took her a moment to realize that instead of the branch, her fingers were wrapped around the cool scales of the snake.

"Whoa!" Elle called out in fright as she let go. The snake hissed at her and Elle reared backward, losing her foothold. She let out a scream as she tumbled to the ground.

"Elle!" Dashwood yelled as he ran over. He leaped up onto the platform and grabbed her as she fell. They both landed heavily on the bamboo, while the snake dropped into the undergrowth and disappeared.

"Ow," Dashwood said as soon as he managed to catch his breath.

"Ow indeed," Elle said. She found herself on top of Dashwood, chest to chest, with his arms around her shoulders from where he had caught her. "Thanks for breaking my fall, just the same," she said.

"You're welcome. Did you get bit by that snake?" He made no move to get up.

"No, just got a fright."

The moment stretched out between them and suddenly things were awkward. Elle started to struggle, pushing herself up and away from his chest.

"Easy there," Dashwood said as he started moving away too, but their platform had not been built to absorb the shock of heavy falls, and in that moment, the rope and vines they had used to lash the bamboo poles together slipped and gave way. With a groan and a crack the platform collapsed and they both rolled over and tumbled into the mud. To add insult to injury, the water that had accumulated in the tarpaulin above them splashed to the ground, drenching them completely and extinguishing the embers of their fire.

"Get off me!" Elle rolled Dashwood off her and sat up. In addition to being soaked, she was now also covered in the most foul-smelling mud imaginable. Dashwood, on the other hand, had missed the worst of the mud altogether.

"And thanks for breaking *my* fall," he said. His teeth were very white against the general dirt on his skin.

He held out his hand and helped Elle up out of the mud.

"Are you sure you're not hurt?" he said.

"No, I think the snake got a bigger fright than I did. Apart from a few scrapes and a bruise or two I think I am still in one piece." She wiped the mud off her face and despite herself, she started laughing. It was the kind of uncontrollable hunger- and fatigue-filled laughter that welled up from deep inside. The kind that cannot be suppressed. She laughed and laughed until she was bent double and gasping for air.

Dashwood started laughing too.

Eventually Elle managed to straighten up. She wiped some of the mud off her brow and flicked it onto the ground. "Well, at least it will deter the mosquitoes," she said.

"I think it might do more than that," Dashwood said. "We had better get you washed off. Even small cuts can get very nasty out here if left untended."

"Well, Captain, then I suggest we follow my bearing to the mountain. That way," she said, pointing ahead of them. "We will either find people or, at the very least, we will be up high enough to spy where we need to go. What do you say? Are you with me?"

Dashwood gave an exaggerated sigh for effect. "Against my better judgment, Mrs. Marsh, I choose to be with you. But if you end up getting me killed, I am going to be very annoyed with you."

She stuck out her hand and shook his. "Then we are agreed."

He wiped off the mud from his trousers which Elle had transferred to him. "A pact sealed in mud," he said.

She pulled out her compass and studied it for a moment. It had, mercifully, survived her fall from the tree. "It's that way," she said.

Dashwood peered into the jungle. "Well, one guess is as good as another right now, so that way it is." He picked up his machete. "Lead on, Mrs. Marsh. Let's hope we can find a nice hotel with running hot water along the way."

CHAPTER 22

The trek toward the mountain through the jungle was not easy, for woman cannot travel on roast spider alone. As the day wore on, it became hotter and hotter. Humidity rose up from the ground, steamy and dank, and threatened to suffocate them. Thirsty and weak from hunger, Elle found that she had little energy for banter. They slashed their way through the never-ending mass of undergrowth and vines with a grim determination, always heading uphill and always keeping an eye on the compass.

After what felt like an eternity of green foliage, the thick undergrowth opened up quite abruptly. Elle and Dashwood stumbled into a clearing, both of them hot, sweating and gasping from exertion.

Elle looked around. Most of the vines were missing, perfectly rectangular rocks were tumbled about as if they had been left there by a giant and in the clearing were some of the biggest trees Elle had ever seen. Between their thick, drooping roots, Elle could make out delicately carved stone arches.

"It's a building," Elle said as they stared at the ruins.

"Looks like a temple," Dashwood said, stepping over a fallen branch.

"Do you think it might be . . . ?" She did not dare say the words. Things never happened that easily. At least not to her.

Dashwood shook his head. "No, I think it's probably another abandoned temple. Looks old, though."

Elle ran her hand over one of the carved lintels. "People lived here," she said. Seeing evidence of other humans suddenly seemed very strange and incongruous here in the middle of the jungle.

Dashwood cocked his head, listening.

Elle strained to hear too. Alongside the relentless din of jungle noises there seemed to be another sound in the clearing too. She could detect a soft hissing on the periphery of her hearing that had not been there before.

"I think I hear water," Dashwood said. "It's this way." He started walking along, following the sound which grew steadily louder.

They clambered up some steep rocks and stood in awe.

"Would you look at that," Dashwood said, panting for breath. Before them, a wide waterfall, about fifty feet high, splashed over fat, dark rocks and into a pool that arched out gracefully before them. A fine mist spread out, covering everything in soft coolness.

"Look at all that water," Elle murmured. At the sight of it, her skin started to itch from the layers of sweat, mud and insect bites that covered her. "And a mango tree!" she exclaimed. To the side of them was a smallish tree, drooping with greenish yellow fruit. "Pass me the knife!"

She ran up to it and pulled the fruit off the tree, using the blade to slice off chunks of mango then biting into the juicy fruit, eating it straight out of the peel.

Dashwood joined her and soon they were both covered in sticky yellow juice.

"I think that's probably the best thing I've ever eaten," Elle said, swallowing.

Dashwood did not answer her, for he was too busy stripping off his clothes and boots.

She looked away quickly, only to see his shirt and trousers land on one of the rocks beside her.

"Perhaps—"

She did not manage to finish her sentence because Dashwood gave a loud whoop and ran toward the pool.

"I was going to say perhaps we should check the water for snakes or crocodiles, or deadly rocks first!" she called after him, her back still turned away from the water. "Also, you're not supposed to swim directly after eating."

He did not answer. All she could hear were the delicious splashing sounds of someone swimming.

She turned round.

Dashwood was immersed up to his neck in the pool and he was busy scrubbing the dirt from his face and hair with much vigor. She could see the sunlight playing on his broad shoulders and farther down his torso as it refracted under the water.

He stopped washing when he noticed her staring at him.

"Oh, come on, Mrs. Marsh. Are you seriously going to play the prim matron? After all we've been through in the last few days?"

She snorted. "I assure you, I am far from prim. In fact, I could probably teach you a thing or two." She immediately regretted her reply, for out loud it sounded so much more provocative and flirtatious than it did in her head.

"Only one way of finding out," he called back. "All joking aside, this water is the best thing ever. And there are no snakes or spiders. Not as far as I can see. Just clean, pure water." He scooped up a handful and drank it down.

She took a step closer. The pool did look very inviting. Dashwood started laughing at her. "Are you really that prudish? I promise you, you don't have anything I've not seen before."

His taunting annoyed her. "Standards are standards, Captain. Without them, we would descend into chaos. Please turn your back until I am in the water." She started unbuttoning her shirt and tugging at the laces of her corset.

"Are you serious?" he said.

"Yes, absolutely. I don't want you seeing me and then having all kinds of lascivious thoughts every time you look at me afterward. Especially since I don't know how long I have to be stuck out here with you. And besides, I am a married woman, so no peeking."

Dashwood sighed with exaggerated exasperation and turned his back to her, continuing to scrub himself.

Elle pulled the last of her laces free, unpinned her hair and stepped out of her clothes. Using her hands to cover herself as best she could, she gingerly stepped across the rocks and pebbles toward the edge of the pool.

The water was cool at first, but she sank into the pool with a groan of relief. Dashwood had been right—the water was like a soothing balm over her skin. It fizzed and whooshed around her with an energy that replenished her tired body. But Elle was too enthralled by the luxurious feel of the water washing over her to care about any errant Shadow tricks, and with great satisfaction, she ducked her head under the surface, feeling the cool against her face.

"See? Was I lying?" Dashwood said as she emerged. He swam up to her, stopping about a foot away in the water.

"Yes, you were. This is even better than you said."

She turned away and ducked her head underwater again to rinse the sweat out of her hair.

But something under the surface made her want to open her eyes. Here, the water was flecked with gold light. It moved and caressed her body with an exquisiteness she had only ever experienced in the Shadow realm.

Was this a place of magic? she wondered as her head broke the surface of the water. She took a deep, cleansing breath to fill her lungs with the cool, rich air.

Shadow and Light be damned, she thought. Right now she honestly did not care one jot about the two realms and all the problems that surrounded them—all she wanted was to bathe here in this place for as long as she could.

She swam across to the waterfall with slow strokes, her body slipping through the water with a sensuous ease. At the edge, she found a rock that had been worn smooth by the water and carved out into a hollow where she could sit. She ducked her head under the splashing water, allowing it to run over the contours of her body and through her long hair, snaking the auburn tresses in rivulets over her pale breasts. Elle lost all sense of space and time and, for a few exquisite moments, she became one with this place. She stayed under the pounding of the waterfall until her skin could take no more. Slipping out from under the spray, she ducked into the water, down into the colder depths of the pool and up again, her sensitized skin relishing the feel of the sun-warmed surface.

"You are the most beautiful woman I have ever seen," Dashwood said softly.

Elle opened her eyes and found herself face-to-face with him. She had been so caught up in the magic of the water that she had completely forgotten about the fact that this man was here with her. But there he was, his large, warm body in the water next to hers.

She started to say something to rebuke his rather obvious flattery, but something in his expression stopped her.

He was being completely and utterly sincere.

He reached up and ran his hand under her floating hair, admiring its red-gold hue with a reverence which made her ache inside.

She swallowed, suddenly overcome with an irrational and urgent desire for him. "I—" she started saying, but he interrupted her by placing his lips over hers.

The touch of his mouth on hers felt seismic. The shock wave of their connection seemed to come from the water itself, fracturing her inhibitions. All the emotion she had been holding back for so long thundered through her like a tidal wave, ripping away all the careful, protective constructs she had built up inside.

Elle was swept away by the deluge; her only lifeline was the man holding her and she clung to him like a drowning soul.

Somehow they found themselves back on the hollow seat, the cool rock against her back as they touched with warm hands and mouths. Then he was inside her and she welcomed him, opening up to him with an urgency neither of them expected. They moved together, the exquisite friction building until she gasped and they both climaxed with such force that Elle could feel the water vibrate around them.

Afterward, he carried her to a sun-warmed rock where they lay in the golden light until they were dry.

"I don't really know what to say," Dashwood murmured. He was lying stretched out behind her, his fingers lazily combing her hair.

"Shh. Don't say anything. Sometimes it's better that way," Elle said softly.

Dashwood kissed the top of her head. "Let's leave this jungle. Forget about the lost city. Come away with me. We can find another ship. Crew it up and fly. We can go wherever you wish."

She did not answer.

Dashwood continued, "I know I don't have his power

or his money, but I can give you a good life, Elle. We are good together, you and I. I'll even go legitimate, if you ask me to."

She turned and put her hand against his cheek, where the soft stubble tickled her hand. "Logan, I can't. I made a vow."

He sat them both up and he looked at her. "Why not?" She saw the hurt in his eyes that she was causing and she felt her heart break. "He's gone and your vows ended when he passed over, Elle. You are free to live your life."

Dashwood was right. The last words Marsh had spoken to her were that he wished for her to live and be happy without him.

And he did not come back for you, even though he knew where you were . . . The thought tore through her.

She reached up and kissed Dashwood again. His hands ran up and over her shoulders to cup her chin. The touch of his fingers sent shivers through her as it had when they were in the water. She felt desire for him stir deep inside her.

She could love this man. She could make the life she had always wanted with him; a ship, the freedom to fly where and when she chose, with someone who saw the world in the same way she did. All of that lay before her, bundled up in the heart that this man had just offered her.

Their kiss ended in a little sob that came from the deepest, most broken part of her heart. How cruel the wyrdweavers were to finally grant her everything she had ever wished for when it was impossible to accept it.

Dashwood looked at her with concern. "Please don't cry," he said.

She shook her head. "It's not that. You don't understand. Hugh was the love of my life. I promised to love him forever and now I don't know what to do."

Dashwood's expression grew stern. "I am here and he is not. Does that not tell you everything you need to know?" he said.

"I know," she said softly. "I need some time to think. To sort things out in my head. It is a very big promise I need to turn away from. Do you think you could wait for me? Even if it is for a little while?"

Dashwood ran his thumb across her cheekbone, rubbing away a few drops of moisture. "I will wait for you," he said softly, and she could see the sincerity in his eyes.

She put her arms around him and they held each other for a long time, sun-warmed skin on sun-warmed skin. Around them, the jungle hissed and buzzed in time to the rushing pulse of the water at their feet.

Elle felt Dashwood's muscles tense for a second. "I think we should get dressed."

Elle lifted her face off his shoulder. "Um, perhaps," she murmured.

"No, I think we should get dressed right away," Dashwood said. "We are no longer alone."

Elle looked over her shoulder and gasped in mortification. On the bank of the waterfall stood a monk dressed in maroon and saffron robes. His head was completely shaven, and in his hand he held a long staff.

"Oh my word," Elle said as she lifted her knees and tucked her feet close to her body to cover herself.

The monk did not move. He just stood gazing across the pool with a serene calmness that made Elle want to shriek with embarrassment.

"Stay where you are, I'll get our things," Dashwood said. He stood up and walked over to collect their clothes, striding along completely naked with apparent nonchalance.

The monk did not bat an eyelid.

Dashwood returned and dropped her things on the

rock beside her. "I will see if I can distract that fellow from staring at your beauty by asking if he can help us," he said as he pulled his shirt over his head and dragged his jodhpurs on.

Elle dragged her shirt over her head and fumbled with the laces of her corset. All her fingers suddenly felt like they had turned to thumbs, but she managed to get into her clothes eventually.

She was busy lacing up her boots when Dashwood strode over with the monk in tow.

"Elle, this is Hari. He speaks French."

"Bonjour," Elle said.

"Bonjour, Madame." The monk bowed. His expression gave absolutely no indication that he had witnessed them in a most intimate of moments just minutes before. For that, Elle was so deeply grateful she almost hugged him.

"He says we have been swimming in a sacred spring," Dashwood said. "There is a temple at the top of this hill."

The monk nodded and pointed toward some rocks that were just visible in the water. "The sacred springs. Carvings of the lingam and yoni. Man part and woman parts," he said, gesturing at the geometric designs, "bring power to the water. Make it strong, fertile for the people."

Elle stood up and peered at the rocks he had pointed out. They were indeed carved in fine bas-relief. "Hold on, are those . . . ?" She felt herself blush as she suddenly recognized the rather obvious phallic shapes of half the carvings. They had simply felt like smooth, round rocks underfoot before.

"I think they are. There are a thousand of them carved in the river around here, if I understand Hari correctly," Dashwood said.

"Very strong energy. 'Specially for someone with the

special energy inside them, like you," Hari said in his broken French. One corner of his mouth curled up slightly in a ghost of a knowing smile.

Dashwood started laughing. "It certainly was that, my friend," he said, giving the monk a hearty pat on his shoulder.

Elle felt herself turn crimson with mortification.

"Say, is there any way you can tell us where we might find food and transport?" Elle said, pointedly changing the subject. "Perhaps the nearest town?"

Hari nodded. "We go to the temple. They give you food and place to sleep. Show you way to the village of Siem Riep. Lots of people there. And airships. People who speak English."

Elle felt her eyes fill with tears of relief. There would be no more being lost among snakes and spiders and other horrible things.

They had found rescue.

CHAPTER 23

The temple at Phnom Kulen was, as Hari had said, a steep trek up the mountain, along a series of wooden footbridges and carved stone steps. The place consisted of an interconnected series of buildings, some with roofs made of palm fronds; others appeared to be caves, hollowed out in the sandstone.

Some were dedicated to worship, others for meditation and then there were the living quarters. Unlike other holy places, this monastery seemed to be a place full of ordinary people.

At the sight of the monk, dark-haired children ran out to see the strangers he was escorting. They smiled and laughed and pretty soon it became a game to see who could get close enough to touch Elle and Dashwood.

The children were followed by men and women, all curious to see who had arrived at the monastery.

Hari started speaking rapidly to them, and after a few nods and instructions, Elle was handed over to a group of women. They took her in hand, sweeping her off to the bathhouse, all the while muttering. Elle could not understand what they were saying, but by the way they were examining her mussed up hair and dirty clothes she was sure they were talking about the state she was in. As she walked, she cast an eye at Dashwood, but his back was turned and he seemed to be deep in conversation with Hari.

After her bath, the women rubbed coconut oil over

her skin and brushed her hair until it dried in soft, glossy waves. Even though she did not speak their language, the universal understanding of all things feminine seemed to carry them along. There was much chatter as they admired the deep auburn color, which they seemed to find exceedingly amusing. Elle in turn admired the women with their rich, glossy hair and their easy smiles. They seemed so free and happy, and she felt sad that her own world was so constricted by protocol and convention.

After what appeared to be much debate, it was decided that frangipani blooms were to be fixed into the braid they were making in her hair.

Elle was given traditional clothes. A tunic and skirt made from soft cotton in a blue-green that echoed the color of her eyes and a pair of leather sandals. Free from corsets and trousers that chafed, the strange exotic dress was surprisingly comfortable. She smiled her thanks for the kindness of these people as best she could, and then she was escorted to the eating hall for dinner.

Elle was surprised to see that it had grown completely dark outside while she had been busy with the women. She was even more surprised to see that the monastery offered food for anyone who might be hungry—as long as they ate with appreciation and mindfulness, all the while observing the vows of silence that most of the monks kept.

Elle was so hungry she could do little to stop herself from falling into the bowls of rice and strange cooked vegetables that were served.

It was here, while stuffing gorgeously fragrant greens into her mouth, that she felt someone sit down next to her. Dashwood. In her hunger, she had not noticed him when she came in.

"Enjoying your dinner, I see?" he said. She noticed that he too had been to the bathhouse. He was also wearing a shirt and a pair of loose cotton trousers she had seen the other men wear.

Elle paused, her chopsticks holding a large piece of food halfway between her bowl and her face. "Um, well it has been a fairly trying few days, Captain. And spiders are not that filling."

"So we are back to calling me Captain now," he said.

Elle put her hand on his arm. "I'm sorry. It's force of habit. Please think nothing of it, Logan."

He smiled at her, but she could see that she had hurt him and she felt terrible for it.

He put his bowl down next to hers. It contained the remnants of a fiery vegetable stew flavored with coconut.

"Are you not eating?" she said.

"I think that might be my sixth helping. If I eat any more, I think I might explode."

At that point, Hari glided up to them.

"My English friends. How are you feeling now? I trust that you are better now that you have taken care of your bodily needs."

Elle smiled at him and inclined her head with gratitude. "Thank you. We owe you our lives."

Hari too inclined his head, returning the greeting. "It is our belief to respect and preserve all that is living." Then he smiled at them. "Would you care to take a walk with me before we take some rest?"

Elle looked at Dashwood. "It's still very early," she said. "It gets dark quickly here in the jungle."

Hari smiled at her benevolently. "Here we go to bed early because we rise before the sun to pray and meditate."

"Well, then we would be delighted. And I am very tired, so a good night's rest is perhaps exactly what I need."

They rose from the bench where they had been sitting

and strolled out into courtyard, at which point Hari started telling them all about the significance of the buildings and fountains around them.

"Hari, could I ask you something?" Elle said, once they had completed the circuit.

"I will answer if I can," the monk said.

"We are looking for a city. A lost city, built centuries ago by the Khmer. They called it Angkor Wat. Do you know of it?"

Hari's face went very still. "I know of it," he said.

"Really?" Elle felt herself grow excited. "Do you know where we might find it? Is there a map or something?"

Hari was silent for a very long time. In fact, he was so still that Elle thought he might not answer.

She looked up at Dashwood, who was standing beside her. The light of a lantern illuminated the side of his face, giving it an eerie glow in the darkness of the jungle night.

"The Temple City is not lost. We have always known where it is."

"You do?"

"It is a very sacred place," Hari said. He looked around, as if searching for the correct word. "The holiest of holy. Is that how you call it?"

"Yes, a holy place. A temple." Elle felt her excitement grow.

"It is no place for outsiders who seek only gold. I do not know what is within your hearts, so I cannot take you there." Hari shook his head.

"Oh, Hari." Elle felt like weeping. "We seek the place because we seek answers. I have come so far to see the *apsara*. I must ask her something."

Hari stared at her for another long while. "You, lady with the light inside and who cast no shadow. You are not like other outsiders I've seen before," he said thoughtfully. "I wonder why that is so?" Hari's French seemed to be growing stronger as he spoke to them as if he was rapidly remembering a language he did not often use.

Elle nodded. "Yes, I am special. There are . . . things about me which I can never speak of, and this is why I must go to that place."

Hari looked very unhappy, his eyes darting about as if he were looking for a means of escaping this conversation.

Elle felt Dashwood's hand on her arm, warning her to back down. "Perhaps it's time to go to bed. We are very tired. Our trek through the jungle was filled with hardship, so please forgive us," he said with a kindly voice. "We are sorry if we have caused offense."

Hari bowed. "In controversy, the instant we feel anger we have already ceased striving for the truth, and have begun striving for ourselves," he said with a serene smile. "Now I must say good night, my friends. I show you to your beds now." He rose and started walking, motioning for them to follow him.

Perhaps it was because they were foreigners, or because Hari seemed to have assumed that they were husband and wife, but Elle and Dashwood found that they had been assigned a hut of their very own, set a little way from the rest of the monastery. They had expected a mat in one of the segregated dormitories that the monastery kept for pilgrims.

The hut was in the traditional Cambodian style, set on wooden stilts and with a wood and roof made of palm fronds. Inside, it was furnished simply with a sleeping mat on each side. These were raised off the floor on a low bamboo platform with a fine mosquito net draped over the top.

Alone inside the hut, in the light of a single candle, the enclosed space suddenly made things seem awkward between them. Elle bumped into Dashwood's elbow as she turned her back to unwind the sarong she had been given.

Dashwood unexpectedly bent forward to untie his boots and their foreheads bumped against each other, which made them both recoil and laugh.

"I think we have been given their very best accommodation. I didn't see any other beds with mosquito nets," Dashwood said.

"Well, I for one am eternally grateful. I don't think I've ever been this tired." Elle yawned.

"You got that one right," he answered.

"I have to admit, lying down on a proper bed, protected from insects, is probably the best feeling yet," she said.

"The very best?" he said with a chuckle.

Elle felt her cheeks grow hot. "Oh, you know what I mean," she said.

"I meant what I said at the waterfall, you know. About us going away together. I still do." He paused for a moment. "There have been many women. A man like me tends to get around a bit. It's just the way things are if you live the life I lead."

Elle did not answer, afraid that she might break his confession.

"I don't know," Dashwood continued. "Perhaps it was this place, but it's never been like that . . . like it was today . . . with anyone." There was a rawness in his voice that made her insides ache for him. This was the real Logan Dashwood, honest and brave, with none of the bravado and theatrics he normally used to protect himself.

"I felt it too," Elle said. The words felt inadequate, but she did not know what else to say, because she also wanted to be honest with him.

They lay listening to the sounds of the jungle spilling into the hut.

"Can I ask you something?" he said after a little while.

"Of course," Elle said.

"You told Hari that you were special. I take it that has to do with the fact that you cast no shadow. Why is that?"

Elle stared up at the moonlit folds of her mosquito net. She owed him the truth, that much was plain, consequences for herself be damned.

"I am the Oracle. I am the force that holds the folds of the universe together." She shook her head. "This is very difficult to explain but I am everywhere at once—in both the Shadow and the Light at the same time and this is why I cast no shadow. I don't understand exactly how it works, but this is how it's been for me, my mother and all my grandmothers before them."

They listened to the crickets outside.

"It also means that I can speak prophesies and slip between the realms of Shadow and Light. You saw me do that when we were in San Francisco. My . . . late husband was on the Council of Warlocks. He . . . fought for my freedom because even though the warlocks are traditionally supposed to be our guardians, they have never treated us well. Instead they use us for their own means and so all the women in my family die young. My own mother died at the hands of such men when I was only a baby."

"So *that's* how you did that neat trick with the golden light," he said.

"Yes, I have learned how to manipulate the barrier. I can shift into the space between the two realms. At least I used to be able to do it, but something is wrong with the barrier and I cannot enter. It has been ever since the *Inanna* crashed."

"Hmm," Dashwood said.

"Hugh sacrificed much so we could be together. We both did. And then I lost him to the Shadow realm. I watched him turn into a wraith before my very eyes and that night my heart broke into a million pieces. Even now, it feels like there is just broken and bloody mush where it used to beat. Hugh worked so hard to keep me safe from those who wished to harm me that he forgot to take care of himself."

As soon as the words started tumbling out, she found that she could not stop. "All of it is my fault and this is why I need to find the temple. Inside it somewhere dwells the queen of the *apsaras*. She is said to have the ability to tell a person the answer to the question that they most ardently desire to know. Gertrude, Dr. Bell, told me about it. I need to know if there is a way to bring Hugh back from the Shadow realm alive. It is the one answer I seek more than anything."

"But there is more than this, isn't there?" he said, and she heard the slight edge to his voice.

"There is a man. Patrice is his name. He is very powerful and extremely dangerous. He is looking for me. I heard in Socotra that he has offered a reward of one hundred thousand pounds sterling to any man who would bring me to him alive."

Dashwood pushed himself up onto his elbow and looked at her. "Damn it, Elle! And you did not think to tell me, your captain, about it?"

She sat up too, clutching the sheet to her chest. "I couldn't tell you. I didn't know he had set a price on my head until I bumped into Salty Ben in the tavern. In fact, it wasn't even then. It was only after I walked away and I heard the men talking."

"And before that? In all the time that has passed, did you not think to tell me that you were in that much trouble? Instead you chose to place my ship and all its crew in mortal danger so you could save your own hide?" He let out a low whistle. "One hundred thousand pounds? No wonder every scrappy two-bit tub within a ten-thousand mile radius was after us! Hell, even the Storm Riders decided to have a go!" He was angry now. She could hear the outrage in his voice.

"Logan, I did not know what else to do. I was all alone and I didn't know you. Not like I do now. In fact, I didn't even know if you had been sent to capture me in the first place. You do remember that you had been hired to kidnap me once. Plus, you put me in your brig and threatened to sell me to the highest bidder! How could I have confided in you?"

"And this whole time, all you wanted to do was find a way to bring your dead husband back. All this time you have been using me to get what you want." Dashwood ran his hands through his hair. "I am such an idiot. This afternoon meant nothing to you. The way you held me like I was the only person in the world . . ." His breath hitched in his throat. "I assume those were all lies too? A little diversion with the captain for fun. Tell me, was it?"

"Don't be like that! You know things are complicated. I have never lied to you about that . . ."

Dashwood flung his mosquito net aside and started searching for his clothes. He dragged on his trousers and flung his shirt over his shoulders, doing up the buttons with his back to her.

"What are you doing?" she said.

"I can't be in the same space as you, Eleanor. You sow damage and wreak destruction wherever you go and I don't want to be your next victim."

"Captain, please," Elle said.

He turned to her. "You don't care one bit about who and what you destroy—as long as you get what you want." He buckled his belt with a little more force than was needed, unhooked his mosquito net and flung it over his shoulder. "I am going to find a bunk in the pilgrims' dorm," he said. And then he was gone. The door frame of the hut shuddered as he slammed the door behind him.

Elle fell back onto her mat and squeezed her eyes shut. Why was her life so awful when she never asked for any of this?

The wyrd-weavers were indeed the cruelest of the Shadow creatures, and in that moment she hated them with every fiber of her being. And so, in the silence of the jungle night, Elle eventually drifted off into a deep sleep, agonizing over the bittersweet irony of it all.

But there would be no rest for Elle that night. The moment she drifted off to sleep, the world started accelerating around her.

"No, please," she begged as she felt herself dragged into the realm of Shadow not sure who—or what—had grabbed her. Faster and faster she slipped deeper into the Shadow than she had ever gone before until she found herself sitting on a marble floor.

She sat up, ready to lambaste Jack for not coming to her aid sooner, but around her was nothing but darkness and silence.

"Don't be afraid. You are safe here. And so very welcome, Eleanor," a woman said.

Elle squinted at the light that flared up. The woman was dressed in dark blue robes, not unlike the ones Elle had been forced to wear when she had been captured in Constantinople. She sat in a tall chair that appeared to be carved out of bone. Her long auburn hair was clasped in an elaborate binding of the finest gold filigree and the braid spilled down over her shoulder and into her lap, where her hands were folded serenely.

"My darling," the woman said. She smiled with kind eyes that were the exact color as Elle's.

"Hello," Elle replied. "I suppose I should start by asking what is this place and, more important, who are you?" She rose and was surprised to note that she was wearing the same robes as the woman before her.

Elle groaned inwardly. The last thing she felt like was more wearisome Shadow business. She scanned the gloomy surroundings for a possible escape route. They seemed to be inside a building of sorts. Tall stone columns rose up on either side of a long, rectangular hall that disappeared into the darkness.

The only source of illumination was two braziers on either side of the chair. They flickered wildly but managed to cast a modest pool of light.

"I am Vivienne." And then, a little emotional, she said, "Oh, I just want to say how wonderful it is to finally speak face-to-face. I never thought I would get the opportunity to do this."

Elle's gaze swiveled back to the woman. "Hold on a second, what did you say your name was?"

The woman's expression lost some of its composure and her eyes seemed to glitter a little. "Yes, my darling," she said with a smile that wobbled slightly. "I am Vivienne Chance. Your mother."

"Oh, for crying in a bucket!" Elle said.

"I beg your pardon?" Vivienne looked slightly confused.

"You have known all along that you could bring me here, yet you have waited all this time to reveal yourself to me? And now when I am saved and not about to die of hunger or thirst or be eaten by a tiger, *now* you choose to come for me?" Elle looked down at herself. "Hang on a second, does that mean I'm dead? Did something just happen to me while I was sleeping?"

"Oh, Elle, you don't understand. Please just listen to me for a moment."

Elle pressed her lips together and folded her arms

across her chest. "You have my undivided attention, *Mother*."

Vivienne took a deep, shaky breath. "We are in the temple of Delphi."

"Oh, rubbish. The city of Delphi was destroyed thousands of years ago."

"Aha, that's what they want you to think." Vivienne sat forward in her chair. "When Delphi was lost to the invaders, the Pythias banded together and used their combined strength to move the temple into the Shadow realm. They hid it carefully, where no one would look, and it has remained hidden here from the warlocks for all this time."

"Which explains the architecture," Elle said, looking up at the columns. "It's very, um . . . Grecian."

"I know you must be very angry at me," Vivienne said. "I know how hard it must have been for you to grow up alone, not knowing why I abandoned you, my darling. But we don't have time to discuss that now. In fact, we have no time at all." Vivienne stood up and looked over her shoulder. "If it is found that I brought you here, it would mean certain death for us both," she said in a fierce whisper.

"But you are already dead," Elle said. "Does that mean I am too? Can someone die twice? You are making me very confused."

"You are very much alive, my dear. I am dead. But I live too." A look of exasperation crossed Vivienne's face. "I don't have time to explain this to you. Later. When the time is right."

Elle closed her eyes for a moment and shook her head. From her experience, most conversations with former Oracles had a tendency to make no sense at all.

"This temple is a sanctuary for all the women who bear the name Pythia. When we die, we leave the realm of Light and our spirits come here where we are safe. It is from here that we foretell the future through the mouth of our chosen one, who remains in the Light."

"So what you are telling me, is that this is the place where the voices come from?" Elle said.

"Exactly. As the Oracles that have departed this world, we cannot interfere with the matters involving the strands of time and fate. Because we can see what may come to pass, our interference would cause untold chaos, as we would be interrupting time and space itself. But it is our duty to guard the living, and so by agreement with the wyrd-weavers and others . . . we are allowed to speak prophesies through the woman who is our conduit. It is up to those who hear us to make choices. We only supply the options."

"So where are the others?" Elle said.

"They are not here. Things work differently here, because in this place the layers of reality are so close together that it is possible to slip into one or another with great ease. I had to search long to find a pocket where we could be completely alone." Her expression grew fearful. "We must hurry, for someone might discover us at any moment." She reached over and took Elle's hand in her own.

"Well, get on with it then. Tell me what you need to say," Elle said. She was growing most impatient with all this.

Vivienne let out a ragged sigh. "With you it was different. When you grew into your power, you were alone and completely unschooled. Never before had an Oracle grown up so completely without guidance. And there was such terrible danger present that I begged the others to help, so we broke our most sacred rule and spoke to you directly. It is a step, I fear, that has caused much trouble and sorrow in the time that followed."

"The voices were not allowed to speak to me?"

Vivienne nodded. "We are only allowed to speak

through you when you tell prophesies. But you needed our help. Something had to be done." Her expression took on a determined look. "I do not regret our actions. Not one bit. No matter what anyone says about it." Vivienne gave Elle a reassuring smile, but she was not very convincing.

"Interesting," Elle said. "So why did they stop whispering in my head then?"

"You banished us, remember?"

Elle nodded. "You were being an enormous nuisance. You were interfering with my marriage rather than teaching me to be an Oracle, if I recall correctly."

"Yes, we erred," Vivienne admitted. "There are usually good reasons for absolute rules. Once my sisters and I started watching you, we found that we could not stop. Following your life through the days was absolutely fascinating. So much so that we ended up doing little else."

Elle felt herself blush. "Are you trying to tell me that I had my wedding night with my mother and every grandmother I've ever had watching?" She put her hands to her cheeks. "Oh, the shame."

"My darling, you must not think like that," Vivienne said. "We are all one here and you are part of that unity."

Elle rubbed her face, trying to clear the horrors her mother's revelation had conjured in her mind. "Please, go on," she said.

"When you banished us, my sisters saw the error of their ways. There was a vote and it was decided by the majority that we would never resume our interference with you again. It was too intrusive. But since then, we've had to stand by and watch as disaster upon disaster befell the world. And all of it as a result of what we did."

"Oh, I don't think it's that bad," Elle said. "So you

were bit nosy, but I really don't think you can call it an epic disaster."

Vivienne shook her head and looked deeply remorseful. "The truth is that time and space are fluid. Everything moves along the threads of fate as it was destined to do. But if you interfere with even one small part, the impact ripples across everything. The slightest ripple of a leaf falling on a pond could set in motion events that would result in an earthquake that kills scores upon scores of people."

"Are you trying to tell me that you are responsible for wars and disasters?"

Vivienne sighed and looked deeply weary. "Much darkness and misery will befall the world as a result of what we have done. There will be big earthquakes; disease and famine will ravage the world. There will be war. Millions will die before the wyrd-weavers can untangle our actions. They are deeply angry about it. If we are not careful, the wyrd-weavers will declare war on us. We will be destroyed."

This revelation made Elle pause. Were the voices really in that much trouble? Perhaps banishing them had been the best thing she could have done even if it had been by accident.

"So what is the important thing that you need to tell me? Someone could show up any minute, remember?" she said, bringing the discussion back to the present.

"Yes, of course. I have taken the decision to reveal the secrets of Dephi to you now, in your lifetime. The danger is so great that I think I am justified in my decision. I am hoping that once you know, you will be able to save us. And stop him."

"Stop who?"

"The Shadow Master," Vivienne whispered.

"Patrice?"

"Do not say his name. He has spies out there looking for us."

"Very well. So tell me the secret then." Elle felt herself grow faintly impatient at her mother's senseless prevarication.

Vivienne put her hands to her cheeks and rubbed her face in a mannerism that was remarkably similar to what Elle had done a few moments before.

"The barrier between Shadow and Light is no longer within the control of the warlocks."

"Is that so?" Elle felt her interest pique.

"There was a terrible disturbance in the barrier recently. It caused an interruption that allowed the Shadow Master to take control of the void. He now controls the aether, and this is a very, very bad thing."

"So that's why I can't access the barrier. It all makes sense now," Elle said. She had tried once or twice when it had been her turn to keep watch and Dashwood was asleep, but it had been to no avail.

"Can't someone tell the warlocks to fix it?" Elle said.

"The warlocks do not understand the origin of their power. They think that when they use an Oracle in order to gain power, that she is drained until she eventually wears out and dies."

"And then a new one appears?"

"Correct." Vivienne nodded. "But, in fact, the complete opposite is true. Every time an Oracle channels power, she grows stronger. But the power is corrosive and the human body as host is not designed to withstand its ravages, so the channeling takes its toll on flesh and skin and bone."

"So we do wear out then?"

"Only our bodies do," Vivienne said. "But when we die, we become creatures of pure energy. We come here." She gestured with her hand. "And, Elle, it is such a wonderful place. I have only brought you here, to a quiet corner of the temple, but you should see it! The whole place is filled with golden light, and we have fountains and gardens with green grass and fruit trees . . ."

"Sounds lovely," Elle said dryly.

"The most important thing is that we are not alone. There is so much love and companionship here. I know you will be happy and you will love this place as much as I do when you join us. We are family."

"But what about those we love who don't come here?"

Vivienne did not answer. Instead she produced a golden plum from the folds of her robes. She held the fruit out to Elle on the palm of her hand. "Please, have something to eat," she said.

Elle stared at the plum. It was absolutely perfect and ripe. It even had a few droplets of dew glistening on its unblemished skin. She felt her stomach rumble and suddenly the temptation to eat the fruit was great, but she managed to stop herself in time.

"It's all right, Mother. I am not hungry."

Vivienne put the fruit back into her robes with a wistful expression. "You are right. Tricking you into staying here with me forever is selfish."

"Please continue," Elle said. Agreeing with Vivienne at this point would only serve to send her mother off on another tangent.

"When the barrier between the realms of Shadow and Light was put up, the warlocks did not take into account the fact that the power they so desperately needed would be placed beyond their grasp. They did not appreciate that we are the ones who maintain the barrier, and the more power that is channeled through us, the stronger we become. They also do not understand that this in turn makes them weaker."

"Ha!" Elle let out a little bark of surprise.

"Ha indeed," Vivienne said. "Elle, what you fail to appreciate is the fact that we are more powerful than anybody knows. As the Oracle, you hold all of that within your hands. The entire realm of Shadow is yours to command. All you have to do is learn how to heal yourself from the ravages of aether channeling. If you can do that, you will be invincible."

Elle nodded slowly. Old Jack had called her his queen once. The reason why he did that made sense now.

She looked at her mother. "But if I don't learn how to heal myself, using this power will cost me my life."

Vivienne nodded. "Everything has its cost, my dear. Every single thing. But in return, you gain immortality filled with such bliss that it is hardly a price to pay at all."

Elle shook her head. "I am sorry, Mother, but I would disagree with you on that."

Vivienne sighed. "This is why I was counseled against telling you all this. From your point of view, it is hard to understand. We had no way of knowing what would happen once we told you. This is why it is so very important that you remember this about your power and how you might use it. The Shadow Master is searching for these truths. He is vain and ambitious and very, very dangerous."

"He is also a former docking clerk, so I would not worry too much about it if I were you. I can deal with him."

Vivienne looked distraught. "No, you are mistaken. He seeks the Oracle because he wishes to use her connection to the aether in order to crack open all of our defenses. If he succeeds, he will gain access to all we have and all we know. Once he has this, he will control everything." Her eyes grew large with fear. "We must not allow this to happen, for that would be far too much power for one individual to hold." She grabbed Elle's hand.

Elle flinched. Vivienne's hands were like ice. "It will be

the end of us all. The end of every living thing if he succeeds," she said.

Suddenly the light in the braziers flared up and then
flickered. For a moment, Elle could have sworn that she
could see Vivienne's skeleton. She pulled her hand out of
her mother's bony grasp and stepped back. The young
and beautiful Vivienne flickered back into view. She
smiled at Elle serenely.

"I'm sorry, but I don't accept what you are telling me
about my future. This place isn't all that either." Elle
looked at her mother. "And so, if it's all the same to you,
I think I might politely decline your offer, Mother."

Vivienne put her fingers to her forehead in a gesture of
measured frustration. "Please, Elle, you must heed my
warning."

Elle sighed. "Look, I will do what I can to stop Patrice.
I know I can manage him, so please don't be so worried.
You may take my word as your daughter on that. But as
for the rest, I think I will choose a different destiny for
myself, if you don't mind."

Vivienne snorted. "What? And you think that silly
stone *apsara* is going to help you?"

"I don't care about dominating everything in the universe. All I want to know is how to bring my husband
back. Nothing more."

"Oh, Elle, the *apsara* is not going to be able to tell you
how to do that!" Vivienne said.

"She will tell me what it is that I most ardently wish to
know. And the knowledge of how to bring Hugh back is
just that, so she won't have much choice in the matter."

Vivienne let out a little noise that sounded almost like
a whine. "The *apsara* will not be able to help you. Forget
about her. You have to believe me when I tell you this."

"No!" Elle said. She heard her voice echo down the
hallway. "I refuse to believe that. Not after everything."

Vivienne glanced over her shoulder into the darkness.

A low rumble started emanating from the gloom behind them.

Vivienne blanched. "Someone is coming. You have to go now." She grabbed Elle by the arm and led her to the chair. "Please, sit here."

Elle did as she was told. The bone chair felt smooth and cool under her.

She watched as Vivienne closed her eyes. Her mother's lips started moving in a fast chant.

Elle felt a strange rush of energy and suddenly reality started spinning and whooshing as she was transported through the portal Vivienne had created.

. . . *remember, I am here waiting for you always, my darling daughter. I love you more than words can say* . . . Vivienne's voice echoed in Elle's mind for a moment before she was catapulted back into the realm of Light.

Elle felt the soupy heat of the jungle enfold her once again. The buzz of insects and the calls of the myriad creatures that prowled the jungle at night filled her ears.

She opened her eyes and lay very still, willing the disorientation to dissipate. She lay there for a long time, just breathing slowly and waiting for the dizziness to settle.

Far off in the distance, Elle heard a wolf howl. It was a deep, unearthly sound which sounded profoundly lonely. She tutted and rolled onto her side. Wolves in the jungle. Honestly, she really was busy losing her marbles.

CHAPTER 24

From the observation deck, Patrice watched the ocean of dawn-tinged clouds turn orange. Dawn would break soon, but so far sleep had eluded him. He stared down at his hands. The little half-moons of his neatly mani-cured nails were a pale blue color, the skin of his fingers pale and clammy. He balled his fists to stop his hands from shaking. Strange things had started happening to him since the night he had reinstated the barrier. Stranger than usual, and he was a man who was rather prone to strange happenings.

"Everything all right, sir?" one of the flight stewards asked politely. "Would you like me to bring you a cof-fee?"

"Yes, thank you," Patrice said with a stiff smile. He had chartered the small passenger ship by buying all the available tickets himself. This meant that he was the only passenger on board a fully crewed dirigible.

It was rather extravagant, but he needed to make sure the ship was attractive bait, and there was nothing more attractive than a defenseless passenger ship. And who knew, the crew might make excellent bargaining tools later.

The steward appeared with his coffee, which turned out to be surprisingly good for airship fare.

Patrice sipped the dark brew appreciatively. They had crossed the Caspian Sea overnight and somewhere out there in the distance before them lay a mysterious mountain range shrouded in clouds. It was here that he would find them. The fabled Aeternae. The storm riders of the Hindu Kush.

He had been most surprised to learn of the air raid that had swallowed up so many pirate ships. The sensational news that the Aeternae had broken cover and were appearing over the skies of Siam had even reached the papers in London. There was much speculation as to whether the Empire was at risk, but Patrice knew that this could only be the doing of one person. And that person was Eleanor Chance.

Once the ingredients were all there, hatching his nefarious plan really wasn't that difficult at all. All it took was a little research and a few carefully placed inquiries.

He pulled out a small leather box from his pocket. Inside was a perfectly polished oval stone attached to a strip of leather. On it, numerous fine characters were carved out in Sanskrit. Carefully he lifted the stone and held it up in the light. It was a summoning stone, cunningly liberated from the vaults of the British Museum. He had orchestrated the theft by means of a series of carefully placed bribes. He pulled his arm back and struck the stone against one of the metal struts that arched up and around the windglass. The impact set off a soft subsonic hum, inaudible to ordinary human ears. Patrice repeated this two more times before carefully placing the stone back into its box.

It was done. He had sent out the call. All he had to do now was wait for the storm riders to answer.

He smiled despite himself. Yes, he knew where the Oracle was. And this time he was going to make sure she would not slip away.

Patrice did not have to wait long for the storm riders to arrive. In fact, he had just sat down to an early lunch when he noticed the crew whispering and walking off as fast as they could without causing alarm. In a way he almost felt sorry for them, he thought as he calmly finished his asparagus and quail egg salad. A steward cleared the table, his face pinched with worry. "I'm sorry, sir, but we are going to have to interrupt your luncheon."

"Why on earth would you need to do that?" Patrice said, dabbing a corner of his mouth with his napkin. He knew the answer, but he was taking pleasure in taunting the man.

"I don't wish to alarm you, but the captain has asked that we escort you to one of the escape balloons. There might be a little trouble with some pirates and we want to ensure that our passenger is safe."

"No," said Patrice.

"But, sir, we need to get you to safety."

Patrice shook his head. "Tell the captain that I am going nowhere. In fact, you can tell him to slow down so my guests can catch up with us. Tell him to open one of the cargo doors, so they may board easily."

"Sir, but these are vicious raiders. They will kill us all if we do that."

Patrice gave him a reassuring smile. "Oh, I don't think that is strictly correct. You see, I have an appointment with these gentlemen. So I think it might be more correct to say that they might kill some of you once they are on board. I, on the other hand, will be perfectly safe."

The steward blanched.

"Now go and tell the captain what my instructions are."

The steward wavered.

"Now!" Patrice barked.

He looked around the dining room of the dirigible with its silver tableware and starched linen. Yes, this would be a good place to await his new allies.

* * *

The dreadnought arrived accompanied by darkening skies. Lightning crackled in the clouds around them, and the passenger ship shuddered as it was boarded amid buffeting winds. Patrice put the summoning stone on the table before him and waited long moments as the Aeternae strode on to the ship. There were four of them. Three were tall and muscular, their skin tunics decorated in a macabre pattern of little bones. Patrice could see the little bones of bird skulls woven into the intricate patterns. The fourth man was small and dressed in a simple gray robe. The electromancer. The one who made the storms for the Aeternae to ride.

"We have been summoned. Who wishes to speak with us?" their leader grunted. Patrice noticed that his teeth had been filed into sharp points.

"Gentlemen, please sit." Patrice gestured for them to join him at the table. "Would you care for something to eat or drink?"

The leader of the Aeternae spat on the carpet. "We are not here to feast. Say what is needed."

"Very well," he said, holding up a conciliatory hand. "My name is Patrice Chevalier and I come with a proposal."

The Aeternae leader struck his chest with his fist. "Ga-Rok," he said.

"Well, I am pleased to meet you, Ga-Rok. How would you like to have access to as many ships as your heart desires?"

Ga-Rok frowned. The skin around the sharp, bony protrusions in his head wrinkled. "We are storm riders. We chase and capture all the ships we wish already. Why should we need more?"

Patrice shook his head. "No, no. What I meant is how would you like to join me? You bring your dreadnoughts and I will provide food and clothes for your wives and children. No one will ever go hungry."

This answer did not seem to have the desired effect, as Ga-Rok roared with indignation. "How dare you pass insult like that? The wives and children of storm riders are not starving or poor. We are good hunters." The other Aeternae were looking at one another and shaking their heads.

Patrice rubbed his forehead in consternation. This meeting was not going the way he had hoped.

"That is not what I meant. I meant that I will give you access to all the gold and riches you desire if you fight for me."

"Who will we be fighting?" Ga-Rok said.

"A war is coming," Patrice said. "Many will die, and I want to make sure that those who are with me are safe and protected. This is why I need you."

"This war is none of our concern. We will leave now." Ga-Rok started to turn away.

"Not so fast," Patrice said.

The Aeternae turned back to him with a look of ill-disguised amusement.

"I am the Shadow Master. I control the barrier between Shadow and Light. I also control him." Patrice pointed at the electromancer who was, at that moment, staring at him with wide eyes. "Just like I control all electromancers." Patrice made a sweeping move with his hand and the little man dropped to his knees.

The Aeternae gasped in horror and drew their wide-curved blades.

"You stop now!" Ga-Rok shouted.

"Come, that is no way to speak to an ally," Patrice said. "You see, you need me. Without me there will be no lightning and storms." Patrice paused and gestured for the Aeternae to put away their blades.

The electromancer in his grasp groaned in pain, and this seemed to galvanize the storm riders into action.

"What do you want, Shadow man?" Ga-Rok said.

"Ah, that's better. Now please sit down, so we can speak properly," Patrice said.

The Aeternae shuffled forward and sat down at the table. They looked hideously out of place and extremely uncomfortable—just the way Patrice liked it. He needed to show these savages who was their master, and this was a good start.

"So, as I was saying," he continued. The electromancer made a few feeble gagging sounds and waved his hands in desperation. His face had turned a peculiar shade of purple.

"Oh, all right, you may live." Patrice waved his hand and the invisible force that held the little man by the throat disappeared.

The electromancer collapsed onto the floor and rolled over clutching his throat. He made terrible gasping sounds as he drew deep breaths into his lungs.

"Do not hurt him anymore. We will listen," Ga-Rok said.

"An excellent decision, Mr. Ga-Rok." Patrice ran his fingers around the edges of the summoning stone. "Now, where was I? Oh yes. I am in need of an army. An army that will strike terror into anyone who hears its name. And you, my new friend, already have a reputation that I envy. So you bring your dreadnoughts when I call, and I will make your electromancers more powerful than they have ever been."

"How powerful?" With the initial shock over and his electromancer safe once more, Ga-Rok's eyes had lit up with the realization that this negotiation did, after all, hold some possibilities.

Patrice sat forward. "Powerful enough to attack cities. With no one to stop you."

The other Aeternae started talking rapidly to one another and nodding their heads.

"And you say we may take what we wish?"

Patrice nodded. "Within reason, yes. Once you have done my bidding, you may loot and pillage to your heart's content. Your wives and children will be covered in furs and gold."

"Gold!" the other Aeternae said with relish.

Ga-Rok crossed his arms. "And who are we fighting?"

Patrice laughed. "Oh, it is an enemy that is feeble. A woman."

This made Ga-Rok frown. "Why do you insult us again? We are strong. We do not fight weak women."

Patrice shook his head. "No, she is a witch with very strong powers. She will launch ships to try to stop me."

"This witch, we think we have seen her in the sky before."

"Ah yes, of course you have. She made half the airship disappear and left the other half hanging in midair, didn't she?"

"It was not a good raid," Ga-Rok admitted.

"Well, it is this witch and her ships that we will be fighting. And we will win the fight. I have foreseen it."

Ga-Rok nodded slowly. "If it is foretold, then we may not say anything about it." He pulled out a small dagger from the folds of his tunic and drew the blade across the back of his hand. A fine red line appeared. He looked at Patrice. "We make this pact in blood."

Patrice pulled a face. "Oh, is that really necessary?"

The Aeternae grabbed Patrice's hand and dragged the knife over his knuckles. Then he pressed the back of Patrice's hand against his own. "Two open hands. The pact is made."

"Wonderful," Patrice said as he pulled out a handkerchief to wipe his knuckles. He would have to go in search of some strong antiseptic the moment this meeting was over. These creatures were none too clean, judging by the pungent odor that emanated from them.

Ga-Rok looked around the dining room. "So now we take this ship. It has many shiny things."

Patrice shook his head. "No, my odiferous friend. I need this ship to go home in. But there will be others. I promise."

The Aeternae started muttering, deeply disappointed to hear this news. Ga-Rok stabbed his dagger into the table. "That is cheating. We have been summoned to plunder. How do you take that away from us now?"

Patrice sighed and reached into his breast pocket. He pulled out a booklet and flicked across the table to where the electromancer was sitting. "I assume you can read?" he said with bored contempt.

The electromancer nodded and picked up the booklet, starting to leaf through the pages. His face lit up as he took in the contents.

"It's the dirigible liner company's flight timetable," Patrice said.

The Aeternae frowned.

"It lists every flight between Paris and Tokyo for the next three months," he said, speaking slightly louder than he normally did.

"We will know where the ships are by this?" Ga-Rok's eyes started glittering with greed.

"You're welcome," said Patrice. "As long as you promise to leave this ship be for the moment. I have very important business to attend to—so important that there will be no raiding unless I complete it. Do I make myself clear?"

Ga-Rok nodded, somewhat distracted by the veritable smorgasbord of air prey the electromancer was describing to him.

"Right, gentlemen, shall I leave you to see yourselves out?" Patrice said pointedly.

Ga-Rok and his compatriots rose. He nodded briefly and they made their way out of the dining room with a stiff formality. This did not, however, extend to the hallway, and they broke into excited chatter as they made their way out of the ship.

Patrice smiled to himself as he took in the black elbow- and handprints that his new allies had left on the starched linen of the seats. Who cared if they were unwashed and horrible? They could fight like demons and that was what he needed.

Yes, nefarious plans really weren't that hard once you got the hang of them.

CHAPTER 25

Elle looked up from the stone bench where she had been sitting. It was mid-morning and the sun was shining, but here beside one of the fountains in the rich shade of a cassia tree, the air was cool and lovely.

She was sitting among trails of exotic orchids that bloomed from the most impossible of crevices, and for the first time in longer than she cared to remember she felt at peace.

She had been studying the battered journal that had traveled with her all this way in her coat pocket. Some of the text had been damaged by mud and rain, but there was still enough to work from.

She had been here at the temple for almost a week now. Dashwood had spoken less than a handful of words to her since their first night here, and she had hardly seen him, save for the odd encounter at meal-times.

This made her sad, because she found that she missed his banter and his easy manner. But despite the under-currents involving the captain, Elle felt well fed and rested. In fact, she found that she was growing increasingly fond of this exotic place.

"Good morning, venerable Hari," Elle said. She bowed her head with respect as she had seen others do during her time here.

Hari returned the greeting, bowing with his hands

pressed together. "*Chum reap sur.* Good morning. I trust that you are well."

"I am," Elle said. "In fact, I cannot remember the last time I felt as well from within as I do here."

"To enjoy good health, to bring true happiness to one's family, to bring peace to all, one must first discipline and control one's own mind." Hari smiled benevolently. "If a person can control his mind, he can find the way to Enlightenment, and all wisdom and virtue will naturally come to him."

Elle pondered this for a few moments. "I had never thought about it that way."

"What is it that you are studying?" the monk asked shyly as he sat down next to her.

Elle showed him the journal. "This was given to me by an archaeologist. A good woman who cared only about learning and understanding the world. Not money or treasure." She opened the pages to show him Dr. Bell's sketches. "She spent a long time reading about Angkor Wat in old manuscripts. She gave me this journal because she knew I had a question that only the queen of the *apsaras* could answer. It is in search of knowledge that I come to this place, Hari. Not anything else."

"I have meditated for a long time on this question," Hari said. "The answer you seek from me is something that I cannot give lightly." His expression was grave.

Elle bowed. "I accept that," she said. "And it is I who must ask your forgiveness for imposing my own desires upon you when I first arrived here. I have only been here for a short time, but I feel as if I have learned much by observing the example you and your brothers set for others."

"This is a good thing, for it is only by example that people truly learn." Hari turned to Elle. "The Temple City you seek is about fifty miles toward the south. To find it, one must simply follow the large canal that feeds into a lake. The city floats upon that lake," he said.

Elle nearly dropped the journal in surprise.

"You will need to walk for most of the way along narrow jungle tracks. Perhaps when we are closer, we can find a boat where the Siem Riep River becomes wider. But the journey will be difficult. I have foreseen it so."

"You said 'we'?" she said cautiously.

Hari inclined his head. "I have decided to make a pilgrimage to Angkor Wat. It has been a long time since I have been there and I believe that you will need me on this journey. The path that pilgrims must tread to Angkor Wat is both a physical and a spiritual journey. I know these ways."

"You will do that for me?"

"I will do that for you and for the captain."

Elle looked away. "I don't think Captain Dashwood would be willing to accompany us. I suspect he will make his own way from this place."

Hari shook his head. "He will come with us. But first you must speak to him."

Elle sighed. "I know. There is much that is wrong between us, Hari. My heart is broken in so many ways. I wish there was some way I could make you understand."

"You can search throughout the entire universe for someone who is more deserving of your love and affection than you are yourself." Hari placed his hands over hers. "That person is not to be found anywhere. You yourself, as much as anybody in the entire universe, deserve your love and affection," he said.

Elle frowned. Hari's words were almost as inscrutable as her mother's. "Oh, Hari, what shall I do? All I want is for all the things that I have made wrong to be right. I just want to fix what I have broken, but the harder I try to do that, the worse I make things."

Hari gave her a sharp look. "To ask of the *apsara* is not a simple matter. She takes away as much as she will give. You must prepare for the journey. You will be tested in many ways."

"I understand," Elle said.

He rose with a graceful rustle of his robes. "I will leave you to contemplate these things, but know that our journey cannot begin unless you make peace with Captain Dashwood."

Elle stared at the water fountain for a few long moments after Hari left. The monk was right. She could not leave this place without apologizing to Dashwood. It was the least she could do. As Hari said, she would just have to endure the journey and see what happened.

She found him in the shade of a hut, sitting cross-legged, cleaning his pistol. Like her, he was dressed in the traditional clothes of the Khmer: a cotton *sampot*—a type of baggy cotton trousers—and a loose wide-necked tunic. Elle's dress included a fine thin shawl, which she used to shade herself from the sun, in much the same way the Bedouin did. The pretty patterned material was cool and draped softly against her skin. Back home people might be absolutely shocked to hear her saying it, but these were possibly the most comfortable items of clothing she had ever worn. She had resolved to find a means to trade with the villagers, so she could take some of these clothes with her back home to England.

Her current outfit had been provided by the kind people of the nearby village. It was an act of charity that Elle had found immensely humbling. These people had little, but yet they gave without hesitation to those who were in need.

Her own English clothes, now washed and pressed, remained folded up in her hut where they had been left for her.

Everyone here walked barefoot, and after taking a long, hard look at her lace-up boots and thick socks, Elle had decided to do the same. She wiggled her toes in the warm dust. The sensation was lovely. The fact that this was the first time in her life that she had ever gone barefoot was a source of much mirth. Her new friends were utterly astonished to hear that people in her world put shoes on babies.

Dashwood's cleaning and maintenance of a deadly weapon in this peaceful place seemed somehow wrong. Incongruous. It was a stark reminder that they would have to leave soon.

He looked up at the sound of her approaching and his expression grew wary. She noticed that his blond fringe, normally so carefully combed back, was hanging over his forehead, and a healthy tan spread over his arms and face. He looked well. Alive.

"May I?" she said, gesturing at a shady spot opposite him.

"Suit yourself," he said.

She sat down, carefully folding her *sampot* under her. She watched him work for a few moments.

"Logan, I have been thinking."

"Yes?" His voice sounded guarded.

"You were right. I should have been more honest with you. If I had, perhaps we could have been more prepared for the attack. Lives would not have been lost. I'm sorry."

He nodded. There wasn't much more that could be said about the matter. All the while, his hands kept working, rubbing the cloth against the smooth metal of the gun.

"Also, I know I have hurt you."

He looked up at her.

"Please know that I never intended for that to happen. I—" Her voice caught in her throat. She wanted to tell him how she felt, but she felt so conflicted that the words simply could not form on her lips.

He sighed. "Oh darn it, enough with the groveling. You did what you had to do to survive, and I can't hold that against you. It's a harsh world we live in, us pirates. We all have to do things we are not proud of some time."

Elle smiled at him. "So you keep telling me."

He put the cloth down and started clicking the bits together, carefully checking that they were aligned.

"I just wanted to say that I am sorry," she said. It wasn't enough. She could see it in his eyes, but it would have to do.

"I am too," he said softly.

"I don't know what to do," she said. "I was fine. I thought I had everything together, that I was surviving. Then that day at the waterfall happened. And it was wonderful. Like you said, it has never been like that before. And it turned my whole world upside down. You must know that I felt what you felt too," she said. "And it has left me feeling more conflicted and confused than I ever thought possible."

He did not answer her. The only sound between them were the click and slide as he disassembled the gun again and started rubbing away some invisible speck of dirt with the cloth.

"It's all right," he said after a while.

"Is it really?" She looked up into his face.

He gave her a lopsided smile. "Of course it is. It's this place. I think all those fertility symbols in the river rocks makes the water do stuff to people. We both got caught in the water magic, is all."

"I think you might be right," she said, not believing a word of it. Let the man at least walk away from her with his pride intact. It was the least she could do after everything that had passed between them.

"Of course I'm right. I am always right. You should try to remember that for the future," he said.

She laughed. Her captain was back, she thought with a tremendous rush of relief.

She took a deep breath. There was one more thing she had to say. The most important of all perhaps. "I have been doing a lot of thinking, as I said."

"So have I," he admitted.

"I must find the city of Angkor. Hari says he's been there and he will take me there on a pilgrimage. It is only fifty miles away. So close." She picked at a thread that was peeping out of the seam of her *sampot*. "I wanted to know if you might find it within yourself to come with us. I need you," she said.

"Hari spoke to me too. I swear that sneaky old monk has been playing us all along," he said. He put his gun back into its holster and started cleaning his hands on the cloth. "Well, then I suppose we had better start getting our things together. Sounds like we have a long walk ahead of us. I'm not going to let you walk away with all that gold by yourself. We had a deal. Sixty-forty, if I recall." He stood up and held out his hand in order to help her up. "What do you say?"

His large hand felt strong and warm around hers when she took it. Close to him, he smelled like sunshine, gunmetal and the coconut oil he had been using to clean his revolver a few minutes before.

"I say we leave first thing tomorrow morning." Elle smiled at him. Here, in the sunshine, she had the sudden urge to kiss him, but he turned away before she could.

Yes, her captain was back, and the knowledge made her very happy even if she did have to ignore the fact that his smile could not quite erase the sadness in his eyes.

CHAPTER 26

The trek along the narrow jungle paths toward Siem Riep was not one for the fainthearted. After two days of walking from sunset to sundown, Elle was hot, sticky and burned from the sun. However, this time, things were different. They had food, water and a guide who knew the way. And so they made their way through the jungle, stopping off at villages and farms where Hari attended to the spiritual duties of his order for people they served.

"How are you doing back there, Mrs. Marsh?" Dashwood looked over his shoulder and smiled at her. They were both out of breath and sweating in the humidity.

"I think I preferred it when I didn't have anything to carry," she said, hitching up the bundle she was carrying, hooked over her shoulders like a rucksack.

Dashwood unclipped his metal water canteen—a gift from Hari—and handed it to her.

"How far do we still have to go today?" Elle said.

Hari, serene in his robes and staff, seemed entirely unfazed by the heat and the jungle. "Not too far. We can stay at the next village."

The jungle tapered off and the landscape opened up as they walked. Before them lay acres upon acres of rice paddy fields, punctuated by houses on tall stilts, their roofs thatched with palm fronds. Women and men shaded themselves from the sun in wide, woven conical hats and worked knee-deep in the waterlogged rice fields, while giant longhorn water buffalo grazed and lowed as they were herded along.

As they passed on the road, people bowed to Hari with their palms pressed together.

"No one would believe me if I told them I walked here," Elle said.

"I don't think they get many outsiders visiting," Dashwood said. Not all the faces watching them were friendly.

"Hari, are you sure this is the right place?" Elle asked the monk as they walked along the palm-lined footpath that led into the village.

"Yes, I have stayed here many times. The chief is very friendly. Big fat man. Very friendly." Hari gestured with his arms to indicate the chief's girth, which did indeed seem considerable.

They had reached a cluster of palm-thatched houses in what looked like the center of the village. People were standing in little groups, staring and pointing at them. This was very unusual because in the culture of the Khmer, staring and pointing was considered most disrespectful.

"What is going on here?" Dashwood said out of the corner of his mouth.

"Your guess is as good as mine," Elle said. "Look!"

An old woman in a brown *sampot* came stalking down the footpath. Her thinning gray hair was tied in a tight knot at the back of her head. As she walked she waved her thin arms, all the while shouting at them.

Hari blanched. He extended his hands in supplication, but the woman would have none of it. She walked up to Elle and before Elle could react, the old woman's bony hands clasped the hair on the side of her head. Her wrinkled face and eyes were alive with anger and she started shaking Elle about, all the while shouting at her in

Khmer. This too was most unusual as the touching of the head was an even bigger insult.

Hari had turned quite pale at the sight of the woman.

Elle was so shocked by the outburst that it did not ever occur to her to do something—until Dashwood intervened.

He grabbed the two women and wrenched them apart. Elle stared at the old woman, unsure what to do. The old woman, on the other hand, was full of energy. She was doing her best to claw at Elle even while Dashwood held her at arm's length.

"Seems like you have a new friend," he said.

"What did I do?" Elle said.

By this time, everyone had come to see what the commotion was. All the people around them were glaring with open hostility.

"Hari?" Elle whispered. "I don't think these people like us very much."

The monk started speaking rapidly and inclined his head, until eventually the old woman stopped fighting Dashwood.

"She says you may let go of her now," Hari said.

Gently Dashwood released his grip on the old woman who stalked off, casting filthy looks at them over her shoulder as she went.

"Come, we must go," Hari said.

"Wait, what about dinner and a dry bed?" Dashwood said.

"Tonight we make camp in the forest. It will be nice. You'll see." Hari started walking quickly along the footpath that led out of the village. It was a good half hour before Elle or Dashwood could get anything more out of him.

"What happened back there?" Dashwood said once they had stopped to rest.

Hari looked distraught. "The old woman is the village

wise woman. She can see things that others cannot. She says that she does not want, forgive me, Miss Elle to be allowed to come into the village. She says a dark thing follows her. Word has spread from other villages and farms. Something terrible came out of the jungle in the night. Something with terrible teeth, growling and sniffing, always searching for something."

Elle felt the blood drain from her face. "Did you say it was following us?"

Hari nodded. "It is probably just superstition, but sometimes superstition is more than enough, so for tonight, we are the guests of the jungle."

"I say we stop here," Dashwood said, looking around the clearing that was just off the road. "It looks dry enough for a fire."

"Yes, let us rest here for tonight," Hari said. "I have some rice we can cook for dinner."

Dashwood looked at Elle. "You don't by any chance happen to know anything about this strange darkness following you?"

Elle swallowed. "I have a theory, but it's not possible. It can't be possible."

Dashwood crossed his arms. "Let's hear it."

"I was warned that something had been sent out to find me. A Shadow creature. It's something between a dog and a wolf. It's a big black beast with two heads. Yellow eyes."

Dashwood frowned.

"But I trapped it in the Shadow realm the last time it chased me. It should be stuck there."

"The last time it chased you?" Dashwood's lips were in a tight line.

"Well, yes. Technically my body was on board the *Inanna,* but my Shadow-self had taken an unexpected trip into the other realm. It's complicated."

"The last time it *chased* you?" Dashwood said again.

"Look, I don't know what's going on," Elle said. "I honestly don't. It may be that it escaped when the barrier went all funny." She looked at her feet, suddenly ashamed. Yet again, she had let everyone down.

Dashwood drew his revolver and checked that it was loaded. "Not much we can do about it now. If it's out there, we'll have to face it one way or another. I'll take the first watch."

"I will stay awake too," Hari said. He was sitting with his legs crossed, his back perfectly straight. "On life's journey, faith is nourishment, virtuous deeds are a shelter, wisdom is the light by day and right mindfulness is the protection by night. If a man lives a pure life, nothing can destroy him."

Dashwood shook his head. "Whatever that means," he said. "Let's get the fire going."

The night was very dark. There was no moon and the sky was littered with a thick crust of stars.

Elle sat staring into the fire. She held a hot mug of tea from the pot Hari had brewed. The monk was still in his spot, sitting very still with his eyes closed. Beside her, Elle watched Dashwood's body move steadily up and down as his breath slowed in sleep. His revolver lay on the blanket next to her, at the ready. Beside the gun lay the storm rider blade they had carried with them from the wreck.

She closed her eyes in frustration. Would the constant parade of monsters and creatures through her life ever stop? She had to admit that the thought of saying yes to Dashwood, so they could get as far away from all the Shadows, was becoming more tempting every time she thought about it. Especially alone here in the dark of night.

High up in the sky no one seemed to be able to find her. Closeted within the iron bones of an airship she would be safe. Up in the sky, who knows, she might even be happy.

But what about when she had to go ashore? The thought niggled. Would she not simply be placing everyone within a half-mile radius in danger? Had not enough people died because of her?

A twig snapped.

Elle looked up and peered into the lush darkness around her. Something was out there. She could feel its strangeness in the air.

Everything went eerily silent. It was as if the very jungle that surrounded them was holding its breath. It was here. She could feel it in the hum of aether that surrounded her.

As silently as she could, she moved so she was crouching. Then she took Dashwood's revolver up in one hand and the blade in the other. She gripped them tight for courage, measuring the weight of the weapons. Then she rose to meet the danger. It was time to face the monster Patrice had sent for her.

Slowly she walked toward the edge of the camp. Her feet barely made a sound on the soft ground.

Outside the light cast by the fire, it was so dark that sight was almost useless, but Elle held firm. She listened. Instinctively her nostrils flared as she took deep breaths of warm night air. Something was watching her. She could feel its eyes following her every step.

"Come on, you bastard. I am sick and tired of all these games. Let's have you then. You and me, what do you say?" she whispered. There was no need to speak louder, for she was sure the creature could hear her heart pounding in her chest.

There was a soft rustle to her left and she swiveled round to meet it, but there was nothing.

"Come on!" she said a little louder. "Enough with the

skulking. Come out and fight like a man. Or a beast. Or whatever kind of mongrel you are."

Those are brave words. Brave but foolish for someone so helpless.

The voice came out of the dark to her right. Elle turned quickly and her breath caught in her throat. From the darkness, the massive black hound stepped forward. His yellow eyes glowed in the light of the fire.

"I am not afraid of you, dog. And I am not afraid to die. So either you do what you have to do right now, or leave this place and never bother me again."

The matter is not that simple, Pythia. You know it is not.

"Oh yes it is. I'll not have you bother innocent people who have no stake in this battle any longer. Enough is enough. You and I are having it out right here. Right now!" She did not bother to speak softly. She doubted it would matter anyway, because she had a feeling things would be over soon.

The hound let out a soft menacing growl and pounced.

Elle managed to fire a shot before the creature got to her, but the bullet went wide.

The weight of him knocked Elle to the ground. She dropped the blade as she fought to keep his massive snapping jaws from her. Round and round they rolled, kicking up a dust cloud filled with snarls and spit.

The creature locked one of his jaws round Elle's forearm and bit down.

Elle squealed in pain as his sharp teeth sliced through skin. She could feel its teeth touching the bone, deep inside her arm.

Holding the beast off with one of his sets of jaws around her arm, she reached back and punched the creature in the center of his other face. Her fist connected with the soft, sensitive wet part of his nose and she felt the bones of her knuckles give as it connected.

The hound let out a yelp of pain and shook his head, but the other set of jaws held her firmly. Slowly, he started dragging Elle away from the fire. As he went, he sneezed and shook his head to assuage his smarting nose.

She panicked. She could not allow this creature to drag her off into the undergrowth to do goodness knows what with her. She dug her heels into the ground as hard as she could, straining against the sheer force of the hound as he held on to her arm. She felt muscles and tendons tear as the dog dragged her.

Suddenly, Elle heard a meaty thump. It sounded not unlike a butcher's cleaver hacking into a side of beef.

The hound yelped in surprise, letting go of Elle's arm in shock as his heads swiveled round to see what had happened.

Instinct took over and, just in time, she rolled out of reach. Five shots rang out as Dashwood emptied his pistol into the dark mass of fur.

The hound yelped and jumped. As he turned, Hari leaped up, Aeternae blade in hand. He raised his arms and brought the machete down on the beast's neck. The hound yelped and scampered off into the shadows, the blade wedged firmly into the flesh between his massive shoulders.

Hari's robes were in a state of disarray and he looked rather out of sorts. "Through violence, one may solve one problem, but in doing so, one inevitably sows the seeds for another," he muttered. He stared with his eyes wide in the direction the monster had disappeared.

"What in the hell was that thing?" Dashwood said as he strode over, still holding his gun.

Elle lay on the ground holding her arm. Bright, hot pain seared through her, making her whole body shake from the shock of it.

"Oh no, Elle." Dashwood kneeled by her. Gently he lifted her and carried her to the fire.

"It's just a scratch," she said through chattering teeth.

"Hari, get some water boiling," Dashwood said as he started rooting through their things. He pulled out a beautiful sarong from Elle's bag. It had been a gift from the women in the village. He unrolled it and started ripping strips from the edge.

"Please, no," Elle started saying, but she was in too much pain to do anything. All of her attention was focused on gripping tight the searing pain in her arm with her spare hand. Hot, sticky blood oozed through her fingers.

"Dog bites are the worst." Dashwood's voice penetrated the fog. "Elle, honey, you need to let go so I can see," he said.

Slowly he helped her uncurl her fingers. She could see from his grim expression that the bites were bad.

"Hari, we need to clean these out before infection and rot set in. Who knows what filth that thing has been chewing on."

He rooted round his bags and pulled out a bottle of fiery rice wine, a strong liquor made from fermented rice and fruit. One of the villagers had given it to him with the instructions to drink a capful every day. Apparently it improved virility, among other things.

Gently Dashwood bathed Elle's arm in the hot water Hari brought. "Hari, I'm going to need you to hold her," he said. "Hold her as tight as you can."

Hari nodded, his face a picture of tension.

Carefully Dashwood extended Elle's arm. Then, working quickly, he uncorked the bottle with his teeth and poured the liquor over the bites.

Elle bucked and screamed as alcohol ran into the tear wounds along her arm. It felt like her whole arm was on fire and she collapsed, shaking from the shock. As carefully as he could, Dashwood dried her arm and bound it tight.

She was still shaking, but the alcohol smothering her injuries had jostled her into consciousness. Dashwood finished tying the wounds off. Then, very gently, he lifted Elle into his lap and cradled her there as if she were a child.

Elle was in too much pain to care. She rested her head against his shoulder, feeling the solid warmth of him.

"It's going to be all right, sweetheart," he said as he held her.

"My beautiful sarong," she whispered.

"It's all right. We'll get you another one in Siem Riep," he said.

"Do you think it will come back?" Hari said as he set about clearing away the mess.

"I emptied my gun into its gut, so it's probably slunk off to lick its wounds. If we're lucky, it will bleed out before morning."

"Let us hope the danger is gone," Hari said. "For us and for the people who live here." He peered off into the darkness, lines of worry furrowing his smooth brow.

"Say, you had quite a swing with that blade. Did you know that? If you ever come to America, I'm sure they'd have a place for you on a baseball team," Dashwood said to Hari.

Hari suppressed a small smile of pride. "It is not our way to kill or harm others, but sometimes great evil must be stopped." He bowed. "I think I will make us some tea now. That will revive and sustain us. I also have something in my pack," Hari added as he brought out a small packet of brown powder.

"Opium?" Dashwood said.

"For emergencies. This is an emergency," Hari said in a matter-of-fact tone. "We will mix it into the tea."

Dashwood helped Elle drink her opium-laced tea and

he held her in his arms until she stopped shaking. Then, ever so gently, he helped her lie down in her sleeping roll.

Elle felt her eyes grow heavy, and slowly the throbbing pain in her arm dissipated as the drug took effect. "We will go hunting for it tomorrow, won't we?" she slurred. ". . . must make sure it's dead. So it can't hurt any of the people here . . ."

"We'll worry about that tomorrow," Dashwood said. He kissed her forehead. "What on earth were you thinking, taking on a creature like that on your own? You are a remarkably brave and stupid girl in equal measures, do you know that?"

"Brave and stupid," Elle agreed. Then she drifted off into an opium-soaked oblivion.

The next morning, the sun was already high in the sky when Elle woke. She sat up quickly and immediately regretted it. Her arm felt three times the size it normally was and it was throbbing. At some stage during her slumber, someone had moved her into the shade of a tree.

Dashwood and Hari were both sitting around with anxious expressions.

She stared down at her arm. The beautiful patterned cotton of her former sarong was marked with brown patches from where the blood had soaked through. When she touched it, her arm felt hot and awful.

"How long have I been sleeping?" she muttered.

"Awhile," Dashwood said.

"I have managed to negotiate the use of an oxcart for us," Hari said. "The chief in the next village will help us. If we can walk there."

Elle struggled to sit up. The world spun around her and she fought a wave of nausea and pain as she moved.

"I can walk. Just give me a moment," she said. But despite her words she started vomiting behind a plant.

"How far is it?" Dashwood said. He looked concerned.

"Not too far. Perhaps less than an hour," Hari said.

"Then let's go," Elle said as she wiped her mouth with her good hand and dragged herself upright.

"Logan, do you think you could help me put this pack on to my shoulders?" she said.

"Elle, you are not going to walk like that," he said.

She gave him a brave little smile. "I will be fine, Captain. You did an excellent job with saving my arm. Remind me to ask you where you learned to do that once the buzzing inside my head has worn off."

There was much arguing in the ensuing minutes. Elle, it seemed, was remarkably stubborn when in a fever-induced state, and it took a huge amount of coaxing for her to agree that Dashwood and Hari would carry her things. Then there was a debate over which direction was better. Elle insisted that they needed her compass even though Hari had already been to the village and back.

And so the three of them set out to walk to the next village where an oxcart awaited them.

CHAPTER 27

Elle woke to find that she was in a proper bed, tucked in between thick linen sheets that smelled faintly of soap. She stared at the woven palm leaves, that lay layer upon layer on the roof tresses, quite unsure of where she was or how she had got there. She was growing mightily tired of these blackouts and awakenings. They were starting to do things to her mind.

A blue dragonfly buzzed in through the open shutters in the window, its iridescent wings humming as it made a slow circuit around the room. It hovered for a moment in the still, warm air before zipping out of the window again.

"Where am I?" she said as she struggled to sit up. Her mouth felt dry and sticky, the sweet residue of fever still on her lips. She flinched as she felt the ache in her arm. She looked down to see that it was covered in white, neatly wrapped bandages.

"Ah, splendid. You are awake." A stubbly-looking man in a white pinafore frock strode over to where she lay. His hair had been shaved the exact length of his beard, which gave the impression that his head was covered in a carpet of graying fuzz. In fact, the only contour to his face was a pair of glasses perched on the bridge of his nose. He stopped by the side of the bed and casted a practiced eye over her.

"May I?" he said, with a reassuring smile.

Elle nodded and he rested his cool hand on her forehead, testing her temperature. "Yes, much better. Normal, I should say."

"How did I get here? Or perhaps first I should ask where am I?"

"You are in the village of Siem Riep. This is the medical outpost of the fever hospital in Phnom Penh. I am Dr. Poulin. At your service," he said.

"I am in the hospital?" Elle felt confused. She had lost time before in her trips to the Shadow realm, but never this completely.

"Oh yes, they brought you here by oxcart. Apparently you lost consciousness somewhere on the road north of here."

Elle frowned. The last thing she remembered was walking along the flat jungle track in the hot sun, but the images were shrouded in a hazy cloud of pain and the opium Hari had given her.

"I—I don't know," she said.

"You've had quite an adventure, haven't you, my dear?" The doctor beamed at her.

Elle looked at him. "I'm sorry, but I don't quite remember what happened." She was suddenly worried about what lies Dashwood had told to get her in here.

"Never you mind about that. We can discuss that later when you are ready." He smiled, making the skin around his eyes crinkle. "We don't want you to fall into a relapse from shock now, do we? So I must insist that you rest. Not everyone who is attacked by a tiger lives to tell the tale. And by the bite marks, I should say it was a big one too."

"Attacked by a tiger?" Elle said.

"Oh yes," said Dr. Poulin. "The news caused quite a commotion. The villages between here and the place where you fell have been in uproar. They even sent a hunting party out to find the man-eater. They found some tracks I'm told, but no tiger."

Elle did not answer.

"Although, I did think it rather strange that there are no claw marks." The doctor contemplated this for a few moments. "People attacked by tigers normally come in covered in long lacerations made by the claws. Your injuries look like dog bites. More like a wolf, but that is impossible of course." He shrugged. "Oh well, he must have missed you. You are quite small, aren't you? Either way, whatever happened I think you were extraordinarily lucky. And I must say, your companions did a marvelous job binding the wound."

"My companions?" Elle looked around. The room was empty. Hers was the only bed occupied. A soft breeze whispered through the mosquito nets that were suspended from hooks in the ceiling above each bed. It made the place seem eerie.

"Yes. And with the penicillin fighting the fever, I should say that with all things going well, you should be on your feet in a day or two." The doctor nodded again. "Yes, very lucky indeed."

"Wh—Where are my companions?" she asked.

"Oh, the monk has gone off to do whatever it is that monks do, and I do believe that the American hopped the mail dirigible to Bangkok."

Elle felt her heart sink. So her captain had decided to leave after all.

"He said he would be back in a day or two, weather permitting," the doctor said, interrupting her thoughts.

"How long ago was that?"

"Oh, the last few days. The airship flights round these parts are not that dependable. Things tend to happen when they do." The doctor lifted a large glass syringe. He depressed the plunger and a fine line of clear liquid shot out of the needle tip. "Now, lie back and close your eyes. I will give you a little more laudanum to numb the pain. It should help you sleep."

She felt the needle press into the skin of her good arm and it was not long before the world became all hazy again. "Perhaps just a little nap," she mumbled, and the world went dark again.

When she woke, it was dark outside and her head felt cool and clear. She could hear crickets chirping, and the windows framed the lush star-speckled night outside. She struggled to sit up in bed, trying to set her mosquito net aside.

Her progress was rather wobbly. She felt as if all her bones had turned to rubber while she had been asleep. How long had she been out? Time seemed such a blur.

A single lamp glowed from the hook next to her bed, casting a pool of light over her so she could view the rest of the room. The ward was dark and quiet. Beside her bed, sprawled in a wicker chair, was Dashwood, fast asleep. His head was turned awkwardly to the side as he rested his cheek against the back of the chair. His shirt was open at the collar and she watched the gentle rise and fall of his chest as he slept.

On the table next to her bed was a wooden tray covered with a cloth. She leaned over and lifted the fabric to find an enameled tin bowl filled with lukewarm soup.

At the sight of the food, Elle felt her stomach growl. With her good arm she lifted the bowl on to her lap and began to devour the soup, her spoon clattering against the sides of the bowl as she ate.

Dashwood sat up and blinked. "Ah, you've come back to us," he said.

Elle nodded as she pulled the spoon from her mouth. "Hello, Captain. Care to tell me what on earth happened?"

Dashwood rubbed the back of his neck. "Well, you kinda keeled over on us on the road. Was a hell of a business getting you to Siem Riep, but lucky for you the

doctor was here. He tells me you will keep your arm."
He gestured at the bandages.

"If I don't starve to death first," she said as she scraped
the last of the soup from the bowl with her finger. How
long had it been since she'd eaten? She wasn't sure.

"So, I have news," Dashwood said when she was finished. He was grinning at her.

"Do tell," she said as she placed the empty bowl on
the bedside table.

"I went to Bangkok on the mail shuttle."

"So I've heard," she said.

"And I found Heller, Atticus and Fat Paul."

"They're alive?" Elle's face lit up. "What about the
others?"

"Well, the doc found another ship and left. The Aeternae got Finn and the boys in Engineering. Elias has decided to go home to his family. Seems that the Aeternae
were so caught up in raiding the other ships that they let
the gliders slip away. Heller and the guys made it to Pat-
taya where they took a boat to Bangkok." Dashwood
shook his head. "You got to hand it to Heller, he's a
clever bugger. He left messages for me in all the places I
might turn up, and we found one another straightaway."

"And what places might that be, Captain?" Elle said.

Dashwood laughed. "Ha, now that would be telling.
All I can say is that lady luck has been smiling on me.
Ask me what I did."

Elle sat back against the pillows. "What did you do?"

"I found us a ship. She's not much to look at, but she's
sturdy. A solid hundred-and-sixty-foot junk with a good
set of canvas balloons on her. Heller and the guys should
just be enough to crew her. Won her in a game of domi-
noes. I thought I'd call her the *Oracle's Revenge*." Dashwood was grinning in that boyish way that did strange
things to her.

"Oh," Elle said, unsure of what else to say.

"Heller's piloting her here. He should arrive in a day or so."

"That's wonderful news, Logan," Elle said, genuinely happy for him.

He sat forward and took her good hand in his. "I could do with a good pilot and navvy," he said. "Come with us. Let's get out of here. Leave the temples and the monsters behind and just go. Once we've hauled a bit of freight and made a bit of money, we can refit her. Make her pretty."

"I have to go on," she said softly.

"I figured you might say that," he said.

Elle took a deep breath. "Logan, I want to go with you. But if I don't do this, I will never be able to move on with my life. I will never be able to give you an honest answer."

"I know," he said.

Elle sighed. "Let's pretend things were different. Say you and I were married and you got stuck somewhere between two worlds. You wouldn't want me to give up on you, would you?"

He shrugged. "I might, if all was lost."

"And if I were the one who was lost? Would you give up on me, if you knew there was even the slightest hope that I might be saved?"

"I suppose not," he said.

"Then will you help me find the temple? If only to prove that he is gone, so I may move on?"

He was quiet for a long time before he spoke. "Yes. I will help you find the temple of Angkor Wat. It goes against every gut feeling I have, but for you, Eleanor, I will do it."

"But what about your new ship?"

"Heller has orders to wait. He will wait for you, as I will." Dashwood straightened the sheets over her. "Hari will be here tomorrow. He says the best time to find the *apsara* is by moonlight."

"Thank you," she said. The two words seemed so inadequate for the gift he had just given her, but it was all she could say.

She dragged herself up, throwing her feet round so her toes touched the ground. She was wearing a linen tunic made of the same fabric as the sheets. "Where are my clothes?" she said.

Dashwood gently swung her back round so she was lying down again. "Silly girl. You are in no state to be running off anywhere just yet."

"I need to get this over with," Elle said.

Dashwood shook his head. "Don't be ridiculous. In case you've forgotten, Hari and I both promised that we would do this thing with you, didn't we?"

"Yes, but—"

Dashwood leaned over and kissed her forehead. "Tomorrow you are going to get this Shadow business out of your system once and for all. I give you my word on that, if it's the last thing I do. I even got you a pith helmet for the trip. It's in my things at the hostel."

She stared at him, nonplussed. "You're staying at a hostel?"

"Hari is too."

He turned to leave.

"Logan," Elle said.

He turned back and looked at her, his face dark against the lamplight.

"You saved my arm. And my life, if the doctor is to be believed. Thank you for that. I really do owe you more than I could ever repay."

In reply, he just smiled. "Get some rest. I'll see you tomorrow."

CHAPTER 28

The oxcart rocked as it trundled along on the rough dirt track. Hari sat perched on the driver's bench in front. Next to him was a young lad of about sixteen or so who held the reins of the cart with the unflustered confidence of someone who drove oxcarts every day.

"This cart belongs to my cousin. He says we must bring it and his son back here safely before sunset," Hari said. He smiled over his shoulder at Elle and Dashwood, who were sitting in the back.

Elle's arm was in a cotton sling strapped close to her body. She was doing her best to be brave, but every now and then she would flinch as the cart went over a particularly bad bump or turned swiftly in the road.

"If the cart has to go back, how exactly are we getting home, Hari?" Dashwood said with a tinge of concern.

"We walk," the monk replied simply.

"Oh great," Dashwood said. "Not another trek though the jungle at night. Haven't we done enough of those already?"

Hari ignored him, keeping his back turned.

"Are you all right?" Dashwood asked Elle as she flinched once more.

She smiled at him. "A little sore, but otherwise just fine. That dog really had sharp teeth, didn't he?"

"I'll say," Dashwood said. "You're lucky you still have your arm."

Around them, the villagers of Siem Riep were going

about their business. Men and women dressed in brightly colored Khmer *sampot* strolled down the streets. Some of them carried high-pointed umbrellas, which they used to keep the sun out of their eyes.

At some point, the son of Hari's cousin stopped the cart in order to allow a small herd of elephants to pass on the way to the river for their afternoon swim. Their herders, skinny boys perched up on the haunches of the beasts and armed with elephant prods, were in high spirits and singing to the elephants. In return, the animals raised their trunks and flapped their ears, seemingly as excited about the prospect of a cool swim after a hot day in the plantations.

Apart from the few curious looks that two foreigners in the back of an oxcart elicited, no one bothered them.

After a while, the village road gave way to jungle track, which carried on for a few more miles and then eventually ran out.

The son of Hari's cousin brought the cart to a halt. The oxen snorted and swished their tails, warding off the flies that buzzed around them in the heat of the late afternoon.

Hari hopped off the front of the wagon and straightened his robes. "This is how far the cart can go. We walk from here."

Elle and Dashwood slid off the back and joined him, studying the dense jungle before them.

"Are you sure this is right?" Elle said.

"Ah, yes. You will see," Hari said. He started walking along what could have been a faint footpath, which was little more than an indentation in the foliage.

"All right. So it's back into the creepy bushes then," Dashwood said. He glanced at Elle. "Are you sure you don't have any more monsters up your sleeves?"

She laughed. "Not as far as I know."

"It's not far," Hari said. Elle could just see the odd

flash of saffron and maroon as he moved through the undergrowth.

Dashwood walked ahead of her, a canvas knapsack casually flung over his shoulder. As he walked, he slashed at vines in a fluid motion with a rather sharp-looking machete he had brought with him. Elle also could not help but notice the brace of new pistols he wore on his belt. Bangkok had indeed been kind to him. This made her happy. Goodness knows, she had caused him enough unhappiness.

Elle looked up from her reverie. Dashwood and Hari were both gone. All around her was silence and green jungle. She felt her heart constrict with fear. Suddenly the cold claustrophobia she had felt just before the hound had reappeared enveloped her. Her sweat-slicked skin was suddenly covered in goose bumps, and the cold tickle of apprehension at the back of her neck was growing stronger by the minute. It was here. Watching her, waiting for the moment she was alone so it could finish off what it had come to do. She was sure of it.

"Dashwood! Hari!" she called, not caring how panicked she sounded.

"Over here!" came the muffled answer.

Elle plunged through the jungle in the direction of the sound, not caring about the vines and branches that clawed at her as she ran.

Then, quite abruptly, the jungle gave way and she stumbled into open ground.

Elle stopped and stared in amazement, her panic completely forgotten.

Before her, the landscape opened up. A vast square lake or moat spread before them. The water was covered in what looked like thousands of water lilies, their heads turned to the setting sun. To the side, a wide walkway lined with multiheaded cobras led into what looked like a massive stone complex. And in the center, five ex-

quisitely carved towers rose up from the foliage jungle—
bravely standing against the encroachment of greenery.
The fine carved stone shone in the light of the setting
sun, and in the soft light it looked as if the whole place
floated on the serene waters that surrounded it.

She was here. They had found Angkor Wat.

"Good grief, it's massive." Elle spoke the first words
that popped into her head.

The graceful arches of the carved towers rose up as
high as any building Elle had ever seen in London.
Maybe even St Paul's Cathedral. The walkway was possibly half a mile long.

Hari chuckled. "Quite hard to lose, you see. So not
really lost. Just a little forgotten."

Elle stepped on to the walkway and looked back at
them. "Well, what are you waiting for? Let's go and find
the fabled lady."

Once through the walkway, Elle stared at the complex
in dismay.

"This is even bigger than it looked from the outside,"
Dashwood said. "And look at all those carvings. They're
everywhere." He pointed up at the bas-reliefs that lined
the walls.

There were pictures of soldiers marching alongside elephants and long-horned cattle. There were exquisitely
dressed ladies dancing. To the side were giant monsters
with sharp teeth and snakes with seven heads.

Dashwood was right, Elle thought in dismay. She had
not bargained on the stone carving of the *apsara* being
hidden among so many others.

"It's going to take us a long time to find her," Elle said
as she studied the growing shadows. "And sunset is
upon us." She paused, then looked at the monk. "Hari,
what are we going to do?"

Hari just gazed at her with his usual serenity. "There

are three things that cannot be hidden. They are the sun, the moon and the truth," he said.

"Oh, Hari, now is not the time for riddles," Elle said. She was exceedingly fond of her friend, but she was starting to understand why people got so irritated with the Oracles. Puzzling out obscure bouts of mysticism was no fun when one was in a hurry.

Hari inclined his head. "Follow your heart. This is the truth of this place. You cannot find the queen of the *apsaras* unless she wishes to be found."

"I guess we're going to need these then." Dashwood pulled three small portable spark lamps from his knapsack and handed them out.

"Let's stay together; there's no way of telling what might be lurking inside these ruins," Elle said. She had not quite shrugged off the terrible feeling of dread that had come over her on the way here, and she was not about to take any chances.

Night in the jungle came quickly. Dashwood, Elle and Hari walked slowly among the ruins, their spark lamps casting an eerie glow in the growing gloom.

"Just look at that," Dashwood said as he cast his light across a bas-relief that spread the entire length of a corridor.

Hari peered at the carving. "It is the legend of the churning of the sea of milk." He pointed at the figures. "The battle between good and evil, the separation of light and shadow. Of immortality, and also the birth of the *apsaras*."

Elle stared at the ancient figures in fascination. They looked as if they had been carved there just yesterday. She cast her light on the rows and rows of graceful dancers, suspended in the stone.

Follow usssss . . .

The sound was a faint whisper, nothing more than the rustle of leaves.

Follow us . . . we will show you the way . . .

"Did you hear that?" Elle said.

"Hear what?" Dashwood's hand went to the hilt of one of his pistols.

"Shh. There it is again," Elle said.

Follow us . . .

Dashwood shook his head. "Nope, can't hear anything. Are you sure?"

Elle put her finger to her lips and studied the figures. Was it her imagination or had the stone carvings moved? All the *apsaras* appeared to be facing the same way, pointing in one direction.

"It's this way," Elle said.

Around her, the roots of giant cassia trees spilled from the rock as if they had been poured and then set in thick molten strands.

Follow . . . follow . . . you do not have far to go now . . . the voices whispered.

Elle turned a corner and the light from her lamp disturbed a group of bats. They poured out of the darkness in a high-pitched cloud of clicks and cheeps and squeaks. Elle ducked and put her good arm over her head as the percussion of a thousand leathery wings passed over her.

Dashwood let out a rather unmanly yelp and ducked behind a pillar.

When the bats had passed, Elle shone the light on him and looked at him with scorn.

"What?" He shrugged. "I hate bats," he said.

"And that from the man who made me eat a spider," Elle said.

Hari just shook his head. "We should respect all living things. This is why I do not eat any meat," he said.

Hurry . . . hurry . . . the moon is rising. You do not have much time . . . the voices interrupted them.

Elle closed her eyes and concentrated on the whispers. *This way . . . keep walking . . . not far to go now . . .*

"We need to go through there," Elle said. She gestured at the dark entrance from which the cloud of bats spewed out a few moments before.

"Man, I hate bats," Dashwood said.

"We need to hurry," Elle said.

They rounded the corner and walked along another corridor.

Almost there . . .

Silver light spilled over the ruins, beaming down between the arches and columns as the moon rose up over the edge of the treetops. Elle turned off her spark lamp, for it was no longer needed, and stared in amazement.

The end of the corridor was awash with soft, white light. And there, on a large block of solid sandstone, was a carving of a beautiful young woman smiling serenely. Unlike the myriad of other carvings, this *apsara* stood on her own. The light spilled over the curves of her body as she posed elegantly as an ancient courtier mid-dance.

Her high breasts and narrow waist were perfectly proportioned. Even her delicate belly button could be seen carefully etched into the stone. From the waist down, the *apsara* was dressed in a gilded *sampot* made from the finest silk. Her upper arms and ankles were adorned with finely wrought cuffs and bangles. Around her neck was a wide, flat collar of gold filigree, worked into an intricate pattern that spread out across her chest and shoulders. Around her wrists were rows of large pearls.

Her long hair, spreading out behind her in thick, lustrous waves, was dressed with fine jewels and flowers. On her head rested a conical headdress that pointed up to the sky. It too was made of gold and encrusted with jewels.

As Elle approached, the features of the carving appeared to move slightly.

In the back of her mind a thousand other *apsaras* were all whispering at the same time in great excitement.

She's here . . . She's here . . . Go to her now . . . Go to her before it's too late . . .

Elle stopped before the carving, unsure what to do next.

With the delicate scrape of stone upon stone, the *apsara* inclined her head slightly. Her arms moved from their dancing pose into the *sampeah:* palms pressed together as if in prayer, the traditional greeting of the Khmer people.

"*Joom Reab Sou.*" The carving spoke the words of greeting. Her voice was soft and gentle, and the words washed over Elle like the sound of rain upon a roof.

Gingerly, Elle lifted her injured arm out of its sling and pressed her palms together in the way Hari had shown her. "*Joom Reab Sou,*" she said, returning the greeting with the highest amount of respect she could.

The carving smiled, apparently pleased with this.

Elle smiled back, but kept her head bowed. Inside her chest, her heart was thumping hard against her ribs. She had found the queen of the *apsaras*.

CHAPTER 29

Slowly, the *apsara* lowered her hands from the greeting pose and brought them round in a perfect arc so that one was over her midriff, palm facing inward with the fingers extended; the other she raised up to shoulder height with the palm out and the fingers extended far back. She cocked her head at Elle in a pose that was impossibly graceful. A moment in dance, frozen for eternity.

"Who is it that seeks me out?" the *apsara* said.

"Me," Elle said. "I have come from very far to speak with you, oh, Great One," she added, just in case.

"And what is it that you seek?"

"I wish to ask you for answers. I am told you can tell me what I most ardently wish to know," Elle said.

The *apsara* turned her blank eyes to Elle. The stone was so finely polished that the spheres of her eyes glowed like opals in the moonlight. "Those who have questions do not always wish to hear the answers. Those who have the answers often wish they did not know the questions."

"That may be so," Elle said. "But my question is a simple one. It is a question I have carried with me for a very long time."

The *apsara* stilled for a few moments as she contemplated Elle's answer. "And you are sure that you wish to know this?" she said after a while.

"I am," Elle said.

"Everything has its price. We all end where we begin," the *apsara* said. Her gaze snapped to Elle's face. "What is the price you pay?"

Elle pulled her compass out of her pocket and placed it at the feet of the *aspara* as an offering. "This is all I have," she said.

The *apsara* stared at her. "I sense much turmoil within you. Answers may bring more strife than peace."

"I have come a very long way and I have battled against so many odds to be here. I am ready. Please, I need to know how to bring him back," Elle said.

"Then let it be so," the *apsara* said. She moved her arms again, slowly rotating her wrists so that her fingers extended in a curve. "Then I call upon the moon goddess to set me free so that I may help those in need."

There was a deep rumble—the sound of fine stone scraping on stone. The air around them fizzed with aether. The wind picked up, as if a sudden storm had blown through, but outside their small circle of light, the jungle was deathly still.

The rumbling increased, and in one graceful movement the *apsara* stepped free from the stone. She stood on one leg with her back impossibly straight, the other leg pulled up with her knee in line with her hips, perfectly poised. She drew her elbows up into right angles.

Elle heard Dashwood's sharp intake of breath. Like Elle, he couldn't help but stand in awe as he took in the astonishing beauty of the stone maiden before them. Somewhere in the background, she could hear the ghostly sound of a Khmer ballet in progress. The soft tinkle of instruments—echoes of music played long ago.

The *apsara* shifted position. She placed both feet on the ground and held out her hand.

"Please. I must see inside you."

Elle took a deep breath and extended her good hand. She felt the cool stone of the *apsara*'s palm against her own as they touched. Elle felt a surge of energy rush through her, the ancient power of the Oracle rising up and filling the space around them.

The *apsara*'s eyes widened in surprise as their energies fused. Elle felt her tense and try to pull away, but the bond had already been sealed.

The *apsara*'s face drew into an expression of complete horror. "Too much!" she exclaimed. "Too many! I cannot—" She leaned back, trying desperately to free her hand, but it was no use.

Elle felt the surge intensify and she too tried to drag her hand out of the *apsara*'s grasp, but she was just as powerless as her companion. She felt her eyes roll in their sockets and she threw her head back as thousands of questions—all the questions ever asked of the Oracle, hidden somewhere deep within her—gushed out and spilled over to the *apsara*.

No! Elle thought as the realization of what was happening dawned on her. Vivienne had been right. She should not have come here.

The *apsara* screamed in pain. Her supersonic screech caused the bats that were flying around them to squeak as they darted about in the sky above them.

Faster and faster the questions flowed, some in foreign languages so old that time had forgotten them; others were new. Elle recognized glimpses of women with red hair, all of them dressed in dark blue robes. They stood and watched in disapproving silence, watching as their collective energy spilled forth through Elle.

The flow of questions was too much for the *apsara* to bear and she started to vibrate violently, her beautiful face frozen in an expression of surprise and horror.

A deep rumble rose up from the stone around them. It made the floor and pillars of the temple shake.

In what looked like an act of supreme effort, the

apsara dragged her arm back, pulling Elle's face so close to hers that they were almost touching.

"You can bring him back. The power to do so is within you," the *apsara* whispered.

Then there was a brief moment of perfect silence. It was as if a sudden and complete vacuum had been left behind where all the questions had been. And then, in a bright flash of light, the *apsara* exploded into a shower of gravel.

The white light went out and everything was silent.

Elle fell to her knees and slumped forward. The gravel on the floor dug painfully into her knees and the palms of her hands.

"What just happened?" Dashwood said, kicking some of the *apsara* gravel off his boot.

"The worst thing that could have," Elle said. "I destroyed her. Just like I destroy everything I touch. I should be taken from this place and locked up in a dark cave, somewhere where I can do no more harm." She rested her face in her good hand: a gesture of defeat, despair and utter exhaustion.

From the shadows came the soft echoes of someone laughing.

"Brava!" a man said.

Elle looked up to see none other than Patrice Chevalier.

He stepped into a shaft of moonlight. "Well done, Eleanor. You never cease to amaze me, did you know that?"

"Patrice," Elle said with a detached coolness. "I see that a life of evil has been good for you."

He gestured to the fine linen suit he was wearing. "As a matter of fact, it has," he said.

"Who the hell are you?" Dashwood said, reaching for his pistols.

"Not so fast, Captain," Patrice said. He pulled a flare

out of his pocket and lit it with his flint cigar lighter. The flare lit in a blaze of bright orange before it launched into the sky, where it hovered casting an astringent light over them.

At the sight of the flare, four black dreadnoughts rose up from the jungle and floated forward with a deadly and ominous precision.

"Storm riders," Dashwood breathed, as they watched black ropes appear beneath the ships and snaking down to the ground. The ropes were soon filled with the ominous shapes of the storm riders as they rappelled to the rooftops of the temple.

"I don't know what your game is, mister, but I'd turn around and go back to where you came from," Dashwood said and took aim.

"Elle, please call him off, will you?" Patrice said. "At the moment, I am the only thing between you and these savages." He gestured to the storm riders. "And they are terribly fond of me. If anything was to happen to me, you would be torn limb from limb in seconds." Patrice pulled his own pistol from his coat pocket and aimed it at Elle. "Now lower your guns or she dies."

Slowly Dashwood lowered his pistols, but he did not put them away.

"So it was you that sent the pirates?" Elle said.

Patrice shrugged. "Who else?"

"What are you doing here, Patrice? This is none of your business," Elle said.

"Oh, I think you will find that it is," Patrice said.

"What do you want? Speak quickly. I don't have time for this," Elle said.

"Ah," Patrice tutted. "Still looking for your husband, little dove? The one who abandoned you to die while he frolicked in the Shadow realm?"

"You keep quiet!" Elle bellowed.

"Now, now." Patrice shook his head. "There is no

need to go off into a rage like that. I am only speaking the truth, you know."

"You know nothing!" Elle said. "Nothing at all."

Patrice laughed. "Oh, Eleanor, I have missed that fire. I really have."

"I don't know who you think you are," Dashwood spoke through gritted teeth, "but I think you should leave us alone. This is none of your business."

Patrice swiveled round to face him. "Really? I think I know more about this than you do. In fact, it is you who is mistaken. Has she told you *all* her secrets?" Patrice sneered. "I would wager she did not. That little harlot has used you and now she will cast you aside just like she does with all men."

"I'll break your neck with my bare hands!" Dashwood lunged at Patrice, but he ducked out the way, laughing at the captain all the while.

"Logan, don't!" Elle said. "Please, this is my fight."

Dashwood stared at her for a long moment and then slowly stood back, scowling at Patrice, his eyes filled with a hatred that spoke of the extreme violence that he held in check.

"Good boy," Patrice said to Dashwood. Then he started laughing. "You know they're here, don't you?" he said to Elle. "In fact, they're watching from the shadows as we speak."

"You are lying," Elle said.

"Oh, I don't think so," Patrice said. "You see, I now control the barrier between the two realms. And I'm the Grand Master of the Council of Warlocks, so it's all in my hands now."

"We'll see about that," Elle said. She rose to face him.

"Well, yes, I do still need a little Oracle to ensure the whole thing remains stable. Which brings me conveniently to the reason for my visit." He paused for a moment. "As you so emotively put it a few moments ago, you do belong chained up in a dark cave where you can't harm anyone, and I have come to make that so."

Elle felt the air slide out of her lungs as she stared at Patrice.

Patrice narrowed his eyes. "Oh yes. You have been running about causing trouble for far too long, what with that stupid husband of yours indulging your every whim. How many more people will have to die before you finally accept your fate, Eleanor?"

Elle looked away. Patrice had hit a nerve—many nerves—and as much as she hated to admit it, his words were starting to ring true.

"See, you agree with me. I can tell. Oh yes, I think that the time has come for me to collect you, little Oracle, and bring you to the place where you belong."

The hound lay down in the shadows of the roots of a cassia tree. He hung his heads, still feeling sick and weary from the hunt. In all the thousands of years he had been alive, he had never felt like this before.

The iron blade between his shoulders was wedged in firmly, and no amount of scratching or rubbing could remove it. He had tried, but scraping against the stump of a tree only drove the blade in deeper. And inside him were bullets of iron. They burned and hissed, dissolving his insides until they were nothing but black slime, but yet he held on.

Heavy drops of dark red blood and pus dripped onto the ground between his paws; his thick black fur was matted with it.

The hound lowered his heads onto his paws to rest a moment. He had followed his prey to the village, but in his weakened state, he could not go after her with so many people about. So instead, he waited in the shadows, growing ever weaker as time wore on.

And here she was, standing in the open, bathed in

moonlight. The hound studied the men that surrounded his prey. There were five of them. Two of them were on the other side of the barrier, in the Shadow side, watching on. The other two were just men, although he decided that he would take great pleasure in later killing the one who had driven the blade into him.

But it was the last man that bothered him the most. This was the man who had been there when he had been summoned to go on this hunt. It was the man who smelled of the underworld, the smell of home. No mortal was allowed to carry that scent. And this made the beast very angry. The man was after the hound's prey and that was unforgivable.

The hound's ears pricked up. Something was about to happen. The air was suddenly filled with the scent of aether.

With great effort, the hound pushed himself up onto his feet. He stumbled slightly as he took the first steps toward the source of the light. It was always there, even in this cacophony of smells. Always just on the edge of the divide between the two realms, the scent of freesias and engine oil.

CHAPTER 30

"No," Elle said the word softly, yet somehow it seemed to fill the entire temple courtyard around them.

Patrice cocked his head to one side. "What was that you said?"

"I said no. I will not do your bidding, Patrice."

Patrice formed his face in an expression of affected shock. "You dare to defy me, even now?"

Elle felt a bright surge of anger from within. She had always been prone to bursts of anger and her temper had got her into a whole lot of trouble before. She had always ascribed it to the fact that she had inherited the Chance disposition, but now, as she stood there seething at Patrice, it all made sense. This was not your ordinary garden-variety temper lost. No, this was something far more complex. This was something that had a character all of its own. And in that moment she knew what it was: It was the unbridled fury of the Oracle.

She turned to Patrice. "And why should I obey you? You are nothing but a docking clerk in an expensive suit." As she spoke, her voice grew louder and thicker with a strange ghostlike quality, eventually sounding like many women speaking in unison.

Elle closed her eyes and she felt the power of her mother and grandmothers surge through her. She smiled. She had nothing to be afraid of. The voices were here and they were fighting for her.

Patrice moved his pistol and took aim. "Move or I

will kill you here, where you stand. I am sure the next Oracle will be far more obedient than you could ever be."

"You have ideas above your station, Warlock," Elle said. "You do not deserve the place you hold."

Patrice let out a laugh of surprise. "Oh no, my dear. You know the rules when it comes to warlocks. You keep what you vanquish, and I vanquished Grand Master de Montague fair and square. I am the leader of the warlocks now." He wiggled the gun at her again. "Now start moving."

"You dare to order us around?" Elle said.

"Aha! So the sisterhood has finally joined us? Don't think I don't know about the existence of their secret little hiding place. Its location is going to be one of the first things I torture out of you when we get home."

Elle remained where she was. She could not have followed Patrice's orders even if she wanted to, for she was holding back so much power that it was impossible to move.

Patrice let out an exaggerated sigh. "Very well then, if you don't value your own life, then perhaps you might value the lives of others." He gave Dashwood a dismissive look. "Not that one. He'll be forgotten before long." He looked around, his eyes narrow. "No, I think I have just the right thing to dampen that little temper of yours. I see you have learned to control it now at least."

As he spoke he moved toward an invisible spot just off the edge of the corridor they were standing in. He stowed his gun and reached into the air with both hands as if he were separating two curtains. He tore into the barrier and a shimmering purple light appeared around the space he had made.

Patrice reached into the gap with his arms, all the way up to his shoulders. Then, in one fast move, he dragged something out through the hole he had just made.

There was a loud whooshing sound and then, quite abruptly, Old Jack and Hugh Marsh fell onto the stone floor.

Elle's fury evaporated the moment she saw him. "Hugh!" She sank on to her knees beside him.

Her husband looked awful. He was as white as bone, and in places the tissue had worn so thin that Elle could see the outline of his skeleton glowing beneath. It was something she had seen in her mother when she had met her in Delphi. It was the mark of those born in the Light who dwell within the Shadow afterlife.

Marsh looked up at her, with his white wraith eyes. "Elle," he whispered.

Patrice started laughing. "See, I told you they were here. Standing with their little noses pushed up against the barrier like children outside the toy shop. Isn't that true, Jack?"

Old Jack stood up and dusted himself off. Then he opened his cloak and drew out a lantern. "Oh, thank goodness. I thought we would never get through in time. First, let's get some light in this place," he said, ignoring Patrice. He clicked his fingers and the lantern sprang to life, sending long shadows shooting up the walls of the temple around them. "That's better. Now I can see. What was that you were saying?" He turned his gaze to Patrice, who was staring at him.

"Doesn't anyone recognize what danger you are all in?" Patrice said, brandishing his pistol. "You must fear my wrath."

"Yes, yes. You are the great warlock and we should all quiver with fear in your presence. We know. Eleanor dear, please don't touch him," Jack said, just as Elle reached out to put her hand on the side of Hugh's face. "You don't want to turn to dust on the spot, now do you?"

Hugh flinched and pulled back. "Please. No touch. Touch will kill you," he wheezed.

Elle pulled her hand back in frustration.

"There is nothing you can do about this, my dear." Jack shrugged. "Some muddles just can't be undone. It's best you take that nice young captain of yours and go and live a life of adventure in the skies. That's my advice, if anyone is interested in hearing it."

"She is coming with me. After I put an end to the both of you!" Patrice interrupted.

"I think the lady can decide what she wants to do all by herself, Shadow Master," Jack said. "And besides, she owes me a favor or three. There's no way of protecting my investment if you have her, now is there?" Jack said.

Elle closed her eyes in despair. She had come so far and fought so hard for something that was not meant to be. The realization sent a fresh wave of pain through her tattered heart; the sorrow was too much to bear.

The *apsara* had said that the secret to freedom would lie within her, that she had the power to do this, but that there was a price to pay. She now understood what that meant.

Marsh was still on the floor before her. He was gazing at her with so much sadness that it was almost too much to look at him.

"Well, I think she should be getting back now, old friend," Jack said to Marsh. "It's not good for you to be on this side for too long. Come along, say your goodbyes. Let the lady go and live her life in peace." Jack lifted his lantern and turned toward the rent in the barrier. "I promise I'll look after him until it is your time to join us," Jack said to Elle. "It won't be too long. A human life passes in the blink of an eye, when measured against eternity."

Elle's vision had suddenly gone blurry with unshed

tears. She blinked them away and looked at Marsh who had made no effort to move.

"I will always love you," he said. "Now go."

The words were Elle's undoing. Marsh was really gone. The creature before her was a pale remnant of the man he had once been. To touch him would instantly drain her of everything she was, but somehow none of that mattered anymore.

"I must fix this," she whispered. "No matter what the price."

She reached out and placed her hand on Marsh's cheek.

His skin was ice cold and dry like withered paper. Marsh recoiled in shock at her touch. Elle felt a deep vibration build inside her as aether rose up, ready to spill over.

"I did this to you. And now I am fixing it," she whispered. "Patrice was right. I should be the one to go. You should live. Perhaps the next Oracle will be better than I ever was . . ."

Elle closed her eyes and let go of the energy she held. It felt as if she was inside a waterfall of golden light. It gushed and spilled around her before she had a handle on it, forcing it to re-form and pour into Marsh where he lay.

Use your control, Elle. Be strong and fight. Control it and it will not destroy you.

Vivienne's voice sounded in her head, clear as a chime.

"It's too much, I can't . . ." Elle said as she held on to Marsh.

You can.

I don't want to die, she thought in the breathless moments of panic that followed.

Then live . . . The voice faded away.

Elle straightened her back as she fought to take control of the waves of aether that streamed through her.

Below her fingers, she felt Marsh's cheek fill out and grow warmer. Slowly his emaciated frame became more substantial.

Elle held on, fighting with every drop of willpower she had, until Marsh sat up. With extreme effort he wrenched his face away and broke the connection.

The sever felt like someone had closed a sluice gate in the middle of a deluge. Elle gasped as she felt herself become the bottleneck in the flow of aether.

I'm going to explode, she thought in a panic. *There is too much. I am going to go the same way the* apsara *did, except messier.*

Control it. Do it now! Vivienne said.

Elle closed her eyes and focused all her concentration on the aether, pretending it was just a small globule of power rather than enough to fill an ocean. Slowly she extended her will, molding it until the flow became more like a river than a tidal wave. Then, slowly but surely, she focused all her strength on pushing the power back from where it came. The gap was no different from the gap in the barrier, and she had closed dozens of those. There was no reason why this should be different. Except it was about a thousand times bigger.

She started to shake from the effort. Large beads of sweat rolled down her back. Every joint and tendon in her body creaked and popped. Her bones ached as if they had been set on fire, but she fought on. And then, with one last supreme effort, she closed the gap.

The golden light went out and Elle fell to the ground, exhausted.

"*Magnifique!*" Patrice said. "That was the most impressive thing I think I've ever seen. And you may believe me when I tell you that I have seen and done many impressive things in my life."

He grabbed Elle by the collar of her shirt and pressed

his pistol against her temple. "But the fun and games are over. You are coming with me now. I have had just about enough of your obstinacy. It's time to go."

Elle tried to struggle but she was exhausted. Her legs were like jelly when Patrice lifted her up from where she was crouching next to Marsh's unconscious body. He lay there, eyes closed and perfectly still as if he was sleeping.

"No. Stop," she said as she reached out to Marsh.

Patrice just laughed and started to drag her along.

He had taken only a few steps when a giant black hound with two heads leaped out of the shadows, the storm rider's blade still wedged deep in the muscle. It let out an unearthly growl before it attacked, launching it-self at Elle and Patrice.

One of its massive jaws closed around Patrice's arm, the one with which he was holding Elle. The other set of jaws clamped down into the soft skin around Patrice's throat.

Elle fell to one side as Patrice went down under the shaggy mass of the hound.

"Elle!" Dashwood shouted. He leaped forward to grab her, but as he moved, Patrice pulled the trigger.

A shot rang out, reverberating in the empty hallways of the temple.

"Logan!" Elle gasped as she watched Dashwood re-coil with the shot. His legs buckled under him and he fell to the ground. His hand went to his chest, where a patch of blood had started to bloom through the cotton of his shirt. He gave her an agonized look. Then his eyes closed.

"No!" Elle said.

The hound let go of Patrice's arm and looked at her with one set of yellow eyes. She could see that it was deciding whether it could manage to grab her too. Patrice made a terrible groaning, gurgling sound.

It was strange how that sound, the sound of an enemy dying, was what galvanized Elle into action. It was time to end this thing, once and for all. She stood up, her back as straight as an *apsara*'s, and reached into the barrier. She was still weak and shaky, but she managed to grip it firmly.

The barrier was a strange and sickly-looking mass of purple and gold swirls, as the various aether energies competed in the space. She stuck her hands into the mass and focused all of the energy she could muster into it.

The result was like air filling a vacuum. There was a loud whistling, sucking sound as the barrier corrected itself.

Meanwhile, Elle heard a horrible growl behind her. The hound had dragged Patrice over to where she was standing. The stupid beast was preparing to attack her while still holding on to Patrice.

She watched the hound leap up; one set of jaws dragging Patrice behind him, the other splayed open, and aimed straight at her throat.

She reached into the barrier and ripped open a hole, then she ducked down low just as the hound reached her. His jaws made a loud clacking sound as the hideous teeth snapped together in the air where her head had been. The momentum of the jump propelled him past her and into the hole she had just made, dragging Patrice with him.

The hound looked back at her, his eyes glimmering with naked hatred. Dark blood dripped from his wounds and over his jaws where he held Patrice.

Elle did not hesitate. She grabbed hold of the barrier and sealed it shut, trapping them both on the other side.

Everything went very quiet as she sank to her knees and everything went black.

CHAPTER 31

"Miss Elle. Miss Elle!"

Someone was shaking her by the shoulder.

"No, leave me," she mumbled.

"Miss Elle. You must wake up. Wake up now!"

Elle opened her eyes a fraction, and slowly Hari's face came into focus. He was looking most distressed.

"You must wake up. Please!"

Elle sat up in a rush. "Hari. What happened? Where have you been?"

"I hid around the corner when the *apsara* exploded," Hari said with a guilty look.

"How long have I been out?" she said.

"Few seconds. Please. Come and help!" Hari said.

"Logan!" Elle crawled over to his still body.

"Hari, we need light. Bring that lantern over there." Jack, it seemed, had forgotten to take it with him when he had stepped through the barrier back into the Shadow realm. The wily old thing must have taken his leave in the midst of the fight.

She lifted Dashwood's head into her lap. In the darkness, he looked deathly pale and his skin was clammy. Elle put two fingers against the skin in the place where his neck and jawbone connected.

"Please be alive," she whispered. Her eyes widened in surprise; beneath her fingertips was a faint and rapid pulse.

"Hari! He's still alive. Quickly we need to get some help."

Another pair of hands appeared on Dashwood's chest. Masculine hands with long fingers that she knew so well.

Elle looked up and straight into the eyes of Hugh Marsh.

He smiled at her. "It's nice to see you again," he said.

"It's nice to see you too." In that moment, despite everything, it was all she needed to say.

Marsh gave her a small smile and a nod, and then looked down at Dashwood. "We must keep pressure on the wound. See if that monk will part with a strip of his robes."

"Of course," Hari said as he started ripping at his hem.

Marsh bundled the cloth up into a makeshift pressure bandage and held it over the wound. He took Elle's good hand and placed it over the bandage. "Press down as hard as you can. I will see if I can stop the bleeding. I am weak, but I will try to use what healing skills I can, if you let me channel through you.

"Sir, do you think you might run for some help?" Marsh said to Hari.

"Yes, I will fetch the doctor." Hari nodded and started running, his feet pattering on the stones of the temple floor.

"Are you ready?"

Elle bit her lip and nodded.

Marsh closed his eyes and they both focused on Dashwood.

There was a gentle stirring of aether as Warlock and Oracle worked together. Slowly Elle felt tissue mending as she felt the aether slip into him. Dashwood's heartbeat slowed to normal and he suddenly felt warmer.

He coughed and opened his eyes.

"Elle?"

"Lie still. You've been shot," she said.

"Hugh Marsh. Pleased to meet you," Marsh said when Dashwood looked at him.

"How do you do," Dashwood mumbled.

"Lie still. We can shake hands later," Marsh said.

After a few minutes, Marsh let go of the connection and sat back, panting. "That's the best I can do for now. He's lost a massive amount of blood and we are going to need a doctor to stitch up the wound. He's definitely not out of the woods, but at least his chances are better."

Elle felt the fizzle of aether fade but kept her hand on the pressure bandage, too afraid to let go.

"You do know that vanquishing Patrice makes you the Grand Master of the Council of Warlocks, don't you?" Marsh said.

Elle looked up in surprise. "You can't be serious," she said.

"I think you might make a rather splendid Grand Mistress," Marsh said.

They heard hasty footsteps approaching.

Hari rushed into the light, his eyes wide with fright. "The wild men! They are swarming the temples, looking for us. I could not escape. What are we going to do?"

Dashwood struggled up onto one elbow. "Damn those storm riders. Here," he said. He handed Hari a flare. "Light it and shoot it up into the sky. I told Heller to come and find us. With a little luck we might still make it out of here alive," he said. He had grown pale and sweaty with the exertion of speaking.

Hari took the flare and ran out into the courtyard. He lit it and a bright yellow light shot into the sky.

A few seconds later, they were met by the blare of a large airship's horn. It sounded across the temple complex, sending bats reeling.

Blinding beams of spark light flooded into the courtyard. It was Heller. The *Oracle's Revenge* had found them.

"It's Heller! I love that big bastard," Dashwood said, as they watched the ship lower a passenger cage to the ground.

In reply to the commotion, the four Aeternae dreadnoughts flicked on their own lights. On the rooftops and buildings, scores of Aeternae rose up, ululating and waving their arms in a cry for battle.

"Would you mind helping me up?" he said as he struggled into a sitting position.

Marsh slipped Dashwood's arm over his shoulder and Elle took the other. Together they helped him to stand, just as the first Aeternae dropped into the courtyard.

"Hurry!" Hari shouted, clambering into the basket. He leaned on it in order to lower the edge so they could help Dashwood in. They fell into the rescue basket in a tumble of limbs just as the face of an Aeternae appeared at the edge of the basket.

Elle kicked it in the face, her boot crushing the sawlike protrusions on its forehead.

"Nice shot!" Dashwood mumbled.

The cables clanked and the basket started to lift off the ground.

Elle looked at Marsh and Dashwood. The two men in her life.

"Um, now what?" she said.

"I'm sure we can sort all this out later," Marsh said calmly. "For now I am just happy to be alive."

"I think I would agree with that one," Dashwood said as the first volley of spears came flying by. The storm riders were definitely still in pursuit. One spear pierced the basket, its deadly tip stopping inches away from Hari's head.

Elle looked at Dashwood and Marsh. "Well, gentlemen, then I say right now: Let's run!"

EPILOGUE

Fat snowflakes sifted down from the heavy clouds that shrouded the Carpathian Mountains, coating everything in a delicate blanket of white.

The *Oracle's Revenge* rested in the air above the rooftops and parapets of the winter palace of the Ţepeş family. The ship bobbed and creaked as she strained against her frozen tether ropes. All was quiet in the gloom.

Inside the great hall everything was not so quiet and peaceful.

The Baroness Loisa Belododia turned from the giant fire roaring in the ancient stone fireplace and smiled.

Before her, the crew of the *Oracle's Revenge* was assembled around a huge table that dominated the room.

"Come. Friends. Eat, drink and be merry. You are most welcome here." Loisa extended a graceful black-clad arm in a gesture of welcome. "But please remember not to walk in the halls unaccompanied after dark. Some of my cousins are not . . . as civilized as we are . . . and they may fall foul to temptation if they find you alone in the dark." She turned her dark eyes to her companion, who was standing on the other side of the fireplace. "Jasper, darling, please see that our guests have enough mulled wine. We don't want them catching a chill. It will be cold tonight."

Jasper smiled at Loisa. The process of conversion into a Nightwalker had brought out angles in his cheekbones that made him look rather suave and distinguished. "Of course, my dear Baroness." He clapped his hands, which brought servants with great salvers of mulled wine who replenished the rapidly emptying plates and cups.

Elle sat at the head of the table and smiled with a deep sense of fondness at the people assembled before her. Heller and Atticus were busy challenging one another to see who could drink the vodka-laced mulled wine faster and, by the looks of things, Atticus was winning. Fat Paul was making short shrift of a roast chicken.

Old Jack had fallen asleep in his chair, his hands folded over his belly and tucked under his long beard. He had joined them on board the *Oracle's Revenge*, and given all he had done for Marsh over the last year, Elle felt that it would have been wrong not to allow him to become part of this company.

There were new crew members as well, recruited while Heller and Atticus were in Bangkok. Elle did not know them well, but the new guys were eating while glancing around nervously at the shadows just beyond the warmth of the lamplight. Most of them had never seen a Nightwalker before tonight.

But it was the two remaining men at the other end of the table who drew her attention the most. Marsh sat on the right side. Apart from the fact that his clothes were a little tattier than they had been, he looked exactly like he had on the day before all this happened. Exactly the same, except for his eyes, which had the haunted look of one who has suffered deeply. He sat quietly, drinking and brooding into his cup.

Dashwood was on the left. Despite Loisa's healing, he still looked a little pale from his injury, but he was smiling and joking with Heller.

Every so often, when he thought no one was looking, Marsh would glance over at Elle and then at Dashwood.

There was so much that was unspoken between the three of them, Elle thought.

"So you set out to save one, and now you have saved both." Loisa spoke in a low voice next to her, making her start. Even though they were the best of friends, Elle could never quite get used to the speed and silence at which Loisa moved.

"That I did," Elle admitted.

"What are you going to do now?" Loisa said.

Elle gave a deep sigh. "I honestly don't know."

"Personally, I think having both of them as husband would be a solution I could live with rather happily. Perhaps you should find a country which allows it and live out your life in bliss." Loisa gave her a slow, knowing smile.

"Oh, Loisa." Elle rolled her eyes. "Trust you to find the most shocking solution to the problem. If only it were that simple."

"Have you spoken with them?"

Elle shook her head. "We spent most of the way here fighting off the Storm Riders. To be honest, finding you here at home saved our lives. I don't think Dashwood would have made it much further had it not been for you."

"I see," Loisa said. "But what exactly happened?"

Elle took a swig of her mulled wine. It was potent stuff, made to warm the bones and fortify the body against the biting cold. "Well, there was no sign of Patrice or of that hellhound after the tear in the barrier was sealed. Jack did have a look later, but he could see nothing. Mostly, we have been concentrating our efforts on escaping from Indochina in one piece. There has been little time for reflection."

"And what of the barrier?" Loisa said. "My men have noticed an increase in Shadow creatures in the forest this winter. Most of them were entirely unprepared for the cold. We have done what we can to help them, but many have died out there."

Elle closed her eyes. The knowledge that she was responsible for the realm of Shadow and all its creatures weighed heavily upon her. "The truth is that no one is sure what Patrice did to the barrier. As best we can tell, he infused it with some of his own power, so when he disappeared, he left us with no means of controlling it."

"So it is still in place?"

"Oh yes, but none of us can access it now. All we know is that he has left it open on the Shadow side."

"So those who pass into the realm of Light cannot return to the Shadow. They are trapped here until something is done?"

"Looks to be that way."

"That is bad news," Loisa said gravely.

"It is indeed," Elle said.

Around the table there was a round of raucous laughter. Fat Paul had joined the drinking competition but had succeeded only in spilling wine all down his front.

"And what of the Council of Warlocks?" Loisa whispered.

"Oh, Loisa, in truth I do not know." She looked at her friend. "I have heard word that they have gathered in Venice and that there is much unhappiness over the way things have turned out."

"That is to be expected," Loisa said.

"But what do I do now? Do I claim the title? And if I do, where does that leave matters with Marsh? Could he ever accept my authority?" Elle put her hands to her cheeks, which glowed from the mulled wine and the warmth of the fire. "I am so confused."

Loisa put a reassuring hand on her arm. "It will all work out in the end. In my experience, things always do."

"I do hope you are right," Elle said. She noticed that both Marsh and Dashwood were glancing in their direction.

Mercifully, at that moment, Jasper stole around the table and whispered something in Loisa's ear. Loisa smiled and raised her glass. "To friends returned safely."

Glasses were raised in response.

"And to new ships!" Heller bellowed. "May the *Oracle's Revenge* bring us riches beyond our dreams!"

There was a roar of agreement.

"And now it is time for tonight's amusement!" Loisa clapped her hands, and, through the side doors, the evening's entertainment arrived. It was a troupe of circus performers, dressed in brightly colored red and green costumes. Among them was a troupe of snow fairies, who flew about covering everything in sparkly fairy dust.

Elle clapped her hands as a fire-eater blew a great plume of flames through the air while jugglers juggled and acrobats did somersaults around them. "Oh, Loisa, they are marvelous! Where on earth did you find them?"

Loisa just smiled. "Let us enjoy tonight and be merry, for tomorrow we have work to do."

"Work?" Elle said.

"Oh yes. Tomorrow, my dear, you and I depart for Venice."

ACKNOWLEDGMENTS

This book is dedicated to the ballet dancers of Cambodia. Anyone who has ever seen a performance will agree that the poise and grace with which these women move is astonishing. It takes years of practice and dedication to achieve something so beautiful.

In 1906, the kinnari dancers of King Sisowath appeared at the Colonial Exposition in Marseilles. They took Europe by storm and performances were attended by thousands.

Unfortunately, the twentieth century has not been kind to the ballet, but despite terrible atrocities and violations of human rights, these women kept dancing. Throughout the years of adversity, the art was kept alive—with woman practicing the dance in secret—often in the face of grave personal danger. Without the dedication of these dancers, the world would have lost something beautiful forever. In my own small way I would like to acknowledge their bravery and sacrifice.

A big thank you to the staff of the USS *Midway* Museum in San Diego, California. Thank you for patiently answering all my strange and silly steam-engine-related questions. It's only once you stand next to the turbine of a 700-foot vessel that you fully comprehend the enormity of such a ship.

I would also like to extend a little hat tip to Joris-Karl Huysmans and Aleister Crowley for their teachings on the occult. Patrice's visit to Café de L'Enfer was my re-imagining of the Black Mass as Huysmans and Crowley would have told it.

Lastly, I would once again like to thank the teams at Del Rey UK and Del Rey Spectra for all your hard work. Without you, this book would never have seen the light of day. Thank you especially, Emily Yau, for all the proofreading.